The
Explosionist

The
Explo

sionist

JENNY DAVIDSON

HARPER TEEN

An Imprint of HarperCollins*Publishers*

HarperTeen is an imprint of HarperCollins Publishers.

The Explosionist
Copyright © 2008 by Jenny Davidson
All rights reserved. Printed in the United States of America.
No part of this book may be used or reproduced in any manner whatsoever
without written permission except in the case of brief quotations
embodied in critical articles and reviews. For information address
HarperCollins Children's Books, a division of
HarperCollins Publishers, 1350 Avenue of the Americas,
New York, NY 10019.
www.harperteen.com

Library of Congress Cataloging-in-Publication Data
Davidson, Jenny.
The Explosionist / Jenny Davidson. — 1st ed.
p. cm.
Summary: In Scotland in the 1930s, fifteen-year-old Sophie, her friend Mikael, and
her great-aunt Tabitha are caught up in a murder mystery involving terrorists and
suicide-bombers whose plans have world-shaping consequences.
ISBN 978-0-06-123975-5 (trade bdg.) — ISBN 978-0-06-123976-2 (lib. bdg.)
[1. Terrorism—Fiction. 2. Bombings—Fiction. 3. Boarding schools—Fiction.
4. Schools—Fiction. 5. Orphans—Fiction. 6. Aunts—Fiction. 7. Scotland—History—
20th century—Fiction.] I. Title.
PZ7.D28314Exp 2008
[Fic]—dc22
2007041942
CIP
AC

Typography by Larissa Lawrynenko
1 2 3 4 5 6 7 8 9 10

First Edition

For my father

The Explosionist

ONE

A S A SMALL CHILD, Sophie used to tell herself the story of her own life, pictures and captions running inside her head just like a real book. Even at fifteen, she found herself now and again transfixed by the sense of her surroundings flattening out into a picture-book illustration: the fair-haired chemistry teacher, beakers and test tubes in racks along the countertops, rows of pupils at their desks, and near the back Sophie's own slight figure, a cone of sunlight conveniently picking out her head and shoulders (gray eyes, snub nose, sallow skin, straight black hair bobbed short with a fringe to keep it tidy) so that there was no mistaking the main character.

The warmth of the sun on her face brought Sophie three-dimensional again. She blinked and breathed deeply, the pungent smell of fresh-cut grass cutting through the fug of waterproofed raincoats and formaldehyde.

"Sophie, don't you know the answer?" whispered Leah Sinclair, Sophie's lab partner.

The answer to what?

Sophie stole a quick look at the blackboard, which held the formula $C_3H_5(ONO_2)_3$. Beside it stood Mr. Petersen looking even more harried and chalky than usual, so that Sophie had to fight a ridiculous impulse to get up and brush the dust off his tweed jacket. His mixture of handsomeness and haplessness brought out in her a painful tender feeling which she had entirely failed to keep secret from the other girls. Sophie *hated* being teased, *really* hated it, but she still couldn't help gazing at Mr. Petersen with an expression of sheeplike devotion. It wasn't surprising the others found it funny.

"Can none of you name this chemical?" said the teacher.

Sophie was about to put up her hand when she heard Leah whisper to the girl on the other side of her. Sophie turned and glared. If Leah had just said something about Sophie being in love with Mr. Petersen, it was grossly unfair; Sophie would never have embarrassed Leah by mentioning the well-known fact of her being in love with the games mistress.

Sophie slouched down in her seat. Through her lashes she could see Mr. Petersen looking surprised, puzzled, even a little hurt. Something in her usually strained to answer him as quickly, as fully, as *perfectly* as possible, but today she kept her eyes fixed on her hands and fiddled with her mechanical pencil.

Mr. Petersen gave a defeated-sounding sigh and crossed his arms.

"I'll give you three clues," he said. "It has a sharp, sweet, aromatic taste."

The other girls' faces were so blank, it made Sophie squirm (oh, why couldn't she just be like everyone else and not know the answers?). It was horrible having everyone think of her as an evil Goody Two-shoes when she really wasn't like that at all. She bit her lower lip so hard she tasted blood.

"It is sometimes used to treat a heart disease called angina."

A long pause.

"It freezes at thirteen degrees centigrade."

This one was such a dud of a clue that Sophie couldn't stop the answer from bursting out.

"Nitroglycerin," she said about ten times more loudly than she meant to.

"Nitroglycerin," Mr. Petersen repeated. He sounded pleased (Sophie absolutely *hated* herself for caring what he thought of her). "The active ingredient in dynamite, one of the most powerful explosives known to man."

The other girls perked up. Explosives were good fun. Sophie had more complicated feelings about dynamite, which was only to be expected: She had been a very small child when both her parents died in an accident at the Russian dynamite factory her father directed.

"Nitroglycerin's a powerful blessing to mankind," Mr. Petersen went on. "Doctors use it to treat heart disease, most often in the form of a patch stuck to the skin, although one patient stuck his butter knife into a toaster and received a modest electric shock that actually caused his patch to explode."

Sophie saw a few girls cough so that they would have an excuse to hide their smiles behind their hands. Was the mind of the fifteen-year-old girl a closed book to Mr. Petersen?

"Even a tiny trace of nitroglycerin placed upon the tongue will give you a pulsating, violent headache," the teacher went on, his voice soft, even, and rather sleep-inducing. "A dog given nitroglycerin will foam at the mouth and then vomit; within seven or eight minutes it will pass out and almost cease breathing."

Sophie could hear Priscilla Banks and Jean Roberts almost choking with laughter behind her. She shrank down lower in her seat.

Mr. Petersen pretended not to notice the laughter, but Sophie thought he looked hurt.

"Roughly seventy-five years ago, in the eighteen-sixties," he continued, "half a dozen terrible factory explosions led the Federated European States to ban the production of nitroglycerin altogether. Soon afterward, a massive explosion near the Wells Fargo building in San Francisco led to that city's nitroglycerin being seized and destroyed, and before long to a prohibition on its manufacture in both the Northern Union of States and the Southern Confederacy. We must be grateful to Alfred Nobel (the patron saint, so to speak, of the Hanseatic states) for stabilizing nitroglycerin by mixing it with a porous earth called kieselguhr. In doing so, he invented the explosive that would change the world: DYNAMITE."

He began rooting around in his pockets. "I hadn't meant to show you this, but look. . . ."

They craned forward to see the thing in the palm of his hand: an orange cardboard cartridge that looked like something from a sweetshop window.

"I have enough dynamite here in my hand," said Mr. Petersen, "to blow up the entire school."

The shuffling and whispering stopped. Sophie sucked in her breath.

"Dynamite," he repeated, enjoying the girls' rare attentiveness. "The word comes from the Greek for 'power.' Dynamite Number One was Nobel's name for his first nitroglycerin compound, manufactured by Nobel Explosives,

Limited. Engineers use it to mine metals and blast railway tunnels through tons of rock, but dynamite also allows Scotland and the other members of the New Hanseatic League to retain independence. By providing the Federated European States with the best explosives in the world, we secure for ourselves the power of self-determination."

It was hard not to feel a little sick, looking at the charge of dynamite in his hand.

"Dynamite is quite stable at room temperature," Mr. Petersen assured them. He tucked the stick back into his pocket. "Today's experiment, however, will give you some sense of the extraordinary power of explosives, even in minute quantities. We will manufacture nitrogen triiodide, which belongs to the same chemical family as nitroglycerin. Then we will blow it up."

Sophie sat up straighter as Mr. Petersen wrote the equations on the blackboard. The first equation told how the chemical was formed, the second what happened when it broke down into smaller parts, releasing a massive quantity of energy:

$$3I_2 + NH_3 \longrightarrow NI_3 + 3HI$$
$$2NI_3 \longrightarrow N_2 + 3I_2$$

"Unlike dynamite, nitrogen triiodide is so sensitive that it will explode when poked with a stick," the teacher warned as he handed around the supplies. "Even the touch of a feather will produce an explosion."

Nan Harris was rolling her eyes. The blood rose hot in Sophie's cheeks and she put up both hands to cool them, hoping nobody would notice.

"You must wear goggles during the experiment," Mr. Petersen continued, "as iodine vapor irritates the eyes and the respiratory system."

"What about my asthma, sir?" asked Josie Humphries.

"Any girl with asthma or other respiratory difficulties is excused from participating," Mr. Petersen said, frowning. "To make up the missing work, she will hand in an extra set of sums on Monday; the first ten problems, let us say, on page two hundred thirty-five in the textbook."

Josie subsided, and the girls got down to work. With Leah watching, Sophie ground the iodine in a mortar and put a few grams of the dark brown powder in a saucer, then poured in ammonia water to cover it. After twenty minutes, she poured off most of the ammonia, the residue going onto two pieces of filter paper, which were dried with ether.

She looked around and saw that the others were dawdling, just as they always did in chemistry lab. It was hard to believe they were the same girls who would race about the tennis courts later on. She could never explain to them why she felt exactly the opposite: chemistry and physics made Sophie lively, while sports practice filled her with lethargy. Fortunately she had an excuse for running slowly: a slight limp that was the only remaining symptom of the broken femur she had sustained long ago in the explosion that killed her parents. Sophie had been thrown clear of the building and found virtually unharmed, except for the injury to her leg and a few cuts and bruises.

When all of the girls were ready, Mr. Petersen distributed the feathers for detonating the explosive. Sophie had imagined herself wielding the cast-off plumage of an ostrich or a peacock whose luxuriant fronds might have decorated a particularly expensive hat. It was a disappointment to be given an ordinary pigeon feather, she thought, dutifully setting up the ring stand with its two filter papers covered with dark powdery nitrogen triiodide.

"Class," said Mr. Petersen, "is everyone ready?"

The girls at the next station quieted down, and they all took their places, lowering their goggles.

Sophie wanted to be the one to trigger the explosion, but fair-mindedness compelled her to offer the feather to Leah.

"You do it, Sophie," Leah said, edging away from the counter.

"On your mark," said Mr. Petersen. "Priscilla, stop chattering and put on those goggles. Ready. Steady. Go!"

The moment Sophie touched the feather to the bottom paper, it exploded, detonating the second sample and releasing a violet puff of iodine gas. All around the classroom the reaction was duplicated in a spectacular demonstration.

They spent ten minutes cleaning up, and then the bell rang. As the other girls collected their books, Sophie jotted down a few more notes. The second bell went, and she hurried to put her things together.

Just before she reached the door, Mr. Petersen spoke behind her.

"Sophie? May I have a word?"

At that exact moment the glass in the classroom windows shattered inward, and a soft, slow thump shook the lab equipment in its mountings. The shock moved through the air like a load of cement.

Seconds later Sophie found herself on the floor, Mr. Petersen crouched over her. The room was strangely quiet, though she could hear the Klaxons outside. She felt something wet on her forehead. She raised her hand to her temple, then looked at her fingers and saw a smear of blood.

Confused and disoriented, she thought for a moment that the dynamite in Mr. Petersen's pocket must have blown up, though if this had been the case, surely neither of them would have survived the explosion.

The shock wave produced by nitroglycerin—why was she

thinking this?—moved at over seventeen thousand miles per hour.

"Damn, damn, damn," said Mr. Petersen, so close she could feel the heat of his body against hers. "Oh, damn and blast it, Sophie, are you all right?"

"Quite all right," said Sophie, struggling to her feet.

Mr. Petersen helped her up. Usually Sophie hated being helped, but now all she could think about was how shaky she felt and also what a waste it was to find herself so close to Mr. Petersen under circumstances not at all conducive to the intimate conversations that leavened her daydreams.

He was pressing a handkerchief into her hand; it was none too clean, but she held it to her head anyway, hoping the blood wouldn't stain her uniform. Her great-aunt would never allow her a new one so close to the end of term.

Afterward she thought his other hand might have rested on her shoulder for a moment, but she was never sure of it.

"Can you make your own way to the infirmary?" he asked. "I need to see that nothing's broken here."

It was an odd thing to say, given the great shards of window glass covering every surface. The floor was littered with the wreckage of test tubes, pipettes, and retorts.

He flushed a little at Sophie's doubtful look, and for the first time she realized that Mr. Petersen was no less capable of mortification than Sophie herself—a strange and liberating insight.

"Go along, then," he said, smiling awkwardly. "The headmistress will want everybody in the assembly room, but you must see Matron first."

As Sophie had her forehead bandaged by Matron, her mind wandered back to the cartridge in Mr. Petersen's pocket. How had an ordinary science teacher gained possession of a stick of dynamite? It was illegal for private citizens to own high explosives without a permit.

She collected her thoughts just enough to retrieve the stained handkerchief from the laundry bin when Matron wasn't looking. Mr. Petersen probably wouldn't think to ask for it, and there was nothing to stop Sophie from keeping it as a token of her hopeless and forbidden love. Was there?

TWO

SOPHIE GOT TO ASSEMBLY too late to join her classmates. She stood at the back of the auditorium and braced herself for the headmistress's speech. Hardly a week of term had gone by without a bomb going off, and Sophie had become used to the sick feeling in her stomach and the awfulness of the special assemblies that followed.

Miss Henchman stood on the low stage, her head bowed.

"Girls!" one of the junior staff members called out, to no effect. "Girls, please, a little quiet!"

As the room fell silent, Miss Henchman raised her head, cleared her throat loudly, and took a sip from the glass of water on the lectern.

"Our city has just suffered another outrageous attack at

the bloody hands of the Brothers of the Northern Liberties, those fiends without conscience," she announced. "The explosion killed four people in a shopping arcade in the Canongate and grievously injured a score more."

A tumult of voices could be heard in response. Miss Henchman sniffed and pushed the gold pince-nez up her bony nose. The girls fell silent again.

"Scotland will never give in to the demands of terrorists," the headmistress said, her left hand going to her large bosom, "even if the price is further loss of life. The Secret Service will not relent until every last one of these ruthless murderers has been arrested and executed, in the name of justice and as a deterrent to the entire wicked cohort!"

Cliché and bombast, thought Sophie. Fair enough to use the word *murderers* for the suicide bombers who strapped explosives onto themselves and went out into crowded shopping precincts, trams, and restaurants to blow people up. But how could killing the terrorists in turn set anything right again?

Sophie didn't realize she'd spoken aloud until the girls nearby turned to stare.

"What is it?" she asked the person next to her, a tall auburn-haired girl she knew only by sight.

But Miss Henchman had already caught the whiff of something forbidden at the back of the hall. There was a strong antipathy between Sophie and Miss Henchman, like a cat and a dog that can't be in the room together.

"Sophie Hunter," said Miss Henchman in her starchiest voice, "have you something to say to us all this morning? I didn't quite catch your last remark."

"Just tell her you're sorry," hissed the red-haired girl. "Say you've got a cough and apologize for disrupting assembly."

"I don't have a cough, though," said Sophie. She caught Miss Henchman's eye. The headmistress had begun to swell—*literally*, her face had gone all red and puffy—with irritation.

"Sophie?" she said in a dangerous voice. "I'm still waiting."

As soon as Sophie opened her mouth to speak, she knew it was a mistake, but she couldn't stop herself. She couldn't bear it when people used language to falsify things. *Justice, deterrence*—these were the words people used to cover up the truth.

"It's wrong when terrorists kill people," Sophie said, stumbling a little over the words. "Really wrong, I mean, not just illegal but immoral as well. But how can it be right for us to talk about killing them right back? If we justify killing them in the name of justice, then they can keep on killing us in the name of liberty. It might be necessary to execute them—I'm not arguing with that—but how is it any better than what they do?"

14

Everyone was looking at Sophie and whispering. Would she be punished for her outburst? But Miss Henchman shook her head, with a sigh that said louder than any words that Sophie existed at a level altogether beneath the headmistress's contempt.

"I hope you will see fit to join with the rest of us," she said, "in praying that the police may apprehend these criminals as soon as possible, and send them to their just deserts. Afterward, all girls will have a free period before lunch; you may spend the time in your rooms, or else in the school library, but any girl found loitering in the corridors will receive a demerit."

Miss Henchman could shift from death to school discipline in a single breath. Sophie said a few private words in her head for the departed and their families, but nothing about vengeance or just deserts or an eye for an eye.

Afterward, Sophie saw Matron go up to the headmistress and speak a few sentences. Both women looked over at Sophie, and then Miss Henchman shook her head again in a maddeningly condescending way. As she swept out, the headmistress stopped for a moment and told Sophie that she must take good care of herself after having had such a nasty shock, and that she should ask Matron for an aspirin if she didn't feel more the thing by lunchtime.

Sophie was dismayed to find herself in the grip of feelings

so strong she had to run a finger along her lower eyelid to catch the tears. Sophie's friends were nowhere in sight—they must have gone back to their room already—and her tears were witnessed only by the awful Harriet Jeffries. Everything about Harriet drove Sophie wild with irritation, from her pink hair ribbons and slight lisp to the namby-pamby way she kept her elbows tucked modestly at her side.

"That's treason, you know," Harriet said, sounding absolutely delighted. "You can't go around saying things like that."

"I can say what I like," Sophie said. The sight of Harriet's smug little face filled her with rage. "It's a free country, isn't it? And if it's not, maybe the Brothers of the Northern Liberties are more right than we know."

Harriet opened her mouth in a comically exaggerated expression of delighted shock. "My father says that people who talk like you ought to be put up against a wall and *shot*," she said.

She was gone before Sophie could catch her breath.

In the dormitory upstairs, Sophie found Nan rifling through the locker beside the corner bed. Nan was a big athletic girl, second captain of the hockey eleven and endlessly hopeful (despite a vast preponderance of evidence to the contrary) that Sophie would somehow turn out to be good at sports after all.

16

"Whatever got into you just now, Sophie?" she asked.

Sophie didn't answer, just threw herself down on the bed by the window. With four beds, the room was rather cramped, but the girls had an adjoining study as well. The other three boarded full-time, as did virtually all the school's pupils, but Sophie's great-aunt had wangled a more frugal arrangement whereby Sophie spent weekends at her house in Heriot Row.

"You'll have to make that bed again if you lie on it, you know," Nan told Sophie.

Sophie only grunted and rolled over onto her stomach. As head girl of the form, Nan's job was to enforce the rules; there was no point holding it against her.

Sophie couldn't understand how the others were so little affected by the morning's violence. Across the room, Priscilla was demonstrating a new hairstyle to Jean, whose mop of curls limited her to admiring rather than emulating Priscilla's sleek hairstyles. Priscilla was fair-haired and conceited and extremely pretty, but Sophie secretly thought Jean's brown eyes and pale skin and cloud of dark hair made her more striking than Priscilla, who looked too much like the girl twirling the umbrella in the chocolate advertisement.

Meanwhile Nan had retrieved a picture postcard, a seaside scene sent by her oldest brother from his posting on the Caspian, from the locker and propped it up on the mantel above the fireplace. She took up her brush, slid the elastic band off her chestnut-shiny hair, and gave it a few brisk strokes, then divided it into three thick strands, which she plaited into a tight fat braid.

"Seriously, Sophie," Nan said as she fixed the tail of her plait with the elastic and tossed the rope of hair back over her shoulder, "you mustn't make such a spectacle of yourself! You were lucky Miss Henchman didn't send you home just now."

Why *had* she been so insubordinate? Sophie couldn't even explain it to herself, let alone to the others. She prided herself on being steady, calm, and rational. If only feelings could be completely eradicated! For the past few months it seemed as though the least little thing was enough to set off a cascade of powerful emotions in Sophie.

"Miss Henchman is a poisonous lunatic," she said finally. "I don't see how you can listen to her without thinking someone should lock her up and throw away the key."

Nan just rolled her eyes, but Jean and Priscilla looked quite shocked.

"I thought the Henchman was rather wonderful this morning," said Priscilla, her eyes wide.

"You would," said Sophie, groaning and covering her head with a pillow. If she was going to cry, she didn't want to do it in front of the others.

Priscilla made a huffy noise.

"Don't mind Sophie," Jean said to Priscilla. "You know

she's got an irrational hatred for Miss Henchman, just as she has an irrational passion for Mr. Petersen."

"I don't—," Sophie started to say.

"Sophie," Nan interrupted to keep the peace. "What did Mr. Petersen want with you at the end of class this morning?"

"I don't know," Sophie muttered from beneath the pillow. "The bomb went off before he could say anything."

Nan reached over to Sophie and seized the pillow. Sophie felt quite naked without it. She blinked a few times and hoped the puffy redness about her eyes would look more like hay fever than crying.

"You were still in the classroom when it went off? The rest of us were all in the corridor by that time. No wonder you're in such a state! That wall of windows was directly exposed to the blast. Are you all right? Is that a cut on your forehead?"

Nan meant well, but Sophie knocked her hand away before she could touch the sticking plaster on Sophie's forehead. She thought she would *die* if she found herself right now at the receiving end of someone's affectionate caress. She liked the other girls, and they had all chosen to live together, but she felt the pressure of their constant presence like a deep-sea diver too many fathoms down felt the pressure of the water above. She scowled and clamped the bridge of her nose between thumb and forefinger to hold back the tears.

"Anyway," said Jean, still smarting at Sophie's having spoken rudely to Priscilla, "blast or no blast, it's no excuse for making that sort of reflection on your friends!"

"Sophie can make any reflections she likes," Priscilla said, "so long as she helps me write up my chemistry notes before class on Monday. I simply cannot follow a word that awful man says."

"Mr. Petersen isn't awful," Sophie said, sitting up. The others began laughing. Sophie's fixation on Mr. Petersen was old news; when he had first arrived in March to replace their former teacher, who had left to be married, lots of the girls decided they were in love with him, but they stopped liking him (all but Sophie) because of chemistry being so boring.

"Look around you in class on Monday morning," Priscilla advised. "Everyone just sits there staring into space. He's the most boring man alive! Besides, Sophie, you can't seriously be in love with a man whose name's Arnold. . . ."

"Mr. Petersen's not awful," Sophie said again. "He's a slightly awful teacher, it's true, but he's not an awful *person*."

Priscilla didn't seem to be listening. "There's something terribly *odd* about Mr. Petersen," she mused, examining her face in a silver compact and licking one finger to smooth down an eyebrow.

Something in the sound of Priscilla's voice made Sophie suspicious. She tensed up in anticipation of one of the personal digs that were Priscilla's specialty.

"He's got a morbid preoccupation with explosives, hasn't he?" Priscilla continued.

"Yes," Jean chimed in, "he's got a bee in his bonnet about bombs."

"It wouldn't surprise me one bit," Priscilla drawled, "if he knew more about the terrorist bombings than he's letting on!"

"That's preposterous," said Sophie. "He was standing right there in front of me when the bomb went off. He couldn't have had anything to do with it!"

"Yes," Jean said, taking her lead from Priscilla, "but he could still be the criminal mastermind running the terrorist cells, couldn't he? Being in class is an awfully good alibi!"

"In a Sherlock Holmes story," Priscilla added, turning her wide blue eyes toward Sophie, "he would have specially timed it so as to avoid suspicion."

"Don't tease Sophie," Nan begged. "You know she hates being teased. . . ."

But Nan's well-meant intervention tipped Sophie over the precipice into absolute fury. She stood up and shouted, an all-out bloodcurdling cry of unhappiness and rage. She didn't think she could stand another minute—another *second*—of this. Then she dragged the small valise from under her bed and began to throw things into it, first her toilet bag and bedroom slippers, then her pajamas.

"What are you doing?" Priscilla asked, rather apprehensive now.

"Sophie?" said Jean.

"I'm leaving!" Sophie said. She stomped into the study for the rest of her schoolbooks and a half-written English essay, which she crammed into her leather satchel. There was something undignified about packing rather than simply storming out, but she retained just enough self-command to know that it would be a disaster to leave without her homework.

"You can't go!" Nan said. "We've still got spiritualist instruction and maths after lunch."

"I don't care," Sophie said. "If anyone asks, tell them I had a headache and went home early for the weekend."

Nan looked horrified.

"It's only the truth, strictly speaking," Sophie added. "Matron will back me up."

"Sophie, are you sure this is a good idea?" asked Jean.

"I don't give a damn if it's a good idea or not," Sophie said, fastening the clasp on the valise and throwing her satchel over her shoulder.

Jean groaned and Nan covered her ears. Even Sophie was a bit shocked at herself for having used a swearword.

"You know I should report you," Nan said.

"Don't worry," Sophie said, relenting at the sight of their worried faces. "I doubt Miss Henchman will expel me." As the words left her mouth, she was overcome with panic. "There's nothing you can say to make me change my mind about leaving."

"If you're going, then," Priscilla said, after a long pause, "best do it now, while the hall monitors are still in their rooms."

Avoiding the main hallway, Sophie made it out through the delivery entrance without a hitch. Closing the door behind her, she heaved an enormous sigh of relief. She still felt as if she might burst into tears at any moment, but at least she was out of range of anyone she actually knew.

The tram stop was almost deserted. Was it because she was so much earlier than usual? No: surely it was due to the morning's attack that the streets were so empty. She shivered in spite of the warmth of the day.

When something moved suddenly behind her, she whirled around to face it, clutching her satchel in front of her chest as if it would shield her from danger. She relaxed when she saw it was only the old man she privately called the Veteran. He had lost both legs in one of the colonial wars and wheeled himself and his belongings around the neighborhood on a little platform on casters. From a distance he could easily have been mistaken for a bundle of old rags.

"Didn't mean to frighten ye, miss," he said, leering at Sophie. "Have ye a penny for a poor wretched beggar, then?"

There was something almost comforting in the familiar small pressure of his extortion. Sophie dug around in her pocket for a coin and gave him sixpence.

He winked at her. "Early you are today?" he said, the rise at the end making it a question.

"That's right," said Sophie, though it was strange and a bit frightening to think of him keeping close enough tabs on her to notice a departure from the routine.

The tram pulled up and she got on in a rush, showing the conductor her student identity card and moving to an empty seat in the middle of the car. She looked back once and saw the Veteran's gaze still fixed on her as the vehicle turned the corner into the next road. Then she scrunched her eyes tightly shut and buried her face in her hands.

THREE

S OPHIE LET HERSELF in at the front door and crept upstairs to her room on the top floor. Bedroom door safely closed behind her, she reached up and pulled the sticking plaster off her forehead, absently rolling it between her fingers as she put away her school things, kicked off her shoes, and threw herself down on the bed. After a minute she crawled under the duvet (Great-aunt Tabitha believed eiderdown quilts made central heating completely unnecessary), pulling it up around her shoulders and tucking the edges underneath to seal herself in a tight bundle.

Great-aunt Tabitha served two masters, and neither one was Sophie. Her deepest affections were reserved for the Scottish nation and the spirit world, though she had taken

Sophie in when she was a baby, which was very good of her, or so Sophie was informed at regular intervals. Great-aunt Tabitha's rare bedtime stories, for instance, concerned Michael Faraday's death-bed revelation about the unity of electromagnetism and spiritualism or the rationalist peer Lord Kelvin's conversion, following his daughter's death, by a spiritualist medium who put him in touch with the little girl.

Sophie woke late in the afternoon with the buttons of her blouse pressing deep into her skin and the pillow beneath her face damp where she had dribbled onto it. Only hunger made her finally drag herself out of bed.

Crossing to the washstand, where her comb and brush sat beside the porcelain basin, she stumbled and stopped short. The temperature of the air had dropped twenty degrees or more.

An icy feeling crept down from her face to her hands and feet. She clenched her fists, breathing fast. What if she tried to move and found she was really and truly frozen to the spot? She took a step forward, and the coldness of the floorboards almost burned the soles of her feet.

She told herself not to be ridiculous. This couldn't be a ghost or anything like that. The newspapers had been saying it was the coldest summer in Scotland since they began keeping records, that was all.

Something itched in her nose and Sophie sneezed, the

sound breaking the spell. The cold melted away and she moved cautiously to the washstand. But when she leaned up on the tips of her toes to brush her hair in the small smoky mirror over the washstand—a mirror placed too high for comfort, so as to promote tidiness without vanity—her own face was nowhere to be seen. Instead she saw the head and shoulders of a very pretty young lady, her hair up in a style that was at once flattering and out-of-date, a gaudy necklace clasped around her neck.

Sophie blinked. It had to be a trick of the light. The mottled surface of the mirror often distorted Sophie's image in unexpected ways.

But blinking did nothing to clear her vision, and as she looked more closely, the smiling eyes in the mirror actually met her own, and the woman reached her hand out toward Sophie as if to caress her hair. She looked very much like a photograph Sophie had of her mother, but the hair and dress bespoke a far distant time and place.

Sophie shut her eyes, counted to ten, and stamped her foot. To her great relief, when she opened her eyes and looked in the mirror, it showed her nothing more unusual than her own face, red lines still printed across her cheek by the folds of the duvet, a scratch on her forehead just beneath the hairline.

She let out a breath she hadn't realized she'd been holding

and picked up the brush. Ghosts were *stupid*; only foolish people believed in them. If only the woman hadn't looked so real! Sophie could almost feel the soft touch of her hand on her own cheek. She attacked her hair with savage vigor, pressing the prickly bristles of the brush deep into her scalp.

Downstairs in the kitchen Sophie found the housekeeper Peggy, her faded reddish hair waved in the rigid curls of her Friday morning wash-and-set, an effect made comical by her stout figure and the beads of sweat that stood out on her bright red face as she stirred the saucepan.

Sophie went over to kiss her, trying not to breathe the fumes from the pan. Peggy was friendly and funny and the closest thing Sophie had to a mother, but she had a sort of negative instinct for cookery, a lack of ability amounting to a perverse genius. Her poached eggs were like golf balls, her fried potatoes soggy and undercooked, the nut cutlets which Great-aunt Tabitha (a strict vegetarian) insisted on having instead of meat as tough and tasteless as the soles of Sophie's school shoes.

"Well, now, Sophie, I didn't even hear you come in," said Peggy, continuing to stir the sauce as Sophie tucked her feet up under one of the rush-backed chairs at the table.

Sophie opened her mouth to explain and then realized she couldn't face the questions that would follow the admission she'd been home much earlier. She always tried to give confession a chance, but concealment was a practice of long standing.

"Your great-aunt wants you to join herself and the other ladies for supper," Peggy continued. "They're invited at half past seven for eight o'clock, and she says you're to go to that séance after."

Peggy said "that séance" as she might have said "that nasty mess the dog made on the floor." Peggy thought poorly of the spirit world; she believed in spirits, of course, but that didn't mean she had to like them. Sophie herself found supernatural things intriguing and worrisome in roughly equal measure.

"Do you think I might have something to eat first, Peggy?" Sophie asked. "I don't think I can wait until supper."

"The poor bairn, famished-like! The dinners at that school aren't fit for pigs," Peggy muttered grandly, slamming around a pan to show partisan resentment. Considering herself in contention with the Edinburgh Institution for Young Ladies over Sophie's heart and stomach, Peggy was liable to single out the school's food for special condemnation. "Shall I fry you up a nice bit of fish, then?"

"No, I don't want to put you out," Sophie said hastily. "You must have plenty to do before supper, with all those ladies coming," she added, aware of perhaps not having sounded very polite.

"Aye, that's so," Peggy said, though Sophie could see she had already peeled the huge vat of potatoes. "Those old witches eat like there's a famine on. You go on into the larder, then, and help yourself. Just mind you don't touch the gooseberry fool; that's for pudding this evening."

Sophie averted her eyes from the bowl of fool, which looked like something a cat might have sicked up. She hacked a hunk of cheddar off the half wheel on the shelf and put it on a small blue-and-white plate, along with an apple that she cut into quarters. Then she helped herself to two gingersnaps and asked Peggy if she minded whether Sophie ate in the kitchen. Peggy liked to have her there, on the whole, but it was best to acknowledge her sovereignty by asking permission.

As Sophie finished her tea, the sitting-room bell rang on the board above the sink. Peggy cast her eyes up to the heavens and began very, very slowly to take off her apron. The bell went again, and Peggy plodded up the basement stairs, mumbling under her breath as she went.

Within minutes she was back.

"Herself wants you in the sitting room," she said.

"Did she say what for?" Sophie asked, hating herself for being such a coward.

"Those that don't ask won't be told no lies," said Peggy, clamping her lips shut, though Sophie guessed her to be just as much in the dark as Sophie herself.

Sophie rinsed her plate off under the cold-water tap in the pantry, the only running water in the house, and wiped it dry. She folded and refolded the tea towel before bracing herself, walking up the stairs to the hall, and knocking at the sitting-room door.

"Come in," a voice called out.

Inside Sophie found her great-aunt standing by the mantel with the mauve-and-gold Louis XVI carriage clock in her hands.

"Clock's stopped again," she said to Sophie.

Great-aunt Tabitha barely topped five feet, but Sophie had once seen her overpower two enormous Alsatians by the force of her glance alone. She still dressed in the style she and her friends had adopted as forward-looking female undergraduates in the 1890s, and today she wore the usual long serge skirt and crisply ironed white cotton shirt of masculine cut, its sleeves rather inky. She had a beaky nose that Sophie was glad not to have inherited and a disorganized wispy bun of hair whose color had reached the shade known as salt-and-pepper (a suitable phrase, Sophie always thought, for someone so very peppery herself).

"Stop gawping like a dullard," said Great-aunt Tabitha. "Really, Sophie, with your mouth hanging open like that, you look almost subnormal."

Sophie shut her mouth and went to have a look at the

clock, a prized family possession bestowed by the second Marquess of Bute on Sophie's great-great-grandfather to mark his thirtieth year of service on the estate. As soon as her hand made contact with its casing, Sophie felt a kind of hiccup, like an electric shock. Her hand jerked back, and the clock began ticking.

"Well!" said Great-aunt Tabitha, looking at Sophie with surprise. "If worse comes to worst, you can always apprentice yourself to a clock maker."

She led Sophie over to the uncomfortable straight-backed chairs by the window, chairs Sophie had hated for as long as she could remember.

"One of these days," she said to Sophie, "you and I must have a serious talk about your future."

"I suppose nothing can be decided until after I sit my exams in August," Sophie ventured. The exams loomed over the fifth-form girls; Jean had actually been sick the other night, she was so worried about calculus.

"Sophie, you must work hard and perform to the utmost of your abilities on those exams," her great-aunt said, looking straight into Sophie's eyes. "If your marks aren't high enough, we won't be able to keep you at school for your final year, let alone send you to university."

Sophie did not need to be told to work. She loved all things academic; the science subjects were her favorites.

"I'll do everything I can," she promised, feeling an ache in her stomach.

"Yes, you're a good girl, Sophie, and I know you will. But given the present situation, it's difficult to persuade the authorities to spare even a handful of girls for university education, what with the need for Land Girls, Women's Auxiliaries, and nurses, not to mention girls for IRYLNS."

The acronym—pronounced "irons"—had loomed large over Sophie's childhood. The mission of this elite government-sponsored training scheme—in full, the Institute for the Recruitment of Young Ladies for National Security—was to supply Scotland's leaders (members of Parliament, captains of industry, doctors, ministers, and so on) with the highly competent assistants they needed. Great-aunt Tabitha was one of its founders, along with several of her university friends, and it had come to represent almost the most prestigious choice a girl could make of career, assuming she wanted one; most of the best Edinburgh families gave up a daughter or two to IRYLNS, rather in the spirit of their long-ago ancestors' willingness to dedicate a son to the ministry.

Sophie desperately wanted to study at university, but hardly any women were accepted to St. Andrews, Aberdeen, Glasgow, and Edinburgh, and in the last few years, most of the academic types at Sophie's school had chosen to go straight to the training program at IRYLNS (Miss Henchman was on the board of governors).

"I'll go to IRYLNS instead, if it's more important," she said, wanting to show Great-aunt Tabitha that she was considering not simply her own selfish desires but also the National Good, a phrase heard frequently in Heriot Row. IRYLNS wouldn't be too bad, not so long as she could assist a team of scientists or engineers or something like that.

"Sophie, you don't know what you're talking about," her great-aunt snapped.

Sophie was taken aback. Though they hadn't talked about it before, she had always imagined her great-aunt would be pleased to find Sophie willing to consider this alternative to a university degree. IRYLNS was her pet project—why would Great-aunt Tabitha jump down Sophie's throat for suggesting it? Did she not think Sophie good enough?

"So long as I have any say in the matter—and it may not be for much longer, not if war's declared—you'll go into IRYLNS over my dead body," pronounced her great-aunt.

"But—"

"I don't want to hear another word," Great-aunt Tabitha said.

It was one of her favorite phrases.

Sophie felt mortified and hurt, but there was nothing she could do about it. How she hated being talked to like a child!

At that moment the doorbell rang.

"That'll be Janet," said Great-aunt Tabitha.

Miss Janet Gillespie was a large, untidy woman, Great-aunt Tabitha's most loyal lieutenant. She idolized Sophie's guardian and had a nasty habit of looking at Sophie and shaking her head, as if to say how fortunate Sophie was to have a relation who didn't scruple to sacrifice her own comfort and peace of mind for the sake of a poor wretched orphan.

"Sophie, I expect you to join the ladies for supper—Peggy's cleared off the dining-room table and laid places for ten—as well as the séance afterward. Miss Hodge telephoned this morning to say she couldn't be here, so you are needed as a sitter."

Dismissed, Sophie slipped upstairs just in time to avoid the inevitable awkward encounter with Miss Gillespie in the hall.

FOUR

AT HALF PAST SEVEN, Sophie changed into a faded pink cotton frock and a soft gray cardigan she had reclaimed from the rubbish after Peggy pronounced a verdict of moth. Sophie hated séances, hated everything about them, but if she had to go to one, she might as well be comfortable.

Downstairs, the sitting room had filled up with ladies of different shapes and sizes. None of them noticed Sophie come in, and she stood by the door and surveyed them in peace. Her eyes kept drifting to a large woman who wore a black dress with jet beading and sat by herself in the corner, holding her heavy body upright like someone not sure of her welcome.

As the mantel clock struck eight and Great-aunt Tabitha

began to round up the guests and herd them into the dining room, the stranger's eyes met Sophie's own. Sophie smiled and gave an awkward half nod—she didn't want to; she didn't like the look of the woman at all—but the woman simply stared at her, not turning away until Sophie's great-aunt arrived at her side to escort her in to supper in the next room (oh, this must be the medium, to prompt such solicitude).

For pudding, there was a choice between gooseberry fool or stewed fruit. Sophie asked for the plums, which were bland and inoffensive. She decided not to take a sponge finger from the biscuit barrel when it came around. Sophie's great-aunt insisted on Peggy making them at home rather than buying the packets of ready-made ones at the shop, which she said were low-class.

As the maid came in to clear the table, Great-aunt Tabitha stood and announced the order of affairs for the rest of the evening. Sophie's great-aunt would examine the medium in private, in the presence of two members of the Caledonian Guild of Spiritualist Inspectors, who had spent the whole of supper silently munching their food at the foot of the table like a malevolent pair of crows. Meanwhile Miss Gillespie would organize the others into a sitters' circle in the conservatory at the back of the house.

Sophie had already got up from her chair and folded her napkin when her great-aunt appeared beside her.

"Sophie, this is somewhat irregular," she said irritably, "but our guest has asked for you to join us upstairs for the examination."

Sophie couldn't imagine why the woman wanted her there. Something about the whole business gave her a bad feeling. She looked over at the medium. Arms folded, expression impassive, the woman's eyes rested directly on Sophie.

She followed the others up the stairs, Great-aunt Tabitha leading the procession, like a brisk but demented mother duck, to the little-used bedroom directly opposite from Sophie's on the top floor. It was wretchedly cold and damp; Sophie pulled the sleeves of her cardigan down over her hands and then clasped them in her armpits until Great-aunt Tabitha glared at her, at which point she let them drop back to her sides.

Though she had read about this kind of inspection, Sophie had a nasty suspicion it would prove quite different to see one in person. What happened next was absolutely awful. Under Great-aunt Tabitha's penetrating gaze, the two inspectors stripped the medium completely naked. One woman searched her—Sophie blushed and looked away when the medium was asked to bend over so that her body cavities could be checked for the concealed lengths of muslin used to fake ectoplasm—while the second inspector carefully examined each item of clothing.

Sophie had never seen a grown-up person without any clothes on. She couldn't take her eyes away from the vast expanse of flesh: the enormous breasts, yellow and goose-pimpled in the cold, the folds of fat over the woman's hips and abdomen, the imbalance between her bulky thighs and skinny calves. Worst were the raw red marks where the woman's steel-boned corset had imprinted her body. In places the chafing had actually broken the skin.

Sophie dared not look at the woman's face until the inspectors had given her back her undergarments and a cloak to cover herself. The rest of the medium's clothes would be kept from her until afterward, so that she couldn't use them to conceal the accessories of fraudulence. When Sophie did look, the woman's expression puzzled her. Instead of the humiliation and anger one might have expected, the medium wore a look of calm satisfaction. As Sophie's eyes met hers, the woman's face broke into a disturbing smile. Why should she look like someone gloating over a private victory?

Sophie's unease deepened as they descended the stairs to the ground floor. In the conservatory, the medium's wrists were tied with cloth tape, the knots sealed with wax, and the ends of the tape tied to the chairs on either side of her. Ten chairs had been arranged in a circle around a black-and-gold lacquered table of vaguely Japanese provenance.

As the guests took their seats, Sophie chose one as far

from the medium as possible. The maid dimmed the lamps.

"Join hands," Great-aunt Tabitha intoned, "to promote the energy flow among the sitters. Spirits of the Great Beyond, we are gathered this evening in the company of your servant Mrs. Euphemia Tansy in the hope that we will be honored by some sign of your presence. We will hear anything you wish to impart about life on the Other Side. We await your instructions."

Most of the women had closed their eyes, but Sophie kept hers open just a crack, enough to sneak a look around the table. She found séances less frightening when she could see what was happening. (But she hoped Great-aunt Tabitha wouldn't start inviting her often—one every six weeks or so already seemed more than enough.) The sitters' hands were clasped together, each pair of hands resting on the table in front of them. The medium was absolutely motionless, her glassy eyes staring off into the middle distance.

When the voice came, Sophie jumped and almost lost her grip on the hands on either side of her.

"Who calls me here?"

It was a man's voice, lightly Scandinavian-accented and seeming to emanate from a point in midair several feet above the medium's head.

"I do," said Great-aunt Tabitha, her voice not faltering at all.

"I cannot tell of life on the other side," said the voice, "for I speak to you from limbo. Though my body has long since fallen to dust, my soul is not yet able to leave its shell. I answer your call for another reason. I am here to speak to the youngest one among you, one whose help I require to release me from my mortal coil."

Sophie looked quickly around her, but there was no doubt about it: she was certainly by many years the youngest person at the table.

Meanwhile the table rocked slightly beneath their hands, and several women gasped.

To Sophie's utter dismay, she felt a slight breeze and the sensation of a hand touching her face. This was too awful, it couldn't really be happening—oh god, could this have anything to do with what she'd seen in the mirror upstairs? Only half aware of what she was doing, Sophie started shaking her head. A small moan escaped from her mouth and she suddenly had a new appreciation for the cliché *paralyzed by fear*. Go away, she said in her head. Leave me alone.

"Sophie, dear child," said the voice, "do not be afraid. I come to warn you of great danger, and to bid you follow the one your heart inclines to. Keep your own counsel, and expect a journey over water before the summer's end."

The hand brushed through her hair and then left in a *whoosh*, like air rushing into a jam jar when the lid is first popped open. Sophie wanted to jeer—she didn't even *believe* in spiritualism, not really, not like Great-aunt Tabitha and her friends. The spirit's words sounded awfully like the hoary predictions of a fairground fortune-teller. Nonetheless Sophie's pulse was racing so fast she thought she might faint.

She clutched the hands of the women on either side of her and felt a welcome squeeze back from one of them. Most of the women had opened their eyes now, though the dim light made it difficult to see much.

The medium groaned. Then her face convulsed into a rictus so horrible it reminded Sophie of a gruesome illustration in a book she'd once seen, a police photograph of a dead woman lying on the floor of a grand Paris apartment with her throat cut. The shadow cast by the fastening on the medium's cloak exactly mimicked the gaping hole of that wound.

Another voice began to speak, but this time Sophie thought she could see a very faint movement of the medium's facial muscles. When the new visitor identified herself as Pocahontas and offered to serve as the spirit control for the evening, Sophie breathed deeply and tried to un-hunch her shoulders. It was awful but true to say that clear-cut fraudulence was vastly preferable to something that felt a bit too much like the real thing. "Pocahontas" transmitted various messages to the sitters from their dear departed: Miss Gillespie's father was glad she had decided to renew her membership at the golf club, Miss Allison's mother was no longer in pain now that she'd Crossed Over, Miss McGregor's fiancé still cherished her memory as a Precious Jewel of his Former Life (tiny shriveled-up Miss McGregor actually cried when she heard the message from her lost love).

Sophie had a terrible itch on her nose, but releasing her neighbor's hand prematurely would mean trouble later on with Great-aunt Tabitha. It was a great relief when "Pocahontas" departed and the medium came back to herself.

"Lights, please," Great-aunt Tabitha ordered, the excitement fizzing in her voice.

All around the table, women were flexing their hands and turning to their neighbors, their voices rising as they began to dissect what they had just heard.

Peggy brought in a tray and began to hand around tea and coffee. She served Sophie first, giving her three lumps of sugar with the tongs and making a funny face that gave Sophie comfort.

"Coffee, cream, and two sugars," the medium said hoarsely when Peggy came around to her. She was shivering, though the room was no colder than usual, and had drawn the cloak closer around her broad shoulders.

"Mrs. Tansy," said Great-aunt Tabitha warmly, "you were simply magnificent. Can Peggy get you anything else to eat or drink?"

"I wouldn't say no to a wee dram of port," the medium said, licking her dry lips and warming her hands on the sides of the coffee cup.

Great-aunt Tabitha visibly recoiled. Spiritualism, vegetarianism, pacifism, and temperance: these were Sophie's great-aunt's gods, and all forms of alcohol were banned from the house except for a rather dusty decanter of whisky kept in honor of Great-aunt Tabitha's long-deceased father.

Several other ladies crowded around Mrs. Tansy, wanting additional details and personal reassurances, but Great-aunt Tabitha brushed them all away.

"Can't you see the poor woman's done in?" she said. "Peggy will show you out when you're finished with your coffee (Peggy, will you bring a glass of lemonade for Mrs. Tansy?), and Mrs. Tansy has thoughtfully provided cards for anyone who may wish to retain her services on a private basis. You'll forgive me if I whisk her away just now for a breath of fresh air."

She helped the medium to the door, jerking her head at Sophie to join them. Sophie followed them to the small study on the half landing, a room her great-aunt rarely used.

Great-aunt Tabitha put the medium into a heavy upholstered armchair (its ancient springs made it less comfortable than it looked; nobody ever sat in it twice) and took the chair behind the desk for herself. Sophie found a seat on the stepladder used for fetching down books from the top shelves.

"Mrs. Tansy, you have greatly exceeded my expectations this evening," said Great-aunt Tabitha once the medium had settled herself and taken a sip of the lemonade. "I had heard very good things about you and your friend Pocahontas, and I was not disappointed. Pocahontas brought wonderful news, and I hope she will pay our little circle many more visits before she passes further on into the Realms of Light."

The spiritualist cosmology, an article of faith with Great-aunt Tabitha, made Sophie cringe. Her terror had gone; she felt tired and crotchety, but also intensely curious as to what had really happened just now. Surely the whole thing had been faked, but what motive could the medium have had for involving Sophie?

"I'm very pleased to hear it, ma'am," said the medium, her voice still hoarse. "I am never aware of anything that passes while I am in the trance state, so I did not know until you mentioned it that Pocahontas had come."

A lie, Sophie thought. The corner of the woman's mouth had turned up just a little, giving her a look of smug contempt. She must think Great-aunt Tabitha a complete fool.

"You earned your fee and more," said Great-aunt Tabitha, pulling out several drawers in search of a clean envelope. She gave a happy grunt when she found one and opened the large handbag sitting on the desk.

The medium colored as Great-aunt Tabitha counted out a small stack of pound notes. The memory of the woman's raw scabbed flesh flooded into Sophie's mind, and she suddenly felt horribly complicit in the nastiness of the night's work. Aside from everything else, it seemed terribly thoughtless of Great-aunt Tabitha not to have let Mrs. Tansy put on her real clothes again.

"I said nothing to you before, so as not to disturb you," Sophie's great-aunt continued, oblivious to the medium's evident embarrassment, "but the conservatory is equipped with highly sensitive equipment designed to detect the electromagnetic disruptions that attend spirit visitors. A device attached to my seat allows me to monitor the proceedings."

"If I'd known," said the medium, in a stolid way, "I'm sure I'd have asked you to turn off the devilish contraption. It might have stopped the spirits from coming at all!"

"On the contrary, my dear Mrs. Tansy," cried Great-aunt Tabitha, throwing her hands in the air, "the readings went off the charts! Particularly during the first part of the conversation, the one with the well-spoken European gentleman who wanted a word with Sophie."

Mrs. Tansy looked really surprised.

"I'm sure I don't know anything about that, ma'am," she said.

Sophie thought she might be telling the truth this time;

she sounded genuinely unsettled.

"Of course you'll have no memory of the words he spoke, or of his very refined aura," said Great-aunt Tabitha in a manner that reminded Sophie of a cobra poised to strike. "But I'd like to know why you asked for Sophie to come and watch you be searched. It struck me at the time as an odd request, and it was impossible not to wonder afterward about the connection between that and the most particular attention the visitor paid to the girl."

It was a relief to learn that the spirit visit had not erased all common sense from Great-aunt Tabitha's mind. The same question had occurred to Sophie, and she eagerly awaited Mrs. Tansy's answer.

"I just had a feeling," said the medium, her eyes sliding away from Great-aunt Tabitha's, "a strong intuition that the young one needed to see there was no fakery about the business."

"What kind of a feeling?" Great-aunt Tabitha persisted. "Was it—?"

As Sophie leaned forward to hear what the medium would say, though, her arm brushed against a stack of books and papers. Sophie reached out her hands just too late to prevent the whole mess from toppling slowly to the floor.

"Sophie—"

"I'm sorry," Sophie gabbled, falling to her knees on the

floor and desperately piling the things together again. What an idiot she was! Stupid, stupid, stupid. . . . "I didn't mean to—I'll—"

Great-aunt Tabitha cut her off. She looked at the enameled watch she wore pinned to her front.

"Goodness, Sophie, it's *hours* past your bedtime. Off you go! No, not a word—we'll talk tomorrow evening after you've finished your homework. Say thank you to Mrs. Tansy, please, and make sure to clean your teeth before you go to bed."

Sophie's great-aunt seemed not to know whether to treat her as a small child or someone quite grown-up. It led to an odd jumble of different kinds of advice. Sophie reached obediently to shake Mrs. Tansy's hand, but when the woman clasped Sophie's hand in her own, Sophie felt a sharp pain in her palm, and then a significant pressure.

She looked quickly up into the woman's face; Mrs. Tansy pursed her lips and gave an almost imperceptible shake of the head. She clearly meant Sophie not to attract her great-aunt's attention.

Once she reached the upstairs landing, Sophie opened her hand. She was holding a miniature metal iron, just like one of the counters on the Capitalism board, and a business card with Mrs. Tansy's name and address on it. How very strange!

In her bedroom, she draped her dress over the back of the chair, pulled on a nightgown, and tucked the card and the metal token into her school satchel for safekeeping.

Mrs. Tansy's words about the "feeling" that made her ask Sophie to watch the disrobing had not been uttered with the same stolid certainty as everything else. Had she been lying? If only Sophie had been allowed to stay for the rest of the conversation!

Great-aunt Tabitha would almost certainly want to determine whether Mrs. Tansy's feeling fell into one of the categories devised by Arthur Conan Doyle, the great detective novelist and theorist of the occult, who divided psychic intuitions according to whether they were based on precognition, telepathy, or some other, as-yet-unknown form of clairvoyance.

Sophie wanted to know something more practical. Who sent the warning, and what did it mean?

Could Sophie have a secret enemy?

It was easy to imagine how Nan, Jean, and Priscilla would react to the words *secret enemy* on Monday back at school.

The thought of her friends consoled Sophie and she rolled over, trying to find a comfortable position. But though her body was bone-tired, she had slept too long in the afternoon to fall asleep now. Despite the house's heavy walls, the door to Sophie's bedroom cleared the sill by almost an inch, and the parquet floors amplified every footfall. She listened to the medium getting dressed again in the room across the hall and being shown downstairs by the maid, and the sounds of the last visitors leaving. She heard Peggy locking the outside door and putting out the lights. She lay awake in bed long after the rest of the house had gone quiet, the hall clock striking three before she finally fell into a restless sleep.

FIVE

THE WEEKEND PASSED in a blur of homework and bad dreams. On Monday morning Sophie was woken earlier than usual by Annie, the maid whose job it was to bring up the brass hot-water can for the washstand. The house had no bathrooms, and Great-aunt Tabitha had refused to modernize on the grounds that what was good enough for her father was good enough for her and Sophie.

The maid blethered away self-importantly as she shook the warm towel off the top of the can and poured the water into the basin. Sophie felt strangely groggy, almost as though she were still dreaming.

"A bomb?" she echoed stupidly, sitting up and trying to collect herself.

"Yes, Miss Sophie, didn't you hear the telephone first thing this morning? The crack of dawn, it was."

Now that Sophie thought about it, her morning dreams (a dark confusing blur of unpleasant emergencies) *had* included the buzzing of an egg timer and the beeping of a radio-wave apparatus for detecting enemy aircraft.

"It was the minister of public safety," Annie continued, opening the curtains and picking Sophie's clothes up from where they had fallen on the floor. "Calling to tell Miss Hunter that a bomb'd gone off in St. Giles' Cathedral."

"But surely the cathedral must have been quite empty?" Sophie said, her brain finally starting to work.

"Aye, that's right," said Annie, "it went off at the wrong time, they say, and the only one in the building was the night watchman, and he was knocked out but said to be doing well in hospital. Hours ago, it was."

Though it wasn't nearly as bad as it might have been, the thought of another bomb going off made Sophie's eyes water. As she washed and dressed and packed her things for school, she pretended not to have heard anything about the latest attack, but she felt jumpy and upset.

To get to school she walked through Queen Street Gardens and down Hanover Street past the George Hotel to the Princes Street tram stop. The throngs of people passing up and down the street seemed more subdued than usual, and

Sophie had the feeling that any small unexpected noise would set off a mass panic.

When the tram came, she wedged herself into a seat near the back as the vehicle began climbing Calton Hill in the direction of some of her favorite Edinburgh landmarks: the full-scale replica of the Parthenon built to honor the Scots who died in the Napoleonic Wars; the column in the shape of a telescope marking the achievements of Lord Nelson, whose great victory at Trafalgar had been the last bright spot before Wellington's awful defeat at Waterloo. Sophie's school sat on the hill's lower slopes. Modeled on a classical temple, the Edinburgh Institution for Young Ladies had an enormous Doric portico with columns in the center of the main building and walkways along either side leading to the two wings.

Not until after supper did Sophie find herself alone with Nan, Jean, and Priscilla, and it was a great relief when they behaved as if nothing out of the ordinary had happened on Friday morning. Priscilla asked Sophie for help with her sums, Nan gave a tedious account of the Saturday afternoon lacrosse scrimmage, and Jean returned Sophie's buttonhook, borrowed the week before when her own went missing. Everything felt so familiar and comfortable that the strange feeling in Sophie's stomach finally went away.

In English that morning they had written responses to a famous writer's assertion that if he had to choose between betraying his country and betraying his friend, he hoped he would have the guts to betray his country. It was almost bedtime, but the girls were still arguing about whether it made any sense.

"No true friend would ask such a thing," Nan said. "A real friend would help you serve your country, not betray it."

"But that's not the point," Jean argued. "Isn't there anybody in the world you care about so much that you'd really do anything for them?"

"I'd give up my life for any one of my brothers," said Nan, looking determined. "But my brothers would kill me—*literally* kill me!—if they thought I was about to betray my country."

"What if your brothers were all up in front of a firing squad and you could only save one of them?" Sophie asked. She liked this kind of conversation. "Which one would you pick, and why?"

"Oh, I couldn't possibly choose between them," said Nan, her mouth set in a stubborn line.

"But you must have a favorite," Jean said, pressing for a better answer. "Everyone has a favorite, if they're really being honest."

"That's not true," said Nan.

"Yes, it is," said Jean. "There are lots of people I love—my mother and my baby brother, for instance—but my favorite person in the world is Priscilla."

Priscilla looked entirely unmoved by this tribute. Typical, thought Sophie, feeling annoyed.

"I'd do anything to make sure Priscilla was safe," Jean continued. "Even if it meant betraying my country—which it probably wouldn't, of course."

"I agree with Jean about having a favorite person," Priscilla said in a softer voice than usual. Sophie looked at her, thinking she sounded almost human for once. "My favorite person's my father. I couldn't bear it if anything happened to him."

"What about you, Sophie?" Jean asked. "Who's your favorite person, the person you'd do anything to protect?"

Sophie couldn't help it. Mr. Petersen's face came irresistibly into her mind, and a flood of heat spread up over her neck and face.

The others began to crow.

"Sophie loves Mr. Petersen," said Jean through giggles.

"Yes," said Priscilla, "in the breast of Sophie Hunter lurks unbridled passion and a love that dare not speak its name. Love for the most boring man in the world!"

Sophie felt upset and mortified. She took a few deep lungfuls of air, a breathing technique Great-aunt Tabitha had learned from a Yogic guru and practiced every day before breakfast. It was meant to calm people down, but it didn't seem to work very well.

Just then the housemistress appeared to check that they were all in bed; Sophie almost felt she should say a prayer of thanks for the convenient timing. A moment later the second bell rang for lights-out.

SIX

ALL THE GIRLS WERE seated and waiting attentively the next morning by the time Miss Chatterjee strode into the room and set her books on the table at the front of the class. Born in Calcutta and educated at Oxford and the Sorbonne, Miss Chatterjee spoke in a crisp, fancy-sounding English accent that stood out amid everyone else's respectable middle-class Scottish voices. She was hands down the most exciting teacher in the school.

Modern European history was a subject one couldn't *not* be interested in, at least in Sophie's opinion. Every one of the abuses and atrocities that filled the daily papers could be traced back in one way or another to the fatal day in 1815 when Napoleon defeated Wellington and slaughtered the British forces at Waterloo.

The previous week they had been reading Edmund Burke's reflections on the French Revolution.

But Miss Chatterjee stymied them all with her opening question. "Why was Edmund Burke," she asked, "so very *angry* with the French revolutionaries?"

"Because the leaders of the revolution were wicked," Priscilla said flippantly when nobody else spoke up.

Miss Chatterjee sighed. "One may denounce the wrongs done by people whose political beliefs one does not endorse," she observed, "without mounting an impassioned assault on the very foundations of their philosophy. I ask you again, why was Burke so angry?"

"Because his whole world was threatened by what was happening in France," suggested a small, very serious girl called Fiona.

"And what features of his world did Burke wish to protect?" Miss Chatterjee asked, perching on the edge of her desk, stretching out one long nylon-stockinged leg and examining the handmade calfskin shoe on her left foot.

"Kings and queens," Nan said.

"Inheritance from one generation to the next," said Priscilla in a submissive voice.

"Private property," offered Harriet Jeffries. Something about the way Harriet talked always reminded one that her top marks were in penmanship and deportment; Sophie still hadn't forgiven Harriet for being so horrible on Friday after assembly. But then, Harriet was always horrible, so there was no point expecting anything different. "Lords and ladies and country estates."

"The English constitution," Sophie said firmly. Harriet sounded much too enthusiastic about the lords and ladies, in a lending-library-romance sort of way. She really was a most awful girl.

"And what do *you* think of those things?" said the teacher. "Were they worth defending with the vehemence Burke musters for the occasion?"

"The constitution was worth protecting," Sophie said, a little shocked by the question. "Look what happened when England lost it. . . ."

Along the line of Hadrian's Wall now stood miles and miles of concrete bunkers and concertina wire. Many girls had lost family members when England fell to Europe in the 1920s, and rumor spoke of concentration camps and mass graves. Ordinary Scottish citizens rarely received permission now to cross at the official checkpoint at Berwick-upon-Tweed; most in any case wouldn't risk passing into what amounted to enemy territory.

"What about the king and queen?" said Miss Chatterjee. "Do you believe monarchy is a political good worth hanging on to?"

Several girls shook their heads, and Fiona spoke up.

"All the countries in the Hanseatic League have abolished their monarchies," she said. "The Scottish parliament voted not to restore the Stuart line after we split with England, and Sweden and Denmark no longer have kings and queens."

"What about Burke's defense of property?" said Miss Chatterjee, her voice rich and smooth, like butter. "How does that sit with us?"

"The Scottish government has raised taxes and death duties on the principle that the very wealthy should subsidize health care and education for the poor," Nan said slowly. "And everybody thinks that's a good thing, even the people who have less money now they're being taxed at higher rates."

"Well, perhaps not *quite* everybody," Miss Chatterjee said, laughing a little, "but certainly most of us do."

"So the answer would be no," Nan continued, answering the teacher's question. "Burke's defense of property seems like almost the opposite of what we would approve of."

Miss Chatterjee nodded.

"Very good, Nan," she said. "Now, what would you say if I told you that most of the models for Scotland's constitution, and for the constitutions of the other Hanseatic states, can be found in the writings of precisely those individuals whom Burke abhors? That the sympathy with which we have read Burke is at the very least ironic, and possibly altogether misplaced? That if Burke represents politics as a matter of 'us' against 'them,' history would align us not with Burke but with his mortal enemies, the revolutionaries?"

But it was the political repression and state-sponsored violence of the European Federation that had their roots back beyond Napoleon in revolutionary France! How did Miss Chatterjee so reliably manage to turn Sophie's brain inside out and make her see things in an entirely new way?

Lunch was much worse than usual: gray meat decorated liberally with gristle; starchy potatoes boiled down almost to mush; the smelly yellowish-green miniature cabbages that had been known as Brussels sprouts until Napoleon made that city his capital; and a disgusting pudding called a "shape," made from milk, water, beet sugar, and gelatin substitute. It was a good thing Sophie was inoculated against disgust by Peggy's cooking. At least at school she was spared the need to assuage the cook's feelings by eating everything on her plate; here one of the dinner ladies would happily scrape whatever was left into a tin bucket for pig swill.

The food still sat heavily in Sophie's stomach as she plodded, lagging behind the other girls, along the strip of land adjoining the New Burial Ground to the school tennis courts. Sophie was such a poor athlete that the games mistress turned a blind eye to her skiving off, so long as she made some pretense of helping to carry the equipment. Sophie had a funny halfway status that gave her more liberty than the real boarders, although a bit less than the school's handful of day girls, but she was careful not to abuse it.

In tennis season, Sophie served as ball girl, and whenever too many balls vanished over the stone wall to the gardens of the houses behind the courts, she would scramble through a hole to retrieve them. That was how she had befriended the professor, a Swedish neurologist now retired from the University of Uppsala and living in one of these houses. After a serendipitous tennis-ball-related encounter, Sophie developed a habit of visiting him once a week or so for lessons in everything from entomology to the Russian language. Unlike most grown-ups, the professor did not tell Sophie that she was too young to understand the sort of thing she liked talking about, whether it was the theology of Count Tolstoy, the novels of Richard Wagner, the verse of Albert Einstein, or the operas of James Joyce.

After they had finished that day's lesson, the professor's housekeeper—a pleasant, somewhat stern woman called Solvej Lundberg, who had come with him from Sweden— would bring in a tray of tea.

Today it was Sophie's favorite, toast with anchovy paste and a Battenberg cake with its checkerboard of pink and yellow cubes. She had picked up the habit of pulling the cake apart and eating each cube separately, a trick that would have earned her a scolding in Heriot Row. When she took a bite of toast, though, she found she wasn't hungry after all. Her eyes had a twitchy feeling that might mean she was about to cry.

"We have a surprise for you today, Sophie," said the professor, cutting into her thoughts.

"Oh?" Sophie said dispiritedly. "What is it?"

Rather than answering, he held a finger over his lips and cocked his head to listen. The street door opened, then slammed shut. The loud footsteps in the hall told Sophie everything she needed to know.

"Mikael!"

Mikael was the housekeeper's nephew. His mother shipped him over to Edinburgh every so often from Denmark when she felt she couldn't manage him, and Sophie was very fond of him.

It was as if Sophie's wish for someone to confide in had been magically granted—Mikael was the cleverest person Sophie knew, with the exception of Miss Chatterjee (but teachers didn't count).

"I didn't know you were coming!" she said after Mikael had helped himself to an enormous hunk of cake.

"Oh, yes. By the way, Aunt Solvej," said Mikael, giving Sophie a sly wink, "I wouldn't say no if you rustled up a new lot of buttered toast, no anchovies."

Two of Mikael's most noticeable traits were his bottomless hunger and his excellent colloquial English, spoken virtually without an accent.

Mrs. Lundberg returned shortly from the kitchen with plain buttered toast and several new kinds of biscuit as well, including chocolate digestives and coconut macaroons with glacé cherries on top. It was surprising how much hungrier Sophie felt now.

"Join us for our repast," the professor urged, but Mrs. Lundberg would never sit down in the presence of visitors. Instead she cleared the cups and plates and rumpled Mikael's hair as she passed.

It was rather a blow when Sophie looked at her watch and saw the time.

"Sophie, you wretch, you mustn't go yet," said Mikael. "I've only just laid eyes on you!"

But Sophie had to leave if she wanted to reunite with the tennis players before they all walked back to school. She kissed the professor on the cheek and said good-bye to Mrs. Lundberg, who pressed a packet of cake and sandwiches into Sophie's hand.

Mikael stepped out into the garden with her. Often these days Sophie came and went by the front door, but the way through the garden and over the wall was quicker and less conspicuous.

"It's good to see you," she said to Mikael outside in the garden, feeling shy now they were alone together. "How long are you here for?"

"Till July," Mikael said, grinning. "Good, isn't it? My mother's really fed up with me; she told me to stay away till she cooled down."

"What did you do this time?" Sophie said.

"Oh, I borrowed someone's motorcar and had a bit of an accident."

"I didn't know you could drive!"

"My brother gave me a few lessons last summer. To tell the truth, though, I really *don't* know how to drive!"

"Will you have to pay for the repairs?" Sophie asked.

"No, fortunately the car belongs to my mother's 'gentleman friend,' and he's simply rolling in money," said Mikael breezily. Sophie looked at him with envy. In his place, she would have been dying of mortification. "Anyway, I've got all sorts of things to tell you about. Friday afternoon, the usual time and place?"

"Perfect," said Sophie.

They stood smiling at each other for an awkward moment. Then Sophie clambered over the wall and returned to school.

SEVEN

THE GIRLS' RIFLE CLUB met that Thursday in the school gymnasium. Standing in a row of girls facing the targets opposite, Sophie bit the paper off a cartridge and poured the powder down the rifle bore, then put the greased bullet in the bore and rammed it down on top of the powder.

An hour of shooting left Sophie filthy and exhausted but much happier than before. (Funny the way firing a gun always put her in a good mood.) She and Nan walked back to their room and changed into their dressing gowns before going to take the extra bath allotted to members of the Rifle Club.

The bathroom had a row of cubicles, each with its own tub and taps, and the two girls ran hot baths, a luxury unknown at the National High School for Boys down the road (Sophie was glad of the hot water but sorry boys and girls should be treated so differently).

"My dad visited on Sunday afternoon," Nan said as they soaked in painfully hot water. "He says that this time it really looks like war."

Sophie admitted that her great-aunt had been saying something very similar.

"Sophie, what will you do if war breaks out? How will you serve, I mean?"

Sophie smiled at Nan's phrasing, but the question demanded serious thought.

"Oh, it's impossible," she said, feeling the back and shoulder muscles that the hot water had loosened snap back into tight bands. "It's easy for you. Your family's been army as far back as anyone can remember."

"Yes," said Nan, the affirmation echoing off the tiles of the cavernous bathroom. Sophie envied her certainty. "I know I'll join the women's army auxiliaries—there's never been any doubt, and a declaration of war will simply speed things up a bit. All three of my brothers are in the army already, of course, and there's no reason for me not to follow them. But what will Jean do, and Priscilla? What will you do, Sophie?"

"If it were fifteen years ago, and war not even on the horizon," Sophie said, thinking out loud, "I suppose it'd be a pretty sure thing that I'd go to university. Miss Chatterjee told me that when she first began teaching here, almost all the girls stayed on for sixth-form work, and quite a few of those went to university as well. Now most of us leave after the fifth form."

"That sixth-form group this year is like a ghost ship," Nan agreed, splashing for emphasis. "There are so many empty seats, it must be terribly discouraging. And last year not a single girl went on to university. All the really academic girls go now to IRYLNS instead. Is that what you'll do, do you think?"

Sophie sighed. "I don't know. You'd think Great-aunt Tabitha would like the idea of me going to IRYLNS, but when I suggested it this weekend, she practically bit my head off. I think she's going to pull strings and try to get me admitted to university."

"Do you think she's got that kind of influence?" Nan sounded impressed.

"I hope so," Sophie said, only realizing as she said it how very much she wanted it to be true. "The auxiliaries would be absolutely dire! Seriously, can you see me in a khaki uniform saluting my superior officer?"

"No, it's true," Nan said, "I can't picture that at all."

"Imagine how poorly I'd do in the PT testing," Sophie added. "I couldn't do a single press-up last time they made us in gym! They'd probably ship me off to some awful farm in the middle of nowhere. Even a factory job would be better than having to work as a Land Girl."

"Oh, I don't know," Nan said thoughtfully. Nan liked the outdoors more than Sophie did. "Farming wouldn't be so bad. But I think you should hold out for university."

"The horrible thing," Sophie said to Nan as they hurriedly dried themselves and put on their pajamas, "is that we're being forced to choose now about things that really should be able to wait till we're older. It's hard to say what's worse, the suddenness of having to choose or the chance that if we don't make up our minds soon, the choice will be taken away from us altogether."

In spite of this disturbing conversation, the evening's exercise and the warm bath had relaxed Sophie, and she lay in bed in a pleasant haze, looking forward to double-period chemistry the next morning. She was asleep before she knew it, a rare thing this far into the summer term, when dusk fell long after even the oldest girls' bedtime.

A few hours later, though, she found herself standing spread-eagled, back against the bedroom door, her throat raw from the shout she'd just unleashed.

A light went on by one of the beds. Priscilla's sleepy face turned toward her.

"What on earth just happened?" she asked Sophie.

By now Jean and Nan were both sitting up.

"Yes, what's the matter, Sophie?" said Nan.

"I don't know," Sophie said, her voice rough. She cleared her throat and cast her mind back. She couldn't remember a thing. Something moved in the shadows, and Sophie thought her heart might actually explode with terror.

"Sophie screamed," said Jean. "That was what woke us, I think."

Sophie spread her hand flat across her neck and collarbone and took another deep breath. Her hands were freezing, the skin of her chest hot and feverish, and she could feel her heart pumping at twice the usual speed.

"You must have had a nightmare," Nan said. "What was it, Sophie? My brother Sam always says that when you have a bad dream, the best thing to do is talk about it."

"But I can't *remember*," Sophie said, deeply shaken. "I might have been in a factory. And someone was having an argument."

"What kind of a factory? Who was there? What were they arguing about? What were you doing there?"

But Sophie could answer none of Nan's questions.

"Go back to bed!" Priscilla finally said. "We're perfectly safe here. A bad dream isn't going to kill you, horrible though it may be."

In bed again, Sophie's feet were freezing cold and she folded her left foot behind her right knee to warm it up, then switched sides to warm the other foot. It took longer for her heart to stop hammering in her rib cage. If this was *perfectly safe*, what must *grave danger* feel like?

In the morning Sophie hardly remembered the interruption to the night's sleep, though she felt irritable and poorly rested. The others didn't let her off lightly, though. They pestered her right up until they got to chemistry and discovered, not Mr. Petersen, but the biology mistress, Miss Hopkins.

"Mr. Petersen can't be with you today," the teacher told the class. "You may use this time to catch up on work for your other classes, and lessons will resume on Monday."

The sound of scratching pens and the rustle of pages soon filled the classroom. Sophie couldn't concentrate, which was most alarming. She was used to being able to work even under the most adverse conditions. It was a great disappointment not to see Mr. Petersen, of course, but there was no reason missing him should make her so uneasy.

At twenty-five past nine, a first-form girl crept into the room to deliver a note to Miss Hopkins.

"Girls," said the biology mistress, speaking abruptly as she ran her eyes over the note, "I must leave you. You may speak with one another while I am away, so long as you moderate your voices. I'll be back in fifteen minutes; Nan, I authorize you in the meantime to discipline any girl who creates a disturbance."

After she left, the girls looked at each other. Sophie tried to get on with her English essay. Many of the others took out the bundles of knitting that had been all the rage that term and began to click away with their needles.

The low murmur of conversation couldn't cover up the noise of Priscilla poking Jean in the side and snickering.

"Sophie," Priscilla called out softly.

Sophie looked around.

"Where do you think Mr. Petersen's gone?" Priscilla said.

Sophie decided to ignore her and turned back to her work.

"If Miss Hopkins comes back and tells us there's been another bombing," Priscilla persisted, "will you admit the odds just got much better on Mr. Petersen being one of the bombers?"

"Yes," said Jean, whose father gambled, "from ten-to-one outsider to four-to-six odds-on favorite."

"Don't be silly," said Sophie, glaring at them both. She went resolutely back to the essay.

Miss Hopkins returned just as Nan threatened to single out two particularly loud girls for punishment.

"Girls," Miss Hopkins said, taking her place before the class, "there's no need to panic—"

Several girls uttered small screams.

"—but I'm sorry to have to tell you that another bomb went off this morning, this time right in the heart of Princes Street."

She looked like someone trying not to weep.

"How many people were killed?" Nan asked, her voice quite calm.

"More than a hundred," said Miss Hopkins. She took off her glasses and wiped them on the cuff of her blouse.

Some of the girls began crying.

Sophie didn't dare look at Jean and Priscilla.

Of course Mr. Petersen wasn't the bomber. He couldn't be. On the other hand, where was he?

Sophie walked in a daze through the rest of the day's classes, earning a reprimand from the maths teacher and an extra essay assignment from the lady who taught spiritualist instruction, an old crony of Great-aunt Tabitha's.

Though she still felt sad and angry and worried and confused—feelings were *awful*—Sophie's spirits lifted just a little when the bell rang to mark the end of the last class. Mikael would be able to help her, she told herself as she ran upstairs to pack for the weekend.

She decided to cram everything into her satchel so that she wouldn't have to carry more than one bag. It was a tight fit. She said good-bye to the others and ran downstairs, earning a reproof from a prefect in the hallway. She would have to hurry if she didn't want to be late.

Lord Nelson's Column—shaped like a telescope and visible from almost everywhere in Edinburgh—was surrounded by a secluded park, an overgrown brick path weaving through the hilly garden thick with rough grass. The tower had five stories all together, each with a few narrow windows. After climbing a hundred and forty-three stairs to reach the small circular chamber at the top, Sophie passed through the tiny doorway, barely a foot and a half wide, and out onto the little balcony, its sturdy low parapet just hip height.

Still panting from the climb, she dumped her satchel on the flagstones and used it as a seat, then leaned her elbows on the parapet to look out. It was so clear that she could see all the way down the coast to North Berwick, where Sophie had spent many summer afternoons paddling in the rock pools while Great-aunt Tabitha played eighteen holes on the links.

Where was Mikael? The trouble with waiting for someone was that it was like not being able to go to sleep, Sophie thought. It gave one altogether too much time to think about things.

She couldn't stop worrying about what it would mean if Scotland and the Hanseatic League went to war with Europe. Even worse, what if Scotland *lost*? Would the streets of Edinburgh be renamed after French and German war heroes? Would troops patrol Calton Hill? Would French become

Scotland's official language, and would a permit from the local prefecture be needed to take the train to North Berwick?

How much longer would the Hanseatic League hold fast?

By the time Mikael got there, Sophie was cold and bored and more than a little hungry. Her delight at seeing him warred with her feeling of grievance at his lateness, but when he smiled, her irritation washed away like a bloodstain under cold running water.

"So which day did you get to Edinburgh?" she asked as Mikael took a seat beside her. The satchel was fine for one person to sit on but small for two, and she shivered at the pressure of his leg against hers.

"On Sunday," Mikael said. "My mum kicked up such a fuss, I reckoned I'd better stay away for a few weeks."

"You'd think your mother would be used to you by now!" Sophie said.

"Yes, it's strange, isn't it? I can never see why she's so upset. It's not like I've ever actually killed anybody, or even put anyone in hospital—"

"You sound sorry for that!"

Mikael laughed. "Actually," he said, "though the car episode was entirely my fault, it's not what's got her so riled up. For once it's my brother, not me, who's in really hot water."

"Your brother? But I thought he was a kind of saint."

Mikael's brother was ten years older and had left home to go to university when Mikael was still quite young. Sophie had never met him, but he was by all accounts (and to Mikael's chagrin) a complete paragon of all the virtues.

"This time my perfect older brother seems to have done something heinous beyond belief. I'm not sure what it is exactly, but he hasn't written home for months, and I think my mum's convinced she's lost him permanently."

"How odd," Sophie said, her own worries receding a little as the puzzle claimed her attention. It was hard to think what Mikael's brother could have done to upset their mother so much.

"At any rate," Mikael continued, "when the police telephoned her about my little escapade, she well and truly flew off the handle."

"What do you think your brother did, then?" Sophie asked.

"Yes, it's quite a mystery, isn't it?" Mikael said blithely, sounding not at all disturbed by his brother's departure from the straight and narrow. "I'll see if I can winkle the real story out of Aunt Solvej. It's probably nothing much, and Mum's simply making a mountain out of a molehill."

They gazed out over the city, Sophie uncomfortably aware of how close they were sitting to each other.

"Sophie, what about you?" Mikael asked, putting his hand on her knee in a way that made her jump. "How are you? I have to say, you looked terribly worried the other day. Everything all right?"

After a pause, a string of incoherent phrases poured out of Sophie: the horror of the bombings, the sense they all had at school of waiting passively for their future to be decided, the impossibility of getting along with the others, her dread of war.

When Sophie fell quiet, Mikael rooted around in his pockets and dug out a waxed-paper packet of sandwiches.

"Cheese-and-tomato or fish paste?" he asked.

"Cheese-and-tomato, please," Sophie said.

In silence they ate the sandwiches, which were squashed and soggy but extremely satisfying.

"Sophie," Mikael said, when they had folded up the wrappers and tucked them into Sophie's bag for later disposal, "you're obviously leaving something out, something big. All that stuff you've been talking about, none of it's much good, but it's not enough by itself to have put you into such a state. No, not even the bombings," he added.

Sophie squirmed on her seat, the words lodged like lumps of suet in her throat.

"It was a séance," she said, steeling herself. "There was this awful medium and she had a peculiar message for me— for me personally, I mean, a sort of warning—and before that, I saw something that looked like a ghost in the mirror—"

"Hold on a minute," Mikael said, putting up his hands.

Sophie braced herself for ridicule.

"Slow down, can't you? I've no idea what you're talking about. Start from the beginning and tell me the whole story."

Sophie told him everything that had happened, her voice growing stronger as she saw his intent expression.

By the time she finished, he looked quite worried.

"Those mediums are really wicked," he said, "preying on people's weak side like that. It should be illegal to pretend to be able to contact the dead. Outright frauds, the whole lot of them."

"It was the creepiest thing you've ever seen," Sophie said. She would like to have believed the medium was a fraud, but if Mikael had been there, surely his skepticism would have been shaken. "Of course it's ludicrous—great danger and a voyage over water and all that. But the way the medium asked for me beforehand so that I'd be sure she didn't have any tricks up her sleeve—"

"What was her name again?"

"Mrs. Tansy: Euphemia Tansy, I think it was."

"All right," Mikael said. He jumped to his feet and pulled Sophie up after him. "We've got to look into this. It sounds to me as though someone may have put the wretched woman up to this business, and if that's so, we should be able to find out who it was and what they wanted."

"I've got her address," Sophie said suddenly. She didn't know why she hadn't thought of it sooner. Having an ally must be good for the brain. She dug through the bits of paper at the bottom of her satchel until she found the medium's card, and handed it over to Mikael. Her hand brushed against that funny little metal iron in the process, but it seemed hardly worth mentioning.

"Excellent," said Mikael, examining the address on the card. "I'll go there right now, and you and I can meet on Sunday afternoon at the library so I can tell you what I've found out."

He must have been able to tell Sophie was frightened, or he would have suggested she come with him. Though she supposed it was what she'd hoped for, she wasn't sure how she felt about Mikael taking charge like this. What if Sophie lost all her self-reliance?

"You'll be careful, won't you?" she said.

Mikael shrugged away her concern. "I'll be fine," he said in an untroubled way. "It's good practice in case I turn out to be a detective when I'm older."

"Do you want to be a detective?" Sophie asked. In December, it had been a fighter pilot, and the summer before, an engineer in the oil fields of Baku.

Mikael blushed and didn't say anything, which made Sophie think he might really mean it this time. How interesting!

And how convenient for Sophie!

She told Mikael as much more as she could remember about the medium and what she had said, then noticed it was almost six o'clock. Peggy would be frantic.

"Oh dear, I must go," she said, brushing off her skirt and settling the satchel back over her shoulders.

"I'll see you on Sunday," said Mikael.

They made their way down from the tower, then parted, Sophie hurrying downhill to the closest tram stop. If Mikael could find out more about the medium, she would be greatly in his debt.

As soon as she got home, Sophie remembered that Great-aunt Tabitha was out for supper, a regular engagement at the Women's Spiritualism Club, and in the kitchen she found a note from Peggy saying she wouldn't be back from the dentist until seven. A few months earlier Peggy's metal fillings had begun picking up spirit voices, and when a long-dead servant from the Stevenson house down the road settled in and began to comment rudely on Peggy's cooking, Peggy had hauled her life's savings out from her mattress and gone to have all the old fillings replaced with the new plastic emulsion ones, which couldn't act as receivers.

In other words, Sophie might have stayed out as long as she liked. She couldn't decide whether to be relieved or offended by this evidence of her own insignificance.

EIGHT

AFTER LUNCH ON SATURDAY Peggy sent Sophie out with instructions to get a bit of sun and fresh air and not show her face at home a minute before teatime. As Sophie was about to let herself out the front door, Peggy appeared in the hall, marched over, and motioned for Sophie to hand over her satchel. She opened it up and took out the detective novel tucked into the front pocket.

"Reading's all very well in its place," she said, holding the book beyond Sophie's reach, "but it's out and about I want you this afternoon, not sitting somewhere cramming your head full of rubbish. I'll keep this for you in the kitchen, and you can have it again after tea."

Sophie begged shamelessly, but Peggy wouldn't relent,

though she did give Sophie a shilling before shooing her away from the house.

"And stay out of crowds!" Peggy called after Sophie, who waved to show she'd heard. Peggy was sure that as long as one was sensible, one would never find oneself on the spot when a bomb went off.

Sophie didn't actively dislike spending time outdoors, but it was hard to know what to do once she was there. In the end she wandered along Heriot Row toward Broughton Street Lane, where she gravitated to the used bookseller in the appealingly seedy row of shops that included a secondhand wig retailer and a little photography studio whose windows advertised the services of Daguerreotype Mediums and Photographic Sitters. She browsed for a while in the book-shop and finally exchanged her shilling for two novels by Ibsen and Strindberg.

On her way out, Sophie stopped to give her last penny to the Veteran, whose injury didn't stop him from wheeling him-self all over town on his little cart. Sophie often saw him away from his usual post in front of the school, though she didn't remember ever seeing him so close to her house before.

With no particular destination in mind, she crossed Leith Walk into London Road and entered the Terrace Gardens through the north gate, formerly wrought iron but now naked wood because the government had stripped the parks of metal for the war-preparedness effort.

Sophie strolled along the yellow gravel path in search of a suitable bench, one colonized by neither the terrifying uniformed nannies with their grand perambulators nor the vagrants who slept in the park during the daytime and hung around the main railway station at night.

A sharp piece of stone lodged between Sophie's heel and the inside of her shoe, and at the next bench she propped her foot on the seat and unbuckled the strap of her sandal. As she shook it out over the walk, she heard someone calling her name.

She looked up and saw Jean. It wasn't surprising that Jean should be here—the gardens were only ten minutes' walk from school, and fifth- and sixth-form girls often spent their free afternoons in the park when the weather was fine. The only surprise was to see her without Priscilla. Sophie said as much, and Jean flushed.

"Priscilla was supposed to come with me," she admitted, "but we had a falling-out last night and she's still furious."

Though Sophie nodded, Jean seemed to feel further explanation was needed.

"It was all my fault," she said, sounding guilty and miserable. "Priscilla had a letter from a boy she met over the Easter holidays, and I got upset when she said she wouldn't show it to me. And then I said lots of awful things, and then she told me I'd better find a new best friend if I couldn't stop being such a jealous monster."

Sophie reached across and patted the other girl's hand. It was impossible not to feel for Jean; the unhappiness in her voice was palpable.

"I expect she didn't mean it," she told Jean. Priscilla wasn't the type to bear a grudge.

"Yes, I know," Jean said, gulping and swallowing, "but meanwhile I'm completely wretched, and the worst is knowing I've got no one to blame but myself."

They sat in silence for a minute, Sophie wishing she were brave enough to invite Jean to do something with her instead. Something about the bond between Jean and Priscilla was so strong as to repel outsiders.

She sneaked a look at Jean and was intimidated afresh by the scowl on her face. Then she told herself not to be such a coward.

"What had you planned to do this afternoon?" she asked, trying to sound noncommittal.

Jean's face lit up.

"We were going to go and look at the electric kitchen in Princes Street," she said.

Sophie felt hopeful. Perhaps Jean would ask her to come along!

Then Jean slumped back down on the park bench.

"It won't be much fun by myself," she said, chucking a pebble at one of the pigeons. The birds flew up and away in a flurry of cries and feathers.

"I could come with you, if you'd like," Sophie said, choosing her words carefully so as not to put Jean under any obligation.

Jean took Sophie's hand in her own and squeezed it gratefully.

"I'd love you to come, Sophie," she said. "I've been wanting to go for ages; it's supposed to be lovely. I'd have asked you before, but I didn't think you'd be interested."

Even if one didn't care about kitchens one way or the other (Sophie didn't), it was certainly nice to feel wanted.

They left the park by the east gate and walked past the grand row of embassies along Regent Terrace until they passed the school, then wound their way through the monuments on the hill and down by way of Waterloo Place into Princes Street.

They stopped outside the showroom, Jean gazing into the windows while Sophie looked up and down the street. This was where the most recent bomb had gone off, but there were hardly any signs of damage. All the plate-glass windows had been replaced, and only the heap of flowers on the pavement in front of the Army and Navy Store told one that people had died here. Following some impulse she didn't understand,

Sophie leaned down and picked up one of the flowers, which she tucked into the pocket of her satchel.

Next to Sophie, Jean's breath was misting up the shop window.

"Isn't it gorgeous?" she said to Sophie.

Sophie reached for her pocket handkerchief to wipe away the mist.

"I'd like that for my mam," Jean continued, pointing to an enormous electric cooker.

Everybody at school knew that Jean's mother was a slave to housework as well as to Jean's father, who was an awful miser. Jean's godmother paid her school fees. The really monstrous thing was that Mr. Roberts refused to electrify the flat despite his being an electrical engineer who dined out every second Tuesday evening at the electricity lovers' Dynamicables Club.

Suddenly Sophie thought of how unhappy Peggy would be to learn that she was right in the middle of the city's most crowded shopping district. She shifted nervously from one foot to the other.

"Come on, then!" Jean cried, grabbing Sophie's hand. They pushed open the door and made their way into the crowded shop. Two girls in black maid's uniforms and spotless white caps and aprons walked around the room with trays of savories cooked in the electric oven, and Jean and Sophie sampled prunes wrapped in bacon and pigs-in-blankets before wandering to the back of the showroom, where an elegant woman had just taken a beautifully golden sponge cake out of the oven and was inviting members of the audience to lay their fingers on the cake's perfect surface.

There was no doubt it looked a lovely cake, but it soon became clear that the woman wasn't going to cut it up and distribute the pieces—perhaps it was needed for another electric cookery demonstration later that afternoon?—and the girls drifted to the only part of the showroom they had not yet explored, the Electric Arbor at the back of the shop. Here fronds of synthetic greenery had been draped over the really expensive appliances.

"But you said it could be delivered later this week," cried a large lady in a fur jacket that made her look like a walrus. She didn't notice Sophie and Jean gazing at her from the other side of a massive freezer chest.

"That was the ordinary model," the shop assistant said. "With the special features you've requested, madam, it will be a month or more before the manufacturer can ship it."

"I don't want to wait a month!" the lady snapped. "I want it right now!"

"Isn't she awful?" Sophie whispered to Jean. It was curiously enjoyable to see a grown-up person behaving so badly in public.

"Yes," Jean said, "but Sophie, isn't there something familiar about her?"

Meanwhile the lady continued to harangue the helpless assistant. "Without the self-cleaning oven and the automatic timer with its on-off feature," she complained, "I really might as well buy an ordinary model at the Co-Op!"

"I'm very sorry, madam," said the shop assistant, flustered. "I can promise you—"

"Sophie?" Jean said, her voice wavering between horror and laughter.

"Yes?"

"I think that woman's Miss Rawlins!"

Sophie frowned. There had certainly been something familiar about the shopper's face and figure. But how could their old chemistry teacher—the one Mr. Petersen had replaced in March when she left to be married—have turned into this fur-clad monstrosity?

"She must have married a millionaire!" Jean exclaimed.

"Let's wait for her to come back out," Sophie said, almost certain that Jean was mistaken. "It might just be, oh, I don't know, her evil twin or something like that."

They hung around looking at the vacuum cleaners and electric hair dryers until the lady emerged from the manager's office, still hanging on his arm but now clutching her checkbook.

Then they edged closer to the counter, where the lady, still oblivious to their surveillance, brandished a massive gold-and-onyx reservoir pen over her checkbook. They could see the gold bangles on her wrists and a pair of diamond earrings hanging from her ears, earrings that Sophie's great-aunt would certainly have called unsuitable.

They saw the name on the checkbook: Miss Ailsa Rawlins.

"It's her," Sophie said under her breath.

At that moment their former teacher looked up and saw the two girls. She drew her coat more tightly around her and sniffed. "Jean Roberts and Sophie Hunter," she said repressively.

It wasn't exactly a warm greeting.

"Good afternoon, Miss Rawlins," Jean said politely.

"Good afternoon," Sophie echoed, barely suppressing a fit of giggles.

"What are the two of you doing inside on such a fine day?" Miss Rawlins asked them. "Have you already had your constitutional?"

Jean and Sophie looked at each other, then shook their heads. Sophie dragged Jean away before they could disgrace themselves by collapsing into outright laughter. They broke into a run outside, ending up breathless in the grass below the monument to Walter Scott.

"Our constitutional!" Sophie said, once they'd caught their breath.

Just the word itself was enough to send them both into fits of laughter.

"Strange, though," Sophie added thoughtfully. "What exactly do you think she was doing in that shop?"

"Well, obviously, buying an electric cooker! It's natural to get everything fitted out new when you're married, isn't it?"

"She left school to be married, you're quite right. But why is she still writing checks in her maiden name?" Sophie sat up and brushed the grass off her hair. "Don't most married women change their names and share a bank account with their husbands?"

Jean shrugged. "Perhaps she kept the account she had before they were married," she said, not very interested in this line of speculation. Then she perked up. "Perhaps the cooker's a wedding present for her new husband!"

Sophie shook her head. "I don't think she's married yet," she said firmly. Something was nagging at her, but she couldn't think what. "She wasn't wearing a wedding ring just now. Bangles, yes, and earrings and some sort of necklace, but the ring finger was bare."

Jean stared at Sophie.

"It couldn't—"

"She couldn't—"

They both spoke at once. Then Sophie succumbed to an uncontrollable fit of giggles.

"I don't like to say it," she said, almost choking with laughter, "but I think Miss Rawlins may have become a kept woman!"

"No!" said Jean, her eyes going wide with surprise. "How completely extraordinary . . ."

"Yes, people do the strangest things," Sophie said, suddenly grave.

"It's romantic, though, isn't it?" said Jean, sounding as if she wanted reassurance.

"Oh, it's not strange that Miss Rawlins would prefer being someone's kept mistress to teaching chemistry," Sophie said, fighting another attack of laughter. "But it's most peculiar that a millionaire should choose someone like Miss Rawlins to put in his love nest, isn't it?"

The two girls shrieked. For an instant Sophie felt that all was right with the world, what with the warm sun and the smell of grass and roses and the delicious prospect of spreading such an excellent piece of gossip back at school. Then a cloud passed over the sun and she shivered.

"We'd best get a move on," Jean said, struck by the same solemnity that had just come over Sophie.

Jean had to pick up a few things at the shops for her mother, who had telephoned school in the morning to say that she was stuck in the flat with the baby on account of colic.

"Do you want to come with me?" she asked Sophie. "I

must be back at school by five o'clock; Miss Bagshawe wouldn't give me a longer furlough, but she saw I couldn't leave my mother in the lurch."

Peggy wouldn't expect Sophie home for another hour. It was strange how nice it felt to be invited to do something quite ordinary; the shivery distress of a minute ago was gone, and she welcomed the prospect of more companionship.

First they picked up a cottage loaf at the bakery, lingering to peer at the fresh floury baps and iced buns and Sally Lunns bursting with currants.

"Have you any extra money?" Jean was often hungry, but she had to pay for the shopping with her own pocket money, which left nothing over for indulgences.

"No," Sophie said, not quite sorry enough to regret the Ibsen and Strindberg in her satchel. If she hadn't run into Jean, she could have begun one of them this afternoon. . . . She cast a guilty look at Jean as if the other girl could read her mind.

Next they stopped at the Buttercup Dairy.

"Half a pound of butter, please."

"Sweet or salted?"

"Salted."

The girl behind the marble counter placed a square of greaseproof paper on the brass scales and cut a wedge off the slab. Dipping her two wooden paddles into a pretty blue-and-white porcelain bowl of cold water, she worked the butter into a perfectly round pat, pressing into it the stamp with its picture of the dairymaid with the cow holding a buttercup to the girl's chin.

Both girls averted their eyes when they passed the butcher's shop, where several carcasses hung on hooks in the window next to a tray of jellied meats with the label "Potted Head."

"Will you come with me to my mam's?" Jean asked, sounding nervous for the first time that afternoon. Then her voice brightened. "You could meet our new bull mastiff!"

Sophie politely declined, secretly relieved she needed to be back for tea at Heriot Row.

"Walk with me another few minutes, then," Jean said.

They lingered on North Bridge, leaning over the edge and looking out onto the central railway station and the chaotic spread of the city's older sections. The bridge spanned the divide between Edinburgh's two halves: the New Town, swept clear of all dirt and inconvenience and irrationality, its grid of elegant three-story houses characterized by their orderly insistence on life conducted without mess, and the Old, a warren of closes and wynds, ancient tenements of six or seven or eight stories, all bursting at the seams with people.

It was probably a moral failing, but Sophie much preferred the New Town to the Old, because of the way it let one insulate oneself from the loud and smelly and generally off-putting lives of other people.

"Do you like living in the Old Town?" she asked Jean, choosing the words carefully so as not to sound critical.

"Oh, yes," Jean said. "When my dad's out at work, my mam's got all the other tenants in the building to be friendly with. The only reason she had to ask me to get the messages today was that the neighbor's children are down with the chicken pox and she didn't want to leave the baby. It's like having a huge extra family. You can make a new friend whenever you like, and there's always someone to talk to."

Sophie tried not to shudder. It sounded like her idea of hell.

The road along the bridge was fairly empty. A few cars went by, and then a brewer's dray drawn by four Clydesdales, an attractive sight against the hoardings plastered with bright advertisements for proprietary brands of dynamite like Atlas, Hercules, and Goliath.

Meanwhile, walking toward them on the pavement was a girl they both recognized at once.

"Sheena Henshawe!" Jean exclaimed.

Sheena Henshawe had left the Institution for Young Ladies two years earlier, trailing clouds of glory. She had been captain of the hockey and lacrosse teams as well as the girls' rifle eight. Sophie still cherished the memory of the evening at supper when Sheena had casually introduced Sophie as her shooting protégée.

"Do you think she'll remember us?" Jean whispered to Sophie as Sheena came up level with the streetlight.

Sheena had gone on to IRYLNS, like many of her classmates, and Miss Henchman had even mentioned Sheena by name in a recent assembly meant to spur the girls on to new heights of patriotic endeavor.

"Of course she will!" Sophie said, outraged at the idea that Sheena might have forgotten her old friends. "She knows you and me both; she was head girl in our house that time when we all had to do detention for booby-trapping the Faraday house entryway, don't you remember? And she often used to give me and Nan tips on marksmanship."

They watched the young woman walk toward them against the backdrop. Several inches taller than either Jean or Sophie, Sheena wore a mint-green linen suit that by some miracle looked neither dirty nor crumpled, despite the warmth of the day and the grime of the nearby trains. The heels of her shoes were so high that Sophie wondered how she could walk in them.

When Sheena came closer, though, Sophie suddenly doubted her own conviction that the older girl would remember them. Girls who'd left school seemed to become foreign creatures, inhabitants of a strange new world.

As Sheena came up level with them, her eyes swept over the two schoolgirls with no sign of recognition.

"Well!" said Jean when Sheena had vanished out of sight at the other end of the bridge. "She looked as though she thought we weren't fit to wipe the bottom of her shoes with! Sophie, she wasn't always such a snob, was she?"

"No," Sophie said, rather more shaken than she wanted Jean to know. "She was much the nicest of the girls in her year. She gave me that set of colored bamboo-fiber pens for my birthday, and she showed me how to work square roots without a slide rule. She can't have forgotten us, she simply can't!"

"Could she be terribly shortsighted," Jean suggested, "and not able to recognize us without her spectacles?"

But Sheena had had the best eyesight of anyone on the shooting team.

"Sophie?" Jean said.

"What?" said Sophie.

"Didn't Sheena look lovely just now?"

Sophie grunted skeptically.

"That's exactly what I've always imagined a first-class secretary looking like," Jean continued. "Those shoes! Oh, Sophie, I'd do anything to become like Sheena. . . ."

Sophie was offended as well as surprised.

"You can't mean to say that you look at that—that creature that used to be Sheena and want to be like that yourself?" she said, almost in tears at the thought of how Sheena's glossy new carapace made her indistinguishable from any other young woman. "It's horrible! I'd rather *die* than grow up and leave school if it means I'll turn into a complete blank."

"If I go to IRYLNS and get a real job," Jean said, her eyes dreamy and placid, "I'll be able to live in a flat with an electric kitchen. My dad would be proud of me then. He often says how much he wishes he had an IRYLNS-trained secretary to help him in his office, rather than the useless one he's got now."

There was no point arguing. Sophie felt the gulf between herself and Jean open up wider than the span of the bridge.

"I must go," she said abruptly.

"All right," said Jean, still mesmerized by the vision of beautiful clothes and a weekly pay packet. "See you in school on Monday, then."

It was a nasty end to a nice afternoon, Sophie thought, walking up Dublin Street to Abercromby Place and from there along the north edge of Queen Street Gardens toward Heriot Row. She sped up as she came near to the house, and the only strange thing was that the Veteran was lurking on his cart just down the road. He didn't ask Sophie for money, but she had an uneasy feeling he was watching her.

If only Sheena had seen them and stopped, or even just smiled to say hello! Was that what growing up meant, abandoning one's memory and friends and reinventing oneself without the least shred of connection to one's former life?

NINE

THE CLOCK STRUCK FIVE as Sophie let herself in at the front door and went to the kitchen to find Peggy amid steam and general flouriness.

"Thank goodness you're home; your great-aunt's been running about the place like a chicken with the head cut off. You're not to have tea in the kitchen after all—herself wants you upstairs for supper with the visitors."

Sophie sliced herself a thick doorstop of bread and took a bite, wondering who the visitors might be.

"There you go again, eating your bread without any butter or jam!" Peggy exclaimed, slamming a pot of raspberry jam down in front of Sophie along with the butter dish and a knife and plate. "And brought up in the most civilized city in the world! Do put something on that; it gives me the horrors to watch you swallowing a dry crust."

Sophie cut her piece of bread into two and spread butter on one piece, jam on the other. She liked jam and she liked butter but she didn't like jam and butter together.

"Who's coming to supper, then?" she asked.

Peggy made a clucking noise of disapproval.

"There's three of them," she said. "A government minister and her gentleman assistant, and a spiritualist lady, and me with no time to get any fish into the house!"

Though Sophie's great-aunt believed it was a very good idea for women to be vegetarians, whenever a man came to dinner Peggy was expected to serve fish, which Great-aunt Tabitha referred to as "brain food."

"Best go and wash and change into something decent before they get here," Peggy added. "Your great-aunt won't like to see you in that awful old jumper."

It was really Peggy who cared about what Sophie wore rather than Great-aunt Tabitha, but Sophie obliged her by changing into a newish marigold-colored frock.

After washing her face, Sophie waited in her room until the doorbell announced the first arrival. She took the stairs slowly, then smoothed down her hair, which she had forgotten to brush, and let herself into the sitting room.

There she found two people engaged in a tête-à-tête. The

taller was an imposing woman of heavy, almost masculine build, her ash-colored hair styled into a rigid armature. Her conversation partner was a young man with thick, wiry, close-cropped bronze hair, a prominent nose, and an athletic figure. Curiously, the minister and her assistant had exactly the same color eyes, a distinctive pale green, though the man's were hooded and deep-set while the minister's bulged out of the sockets almost like peeled grapes.

They broke off talking to look at Sophie but turned back to their conversation without introducing themselves. She was relieved when Great-aunt Tabitha burst into the room and swept Sophie over to meet the visitors. The older woman was Joanna Murchison, the minister of public safety (Great-aunt Tabitha quite often had members of the cabinet to supper); the young man was Nicholas Mood, the minister's devoted assistant. Great-aunt Tabitha and Joanna Murchison had been at school together, though Sophie thought the two women regarded each other with more wariness than affection.

Amid all the introductions the doorbell rang again, and a moment later Peggy ushered into the room a very attractive woman, thirty-five years old at the most, her sleek black hair cropped close to her head to show off the diamond studs in her ears; she wore a midnight blue silk blouse and a long, narrow black velvet skirt with high heels.

"Miss Grant, how delightful to see you!" said Great-aunt

Tabitha. "Let me introduce you—Joanna Murchison, Ruth Grant, Nicko Mood. Sophie, this is Miss Grant, one of the most talented spiritualists in the Society."

The Society was the Scottish Society for Psychical Research—but Miss Grant couldn't be a spiritualist, she was much too nice-looking. . . .

"I'm the kind of spiritualist," said Miss Grant, smiling at Sophie's expression, "who *doesn't* have drifty tresses and lots of scarves and rings with locks of hair in them."

It was as if she could read Sophie's mind! Sophie resolved to keep her face completely expressionless for the rest of the evening.

The party fell naturally into two groups: a main one composed of Great-aunt Tabitha, the minister, and her assistant, and an onlooker one made up of Sophie and Miss Grant.

After they had watched the others for a few minutes, Miss Grant turned to Sophie and began speaking in a quiet voice.

"It's an interesting dynamic, isn't it? That young man is in the *agonizing* position of being caught between two powerful women, not quite sure which one it's more politic for him to concentrate on pleasing this evening. . . ."

It was true that Nicko Mood's body language was showing an alarming twisty-turny aspect as he reoriented himself to whichever woman was speaking. Sophie felt too shy to say anything in response, but she liked the way Miss Grant spoke to her almost as an equal.

"Your great-aunt invited me here this evening to assess the minister's real state of thought on various political affairs," Miss Grant confided. "Pay attention to the conversation at supper, and see what you think—it never hurts to get another perspective on these things."

"I don't think Great-aunt Tabitha would put much weight on my judgment," Sophie confessed. "She doesn't think I'm old enough to have an opinion."

"Well, then it's about time she started paying a bit more attention, isn't it?" said Miss Grant. Sophie wished she could have even one-tenth the woman's poise and confidence. "Personally, I'll be interested to hear what you make of young Nicko. I find there to be something vaguely sinister about him, but he likes to pass himself off as something of a lightweight."

Her voice had returned to full volume by now, and the word *lightweight* fell into a moment of silence. The other three turned toward Miss Grant, who promptly burst out laughing.

"My mother says my brother's had the most terrible effect on my language," she said with disarming breeziness. "He likes to box, and she's constantly reproaching me for the awful slang I've absorbed."

Sophie was horrified and impressed at the cover-up. Did Miss Grant even *have* a brother?

Over dinner, Sophie learned only that the minister was overbearingly talkative. The conversation was so boring that even Nicko looked hard put to maintain his expression of avid interest. Miss Grant fiddled a lot with her napkin and drank several tumblers of water, while the thin pinched line of Great-aunt Tabitha's lips told Sophie how trying she was finding it to stay quiet as the minister's words rolled over them in great waves of bureaucratic bossiness.

After Peggy had brought in the cheese and fruit and served the coffee, Sophie's great-aunt rapped her saucer with a silver teaspoon.

Everyone turned to look at her, the minister stopping in midsentence and affecting an air more astonished than displeased at the interruption.

"Joanna, you've been waffling on all evening like a talking press release," said Great-aunt Tabitha. "What I want to know is what on *earth* you mean to do about these wretched assassins?"

Trust Great-aunt Tabitha to go directly to the point!

"How would you respond," said the minister, leaning back in her chair and taking a sip of coffee, "were you to learn that the European Federation has been funneling money and explosives to the Brothers of the Northern Liberties?"

The minister's question made the other two women in the room flinch. Nicholas Mood had chosen a pear from the shallow bowl at the center of the table; his peeling technique was admirable, and the yellow-gold skin descended to his plate in a single mesmerizing spiral. Now his knife faltered.

"Surely that's simply a conspiracy theory," Miss Grant interjected, her eyes bright, "a farfetched story meant to damage ordinary people's confidence in the integrity of the government? The Brothers of the Northern Liberties are run-of-the-mill separatists. They despise government meddling and the centralized power that Europe exemplifies. It beggars belief that the Brothers should choose the Europeans for their allies."

"My dear Miss Grant," Mood broke in, "such charming naïveté! Did the minister say the Brothers supported the European government? She merely asserted that they have accepted material aid, in the form of money and ordnance, from them. Did you never hear the expression, 'The enemy of my enemy is my friend'?"

Showing no offense at the young man's rudeness, Miss Grant poured herself another cup of coffee. Sophie admired her calm. The nastiness of Mood's tone had something to do with Miss Grant's being quite young and pretty and not yet very important. Why couldn't men talk to women exactly as they spoke to other men?

"What are you getting at, Nicko?" asked Great-aunt Tabitha, giving him a hard look. "Rumors about Europe's supporting the Brothers have been circulating for months. There's no reason to think there's any substance to the stories."

Mood looked to the minister for permission; receiving a small nod, he puffed up his chest with consequence.

"We stand poised on the verge," he said (it was uncanny how closely his speech patterns followed the minister's), "of acquiring hard evidence of their involvement. Irrefutable evidence, and we'll soon make it public."

An indrawn breath from Miss Grant, some flinching on Great-aunt Tabitha's part: Sophie felt frightened. Great-aunt Tabitha was impervious to intimidation; if *she* was afraid . . .

"The next step, of course," Mood continued with suppressed excitement, "would be to mobilize our own troops in preparation for declaring war on Europe. If we are able to offer the Diet at Stockholm decisive proof that the Europeans have contributed to cause civilian deaths on Scottish soil, the other nations of the Hanse will be obliged to support us."

"War between Europe and the Hanseatic states?" said Great-aunt Tabitha, her voice fainter than usual. "You can't mean it. Surely we've not forgotten the destruction the last war wrought. . . ." She trailed off.

"The European Federation threatens our sovereignty by its very existence," Joanna Murchison said, then heaved a sigh that to Sophie's surprise sounded quite heartfelt. "The last ten years have seen the slow erosion of civil liberties—"

"Yes, and at your own hands, too!" said Great-aunt Tabitha, giving the rim of her coffee cup a quick rap for emphasis. "For shame!"

"I don't deny it," Joanna Murchison said, looking almost bowed down with the weight on her shoulders, "but it has been vital to national security. You know perfectly well that in times of war, small personal liberties must be suspended for the greater good. Afterward—ah, then we will be able to remake the Republic of Scotland as its founders conceived it."

Sophie was confused. She hated the feeling of not knowing enough to understand, and made a resolution on the spot to begin reading the newspapers religiously.

"You genuinely believe what you're saying, don't you?" Miss Grant said suddenly, throwing aside her napkin and pushing her chair back from the table.

"Why do you suspect me of dishonesty?" said the minister. "I only have the country's best interests at heart."

The silence that followed felt almost suffocating. Nicko was eating bites of his pear, licking the juice off his fingers with disgusting voluptuary greediness.

"Nicko!" said the minister.

"Minister?" he said, setting the last slice of fruit down on his plate uneaten and turning to her with unctuous readiness.

The minister stood up, her napkin falling to the floor, and Nicko followed suit.

"We must make our farewells. No, Tabitha, we are fully capable of seeing ourselves out. Good night, Tabitha. Good night, Miss Grant."

The minister shook each woman's hand, ignoring Sophie. Nicko Mood bowed to them both and nodded at Sophie.

"You meant exactly what you said, didn't you?" said Sophie's great-aunt to Miss Grant as soon as the others had left.

"I'm sure Murchison wasn't lying," said Miss Grant. "She sincerely believes that only war with Europe will make Scotland safe. That is not to say, of course, that she doesn't have other motives beyond that oh-so-noble desire to protect the country. She holds half a dozen directorships in munitions companies, for one thing, and she'll not turn down the chance of amassing a small fortune in the event of war. But money's far from the primary goal here. No, Tabitha, though I despise her, I fear there's no way around it. The Society for Psychical Research will have to support her, if indeed it comes to that."

What? Sophie thought she must have misheard.

But Great-aunt Tabitha was nodding her agreement. "It's a great tragedy," she said. "I'm almost certain that any evidence linking the Europeans to the Brothers of the Northern Liberties will have been cooked up for the occasion. But whether or not that's so, the story will be virtually impossible to refute once it's made public."

Now Great-aunt Tabitha sat back in her chair and put a hand over her eyes. Sophie thought she had never looked so old and tired, as if the surge of energy just now had burned out her circuits.

"Isn't there something you can do about Nicko Mood?" Sophie ventured. "He seemed so—so *cunning*. . . ."

The two women looked at each other. Then Great-aunt Tabitha gave a grim laugh. "Don't worry about *him*," she told Sophie. "Nicko knows I've got his number. Unlike Joanna, who's dangerously idealistic, Nicko's in this for the sake of one thing only, the personal advancement and professional ascendancy of Nicholas Mood. If the minister's star were no longer on the rise, Nicko could be easily enough persuaded to make *quite* different choices about where to devote his energies."

Sophie thought there had been something vaguely fanatical about Mood that Great-aunt Tabitha didn't seem to be taking into account, but there was no point persisting.

"Sophie, I count on you to keep this completely secret," Great-aunt Tabitha added. "Not a word to anyone. Understood?"

"Oh, yes," said Sophie, rather thrilled to be trusted for once.

"Off to bed, now. Peggy will give you a cup of warm milk in the kitchen if you can't sleep. Try not to think about what you've heard this evening. And remember, things may turn out perfectly all right in the end."

She didn't say it as though she meant it.

On an impulse, Sophie crossed over and kissed her great-aunt on the cheek before saying good night to the two women. She went straight upstairs to bed without stopping in the kitchen; Great-aunt Tabitha never remembered that Sophie hated milk.

War, she said to herself, lying in bed and trying to fall asleep. If the minister gets her way, the country will be at war by the end of the summer. At war not because of justice or the need to protect national boundaries or save lives, but simply due to one woman's desire to force the world into alignment with her vision.

Sophie distracted herself by translating the sentence into Latin. The Latin version was different from the English because you had to put both parts into the future tense: If the minister will get her way, the country will go to war.

She drifted off to sleep with the grammatical constructions running through her mind like sand through one's fingers at the beach.

TEN

O N THE WAY TO MEET Mikael after a reassuringly indigestible Sunday lunch, Sophie found the streets almost empty. Her destination was the foyer of the central branch of the public library, but as she passed under the Corinthian colonnade through to the grand marble entrance hall, Sophie got a nasty shock. A loud clatter sounded just behind her, and she turned and saw the Veteran on his cart. He leered at Sophie, and she hurried up and made her way inside without delay.

How unusual—how *unpleasant*—to see him on Saturday and Sunday as well as during the week. Usually she only saw him hanging around school.

She tried to push him out of mind, rubbing her temples

with her fingers to dispel a slight headache. She had to stop being silly and concentrate on the task at hand.

Mikael was waiting in the lobby, lounging in a way that proclaimed great satisfaction at his having got there before Sophie.

"Sophie, what kept you?" he said virtuously.

"I'm not late!" Sophie protested.

"No, it's true," he said, laughing. "I was here early, but I knew just what you'd say if I hinted you were late."

Sophie kept her face still so he wouldn't know she was upset, but inwardly she seethed. Why, oh why couldn't she have been born with the sort of thick skin and easy temperament that made Nan, say, completely impervious to teasing?

Something else had caught Mikael's attention.

"What are those things?" he asked, pointing to the row of booths running all along one side of the lobby.

"Those?" Sophie said, surprised. "Don't you have them at home?"

"I can't tell you if we do until I know what they are! Seriously, are they for voting in elections, or perhaps for getting your photograph taken automatically?"

Sophie had forgotten the way Mikael's insatiable curiosity made her notice things about Edinburgh she normally took for granted.

"You really don't know, do you?" she said, still not quite

certain he wasn't pulling her leg. Everybody knew what the machines were for, though it wasn't much talked about.

"No, I don't know, and if you don't tell me, I'm not going to help you find this quack medium of yours, either! Only one person's gone into a booth while I've been here, and he hasn't come back out yet, or I'd ask him instead. There was an old lady who wanted to, but a younger woman—I think it must have been her daughter—stopped her."

It was hard to find the right words to explain.

"You said someone did go in?" she asked.

He nodded.

"How long ago?" she said.

"Oh, five or ten minutes," Mikael said.

"Watch, then."

They turned to face the machines.

"What am I looking for?" Mikael asked after a bit. He was still grinning and seemed to suspect Sophie of playing a minor practical joke.

"You'll know when you see it."

A minute later, two ambulance men came in through the front door, carrying a stretcher and accompanied by a constable in uniform. Clearly they were in no particular hurry; they stopped to chat with the porter on duty before they sauntered over to the third machine in the row of eight.

The constable took a key from his belt and inserted it into

the lock, then held the door open as the ambulance men leaned in and pulled out the corpse of the man Mikael had seen.

The way they handled the body made it quite clear he was dead.

"What happened to him?" Mikael gasped. "Did he die of a heart attack? How did they know where to find him?"

"A signal went off at the police station," Sophie said. Oh dear, she could see she'd have to say it outright. "Mikael, they're suicide machines. Machines for the Voluntary Removal of Life, that's the official name. I thought they had them in all the Hanseatic states. Have you really nothing of the sort in Denmark?"

"Sophie, in København, they'd throw you into prison just for suggesting it! Suicide is illegal in all civilized countries. Do you mean to say that a man can go into one of those things and kill himself, just like that?"

"Well, you can't get in without a special token," Sophie said. The expression on Mikael's face made her flush a little, but there was nothing to be ashamed of, was there? "You can get one from a member of Parliament, a doctor, a minister, a licensed spiritualist, or the senior librarian," she added, hating how defensive she sounded, "but they're not supposed to give you one unless they're convinced you're in your right mind."

"In your right mind, but bent on suicide? Impossible!"

Sophie could perfectly well imagine being in her right mind and yet at the same time wanting to die, but Mikael wasn't the kind of person who would understand.

"Once you insert the token and go in," she continued, deciding to stick with pragmatic rather than philosophical considerations, "the machine kills you with an electric shock and then it summons the police. There's another lot of machines at the main post office, and almost every village has one now too, even the places too small for a Carnegie library."

"And the government actually lets people commit suicide?"

"How can suicide be prevented?" Sophie countered. "Even in olden times, people found ways of killing themselves. It's much more sensible to make it safe and legal."

"Safe? Sophie, just listen to yourself!"

"I don't see why you're getting so worked up about it," Sophie said, uneasily conscious that it had taken Mikael's reaction to reveal what was troubling in the familiar practice. She suddenly wondered whether she might be blind to other things about Scotland as well. But the Scottish government was the best in the world; that was what Great-aunt Tabitha said, and Sophie's great-aunt was always right about politics, even if she didn't seem to understand much about Sophie.

"This country's got an awfully distorted relationship with death," Mikael said, gesturing around him in disgust.

"Enough of this arguing, Sophie. Let's go and see what we can discover about that medium."

"Did you find her the other day?" Sophie asked.

"It was really strange, Sophie," Mikael said. "I went to the address on the card—it was a seedy place in the nastier part of the Old Town—and knew at once I'd found the right spot. The lady in the shop next door described Mrs. Tansy perfectly, and I found a pack of kids who told me she used to be picked up most evenings in a chauffeured motorcar and taken off to her appointments. But the flat was completely empty, and the landlady couldn't—or wouldn't—tell me where she'd gone, or when."

"I don't believe it," said Sophie, puzzled. "Why would she have given out a card if she didn't mean to stay at that address?"

"Fishy, isn't it? It wasn't hard to track down the carter who took her things, but that didn't get me much further. He'd taken her goods to a long-term storage warehouse in Leith, where she paid on the spot for six months' storage. She didn't leave a forwarding address."

"It's most suspicious!" Sophie said. "What can she be up to?"

"It's possible, of course, that Mrs. Tansy's left the city, or even gone out of the country," Mikael continued. "On the other hand, the landlady gave me the distinct impression that she was still fairly close at hand."

"What did she say that made you think that?" Sophie asked. Though the thought of seeing the medium again made her skin crawl, Sophie really did want to talk to the woman. It would be impossible to find out the meaning of her warning if she had left Edinburgh.

"It wasn't anything she said, not exactly. Well, I suppose it was. Oh, it sounds silly now. . . ."

"No, tell me," Sophie pressed him. "What was it?"

"Well, the landlady had a bird in a cage—a budget, is that the word?"

"Budgie!" Sophie said, amused by his small mistake.

"Budgie, then. But there was an enormous black cat stalking about the flat. Several times the cat actually made it up onto the shelf and got his paw through the bars before the landlady noticed. She saw me looking and said she was only keeping the cat for a few days. If her friend hadn't come for it in a month, she'd throw the wretched animal out into the street."

"That's a real Sherlock Holmes move, isn't it?" Sophie said, full of admiration for Mikael's perspicacity. "It does seem likely the cat belonged to Mrs. Tansy; you could see her thinking a big black cat would be a good prop for a medium."

"Afterward I checked with the children outside," said Mikael, clearly pleased. "That cat *definitely* used to live with

Mrs. Tansy. She doted on it and paid the kids off to make sure nobody would hurt it."

Sophie congratulated Mikael on having found all this out.

"It wasn't hard," he said, brushing away the compliment. "The trick will be to find where she's gone now. I can't watch her old place. I've bribed a couple of those kids to get me word if she shows up, but we can't count on them."

"Where do you think she's gone?"

"Hard to say. If she's holed up at a friend's, we may never find her. On the other hand, she hasn't taken much with her, and I think there's a good chance she'll have gone to a hotel. Would that fit with what you saw of her that night at your great-aunt's?"

Sophie thought about it.

"Yes, I think so," she said after a minute.

"So what we must do now is get a list of Edinburgh hotels," Mikael said, "and then I can check whether she's registered at any of them."

"Surely she won't have registered under her own name? It would be pretty idiotic to go to all that trouble not to be found and then leave your name for anyone who thought to come looking."

"No, but the wretched woman cuts such a distinctive figure, she won't find it easy to conceal herself," said Mikael. "Even if I don't have the right name, I'll be able to describe her—you know, jet beads, heavy build, that sort of thing, just like you said—and explain to the people at the front desk why they should let me up to see her. By pretending she's the only person who can help me get in touch with the ghost of my dead mother, for instance."

"You'd pretend *that*?" Sophie said, surprised that the séance-despising Mikael would even fake a belief in spiritualism.

"All in a day's work," Mikael said. "Seriously, if you really mean to find things out, you can't stand on principle."

He seemed to have grown up quite a bit since his last time in Scotland. He even looked quite handsome, Sophie thought, if not altogether up to the Mr. Petersen standard.

"Let's get the list of hotels from the telephone book in the main reading room," she said.

"Good idea."

They left an hour later with a list of thirty hotels.

She felt remorseful that obligations at school would stop her from being much use, but Mikael waved away her apologies.

"It's my pleasure, Sophie," he said. "Things get pretty quiet at the professor's, and at least this will keep me out of trouble."

A sharp shooting pain made itself felt above Sophie's left eye. "What if it gets you into trouble instead?" she asked, feeling slightly sick. For some reason thinking about the medium made Sophie's head hurt.

"I'm used to getting in trouble," Mikael said. "You could even say I like it."

"Oh, if this goes wrong, your aunt will never forgive me!" said Sophie.

"Nonsense. Stop worrying. You'll see, I'm good at this."

Just then Sophie's headache came on so strongly that she decided not to fuss any more over Mikael, who promised to let her know as soon as he found anything out. She walked home in a daze, her head so painful that she hardly noticed the figure on the cart following her back to Heriot Row.

At home, Peggy took one look at Sophie's face and put her straight to bed with an aspirin and a mug of hot lemon-barley water. She wouldn't even listen to Sophie's pleas to be allowed to finish her homework. Secretly this was a relief, though Sophie would never have admitted it.

ELEVEN

O N MONDAY NEITHER JEAN nor Sophie mentioned having seen Sheena, in unspoken agreement that it had been too troubling to turn into a funny story. It was Priscilla, that evening, who put into words the strangest thing about their having seen their old chemistry mistress.

"It doesn't make any sense," she said. "Miss Rawlins wasn't *pretty* enough to be a kept woman, not the kind of kept woman who gets given fur coats and electric cookers, at any rate. I don't dispute what you say about her not really being married, but there's got to be some other explanation."

"Perhaps her fiancé stood her up and she's buying furs and electrical appliances now in order to console herself," Sophie suggested, though she could hear how thin it sounded.

Really it was what had happened to Sheena that Sophie considered the greater mystery—a mystery she could hardly bear to contemplate.

"That can't be it," said Priscilla. "If you don't mind my being blunt, women usually become better off when they marry. Miss Rawlins didn't have any money when she was our teacher, and if she hasn't married after all, where's the money come from?"

"How do you know she didn't have any money?" Nan asked.

"Oh, she hadn't a penny beyond her salary," Priscilla said, confident in the way of someone who came from money herself. "Don't you remember that awful caoutchouc mackintosh we used to joke about when we had her for first-form science? No self-respecting woman with a private income would wear a raincoat like that for a day longer than she absolutely had to."

"Yes," said Sophie, "but couldn't she have had her mind on higher things? Some people don't mind what they wear."

"Sophie, we all know *your* mind's on higher things," Priscilla said, laughing in an annoyingly superior way, "but even that dreadful cardigan of yours must once have been quite good. At least good clothes age gracefully. Don't you remember the revolting carnation scent Miss Rawlins used to wear, and the amber brooch that looked like something out of the lucky dip at a village fête? I'm not at all surprised to hear of her wearing a fur jacket in June. She hadn't good taste, and yet she hankered after expensive things."

"Yes," Jean interjected, "that jacket must have cost fifty guineas or more!"

"I think Miss Rawlins lied when she said she was leaving to be married," Priscilla continued. "And here's a thought: what if somebody paid her off to leave her job partway through the school year?"

"Why would someone pay her to leave her job, though?" said Nan.

Instead of giving a direct answer, Priscilla asked another question.

"Who benefited from her leaving like that?" she said.

"Priscilla, you're not saying—," said Jean, drawing in a breath and then falling silent.

"I most certainly am," said Priscilla, an evil glint in her eye.

Sophie had a bad feeling about what was coming next.

"Let's suppose," Priscilla said, "that Mr. Petersen paid off Miss Rawlins so that he could take her place. This job gives him the perfect cover for his secret life! And of course it explains why she might have come into money—the false marriage story would have simply been a pretext for her change of fortune."

Sophie groaned. The whole business about Mr. Petersen leading a double life was absurd. Priscilla was doing this just to torment her.

"Are you harking back to the notion that Mr. Petersen might have had something to do with the bombings?" Nan asked, looking up from her history essay. "I don't see a school providing very good cover for a terrorist, if that's what you're getting at. Surely there are other jobs where one might come and go more freely without anybody noticing?"

"Yes," said Priscilla, "but this place is so respectable, it makes up for not allowing you the freedom of movement you'd have as, say, an insurance salesman. Besides, my father says the police have tests now to find out whether you've recently handled explosives. Since he's teaching chemistry, he's got a perfectly good excuse for the tests coming back positive if they arrest him and find traces of chemicals on his hands."

Sophie stood up. "I'm going to bed," she said. It would be too awful if the others could tell how upset she was.

"Sophie, you can't pretend you don't suspect him yourself, just a little bit," Priscilla called after her as she retreated to the bedroom.

Sophie couldn't help giving it some serious thought. Was Priscilla right? Sophie had Mr. Petersen's handkerchief under her pillow. Her hand went to it involuntarily now, and she twisted the muslin into a knot around her fingers.

As for suspecting him in the bombings, it was impossible to see Mr. Petersen either as a political ideologue or as a criminal mastermind. But what if the teacher had some quirk in his mental makeup that made him know he was doing something wrong without being able to stop himself?

It took Sophie a long time to fall asleep.

Miss Chatterjee started class the next morning by holding her left hand up in the air, fist clenched, and asking the girls to guess what she was holding.

"It has something to do with what we're learning this week," she said when the girls begged for a hint.

"Is it a key?" Jean said doubtfully. "A key to a museum of historical exhibits?"

Miss Chatterjee shook her head.

"A coin," Fiona suggested, "a coin with Napoleon's head on it!"

"You've both come close—it's certainly a small metal object—but you haven't yet fastened on the right thing. . . ."

In fairy tales, two wrong answers always came before the right one. Sophie closed her eyes for a moment and let her mind go blank. The picture of a small metal thing swam into view.

"It's a bullet," she said, opening her eyes in time to see

Miss Chatterjee smile as if Sophie had said something very clever. It wasn't at all clever, of course, just a good guess.

"It is indeed a bullet, and not just an ordinary bullet but one that was actually fired on the battlefield at Waterloo," the teacher said, holding up the slug for them to look at. "It lodged in the shoulder of our school's founder and was removed later on by an army surgeon; if you look closely, you can actually see the marks of the doctor's tweezers and the distortion that comes when soft lead meets solid flesh."

Some of the girls looked sick.

"Yes, stomach-turning, isn't it?" said Miss Chatterjee. "But we mustn't be high-minded about violence. If we woke up tomorrow and the world had no more use for top-quality munitions, the days of the Hanseatic League would be numbered. But how does Scotland reconcile its identity as a leading exporter of arms and explosives with its commitment to peace?"

There was a long silence. It took some nerve for Sophie to speak up, but she felt she had to.

"Is that a rhetorical question, Miss Chatterjee, or a real one?" she asked.

"A real one," said Miss Chatterjee, her voice silkier than ever.

Sophie took a deep breath and readied herself to talk the thing through. "Arms are compatible with peace," she said slowly, "because we've adopted a philosophy of deterrence. If there are two great powers, and each one can release enough force to destroy the other, it produces a stalemate."

"If we start bombing each other," said Priscilla, "people are going to die. *Lots* of people."

Sophie saw Nan's face go quite pale. She must be thinking of her brothers.

"When we observe Waterloo Day, let's say, as we will do this weekend," said Miss Chatterjee, tilting her head to one side as she looked at the class, "how do we orient ourselves toward the war dead?"

"We celebrate their sacrifice," said Harriet.

"We mourn their loss," Fiona added, her fair, freckled skin flushing with embarrassment at having said something that might sound pompous.

"How do you think it looked, then, to the Duke of Wellington that day in June, a hundred and twenty-three years ago?" Miss Chatterjee said, her voice quiet and passionate. "Say you're Wellington, in charge of the Allied Army. You're a few days away from what you already suspect will be a decisive engagement, one that will determine whether you crush Napoleon and preserve Britain's status as the world's great imperial power or instead precipitate the long slow loss of English sovereignty in years to come."

"You'd do anything to stop him," Sophie said, her voice

sounding too loud in her ears.

"And what if you were Wellington," said Miss Chatterjee, "and a time traveler from the future arrived in your tent the night before the battle and told you that you could save tens of thousands of lives by retreating?"

"When it comes to a decision like that," Nan said, "a general couldn't listen even to a very respectable time traveler. It would be treason. Besides, if history had unfolded differently, Wellington might have actually *beaten* Napoleon at Waterloo. Imagine: Scotland and England might still be one country, and the Austro-Hungarian Empire a major European power. Why, by now the world might have achieved universal peace!"

They all sat for a moment contemplating Nan's vision of world peace.

"Might one lesson of Waterloo, then," said the teacher softly, "be that a heroic but ultimately self-defeating gesture, though it may guarantee the deaths of many thousands of men, is sometimes preferable to diplomatic means as a way of resolving conflicts between nations?"

But Miss Chatterjee was a pacifist! She *couldn't* be saying this.

"It sounds as though you're suggesting that war is sometimes more effective than peace," Nan said, her outrage audible. "That's certainly what *I* think, Miss Chatterjee, but you've always wanted us to believe that peace is better than war!"

Her eyes accused Miss Chatterjee of betrayal.

"It is not my job," said Miss Chatterjee, raising one eyebrow, "to indoctrinate you in the ideology to which I personally subscribe."

"But you're a pacifist! That's not an ideology, it's a belief," said Fiona, clearly at least as crushed as Sophie and Nan.

"Pacifism is an ideology like any other," said the teacher, "and you would do well to remember it. Four sides, please, for tomorrow, on the lessons of Waterloo for our own time."

TWELVE

FOR THE SAKE OF THE war-preparedness effort, Miss Henchman had recently decreed that all fifth- and sixth-form girls must have regular driving lessons. Sophie's first session fell that Tuesday afternoon. As she and a handful of other girls waited in front of school, Miss Chatterjee drew up in her dashing Crossley roadster.

Sophie would have loved to go for a drive with Miss Chatterjee, but a mantle of shyness held her back. When Miss Chatterjee patted the seat next to her, a sixth-form girl hopped in; the teacher tooted the horn at the rest of them and drove off.

Miss Henchman herself pulled up next in a sedate black Austin and was joined by Fiona.

As the next few cars came by and girls jumped in and drove off, Sophie's hands grew clammy. It was a relief not to have to go with Miss Henchman, but what if they ran out of teachers?

Sophie and another fifth-form girl called Jenny were the last ones standing when two cars pulled up in quick succession. Jenny got into the first, a saloon driven by Matron, and Sophie found herself—oh heavenly good fortune!—climbing into the passenger seat of Mr. Petersen's adorable little bottle-green PG.

"Hello, Sophie," he said as he pulled back out into the road. "I thought I'd drive us out toward Arthur's Seat, and then we'll switch places and you can take a turn or two around the hill. The thing for today is to begin getting a feel for the machine; it'll be fairly deserted out there at this time of day, so you needn't worry much about other cars."

It was both thrilling and terrifying, Sophie discovered, to find herself alone in a car with the object of her affections. Fortunately she didn't have to look directly at Mr. Petersen. He had rolled up his shirtsleeves, and her gaze fell to the veins and muscles of his forearms. People talked utter rubbish about the differences between men's and women's minds, but it was hard not to be struck with the difference between their hands.

She would die if he ever found out about her crush!

All too quickly they reached the lower slopes of Arthur's Seat. The road up the hill was barely wide enough for two cars to pass. As Mr. Petersen pulled over in the Cat's Nick lay-by, Sophie fervently hoped they wouldn't meet a car coming in the opposite direction.

Terror at the idea of operating the motorcar suddenly pushed everything else out of her head. What if she crashed it? A small whimper came out of her throat.

Mr. Petersen politely pretended he hadn't heard.

"You won't find it difficult, you know, Sophie," he told her as they got out of the car and switched seats. "Just remember, left foot on the accelerator, right foot on the brake, right hand for the manual brake. Your left hand should always rest on the navigation wheel."

The car's electrical system included a dynamo, a starter motor, and a battery. Sophie put her hand on the plastic knob of the starter and pulled it out as far as it would go. Then she took a deep breath, released the knob, and felt the car's motor spring to life.

"Harder on the accelerator. That's right, rev it a bit. Feel the power?"

Sophie experimented with different levels of acceleration. It was certainly comforting to think of the hand brake holding the car in place even if she did something stupid.

"All right, let the hand brake go. Go on. You know, the

car's not going to run away with you, you can take it a bit faster than that. . . ."

Once she had pulled out of the lay-by and around the first corner, Sophie relaxed a little. Mr. Petersen continued to talk, a stream of babble that calmed Sophie down rather than teaching her anything she didn't already know.

"Most motorcars in Scotland are powered by fuel cells. A fuel cell is similar to a battery, except that whereas batteries run down, you can keep fuel cells going indefinitely by pumping in more chemicals. Thomas Edison invented this particular version in the 1880s; you put in hydrogen and oxygen, and the cell converts them into electricity, the only by-product being perfectly pure drinking water."

Sophie had a moment of panic when she pressed the accelerator by accident instead of the brake and the car surged forward, but Mr. Petersen didn't stop his monologue, and she soon calmed down again.

"Ironically, given that Edison was an American, his invention never really caught on over there. You'll find a few fuel-cell enthusiasts in the Americas, of course, but most of their motorcars are powered by a filthy and wasteful method called internal combustion. All very well if you're an American sitting on top of huge petroleum reserves, but that kind of reckless consumption doesn't suggest a very sensible attitude toward the future!"

Mr. Petersen proved better at teaching practical things than abstract ones. He did not object when Sophie asked him to draw a diagram to clarify the principle behind the three-point turn or get angry when she couldn't make the car go in reverse.

"It's an old car, and the transmission's a bit dodgy," he said. "I've been meaning to take it in to be serviced. Consider this a useful reminder."

After an hour and a half, Mr. Petersen checked his watch.

"Ready to drive us back to school?" he asked.

"No!" Sophie said. Her hands were aching with the strain of holding the navigation wheel, and the muscles in her legs felt extremely shaky.

If only she hadn't had to concentrate so hard on driving! It certainly wasn't at all what the phrase *romantic tête-à-tête* brought to mind.

"Sophie, I'm disappointed in you! I thought you had a more adventurous spirit. I'll take over, shall I?"

"Thank you," Sophie said.

They switched seats and drove back toward school.

"I hope we'll have time for another lesson before the end of term," Mr. Petersen said.

Oh, he must think Sophie a complete idiot for being so tongue-tied! She forced out a few words at exactly the same moment as Mr. Petersen started speaking again.

"I'd like that—"

"I've been meaning to ask—"

The wheel jerked in the teacher's hands and they narrowly missed hitting a lady crossing the road at the corner.

As the lady shook her fist at them, Sophie suddenly realized that Mr. Petersen was at least as nervous as she was.

"Good thing I wasn't the one driving just now, eh, Mr. Petersen?" she said, hoping her voice didn't sound too quavery. "What were you about to ask me?"

"I'm looking for someone to help me for a few hours a week in the laboratory," he said hurriedly, his eyes fixed on the road. "Would you be willing to put in some time reorganizing the supplies in the balance room?"

This was so much the kind of invitation that Sophie received in her daydreams, she was afraid at first she must have misheard him.

"*Would* I?" she said.

But Mr. Petersen was shaking his head.

"What am I thinking? Of course you wouldn't. You're probably absolutely swamped with work between now and finals—forget I ever mentioned it; I'm sure I can find someone else—you must think I'm a thoughtless idiot—"

"No," said Sophie, finding her voice, "that wasn't what I meant at all. Oh, *please* let me do it!"

"Are you sure, Sophie?" said Mr. Petersen. Sophie

thought he sounded both guilty and relieved. "I'm confident you're the best one for the job," he went on, "but the last thing I want is to put you in a difficult position. I won't think any less of you if you say you won't do it, you know."

"I really want to do it!" Sophie said. She would simply *die* if he refused her services out of misguided scruples.

"Well, if you're sure, I'm going to accept," said Mr. Petersen in an apologetic manner, "but you can always back out later if you find the arrangement's more trouble than it's worth. When will be the best time for you to fit the work in? Tuesdays and Thursdays, perhaps?"

Inwardly glowing, Sophie agreed to meet him at half past two on Thursday afternoon. This must have been what he meant to ask her the morning the bomb went off. Surely Mr. Petersen was the kindest and most gentle person imaginable!

By now they were back at school. Mr. Petersen let Sophie out at the side door and drove off.

THIRTEEN

"**D**ID MR. PETERSEN REVEAL his *dark secrets* while you were in the car together, Sophie?" said Priscilla.

Sophie grunted a denial and kept her head buried in her history textbook.

"Perhaps Sophie used her feminine wiles to get him to tell her about the bombings?" Jean added.

"*What* feminine wiles?" countered Priscilla.

Both girls went into fits of laughter.

While Sophie tried hard to ignore them, a knock came at the study door. Jean opened it, letting in one of the younger students.

"I've got a message for Sophie," said the girl, eyes fixed on the floor. Sophie took the folded note from her hand and began reading.

"Where did you get this?" she asked the little girl.

"From a boy," the girl said. "He came up to the fence at the back of the playground and called me over to him. When I told him we weren't allowed to receive messages from boys, he said he was a good friend of yours and that Matters of the Utmost Importance depended on your getting it."

"What did he look like?" Sophie asked, ignoring the others' snickering.

"Tall and fair, I suppose," said the child doubtfully. "Oh, and he sounded as if he might be a tiny bit foreign, though he had very good English."

"Thank you," said Sophie. "If you see that boy again tomorrow, tell him I'll be there when he says. Not a word to any of the teachers, mind."

"Oh, no," said the little girl, looking absolutely terrified.

As soon as she had gone, the others demanded to know what was going on.

"It's a friend of mine," she said reluctantly. "You know, that Hanseatic boy I see sometimes at the professor's house, the housekeeper's nephew."

"Sophie, you never said anything about a boy!" Nan said. "You were supposed to go to the professor for language lessons, not for secret assignations!"

"Don't be such a bad sport, Nan!" Priscilla said. Priscilla was often accused of being boy-crazy while Sophie was famous for not being interested in boys, so it was natural for her to leap at the possibility of Sophie coming over to the boy-liking side of things. "I think it shows real initiative, Sophie, going off like that to meet a boy. Are you in love with him?"

"Of course not," Sophie snapped. "Mikael's my friend." She couldn't stop herself from blushing. "It's not what you think," she added helplessly.

"Sophie's meeting a boy!" Priscilla crowed. "Sophie, is he desperately in love with you?"

"No, he's not," said Sophie, hating how stiff she sounded. How nice it would be if someone *was* desperately in love with her—but it seemed a wildly unlikely prospect, and Mikael had certainly never thought of such a thing. "Mikael does want me to meet him tomorrow at four o'clock in the groundsman's shed," she said. "You'll help me do it, won't you?"

In the end, though Sophie waited in the shed for more than half an hour, Mikael never came. How maddening of him to be so careless about the time! She would be in hot water if she didn't hurry back to the dormitory, and think of how mortifying to have to explain to the others that she'd been stood up.

Beneath the irritation, though, Sophie felt a twinge of worry. What if something had happened to Mikael?

It was with a horrible sense of inevitability at supper that Sophie looked up to see a pair of uniformed police constables enter the refectory.

A teacher pointed toward Sophie, and a moment later they began to move in her direction. For one frightening moment she was sure they had come to arrest her for breaking the out-of-bounds rule, before realizing how preposterous that was.

Sophie was still chewing a stringy mouthful of gristle when the constables stopped on the other side of the table.

"Sophie Hunter?"

Sophie nodded.

The other girls at the table stared. Priscilla reached for Sophie's hand and squeezed it in reassurance.

"I'm WPC Taylor and this is my colleague PC Martin," the woman constable said. "We've been sent to fetch you down to the central police station. We believe you may be in a position to clear up certain aspects of the story told by a young man who was apprehended earlier this afternoon at the Balmoral Hotel."

Sophie folded her napkin and set it beside her plate, carefully adjusting the knife and fork. Her legs felt trembly when she pushed the chair back from the long table and stood up.

"My friend's not a thief," she said urgently. "He—"

"Oh, it's not a question of burglary," said the other constable, smacking his lips. "The boy was found standing over a dead body. He's a murder suspect."

Murder!

"Mikael would never—," Sophie began to protest.

The woman constable laid a hand on her shoulder to silence her.

"No names, please," she said, glaring at her partner as if he'd already given too much away. "The investigation has been turned over to the antiterror squad, and as far as they're concerned, the less said the better."

Whatever could the antiterror squad want with Mikael? This was worse than Sophie could possibly have imagined.

"Because you're a minor," the constable added, "you'll need an adult to come with you to the station."

Sophie looked helplessly around her. The teachers all looked as stunned at the girls.

Then Miss Chatterjee stepped forward.

"I will accompany Sophie," she said. "Miss Hopkins, will you please tell Miss Henchman where we have gone?"

"When will you be back?" asked the biology mistress.

"We can't guarantee the girl won't be needed for a considerable amount of time," said the constable ominously.

"Nonsense," Miss Chatterjee said with great firmness. "Sophie must be back at school by ten o'clock at the very latest. If you need her for longer, it'll simply have to wait until tomorrow. You can't keep the child hanging about the police station until all hours. In fact, it occurs to me that we might be well advised to wait until tomorrow in any case, and to telephone the school solicitor in the meantime."

The woman constable flinched at the word *solicitor*. "That won't be necessary, madam," she said, her manner more conciliatory than before. "There's no question of Miss Hunter being considered a suspect. But this is a matter of national security, and it's essential we resolve matters as soon as we can."

"Very well, then," said Miss Chatterjee. "Perhaps I'll just mention, though, that our headmistress is quite close to the advocate general; I hope she will not feel any need to call upon that friendship."

Then, as the constables stood speechless, she added, "Well? What are we hanging about here for? I received a distinct impression of there being no time to waste."

She turned her head and gave Sophie an almost imperceptible wink, a gesture of solidarity that brought tears to Sophie's eyes.

FOURTEEN

THE POLICE CAR WAITED outside, a massive black Wolseley. Sophie and Miss Chatterjee were put in the backseat behind a metal grille. When Sophie tested the handle, the door wouldn't open from the inside.

After they passed the Balmoral Hotel, Sophie knew they couldn't be headed to the central police station in Conan Doyle Close. It would be the Castle, and that meant they really were serious about this national security business. Beads of sweat stood out on her forehead, and she was afraid for a minute that she might actually be sick.

They drove in silence across North Bridge into the Old Town. Just before Castlehill, the car pulled off the road into a secure lot, and the woman constable let Sophie and Miss

Chatterjee out of the car. They walked together across the esplanade and right up to the main gate, where four soldiers with machine guns stood at attention.

After passing through a series of gates and checkpoints, they came to Crown Square, the most secure section of the entire complex, where another team of armed guards searched them for hidden weapons. Even Miss Chatterjee seemed to quail a little as they followed the circuitous path from the Great Hall to the Vaults, which had housed prisoners of war since the eighteenth century and had been lately modernized at great expense as a high-security facility for holding terrorists.

They passed through a warren of empty graffiti-covered cells and then a long underground tunnel.

Passing through an austere waiting room, they were ushered into a spacious room decorated disconcertingly like something out of a luxury ocean liner, including a chrome drinks cabinet, a set of angular couches covered in red leather substitute, and a white fur rug.

The man whose office it was saw Sophie scanning the interior and laughed.

"Yes, it's a distinctly peculiar style, isn't it?" he said, grinning at her. Sophie sensed him turning on his charm to warm her up; it made her bristle with irritation and inward resistance. "Particularly in a Gothic hulk like the Castle!"

Though his manner annoyed Sophie, the officer was extremely handsome, with dark hair and a toothbrush mustache exactly like the one worn by the current European chancellor. Unlike the chancellor, who was never photographed except in military uniform, he wore a casual dark lounge suit and shiny leather shoes. He missed being drop-dead gorgeous only because of legs too short in proportion to his top half.

If war were to be declared, Sophie thought, he would definitely have to shave the mustache.

"I'm Commander Brown, by the way," the man added, in the annoying English drawl lots of Scottish officers still used as a matter of course. Great-aunt Tabitha said that Scottish people who spoke with an English accent should be repatriated south of the border and see how they liked it.

The commander reached his hand out, and Sophie shook it.

"You're Sophie Hunter, of course, and the lady with you—"

"Mira Chatterjee," the teacher said.

He held out his hand again, but Miss Chatterjee did not reciprocate, and after a moment he pulled his arm back.

"Sophie—do you mind if I call you that?—you're here this evening because we need your help. Your friend Mikael was found this afternoon at the Balmoral Hotel standing over the dead body of a Mrs. Euphemia Tansy, whom I believe to have been a medium of your acquaintance. I hasten to say that after a brief initial misunderstanding, we quickly abandoned any idea of Mikael's being an active suspect in the medium's murder. But we've got a strong feeling he hasn't told us everything, out of some mistaken motive of chivalry."

"Mikael's not chivalrous," Sophie said, too giddy with relief to be polite. The constables must have lied about Mikael's being a suspect in order to make her more afraid. "Mikael wouldn't want to get a friend in trouble, it's true, but he gave you my name, didn't he? He's not completely lacking in common sense!"

"Yes, and we're grateful for it," the commander said. His barely concealed impatience made Sophie feel suddenly rather frightened. "But all the boy would say was that you'd had some kind of a run-in with the woman, and that he'd promised to find out whether someone had put her up to it."

"But that's just right," Sophie said. She didn't understand what else he wanted to know. "It's exactly what happened. Mikael wants to be a private investigator when he grows up, and since he's here on holiday with nothing much to do, he said he'd look into it for me."

The commander exhaled loudly, then pressed his fingers to the bridge of his nose. Sophie felt an intense surge of dislike for the man. Surely he did not need to show quite so clearly that he thought her a troublesome encumbrance to his inquiry!

"You don't seem to understand the difficulty, Sophie," he said, speaking, Sophie thought, as though to a mentally deficient ten-year-old. "Mrs. Tansy was a distinctly suspicious character. She happened to be on the government payroll, like any number of other spiritualists, but we think she may also have been taking money from several other parties, including the Nobel Consortium and possibly even the Brothers of the Northern Liberties. We've had her under surveillance for some time, but she eluded our team several weeks ago in a department store in Princes Street, and by the time my man reached her home, she'd absconded—she must have planned it in advance. We saw neither hide nor hair of her until she turned up with her throat cut in a suite at the Balmoral. Help me out, Sophie. What on earth had an ordinary schoolgirl like yourself to do with that b—"

A look from Miss Chatterjee prevented him from using a word he would regret, and he ended simply by clearing his throat.

"Your friend Mikael," he added, "doesn't seem to have a very clear idea of how it came about that you met her."

"It was at my great-aunt's house," Sophie said. "Didn't Mikael tell you?"

"Sophie's great-aunt," interrupted Miss Chatterjee, "is Miss Tabitha Hunter."

The commander's head jerked around.

"Miss Tabitha Hunter," he said slowly, failing to conceal his surprise, "president of the Scottish Society for Psychical Research?"

"Oh, I see," said Sophie suddenly. "Mikael would only know her as Great-aunt Tabitha, not as Tabitha Hunter, and besides, he's probably never heard of her, not being Scottish. I mean, she's quite well known in Edinburgh—"

"Indeed," the commander muttered under his breath.

"—but not in Denmark, where Mikael's from."

"A séance at Miss Tabitha Hunter's, and Mrs. Tansy no doubt the distinguished medium," the commander said meditatively.

Though it did not sound like a question, Sophie answered as if it had been.

"Yes, that's right," she said. "And she said some very odd things—I can't really describe it, but there was something *off* about the whole business. I couldn't get it out of my mind. So when Mikael offered to help me find out more about her, it seemed like the perfect solution. Was—was her throat really cut?"

Commander Brown made a graphic sweep with his hand across his throat, and Sophie thought she had never disliked anyone so much in her life.

Miss Chatterjee frowned. During Sophie's last words she had taken a small diary from her handbag and written a few notes with a silver pencil.

"That gesture was quite inappropriate, Commander," she said. "Do you intend to hold the boy overnight, or have you finished with him? I think Sophie might like to see he's all right before we go."

"And who's to say we've finished with Sophie, let alone with the boy?" said the commander in a menacing way. "It's within my mandate to keep the girl here for seventy-two hours, so long as I notify her guardian and allow her to speak to an advocate."

"An empty threat," said Miss Chatterjee, rising and tipping her head at Sophie to let her know she should stand. "Sophie's told you what she knows. You can find her during the week at school or at her aunt's on the weekend. In either case, I suggest you telephone in advance."

The commander raised an eyebrow, but said nothing.

"My other suggestion," the teacher continued, "is that you release the boy at once. I believe that under the Hamburg Convention of 1919, you need a judge's warrant to hold a Hanseatic national overnight without legal representation."

The commander's jaw dropped.

"Ah, I thought you might have forgotten about that

provision," Miss Chatterjee said. "I can assure you, however, that the other states in the League take it very seriously, especially in the case of a minor. If necessary, of course, I will telephone my friend at the Danish embassy first thing tomorrow morning to tell him you are in breach of the agreement."

The commander's face suddenly relaxed. He laughed and stood up.

"Miss Chatterjee, anyone foolish enough to tangle with you will doubtless find a formidable adversary. Happily in this case we're on the same side. All I want is to put a stop to the bombings, and occasionally this leads me to measures of which you doubtless disapprove. The boy is being held in a cell here in the Vaults, but one of the subalterns has already telephoned his aunt and asked her to come and get him. When she arrives, he will be released into her custody. You're welcome to see him now, if you like."

He picked up the telephone and spoke a few words to the aide, who appeared a minute later and took them back out into the waiting room, where he offered them tea or coffee. When they declined, he vanished.

Sophie turned to Miss Chatterjee as soon as they were alone, and opened her mouth to speak. Miss Chatterjee pressed a finger to her lips and rolled her eyes at the ceiling.

"You mean—listening devices?" Sophie said stupidly.

Miss Chatterjee nodded and Sophie fell silent.

Fifteen minutes later, the aide reappeared at the head of a retinue that included Mikael and four armed guards.

"Sophie!" Mikael said. "I had to give them your name, there was no way around it. I hope you're not in too much trouble—I know you're not much used to it."

Sophie ignored Miss Chatterjee's grim amusement. "Don't worry about that," she said, tormented by the idea of what Mikael had just gone through on her account.

She was afraid to go closer while the guards' semiautomatic machine guns remained on him. Now, as if reading her mind, one of the guards used the ring of keys at his waist to free the boy's hands from their shackles.

"You're free to go, sir," said the aide, "as soon as your aunt gets here, but the commander thought you might like a word first with Miss Hunter."

There was nowhere, really, to have a private conversation, but after looking at Miss Chatterjee for permission, Sophie led Mikael to one end of the bench.

Mikael looked pale and exhausted and somehow younger than the last time she'd seen him. His skin had a whitish green pallor under the lights of the Vaults, and he looked as diminished as a newly shorn sheep.

"Was it awful?" Sophie whispered, not sure if she was asking about the cells or the dead body.

"Oh, Sophie, I'm so glad you didn't have to see her," said

Mikael, burying his face in his hands. "She was just lying there in a pool of blood with her throat gaping open. . . ."

Sophie felt sick. She remembered the shadow like a wound on Mrs. Tansy's neck the night of the séance. Great-aunt Tabitha would have called it a premonition.

"I don't blame the first officers on the scene for thinking I'd done it," Mikael said, uncovering his face, though he still wouldn't catch Sophie's eye. "It looked awfully bad, but of course as soon as they saw there wasn't any blood on me, they knew I couldn't have done it."

"How did it happen that you were there?" Sophie asked.

"Well, I did quite a bit of footwork, and after talking to what must have been twenty different cabdrivers and visiting a dozen or more hotels, I finally tracked her down at the Balmoral. I wangled an appointment—she may have been staying there under another name, but everyone knew she was a medium, and she was certainly still receiving clients. That's when I sent you the note. I thought I'd be able to tell you all about the meeting by the time I saw you; I was going to surprise you. You did get my note, didn't you?"

"Yes, and there I was, cursing you for forgetting about our appointment! Oh, Mikael, I'm so sorry," Sophie said, pounding his arm with one fist and wiping the tears from her eyes with her other hand. "Are you sure you're all right?" she went on when he didn't say anything. "You look awful!"

"I think I had a very near miss," said Mikael slowly. "I went up to her room at one o'clock, as we'd arranged, and she actually let me in herself and called room service to order lunch for the two of us."

"I don't understand," said Sophie. "Wasn't she dead when you got there?"

"No," said Mikael, "it was much worse than that. While she was on the telephone, a knock came at the door. She looked rather frightened and motioned at me to hide. I threw myself into the wardrobe, feeling pretty silly. Once I'd got in, she actually locked the door from the outside!"

"You were locked in?" Sophie said. "But—"

"I can't tell you exactly what happened next," he said. "I heard her open the door to the room. Before she'd said more than a few words, though, I heard all sorts of noises: a thud as she fell to the ground, I expect, and some cries and blows and then a horrible gurgling sound. I think the intruder must have cut her throat. Naturally I started pounding on the door of the wardrobe and calling for someone to let me out, but the murderer had vanished by the time I kicked open the door."

"You could have been killed!"

"But I wasn't," Mikael said somberly. "It was she who was killed. It was completely vile, Sophie! And then the room service waiter got there, and he telephoned for the police, and it took a lot of time to clear things up."

"We did right by you, though, didn't we, sir?" said one of the guards.

Sophie had forgotten they must be listening in. She looked up now at the guard, who smiled. Miss Chatterjee was standing in the corner and attending closely to everything that passed between Sophie and Mikael.

"Yes, certainly, Sergeant Fettes," said Mikael, standing up and shaking hands with each guard in turn. "Can I have my things back again?" he added.

The aide disappeared and came back a few minutes later with the duty clerk and a medium-sized metal box.

"One key, a ten-shilling note, two shillings and threepence in coin, one pair of shoelaces, one pocketknife, three safety pins, a length of fishing line," the clerk read out from a form.

Mikael signed the form, swept most of the things into the front pocket of his trousers, then knelt to feed the laces through the eyes of his boots. His hands were shaking.

Mrs. Lundberg arrived just then, the worried-looking professor in tow, and pounced on Mikael with a little scream.

Minutes later they all found themselves thankfully outside the Castle walls.

"Mikael, you look done in," his aunt scolded. "And whatever will your mother say? She'll be furious with me for not doing a better job at keeping you out of trouble."

"Mrs. Lundberg," said Sophie, feeling quite sick with the

need to confess, "you must know that it's all my fault. It was because of something I asked Mikael to do that he ended up in this mess. I am so sorry and I beg your forgiveness, I really do."

Miss Chatterjee looked mildly pleased at Sophie's taking responsibility for the whole thing, but Mikael's aunt shook her head. "I'm sure you're very sorry, Sophie," she said, "but I wish you'd thought of this beforehand and been more careful."

"Don't be angry with Sophie!" Mikael said, tugging on his aunt's hand.

"I'm fed up with both of you, that's the long and short of it," said his aunt, "and don't expect me to forgive either of you before next Thursday at the very earliest."

She climbed into the front seat of the professor's car.

"Mikael, get in the back," said the professor. "Sophie, I believe that was an invitation. We hope to see you at teatime on Thursday next week, just as usual. Will you be all right getting home?"

"Yes," said Sophie. "Miss Chatterjee will take care of me."

"We'll drive the girl home," added the woman constable, who had reappeared as they passed out through the gate into the esplanade.

Sophie and Miss Chatterjee were back at school by ten o'clock, whereupon the teacher sat Sophie in a chair and gave her a thorough dressing-down.

"I hope you know the trouble you've caused," she said. "I have ahead of me what will no doubt be a long and unpleasant conversation with Miss Henchman, one in which I fear I'll be hard put to persuade her not to suspend you. And yet I suspect that Miss Henchman is the least of your worries."

Sophie didn't know what to say.

"Thank you," she finally said. "Thanks for coming with me tonight, and for knowing how to talk to that awful man."

"That type," said Miss Chatterjee disdainfully, "will never understand why he is not so prepossessing as he thinks."

"You're my hero," said Sophie.

The teacher gave a wry smile, as if it pained her.

"Heroism is a fairy-tale concept, Sophie," she said, her voice sharper than before. "The real world corrupts everything it touches. Don't make me out to be anything more or less than a real and quite imperfect person."

Though the others were all agog to hear what had happened, Sophie used the excuse of it being after lights-out to postpone explanations until the next day. She fell asleep almost at once, her dreams haunted by the bulky shape of a female body splayed out in a pool of blood.

FIFTEEN

A T HERIOT ROW ON Friday evening Sophie suffered through a lecture from Great-aunt Tabitha that was an almost exact reprise of one she had received from Miss Henchman the day before, and on Saturday morning she presented herself in the hallway in the regulation white dress that all the girls wore to the Waterloo Day celebrations at school. Great-aunt Tabitha had booked a taxi for nine thirty. When they got to school, she paid the driver and escorted Sophie to the playground, rigged up for the occasion as a kind of amphitheater. There she plowed through the crowd to a pair of seats in the area cordoned off for Very Important Visitors, Sophie trailing in her wake. As a member of the school's board of governors, Great-aunt Tabitha was entitled to sit here, but Sophie would have preferred to join the other fifth-form girls and their parents. Jean and Priscilla waved at her from across the way, but she saw several other girls pointing her out to their families, and the feeling of being stared at was not at all pleasant.

Once everyone had taken their seats, the school orchestra fell silent, and Miss Henchman stepped up to the podium. Seated behind her on the platform were half a dozen visiting dignitaries, including a figure whom Sophie recognized only when Great-aunt Tabitha gave a quiet hiccup of indignation. It was the minister of public safety, their war-loving dinner guest from the week before. Sophie couldn't see Nicholas Mood on the platform but felt sure he must be lurking nearby.

The headmistress gave the same speech every year. Sophie's attention began to drift, and Great-aunt Tabitha took out a tablet and began jotting down notes for a forthcoming lecture to the Glasgow College of Psychical Science.

Half asleep, Sophie realized that Miss Henchman was introducing a second speaker. It was the minister herself!

"I am indebted to your headmistress for this wonderful opportunity," said Joanna Murchison. "*Waterloo* . . . we associate the word with the deaths of men who gave up their lives to keep this country safe. To our neighbors on the Continent, though, the word's a synonym for Nemesis, something that might stop a respected adversary in his tracks. Schoolchildren in France are taught that Wellington 'met his Waterloo' on the eighteenth of June in the year 1815.

"Speaking to you now," the minister continued, "exactly a hundred and twenty-three years after that defeat, I say that it is time for us to reclaim Waterloo for ourselves: to embrace the idea that we may engage European troops once more on European soil, and that this time, not we but *they* will meet their Waterloo!"

The crowd had begun to mutter, but the minister continued speaking. "Only one thing will let us reclaim the legacy of Waterloo. We must meet the combined forces of the European Federation on the battlefield, and we must beat them!"

The noise in the audience rose. A small disturbance had broken out in the aisle leading up to the speakers' platform. Suddenly something very low to the ground shot out past the front row, and a small squat figure swung up the metal scaffolding onto the platform itself. It was the Veteran. He had made his way on his low wheeled cart past the security detail, and as the audience looked on, he grasped the minister's legs and pulled her to the ground, calling out all the while a string of words that sounded to Sophie like "Where's my money?"

Within seconds the guards reached the platform and tore the assailant off the minister, who got to her feet, looking shaken but not hurt. She was immediately surrounded by four of the bodyguards, and there was Nicko giving his arm to her and leaning over to whisper something in her ear. They all began to move at once, and in a flash she had been whisked away into a bulletproof chauffeured car.

Meanwhile several other security officers had hauled the Veteran away, and a minute later the only trace of the assailant was the overturned dolly, its wheels spinning uselessly in the air.

After a brief consultation behind the podium, Miss Henchman stepped up to the voice-broadcasting system.

"Ladies and gentlemen, do not be alarmed," she said, sounding self-important. "The man who just accosted the minister is a local vagrant with a grudge against the government. The minister was never in any real danger, but unfortunately the security staff have decided she must leave at once. Sorry as we are to be deprived of the rest of what promised to be a remarkably rousing speech, we must put the minister's safety before our own enjoyment. A round of applause for the minister!"

Her request prompted only sporadic clapping, perhaps due to the suggestion that the minister's safety mattered more than everybody else's.

"I always said Joanna hadn't any spine," said Great-aunt Tabitha after the school song and the moment of silence. They stood in a pocket of stillness amid a mad rush for refreshments. "Sophie, I simply can't afford to take the time to negotiate that tea tent, and I don't want to leave you here without a chaperone, not after what happened the other day. You're to come with me now to IRYLNS, and while we're there, I expect you to keep your eyes open and your mouth shut."

IRYLNS? Sophie had always wondered what IRYLNS was like. It was a pity her curiosity would only be satisfied as a sort of penalty for misbehavior.

They got into one of the taxis waiting outside the school.

Great-aunt Tabitha asked the driver to stop in front of the Braid Institute for Neurohypnosis in Buccleugh Place, near the university. The cabbie had sized up Sophie's great-aunt as soon as they got into the cab and shook his head with resignation when she didn't give him a tip.

As the car pulled away, Great-aunt Tabitha took Sophie's hand and virtually dragged her ten yards further along the pavement to the front door of an ordinary-looking house next to the Braid Institute, a door whose brass plaque read ADAM SMITH COLLEGE.

Great-aunt Tabitha rapped the knocker, which was decorated with a knobbly pair of hemispheres like the meat of a walnut. Just as Sophie realized they were bronze casts of the halves of the human brain, the door opened to admit them, and she had no time to puzzle out the meaning of this sinister icon.

SIXTEEN

A PRETTY GIRL IN A NURSE'S uniform escorted them
down a long corridor to a pair of bolted doors at
the back of the building.

"Have you permission to bring in the girl, Miss Hunter?"
she asked.

"Not yet," said Great-aunt Tabitha. "I suppose you'll have
to telephone Dr. Ferrier and see if it's all right?"

"I'm sorry, Miss Hunter, but the rules are quite clear
regarding visitors, and I couldn't—"

"Yes, yes," said Great-aunt Tabitha. "I wrote the instructions myself, and I'm well aware you could lose your job for
letting anyone in without the proper authorization. Well, get
on with it then, why don't you? We haven't got all day."

The girl dithered for a minute, then hurried back the way they'd come.

Great-aunt Tabitha tapped her foot with irritation, then turned to Sophie, who tried to erase the puzzlement from her face. Why were they here, and what was Adam Smith College?

"What are you thinking?" her great-aunt asked her.

"Are—this isn't IRYLNS, is it?" said Sophie.

"Indeed it is," said Great-aunt Tabitha, her voice neutral at first but warming into enthusiasm. "IRYLNS represents the fulfillment of the vision of humanity sketched out long ago by Adam Smith in his *Theory of Moral Sentiments* and brought up-to-date by modern medicine in light of a twentieth-century understanding of the social psychology of the Enlightenment. What a good thing—what a *very* good thing—that people can now be made incomparably happier and more productive by the rationalization of the emotions!"

Just then the breathless young nurse reappeared, full of apologies, with the doctor's note and a fistful of forms for Sophie to sign. Not wanting to annoy her great-aunt by taking the time to read through them properly, Sophie scrawled her name at the bottom of each sheet, though it gave her a pain in the pit of her stomach when she caught a glimpse of the phrase *Official Secrets Act*.

The hallway in which they next found themselves was bright and airy and led to an attractively furnished common room looking out over the garden at the back. Girls not much older than Sophie occupied themselves here with all kinds of activity, several of them knitting stockings and scarves, others winding skeins of wool into balls, and a whole row of girls in blindfolds practicing touch typing, their machines muffled to prevent the noise from disturbing the others. Though the blindfolds added a bizarre touch, the sight of the girls with their bright-colored dresses and glossy bobs was otherwise a pretty one.

Great-aunt Tabitha strode through this hive of activity without stopping, Sophie hurrying to keep up with her, and turned into another hallway. At last they arrived at an office into which Great-aunt Tabitha flew like one of the new aerial assault drones. She barged past the receptionist in the outer room and straight into the big inner office.

The room suffered from not having any windows, but provided one didn't mind the bunkerlike feel, it was attractively furnished, with clusters of delicately wrought chairs arranged around several small circular tables and a comfortable-looking chaise longue in the corner beside a long narrow table that evidently served as a desk.

Fearing Great-aunt Tabitha's speed meant something ominous, Sophie relaxed when the elderly woman seated at the desk jumped up and flew into Great-aunt Tabitha's arms.

"Tabitha, what a delightful surprise! I didn't like to ask

you to take the time on a Saturday—a national holiday—"

"Not another word," said Great-aunt Tabitha, beaming at her friend. "I've brought my niece with me today; Sophie, this is Dr. Susan Ferrier, one of my oldest friends and a very dear colleague."

"Delighted to meet you, Sophie," the doctor said, wringing Sophie's hand with bone-cracking enthusiasm. "I've heard so much about you, and it's a great pleasure to make your acquaintance in person; I had almost begun to feel you must be a figment of Tab's imagination!"

"No, Sophie's quite real," said Great-aunt Tabitha, sounding rather sorry that this should be so. "She's generally a good girl, but she got into a mess this week and I thought it time for her to get a good look at what we do here. Show her why she'd better keep her nose to the grindstone and earn a place at university. . . ."

Was Sophie here to be taught a lesson?

"Tabitha, Tabitha," said the doctor, shaking her head. "You know the work we do here has almost invariably positive results. Most girls who go through the program benefit immensely."

Great-aunt Tabitha sniffed. It sounded as though they must have had this argument before.

The doctor turned to Sophie. "You wouldn't turn up your nose at working for a cabinet minister, a brigadier general, a museum director, or the rector of a university, would you?"

Then, when Sophie said nothing: "*Would* you?"

"I didn't know it was the kind of question that wanted answering," Sophie said, not sure why the doctor sounded so angry. She was starting to get a bad feeling about IRYLNS. What weren't they saying? "Of course I wouldn't turn up my nose at a job like that!"

"Almost all the young women in the civil service have passed through our doors at one time or another," the doctor said huffily. "Last year we sent half a dozen girls to the office of the prime minister himself!"

"Is that the kind of thing most girls do when they leave IRYLNS?" Sophie asked in her most polite voice, the one she didn't usually use because it made her feel so smarmy and Harriet Jeffries–like.

"Yes, indeed, and it's very naughty of Tab to suggest you'd be better off at university."

"If you or I had been trained somewhere like this rather than at university," said Great-aunt Tabitha, not bothering to hide her impatience, "neither of us would have been able to contribute an iota to IRYLNS."

"True, true, but who's to say that would have been for the worse?" said Dr. Ferrier, her mood sunny again. "Someone else would have made the contributions and got the credit— but they also serve who only stand and wait, as the poet says.

Besides, neither one of us was pretty enough to be a top-notch candidate for IRYLNS!"

Though Great-aunt Tabitha greeted this remark with hearty laughter, Sophie couldn't see what the two things had to do with each other. People said sometimes that someone wasn't pretty enough to get married, though one met some very plain married women and some very pretty unmarried ones. But what did prettiness have to do with being a good secretary, which was presumably the main point of the training one received at IRYLNS?

The doctor ushered them over to one of the little tables and used the speaking panel on the wall to order tea from the receptionist.

"Sophie, do you know much about the work we do here?" she asked.

Sophie confessed her ignorance.

"The name *Adam Smith College* isn't just a cover story, a red herring, or a silly joke," said the doctor. "Adam Smith was the first person in Scotland to come out and say explicitly that human emotions and passions—those things that gave the ancient Greeks so much trouble—should be redirected for the good of the community. His ideas lie at the heart of the philosophy of the Communitarian Party, which operates on the belief that individuals have a moral obligation to put aside selfish desires to promote the good of the group. Thanks to modern medicine, we've been able to take the concept several steps further. The crucial insight—"

"*Susan's* crucial insight," Sophie's great-aunt interjected.

"Your great-aunt's name joins mine on most of the patents," the doctor told Sophie, affecting a not-very-convincing modesty. "Tabitha's downplaying her own role in all of this."

Patents? What on earth could they be doing here? Feeling equal parts confusion and alarm, Sophie paid close attention to the woman's next words, though they did not much clarify things.

"It's long been said," said Dr. Ferrier, "that behind every successful man stands a good woman. When people say that, they're usually thinking of his wife or his mother, but in truth it's more often a secretary or a head nurse or a really excellent administrator who makes sure everything runs smoothly in a man's personal and professional life. The ideal assistant must be cheerful, flexible, reliable, patient, and thoughtful of others. She must also be willing to toil without recognition, often without getting even the most cursory thanks; Tabitha always jokes that we should institute a supplemental training scheme to teach men how to treat our young women properly."

"Important men don't usually know what to do with their negative emotions," said Great-aunt Tabitha, "other than to bluster at people and browbeat them and generally make everyone miserable, including themselves. They also tend to be selfish and inattentive to the needs of others. The real problem is that the women who marry them or work for them have needs too, and when those needs go unsatisfied, everything stops functioning."

It sounded like the men were the real problem, not the women. Why didn't Dr. Ferrier and Great-aunt Tabitha develop a scheme to make men less selfish and angry, and leave the young women alone? Sophie's stomach growled. It must be almost lunchtime.

"Fortunately the central procedure we perform here—the J and H procedure, we call it—makes that fact about human nature completely irrelevant," continued the doctor. "After they undergo a modest amount of surgery and a battery of hormonal and behavioral therapies, our girls are no longer capable of *having* needs. They can't be offended by some imagined slight or by a pattern of overwork, neglect, and verbal abuse. They're happy, well-adjusted workers with all their intellect intact, and yet with none of the temperamental disadvantages—self-absorption, irritability, laziness, a tendency to feel hard done by—that limit the utility of the common secretary. Indeed, in the cases where we see the best outcomes, these young women are even able to become repositories for the anger and desire of the men they work for, rather like human lightning rods."

Human lightning rods? It wasn't a very reassuring comparison. Nicko Mood was very devoted to the minister's interests, but he didn't seem to serve as a repository in this way—it must only work for male employers and female assistants. Sophie couldn't quite follow the underlying principles, although she thought as long as Great-aunt Tabitha was involved, it couldn't be too bad. Sophie's great-aunt might sanction girls undergoing a rather difficult and painful training scheme, but she wouldn't put people into actual danger. Would she?

Suddenly this pleasant room felt almost as dangerous as the vaults beneath the Castle.

"Do you have any questions?" said the doctor.

"What do the letters *J* and *H* stand for?" Sophie asked almost at random, not daring to ask about anything of substance.

The way they responded told her she'd blundered. The two women looked at each other, then both spoke at once.

"No, you first," Dr. Ferrier said.

"The letters *J* and *H*," said Great-aunt Tabitha with a sly look at her friend, "stand for *Joy* and *Happiness*."

There was an embarrassing sound to the words that made Sophie feel as she had the year before when Miss Hopkins lectured them on the birds and the bees.

"And how does the procedure work?" she ventured.

"Oh, you wouldn't be interested in the technical details," said Dr. Ferrier.

There was something ominous about the doctor's obvious reluctance to specify, but they were interrupted at this point by the receptionist's arrival with tea and biscuits. Though she felt like the condemned man eating a hearty meal, Sophie had three biscuits and a piece of cake.

As they finished their tea, Great-aunt Tabitha looked at her enameled watch. "We must get down to business, Susan," she said. "I've worked through the numbers on the last several rounds of graduates, and a few ideas come to mind for improving the next set of statistics. Have you got anybody who can take Sophie around while we work? It's a pity for her not to see the rest of the place while she's here."

The words sounded almost menacing.

The doctor thought for a minute.

"Yes," she said, "that won't be a problem—Alison can take half an hour to show Sophie the sights, then park her in the garden until we've finished."

Having disposed of Sophie, they turned to a stack of files and were at once immersed.

SEVENTEEN

SOPHIE LOITERED OUTSIDE the office under the reception-ist's supervision until her guide showed up. A short stocky woman with a lazy eye, Alison Mackay intro-duced herself and asked Sophie what she would like to see.

"I don't know," said Sophie. What she really wanted was to be allowed to wait for her great-aunt in the street outside. But she hadn't any choice in the matter, and she supposed she might as well get a look at what went on here while she had the chance. It would be worse not knowing. "That is, I'm interested in anything—everything."

"Well, why don't I show you the treatment rooms and tell you a bit more about what we do here? Then we'll look in on one of the occupational therapy classes, and after that you can play in the garden while you wait for Miss Hunter and Dr. Ferrier to finish."

Play! A brief surge of contempt took the edge off Sophie's panic, and she mentally labeled Miss Mackay another one of those grown-ups who couldn't tell the difference between a person who was fifteen and one who was five.

But Miss Mackay's cheerful tones only underlined the horror of what she revealed to Sophie. Spotlessly clean, the first treatment room held an examining table, a glass drug cabinet, and an electrical apparatus that looked like a cross between a medieval torture device and the equipment the comic-book scientist Dr. Maniac used to convert innocent chimpanzees into killing machines of preternatural strength and intelligence. Just such an imagination might have conceived the set of electrodes where the head would go, the metal bands to hold down the torso, the stainless steel cuffs for wrists and ankles. Sophie's own wrists tingled in sympathy.

"I'm afraid I won't be able to show you the operating theater on the other side of the premises," said Miss Mackay. "Visitors aren't allowed. We have several other rooms like this one, of course, which we use to administer significant electric shocks and recondition the synapses of the brain. Dr. Pavlov's work in Russia has been most useful here as a precedent, as well as the contributions of Dr. James in America."

She held up a chunk of solid rubber.

"Each girl has one of these in her mouth to stop her from biting her tongue off." She uttered the phrase with relish, caressing the hideous three-dimensional gag before she replaced it on a shelf with others graded according to size.

Sophie's head was pounding now and her stomach churned. She swallowed a few times in hasty gulps, then took a deep breath. She had to calm down. Great-aunt Tabitha wasn't an angel, but she wouldn't let people be treated like this if it were anywhere near as bad as it looked.

"Many different doctors and researchers have contributed to make the treatment as effective and comfortable as possible," Miss Mackay continued, oblivious to Sophie's physical distress. "Located so near to a university, we are in a wonderful position to incorporate the very latest developments in the science of the mind."

They passed by the next few rooms, which Miss Mackay said were identical to the first, and turned right at the end of the hallway.

"On our left," said Miss Mackay, "the pharmacy, where we keep our hormones, amphetamines, and tranquilizing agents. Shall we just look in briefly?"

She unlocked the door and showed Sophie: stoppered glass tubes of tablets in attractive pastels, vials of gleaming pink and blue capsules, ampoules filled with honey-colored liquid, and hypodermic needles in all different sizes, sinister and beautiful as a vampire's fangs.

"The Duke of Wellington himself," said Miss Mackay, "once responded to a friend's suggestion that habit was a second nature by saying, 'Habit a second nature! Habit is ten times nature.' Here we use electrobiology and human chemistry to lay down new patterns in the brain, then confirm and reinforce those patterns by behavioral conditioning. Why don't we pop down the hall to the training center and see if we might catch the tail end of a therapy session?"

She let them into a private observation area, a small, dark booth at the back of a bright, sunny classroom.

"On the other side of the window is a one-way mirror," said Miss Mackay. "In other words, we are fully concealed."

The room held three long tables, each one seating four girls. Every girl had a small mirror on a stand in front of her. Sophie homed in right away on the middle table, second girl from the left. It took her a minute to remember the girl's name: Hannah Jacobs, that was it. She'd taken awards in music and maths on Prize Day the summer before.

In Sophie's memory, Hannah had an unusually expressive face, a face that spoke so vividly as to make words almost unnecessary. As Falstaff in a school production of *Henry IV*, Hannah had brought the house down.

Now Sophie watched as Hannah's facial muscles worked in perfect synchronicity with the others'. The identical movements were uncanny. The girls were physically alike only in age and general prettiness, but their smiles could have come off a factory production line.

"Smile," said the instructor. "There. Look at your reflection. Smile in response to your own smile. Good. By moving the muscles of your face, you release a flood of neurotransmitters to tell your brain you are happier than before. And again. Wider, please, and be sure to involve the eyes."

"Wonderful, isn't it?" said Miss Mackay, sounding like a proud parent. "These girls have been here scarcely six months, and look at them now. Quite different from when they arrived. Why, a couple of them cried themselves to sleep the first few nights out of homesickness! They're treated to every luxury while they're here; they're not allowed out unaccompanied until the training is complete, of course, but we arrange special excursions to boutiques and beauty salons so that they have all the nice things they'll need once they leave. And they receive lessons in how to make themselves up, dress attractively, and so on."

Sophie couldn't understand why the government should pay for the girls' hairdressing. What had these pretty paragons to do with the torture chambers she'd seen just moments earlier? Had all the girls she saw passed through the course of treatment, and what had it done to them?

"These ones will be ready to take up first-rate positions by the end of the summer," Miss Mackay added, "and we stagger the groups so as to produce a new crop every three months. If we go to war, of course, we'll need to speed that up."

Crop was such an agricultural word, as if the girls were lambs being fattened for the slaughter! Even as Sophie thought this, a girl at the back of the class began to flail around in her chair. An alarm rang, and two attendants appeared in an instant. They rushed to the girl's side and held her down as the seizure racked her body. Sophie flinched.

Miss Mackay pushed a button and the window went cloudy.

"Don't mind that," she said. "A few girls experience side effects, sometimes from the surgery itself but more often from the drugs administered afterward. That girl will be treated at once, and it is most unlikely the seizure will recur."

She looked at her watch.

"I'll show you into the garden now, Sophie," she said, leading Sophie back into the corridor, "and you can amuse yourself there like a good girl. I'll make sure Miss Hunter knows where to find you."

She unlocked a door and shooed Sophie out of the building.

Sophie felt rather shattered. What if she had to enroll at IRYLNS and become one of those pretty, polished girls? Would it be possible to do that and still be Sophie? Perhaps this was what had happened to Sheena. Why, Sheena hadn't even recognized her the other day!

After a little while Sophie dug her book out of her satchel and took a seat on one of the benches beneath the tree at the bottom of the garden. Unfortunately the book was *Mansfield Park*. She'd already read it at least four times, and it was altogether too somber in tone to console her now. But having a book in one's hands was good protective coloration. Sophie gazed at the back of the institute. Through the windows on the right, she could see the girls in the common room, their placid expressions and general air of contentment now taking on a far more frightening aspect.

Blinds covered the windows to her left, but as she watched, a second door to the garden opened, the door from the side of the house Sophie hadn't set foot in. Two nurses came out, each pushing a wicker Bath chair with a small bundled occupant. They trundled their charges over to a sunny spot by the fence, parked the chairs and left them, then began an intense chat on the paved terrace at the top of the garden.

Looking at the two figures in the chairs, Sophie wondered for a moment whether the other half of IRYLNS housed some kind of program for the elderly. The people in the chairs were small and motionless. But the smoothness of their skin suggested they were quite young. What was wrong with them?

Trying not to attract the nurses' attention, Sophie crept closer until she could see that both patients were girls not much older than herself. One had a surgical scar reaching down along her left temple from beneath a turban of bandages; the other was covered with scabs and bruises, including a black eye that made her look as though she'd gone ten rounds with the heavyweight champion of the world.

"All right over there?" one of the nurses called out, not looking up from the discussion of the second nurse's sister's prolapsed uterus and the general iniquity of husbands.

One of the girls mewed, a thin keening sound like a baby seagull. The other simply stared into space.

Sophie had never seen anything so dreadful in her entire life, not even the tortoiseshell kitten squashed flat in the road outside the house in Heriot Row. These weren't kittens, they were girls, real live girls like the ones at school, somehow stripped of their humanity and reduced to damaged husks.

Was this what Sheena would come to in the end?

Was this what would happen to *Sophie*?

Sophie's great-aunt found her pale and shivering. She gave Sophie a sharp look but said nothing until they reached the street.

"Do you know the age of the youngest person ever prosecuted for breach of the Official Secrets Act?" she said.

"No," said Sophie, her teeth chattering despite the day's warmth.

"Twelve," said Great-aunt Tabitha, hailing a taxi and

directing the driver to Heriot Row. The hand clutching her purse looked like the talons of a bird of prey.

Sophie jumped out of the cab and let herself into the house before her great-aunt even finished paying the driver. She raced upstairs and threw herself into bed. Only when she'd pulled the duvet up around her neck and curled into a ball did she begin to feel safe.

EIGHTEEN

L ATER THAT AFTERNOON Peggy knocked on Sophie's bedroom door and came in without waiting to be invited.

"Didn't you hear me calling you from downstairs?" she asked, picking up a jumper from the floor and folding it before replacing it in the chest of drawers.

Unable to fall asleep and unwilling to get up and tackle her homework, Sophie had tried to banish all thoughts of IRYLNS by reading her favorite novel, not *Mansfield Park* but *Pride and Prejudice*. Her copy had been read so many times it had almost fallen to pieces, but the story never lost its power to transport Sophie out of her real life.

She apologized to Peggy for making her come upstairs.

"It's not me who's missed an important telephone call," Peggy said, straightening the oilcloth on top of the chest and looking with disgust at the dust that came off on her fingers. "Sophie, why don't you tell me when Annie does such a poor job of cleaning in here?"

Sophie's senses finally came back to her. "Do you mean to say there was a telephone call for me?" she said.

"Yes, and I wrote down the message like the young gentleman asked. Disappointed, he was, not to speak with you yourself."

"Oh, Peggy, you should have come and fetched me while you still had him on the line!"

"Some people put their face in a book and go dead to the world," Peggy said, sniffing and tossing her head. "I did give you a shout, Sophie, and you didn't answer. It was a boy called Michael, well-spoken but foreign, I'd say. Your great-aunt would have a fit if she knew you were getting telephone calls from young men; and it's not just any young man, is it? Isn't it the one the police had in the other day?"

"Peggy, I must telephone him at once!"

"Oh, he left a number," Peggy said, relenting at the sight of Sophie's unhappy face. "Better make the call while your great-aunt's out, Sophie; she won't like you talking to that boy again."

Sophie raced downstairs to the message tablet by the

instrument in the hallway. It was characteristic of Great-aunt Tabitha to have rejected hot and cold running water as unnecessary luxury while thoroughly embracing the technology for transmitting and receiving the human voice over distance, the brainchild of Aleksandr Tolstoy Bell, son of an eminent Scottish educator of the deaf and his glamorous Russian wife. The tablet usually held reminders about the times and locations of various spiritualist meetings. Now the top sheet bore a telephone number in Peggy's careful hand.

Sophie picked up the receiver. When the operator came on, she asked her to put through a local call.

It went through almost at once, and Sophie heard Mikael on the line.

"Sophie!" he said, his voice high and thready. Perhaps it was just the distortion of the instrument, but Sophie thought he sounded really upset. "Are you coming for tea on Thursday?"

"Yes, of course," said Sophie. "Mikael, is something wrong?"

"Not exactly," he said. "Look, what do you know about how your great-aunt met up with this Mrs. Tansy?"

"Not much," said Sophie. Did it really matter? "She tends to hear about pretty much any medium above the level of a fairground fortune-teller. They all seem to come to our house sooner or later."

"That Commander Brown had me back in yesterday after-noon," Mikael said.

Sophie groaned. "Your aunt must be livid," she said, wishing she and Mikael were in the same room talking. The way the telephone didn't show one the other person's face made it hard to tell what he was thinking.

"No, it's all right," said Mikael, sounding a little more like himself. "He's satisfied I couldn't have had anything to do with the murder, and he told me a few interesting things. Apparently someone paid the medium off to approach your great-aunt; they found a note in her records, no information about who it was. And wait till you hear this: the Monday morning after the séance, your great-aunt called a friend at the ministry of public safety and asked him to have Mrs. Tansy put under surveillance."

"But didn't Commander Brown say the other night that his people had been following her for some time?"

"Yes, but they lost her shortly before the night you met her—that was why they didn't know she'd been to your great-aunt's house. I think that when your great-aunt sicced the people from the ministry on her afterward, Mrs. Tansy must have got the wind up and gone to ground at the hotel."

"What else did the commander tell you?" Sophie asked.

"Mostly he asked me more questions. They took me back to the Balmoral—"

Sophie heard the shake in his voice.

"—and had me look at everything again, to see whether the murderer might have left something behind him."

"Did you see anything?"

"Not really. There were some strange tracks on the carpet that weren't there when I first arrived, but they may well have been left by the room service cart or the police photographer's tripod; I'm not sure. But I did learn a few other things. Sophie, it's quite clear from the questions they asked that they believe there's some link between the dead woman and the Brothers of the Northern Liberties."

They both fell silent, listening to the hiss of the line.

"Sophie, are you there?" said Mikael.

"I'm here. What kind of link?"

"I've got no idea, and I don't think they have much of one either. I phoned just to pass this on and to ask you to be careful. Really careful, Sophie. If you'd seen the blood . . . these people have no qualms about taking lives. It's different for me. But you're a girl. I want you to stay well out of it."

"A girl?" Sophie said stupidly. Of course she was a girl, but what difference did it make? Mikael's words made Sophie feel irritable and aggressive, like wearing a scratchy wool vest a size too small for you.

"Look, Sophie, I've got to go. I'll see you on Thursday, all right?"

Replacing the receiver in the cradle, Sophie felt so weary that she actually sank to the floor and started to cry. When Peggy found her there, she dragged Sophie into the kitchen and made her a cup of tea, but Sophie could not be consoled. She decided to try and get through some of her mountain of homework, but after arriving at three different answers to the same sum, she finally packed everything back into the satchel and retreated upstairs to the solace of Jane Austen.

The most surprising thing of all happened on Sunday evening as Sophie lay on her bed reading the chapters Miss Chatterjee had set for Tuesday.

A knock came at the door.

"Come in," Sophie called out, though she knew Peggy always came in a moment later regardless of whether Sophie had invited her or not.

But it wasn't Peggy. It was Great-aunt Tabitha, who hadn't set foot in Sophie's room for years, not since Sophie had had whooping cough when she was eleven and received an awkward visit from her great-aunt bearing a toy from her own youth, a stuffed woolly sheep that may or may not have been responsible for the later infestation of moths in Sophie's wardrobe.

Equally surprising was the fact that rather than offering a tart remark about girls who chose to ruin their posture (and, it was implied, their morals) by lounging around reading in bed, Sophie's great-aunt paused for a minute at the door, then crossed the room, sat down beside Sophie, and awkwardly patted her shoulder.

When Sophie flinched away from her—she couldn't help it; her flesh recoiled at the thought of the gags and the electrodes—Great-aunt Tabitha took off her spectacles and pinched the bridge of her nose between her thumb and the tips of her fingers.

"Think of how much energy we waste," she said, sighing heavily, "when we experience unwanted emotions."

This was unexpected enough to cause Sophie to roll over to look at her.

"If only we could altogether suppress the irrational," Great-aunt Tabitha continued, "and manage our feelings with the efficiency of a dynamo! Our own personal feelings are good for nothing; the perfection of human nature is to feel much for others and little for ourselves."

Sophie was dismayed to find she didn't disagree. It *would* be a good thing if nobody ever felt anything beyond the mild ups and downs of anticipation and enjoyment and occasional disappointment. And yet there must be something terribly wrong with this philosophy of self-control and self-sacrifice, mustn't there, if it culminated in those drooling wrecks in the garden?

"Sophie," Great-aunt Tabitha went on, "I want you to

know that I've been wrestling with my conscience over this business of IRYLNS. Of course the institute contributes an enormous amount to the good of the country, but I've had doubts. . . ."

"What kind of doubts?" Sophie asked, prompting Great-aunt Tabitha to withdraw her hand and begin pacing across the room.

"Doubts about the associated costs," said Great-aunt Tabitha. "Don't misinterpret what I'm about to say, Sophie. I will never withdraw my support from the program. It does too much good, and I continue to subscribe to the enlightened social psychology. But the thought of what happens to those girls as they become sophisticated machines for the suppression of feeling . . . well, if I could go back to the way I felt before," she added, "it would certainly be a blessing."

"What changed?" Sophie asked, afraid but also really curious to hear what Great-aunt Tabitha would say.

"*You*," said Sophie's great-aunt, spitting out the word. She stopped in the middle of the rug, fists clenched by her sides. "Various philosophers have wrestled with the problem of how to restrain the excessive attachment that we are disposed to feel for our own children above those of other people. . . . I never understood the vehemence with which they treated the topic until one day I looked at you (you were doing your homework at the other end of the dining table) and surprised myself by realizing I didn't *want* you to go to IRYLNS."

Sophie didn't know what to say.

"Believe me," her great-aunt added, "I struggled for some time to dismiss these feelings as a momentary aberration. It simply couldn't be, I told myself, that I thought an exception should be made for my great-niece because I loved her."

Oh, how typical, how *maddening* of Great-aunt Tabitha only to say she loved Sophie in the shadow of a future in which Sophie's present self might cease to exist! Sophie sat up and swung her feet to the floor. It was a terrible disadvantage to be lying in bed talking to a person who was standing up.

"It soon became clear," said Great-aunt Tabitha, her voice even drier than usual, "that my feelings were not about to go away. I did not want you to go to the institute, and that meant I did not wholeheartedly endorse what happened there. I began to suspect that a truly ethical person would withdraw from the institute; indeed, she might well resolve to make it her job to bring the program to a halt. If one wouldn't choose to have one's own loved ones undergo the procedure, fairness would seem to dictate that one should prevent its being exercised on one's fellow citizens."

"So will you try to make it stop?" Sophie asked, though she felt more despairing than hopeful.

"I am a pragmatist and a patriot, Sophie," said Great-aunt Tabitha. "I place the good of my country above that of any

189

private citizen, including myself."

"What are you saying, then, Great-aunt Tabitha?" Sophie said, unable to stop her shoulders from slumping. "Are you telling me I'll have to go to IRYLNS after all?"

"Don't look at me like that!" And Great-aunt Tabitha actually turned away from Sophie and resumed her unhappy pacing, avoiding Sophie's eyes. "With any luck, it won't come to it. I will do everything I can, within reason, to keep you out of the program. What you don't seem to realize, though, is the extent to which my hands are tied."

"I don't understand," said Sophie. "It sounds as though you think what happens at IRYLNS is quite wrong. Those poor mangled girls in the garden! I suppose I can see the point of the argument for the national good. One of Nan's brothers lost his leg in the army, and everybody who goes into the service has to take the chance that something will go terribly awry. But it wasn't just the girls outside—can it be right to turn the others into a sort of machine? Isn't it almost as bad as killing, to reshape someone so completely? How can their parents let it happen? If everyone really knew what goes on there, wouldn't they put a stop to it?"

Great-aunt Tabitha was silent so long that Sophie thought she wouldn't answer. Then she sighed and turned back to Sophie.

"Of course a few parents get upset. There've been lawsuits,

threats to expose the damage . . . but in the last analysis, everyone understands the program's value greatly exceeds its costs. And of course it's only a handful of girls who have really poor outcomes. Those excepted, the girls of IRYLNS are really invaluable, not just because of their secretarial skills but for other reasons, reasons you're too young to understand. The same way parents give up their sons to the army, knowing that those young men risk grave injury or even death, they accept the need to allow their daughters to serve."

"But this isn't like losing your leg or even your eyesight," Sophie said. "Those girls—they've lost their *selves*. Even the healthy ones. Surely that's the worst fate of all?"

"Nothing I have ever felt in my life," said Great-aunt Tabitha, the words strong and unadorned, "has persuaded me that I wouldn't give up *all* my feelings, every single one of them, assuming the effects on the intellect to be negligible."

Sophie felt this like a blow. Did Great-aunt Tabitha really have any fondness for Sophie at all, if she would speak like this of sacrificing it?

Great-aunt Tabitha cleared her throat and took on a brisker tone.

"I've got a meeting with Augusta Henchman next week to talk about your future," she told Sophie. "I expect you'll do very well on your exams, assuming you're allowed to sit them. But if Parliament passes the bill that's currently under review, the government will have the right to dispose of you as it sees fit, exams or no. And with that academic profile, IRYLNS'll snap you up in a flash. Girls like you are just what's needed."

"But couldn't you somehow get me exempted?" Sophie asked, though she knew that Great-aunt Tabitha didn't believe in bending rules.

"Imagine what the newspapers could do with that," said Great-aunt Tabitha, shaking her head. "One of the most stalwart supporters of IRYLNS pulling strings to get her ward exempted from the scheme? Why, it might even be enough to topple the government! And that's where I draw the limit. Sophie, I would lay down my life for you without a moment's hesitation, but in the scenario I've just laid out, it wouldn't be my own life at stake, it would be the safety of the country as a whole."

"Is there anything I can do?" Sophie asked. "To protect myself?"

"Stay away," said Great-aunt Tabitha. She had picked something up from the top of the chest of drawers, where Sophie always dumped the contents of her school satchel, and fiddled with it as she talked. "Stay out of trouble and stay away from IRYLNS. I took you there to show you what's at stake. I don't want you even to *think* about telling anyone what you saw."

Sophie said nothing.

"The sleep of reason makes us all monsters," said Great-aunt Tabitha in the special voice she used to mark a quotation, though Sophie had no idea where the words came from. "What about finishing your homework before bedtime, Sophie?"

She set down on top of the chest of drawers the little thing she'd been playing with. After she had gone, Sophie got up to see what it was: that small token Mrs. Tansy had pressed into Sophie's hands—the iron . . . IRYLNS! Had the object itself been a concrete warning, a signal that Sophie simply hadn't had enough information to understand at the time? But how would Mrs. Tansy have known about IRYLNS, and why would it have mattered to her that Sophie should be warned?

Sophie felt like Bluebeard's wife. When Bluebeard gave his wife the keys of the wardrobes and strongboxes and caskets of jewels, when he handed her the master key to all his apartments, when he told her that she could go into any one of them except the little closet at the end of the ground-floor gallery, Sophie's whole body always flared up in scorn, though she knew this wasn't the real moral of the story, for the weak-willed wife. Why couldn't she have kept her promise? Sophie always wanted to cry out, "Don't! Just don't unlock the door! Be perfectly obedient and you won't get hurt!"

Could Sophie live with herself, though, if she didn't try to find out what really happened behind the closed doors of IRYLNS—find out and perhaps try to put a stop to it?

NINETEEN

O N TUESDAY AFTER LUNCH it was Sophie's turn to supervise the younger girls on the playground. She'd been walking around like a zombie since Saturday. Fortunately playground duty didn't involve much beyond making sure the children didn't actually kill one another, and though Sophie's eyes rested on a group of girls playing hopscotch, her thoughts were elsewhere. The other little girls were scampering over the climbing frame or running around playing tag, one particularly noisy bunch amusing themselves by shooting one of their playmates back and forth across the tarmac on some kind of cart.

In her mental haze, Sophie at first hardly noticed the police arriving, but within minutes the entire playground was overrun with uniformed officers. What on earth was going on? Recognizing the woman nearby as the constable from the week before, Sophie took a chance that she would be friendly.

"What's happening?" she asked.

"The interrogation of the man who assaulted the minister of public safety here on Saturday has yielded information that may lead to a breakthrough in another case," said the young woman, smiling at Sophie. "We're here to pick up a crucial piece of evidence, but they've sent the bomb squad as well, in case it's booby-trapped."

"I've found it!" shouted an officer.

A team of men with Alsatians ran to join him. Once the bomb-sniffing dogs gave the all clear, the men moved away far enough for Sophie to see.

It was the cart the girls had been playing with, and a second later she realized it must be the Veteran's transport, left behind the other day after his arrest.

"Why didn't they take it away on Saturday?" Sophie asked, since the woman constable hadn't moved away.

The woman shrugged and laughed a little. "Nobody ever said we were perfect," she said, sounding quite human.

If there *had* been a bomb, Sophie couldn't help thinking, several of the little girls might easily have been killed. She felt a surge of anger, the kind that was a mixture of scaredness and relief at surviving a danger one hadn't even apprehended.

The bell rang to mark the end of recess, but most of the girls ignored it to watch the police, now huddled together.

By nighttime, everyone knew the Veteran was to be charged with the medium's murder, but the story in the evening paper wasn't very forthcoming, and nobody was at all sure how the police had linked him to that crime or why he had attacked the minister.

Nan thought he might have been angry because of the government's decision to reduce pensions for veterans. She had also heard that the minister had annoyed the school servants by not tipping any of them after the lavish ceremonial breakfast. (Miss Hopkins had supposedly caused an uproar afterward in the staff lounge by commenting that she wouldn't turn down a tip herself if a parent tried to give her one.) Nan wondered whether the minister might have offended the Veteran by not giving him money. That was easy enough to imagine, but it didn't really seem grounds for actually attacking a person, Sophie decided, even if the Veteran had a screw loose.

Jean hadn't heard anything.

Priscilla had learned from a well-informed friend that the police had now definitely tied the Veteran to the murder at the Balmoral, but that he still refused to tell them why he'd attacked the minister.

"A friend!" Jean said, curling her upper lip and turning

away. "Boyfriend, more like."

Priscilla smiled her pretty, teasing smile.

"James isn't really a boy," she said. "He's a man; at least, eighteen's old enough to be allowed to get married."

Jean slammed her chemistry textbook shut, knocking a small china dog off the desk and smashing it on the floor.

"You're not going to marry him, though, are you?" she asked Priscilla. "Promise me you won't!"

"Surely you're not going to stand in the way of my union with my one true love?" said Priscilla, in the same light tone she might use to reproach someone for not passing the sugar for her tea.

Sophie and Nan exchanged glances, but there was nothing they could do to avert the inevitable clash.

"Priscilla, you made me a promise that when we leave school, you'll share a flat with me while we both do our certificates at the School of Electric Cookery," Jean said. She was almost in tears by now.

"I said we *might* share a flat," Priscilla said, calm as always. "I never made any promises. It's important to keep my options open at this point; that's what Daddy always says."

"But what about me?" Jean cried out. "I can't possibly afford a flat on my own. Besides, it wouldn't be the same without you. Why do you like those wretched boys so much?"

Now Priscilla looked really annoyed.

"You're acting like a baby," she said to Jean. "You talk as though you'd like to stay a schoolgirl all your life. Now, that's all very well for girls like you and Sophie, but I know there's better stuff waiting when we leave this place, and nine-tenths of the fun will involve men. I want to have a good time before I settle down. But James is truly sweet, Jean; I wish you could have seen him last weekend, kneeling on the ground in front of me and holding my hand and telling me he adores me. . . ."

The image of James at Priscilla's feet was more than Jean could bear. She uttered a strangled yell and fled.

Priscilla began laughing. "Oh, it's almost too easy," she said. "I really shouldn't, but poor Jean does expose herself so, and I simply can't resist. . . ."

"Are you really going to marry James?" asked Nan, who approved of James because he was captain of the boys' cadet corps at the Edinburgh Academy.

"Of course not!" said Priscilla. "I'm much too young. I think twenty-one's the perfect age to get married, don't you? I'm not one of those awful Brides-to-Be!"

The Brides-to-Be were the girls who dropped mathematics, science, and classics in their fifth year to take the Housewife's Certificate. Priscilla was scathing about them. "I certainly don't expect to do my own cooking and mending and washing once I'm married," she'd said in class once when the domestic science instructor begged her to keep her mind on the lesson. "Talk about a waste of time!"

"My father thinks I should take a degree in law," Priscilla said now. "He says that even if I'm married, it can't hurt to have another string to my bow."

"I don't mean to criticize," said Nan, "but it's quite cruel of you to torment Jean like that. Won't you go and find the poor girl and tell her you're sorry?"

"But I'm not sorry," said Priscilla, sounding surprised. "She asked for it. She's got no business being so jealous. Let her stew."

And with that remark, Priscilla returned to her English essay, leaving Sophie rather impressed with her ruthlessness.

When the housemistress came by to tell them to begin getting ready for bed, the three girls put their things away, turned out the study lights, and went into the bedroom, where they found Jean sitting shamefaced on Priscilla's bed, her hands clasped together in her lap, her eyes swollen and red.

"Priscilla, I'm so sorry," she blurted out. "It's none of my business what you do when we leave school. I promise I'll never pester you about this again. Only I would love it if we could share that flat. . . ."

"Well, let's wait and see," said Priscilla, sitting down next to Jean and putting an arm around her shoulders. "You're a goose sometimes, but you're my best friend. I won't do anything without telling you first. Don't worry, all right?"

"All right," said Jean, forcing a smile.

Thinking about possible futures made Sophie's mind run again over everything she'd seen at IRYLNS. What if Jean decided to go there? How would Sophie persuade her not to, without breaking the injunction to secrecy laid upon her by Great-aunt Tabitha? Would Sophie be able to save even herself from IRYLNS?

TWENTY

On Thursday afternoon Sophie went for tea at the professor's. She had to nerve herself up for it. Assuming Mrs. Lundberg was still angry with her, she went around the front way, with a vague sense that she'd forfeited the privilege of entering through the garden.

She rang the doorbell and waited. What if they didn't want to see her?

But when the housekeeper opened the door, she threw her arms around Sophie and hustled her into the sitting room toward a particularly lavish spread of cakes and sandwiches, just as if nothing had happened.

When Mikael came in, Sophie's mouth went all dry and she couldn't swallow. It wasn't as though they'd actually had an argument, but there had been something painful and unpleasant about the end of their last telephone conversation.

"Sophie?" he said quietly, speaking into her ear as his aunt piled his plate high with food.

"I don't know what was wrong when we talked the other day," Sophie said, the words tumbling out. She licked her lips and swallowed. "I didn't mean it. I—"

"Don't be silly! You've got nothing to apologize for. I was in a bit of a mood myself. Pax?"

"Pax," said Sophie, and as he squeezed her hand, the relief made her want to shout.

Over tea the professor told them about an Uppsala colleague who kept a pack of colobus monkeys in a two-acre enclosure, artificially heated at quite amazing expense, where the monkeys lived as they would in the wild. Nobody else said much. When Mikael had eaten his fill, he sprang up out of his seat and invited Sophie to join him in the garden, where, he said, a huge number of weeds awaited them.

Sophie looked at the professor to see if he wanted them to stay inside and keep him company, but he waved her away.

"If you two go outside now, I may finish with the proofs of my article in time for the last post," he said. "Sophie, I trust to see you again before many days pass?"

Sophie assenting, the professor retreated to his study, and she and Mikael went through the glass doors into the garden.

"Are we really going to weed?" she said to Mikael once they were alone.

"Do you know how to tell weeds from flowers?" Mikael asked.

"No," Sophie admitted.

"Neither do I. I really just wanted to get you out of earshot."

They sat down on the bench beneath the tree at the bottom of the garden. Mikael pulled a branch from a bush and began to strip its leaves off one by one.

"Sophie," he said, his uneasiness making Sophie fidgety, "the real reason I was in a bit of a state when we talked the other day is that there's something I still haven't told you about what happened in that hotel room."

Remembering Mikael's mix of self-possession and panic that night in the Vaults, Sophie realized she wasn't really surprised.

"What was it?" she asked. "Why didn't you tell me before?"

"It didn't seem wise."

"Well, what made you change your mind, then?"

"I can only tell you if you promise to keep it a secret."

"I promise," Sophie said, though the words seemed to scrape in her throat.

Rather than saying anything, Mikael took a pocketknife out of his trousers. Sophie remembered seeing it with the rest of his things at the police station.

"So?" she said. "It's your pocketknife. What about it?"

"Sophie, this knife *isn't* mine, though I said it was. When I finally got myself out of that awful wardrobe at the Balmoral and found Mrs. Tansy's body on the floor, I sort of staggered back and sat down on the couch. I didn't mean to, but my legs wouldn't hold me up properly. And then something hard pressed into my leg, and I felt for it without even thinking, and it was this."

Sophie still didn't understand.

"Sophie, this isn't just any old knife," he said, turning it over in his palm. "I recognized it at once. Look where it's chipped. You can see the spot's just the shape of the British Isles."

Sophie examined it.

"So it is," she said, "but what does it matter?"

"The knife isn't mine," Mikael said again. "But I'm one hundred percent sure it's my brother's. It was our father's, before he died, and then it passed down to him."

"It's your brother's?" Sophie said, feeling stupid. "Your older brother, the one who's so exemplary? But that's impossible. What on earth would your brother have been doing in Mrs. Tansy's hotel suite? Are you sure you didn't somehow have the knife with you, and drop it yourself without knowing?"

"Quite sure," said Mikael.

"Your brother's not in Scotland, anyway," Sophie said. "He lives in Denmark, doesn't he?"

"Well, Sweden, usually, but he could just as easily be in Scotland," said Mikael. "Nobody's heard from him for months."

It didn't take Sophie long to see what this meant. "You don't think—"

"I do," said Mikael, a grim look on his face. "It's unmistakably his. And the knife wasn't there before. I'd been sitting in exactly the same spot on the couch before the murderer got there, and I'd have felt it beneath me if it was there."

"How do you think it turned up?"

"Well, I suppose it's just within the bounds of possibility that my brother himself actually came to the room and killed Mrs. Tansy."

"Surely not!"

"I agree, it's pretty much inconceivable. Whatever else he's been doing, I simply can't imagine my brother's become a murderer. What's more likely is that someone took the knife off him and planted it there to incriminate him. But how did they get the knife from him in the first place? I must face it: there's a real chance he's hurt or even dead."

"Dead! But Mikael, he can't be; wouldn't you have heard something?"

"Normally, yes, but he's been completely out of touch

with everyone in the family for several months now."

"Even so, I simply can't believe it. Pretend for a minute that we're in a detective novel: If he was actually dead, someone would have found the body and the police would have identified him and got in touch with your mother."

"Believe me, I hope you're right. I'm pretty worried, though."

"I can see it's terribly worrying. But you know, Mikael, you really can rule out the idea that your brother committed the murder himself. Didn't you see in the papers? The police are holding the Veteran, that homeless man who's always hanging around, for the murder. They seem quite certain he did it; in fact, they were at school just the other day to pick up the trolley he left behind after he attacked the minister of public safety on Waterloo Day."

"When you say *trolley*," Mikael asked urgently, "what exactly do you mean?"

"A little wooden platform on wheels," Sophie said. "He rode around on it because of not having any legs; he lost them at war."

Mikael sprang up from his seat and began pacing back and forth.

"Sophie, you're absolutely right," he said. "It must have been your Veteran at the scene of the crime—"

"He's not *mine*," Sophie interjected. "That's just the name

I have for him in my head."

"When the commander took me back to the hotel, he was especially interested in the marks on the carpet, marks I thought might have been made by the wheels of the room service cart. But they must have been the Veteran's tracks!"

"I'm sure that's right," Sophie said. "What I still don't understand, though, is why he'd have *wanted* to kill Mrs. Tansy. It's all a bit random. Could someone else have hired him to do it, do you think?"

"There's another connection that might perhaps be important," Mikael said thoughtfully. "Commander Brown thinks the medium may have tried to blackmail someone high up in the Brothers of the Northern Liberties."

It was easy to imagine Mrs. Tansy resorting to blackmail. She must have known all kinds of things, many of them very nasty. Perhaps she'd learned the identity of the man behind the bombings and decided to turn it to her advantage.

"Say it's true," Mikael went on. "Then the man who's being blackmailed—the leader of the conspiracy, that is— hires the Veteran to kill Mrs. Tansy."

"Yes, all right, but why do you think the Veteran attacked the minister of public safety?" said Sophie.

It was all most confusing, and it made Sophie wonder how the authors of detective novels kept their clues straight. She shivered when she remembered how many times she'd seen the Veteran in the last few weeks. She had been close enough to touch him—to touch the hands that murdered Mrs. Tansy. Or for his hands to touch her. Had Sophie herself been in danger?

"The minister's main job is to stop the terrorists," said Mikael. "I suppose the leader of the Brothers might have very good reason to want her out of the way."

"That makes sense," Sophie admitted, "but it still leaves an awful lot out. For one thing, why was the Veteran so useless when he attacked the minister? He seems to have done away with the medium in a most gruesome and effective manner, but the minister wasn't even hurt. A good assassin would have used a bomb or a sniper's rifle."

"I see what you mean," Mikael said, sounding pensive. "Well, then . . ." His voice trailed off.

"I don't suppose there's any way one of us could get in to talk to the Veteran?" said Sophie.

"No," said Mikael, "and he'd have no reason to talk to us in any case. But Sophie, what can my brother have had to do with it? Let's assume he's not hurt or killed. Could he have been there in the hotel along with the Veteran? And if he wasn't, why would anybody want to implicate him by leaving the knife?"

"Did you ever work out exactly what your brother did to make your mother so angry?" Sophie asked. "If we knew that, perhaps we could find out where he is now and what he's doing. Then we'll know how his knife came to be there."

"Oh, it's too stupid for words," said Mikael. "Nobody but my mother would have made such a fuss; Aunt Solvej told me the whole story the other day. My brother's spent the last four years working for a pharmaceutical company in Stockholm, but it turns out that recently he left that job for a new one with the Nobel Consortium, even though our mother told him she'd never speak to him again if he took a job working for Nobel."

"The Nobel Consortium?" Sophie said, surprised. "But they're quite respectable! They sponsor a conference my great-aunt goes to every summer in Finland, the International Society for the Promotion of Peace."

"Yes," said Mikael, "but the Consortium's got a pretty sketchy reputation these days, in Scandinavia and the Baltic states at least. You see, it's so wrapped up now with the dynamiteurs and the munitions companies that some people say it's lost sight of its original goal of keeping the peace. The Consortium was implicated in the death of Norway's prime minister last year—"

"The man who said there was no point in the Hanseatic states adhering to the Geneva Conventions?"

"Yes, that's the one. Dead as a doornail. Poisoned. And the Consortium's definitely had a hand in the deaths of a few

French industrialists. Aunt Solvej says my mother has convinced herself that my brother's joining the Consortium is tantamount to his becoming a murderer himself."

Mikael fell silent.

"That's ridiculous," Sophie said firmly. "Just because the Consortium's unscrupulous doesn't mean your brother's done anything wrong. I've never met your brother, but I'm sure he hasn't suddenly turned into a murderer."

Then she thought of something else.

"Do you remember the commander saying that the medium was probably somehow connected to Nobel," she asked Mikael, "as well as to the Brothers of the Northern Liberties? Couldn't your brother have been there at the hotel to see her on perfectly legitimate business, and left the knife by accident? And don't say it," she added when Mikael showed signs of interrupting, "I know you said it wasn't there before, but when things fall into the cracks of a couch, the ordinary rules of matter in the universe don't exactly apply."

"Whatever it is," said Mikael, "I must find him. I wouldn't cover for him if he did it; if he cut that woman's throat, he must have completely lost his mind. But I don't think he did anything of the sort. I'm afraid he's in trouble."

Sophie's thoughts had gone off on another track.

"What we must do first, then," she said, "is find the person who commissioned the Veteran to kill the medium—"

"We don't *know* that someone commissioned him," Mikael interrupted.

"—because that way we also learn who's behind the Brothers of the Northern Liberties," she finished up. "Then we can stop the attacks, and perhaps save hundreds of lives."

"Sophie, that's not our problem! The intelligence officers are working around the clock to arrest the terrorists. What can we do that they can't perform a million times better?"

Sophie struggled to explain. "It's not just the bombs themselves that are so dangerous," she told Mikael. "I promised my great-aunt I wouldn't tell anybody, so you must keep this a secret, but it seems that the Brothers of the Northern Liberties may be secretly accepting money from the European Federation."

"What?" said Mikael, looking at Sophie as if she'd lost her mind.

"It's quite true," said Sophie. "And you see what that means. If it's proven, Scotland's got the right to force the other Hanseatic states to declare war on Europe."

"But that would mean—"

"Yes," said Sophie. "Death and destruction on a scale greater perhaps even than the Great War. We can't imagine it."

"All right, then," Mikael said, rolling his eyes. "It's not much of a job, is it? I've got to find my brother—who could be anywhere in the Hanseatic states—and prove he didn't commit murder. You've got to work out who hired the Veteran, bring that person to justice, track down the terrorists, and cover up Europe's part in the business so as to stop Scotland from going to war. Have I left anything out?"

"You can poke fun all you like," said Sophie, wishing she dared tell him about IRYLNS as well—but IRYLNS didn't even bear contemplating. "We may not be able to pull it off, but we must try."

She jumped when Mikael whacked the naked branch hard against the back of his hand.

"Sophie, I'm really worried about my brother," he said.

The savage unhappiness in his voice gave Sophie a pain in her insides. If Mikael's brother had been anywhere near that suite in the Balmoral, he probably was in big trouble. Sophie wished she could tell Mikael that she was sure his brother was all right, but there was no point saying something she only half believed.

"You know, Sophie," he added, "if you really *do* have any rapport with spirits, now might be the time to start calling in a few favors . . . maybe they can give you some information that will help sort things out. Or at least find my brother for me!"

"I must get back," she said hopelessly. She couldn't tell whether he was joking about the spirit business. "I'll find out whatever I can."

Mikael put his hands together and gave Sophie a leg up to the top of the garden wall.

"Will I see you this weekend?" he asked.

"I've got an awful lot of homework," Sophie said doubtfully. "Also Great-aunt Tabitha's not likely to let me go out for long; I'm still being punished. Shall we meet on Saturday afternoon next weekend?"

"Where?"

"You wanted to see the Hanseatic Exposition, didn't you? Why don't we meet at half past one in Jawbone Walk?"

"What a strange name!"

"Someone put up an enormous whale's jawbone there, an arch tall enough to walk through. It's in the Meadows just south of the university."

"All right," said Mikael. "But phone me if anything else comes up in the meantime, all right?"

Sophie nodded, but she didn't look back as she went over the wall and returned to the tennis courts to watch the last set. Nan and Jean's crushing defeat of Harriet Jeffries and a sixth-form girl called Marjorie gave Sophie great satisfaction, especially when Harriet greeted the final score by slamming her expensive new racket to the ground and storming off the court.

Back at school, Sophie let herself into the balance room with the key Mr. Petersen had had cut for her and waited for him to arrive and show her what he needed her to do today.

Ten minutes later, he still wasn't there. She checked her watch and racked her brain to see whether she could possibly have misremembered the time of their appointment. Most likely the teacher had simply forgotten.

It was stupid of her to feel so completely crushed with disappointment.

She decided to leave Mr. Petersen a note to let him know she'd been here. The trick would be to write it in a way that didn't sound at all reproachful or upset. She looked about for pencil and paper. The top drawer of the desk stood halfway open, and she pulled it a little further out. Surely Mr. Petersen wouldn't mind.

There was the distinctive dark green passport recently adopted by all of the Hanseatic states.

She knew she shouldn't look at Mr. Petersen's private papers. She *really* shouldn't look at them.

But if she looked at his passport, she could find out his birthday and see what he looked like when he was younger. She could see if he had a middle name she liked better than that awful *Arnold*.

Surely it could do no harm to take a quick peek.

Knowing she was doing something that was enough to get her expelled from school if she was found out, Sophie drew a deep breath and flipped open the passport.

The first thing she noticed was the date. Mr. Petersen had been born on the fifteenth of January 1912. That meant he was twenty-six, only eleven years older than Sophie.

The next thing she noticed was an anomaly. She had assumed Mr. Petersen must have been born in Scotland. But his national affiliation was marked as Swedish. In fact, his first name as it was given here wasn't Arnold at all, but the much more Scandinavian-sounding Arne!

There was nothing inherently suspicious about being called Arne or having been born in Sweden, but why was Mr. Petersen passing himself off at school as a Scottish person?

She flipped through the pages, and was even more alarmed to find them stamped full of visas and entrance permits to all of the Hanseatic countries. Why, it seemed as though he had traveled to Sweden alone at least half a dozen times since he'd begun teaching in Edinburgh—almost every single weekend! And yet he'd never said a word about it.

There was only one conclusion. *Mr. Petersen was not what he seemed.*

He can't be connected to the bombers, Sophie said to herself, hands sweating as she pushed the drawer closed to exactly where it had been before. He simply can't.

But taken in conjunction with his fixation on explosives, the evidence of the teacher's journeys seemed rather more alarming. Might he even, like Mikael's brother, have some connection with Nobel, whose name was virtually synonymous with Sweden?

In the end Sophie decided not to leave a note. She locked the door behind her and raced down the hall to the refectory. All through supper, she tormented herself about what she should do.

If there was any chance that Mr. Petersen was the bomber, she had to find out. The lives of others were at stake. But if Mr. Petersen was mixed up with the terrorists, it wouldn't be safe to confront him directly.

In class Friday morning Sophie couldn't keep herself from examining Mr. Petersen for signs of treachery. She felt the strangest mix of feelings for him: admiration and love muddled up with fear and suspicion and guilt. She broke a beaker when she caught him gazing at her, and hardly noticed when the others teased her about it at lunch.

The solution came to her halfway through the meal.

Sophie couldn't risk confronting Mr. Petersen in person, and even all those visas in his passport wouldn't serve as grounds for taking her suspicions to the police. What if he were perfectly innocent?

The people who really had the answers she needed—the medium, the suicide bombers—were all dead. They would be able to tell her whether Mr. Petersen had any part in the business, and what the medium knew that got her killed, and possibly even where Mikael's brother might have got to.

Everybody knew that radios could capture transmissions from the spirit world. It happened all the time; indeed it was often most inconvenient. Surely it couldn't be hard to tune in to the particular voice one wanted?

In school the year before they had built a proper wireless set, with valves and everything. Sophie knew it would be far simpler just to put together the essentials with a pair of head-phones. She would get the things at the ironmonger's after school and build the apparatus over the weekend at home.

She still didn't know what to do about IRYLNS. But working out what exactly had happened to the medium and whether it had something to do with the Brothers of the Northern Liberties seemed like Sophie's moral responsibility. And if she could clear Mikael's brother, not to mention find out why Mr. Petersen had bothered to conceal his identity and how the stick of dynamite had come into his possession, she'd really be doing well.

Feeling for the first time in weeks that she had actually taken charge of her own life, Sophie tore a piece of paper out of her exercise book and began to make a shopping list: the shiny metal lump called a crystal, the length of wire known as a cat's whisker.

Everything needed to build a radio for receiving the voices of the dead.

TWENTY-ONE

OPHIE WAS NOT INVITED to join that Friday evening's séance, an omission she took as a reprieve in the guise of punishment. Instead, she locked the door of her room from the inside and took out the kit she had purchased that afternoon on her way home from school, an assortment of odds and ends in a tin the size of a cigarette packet. The bright red tin said MIGHTY ATOM in lurid yellow capitals; it included tweezers and directions, as well as the galena detector crystal and the cat's whisker for the semiconductor junction.

The directions in the kit could not have been simpler. Sophie had already fashioned a coil with a slider that would let her tune the apparatus to different frequencies, and she had a flimsy set of headphones left over from a similar project—similar but non–spirit contacting—the year before. She fiddled with the parts until she had successfully installed the crystal inside a brass eggcup borrowed from the kitchen, then connected it to the iron springs of her bed (which would double as an antenna) and grounded it to the lightning rod outside the bedroom window.

They had learned about Marconi waves and other electromagnetic phenomena the year before at school. Thanks to Hertz, Tesla, and the other pioneers of wireless telegraphy, one could tune across the whole Marconi spectrum to a huge array of programs broadcast on different frequencies, and here and there spirit voices found a wavelength that would carry their words back to the world of the living.

Headphones on, everything in place, Sophie tried running the slider back and forth along the coil. She caught snippets of speech, including a woman talking about how to get rust stains out of linen and a man speaking in heavily accented English about something called the death drive. She stopped to listen: it was the great underground Marconi guru Dr. Sigmund "Thanatos" Freud, who broadcast an illegal show out of Hansestaat Hamburg that was picked up and redistributed on local frequencies by pirates all over the Hanseatic states and Europe.

Sophie wasn't staying up past her bedtime, though, to listen to the learned but peculiar ramblings of Dr. Freud, who proposed a new psychology of desire, in which he postulated that the denial of longing damaged one's mental and physical health. She had assembled a small pile of things to help her. From the bundles of old newspapers in the coal cellar, Sophie had obtained a decent collection of clippings about the attacks in Canongate and Princes Street.

She was a little scared of touching the medium's thoughts—and of what might happen if she invited such a powerful personality back into the world of the living. She had decided as a result to start instead by trying to contact the two most recent suicide bombers. If the dead bombers knew anything about their leaders, there was surely no reason they shouldn't tell it to Sophie. And unlike Mrs. Tansy, these men had chosen to die, making it less likely they would latch on to Sophie in anger and try to drain the life out of her, a form of attack known to have been attempted by spirits wrenched unwillingly from the world.

The dead lingered for some time where their lives had been lost, particularly when they died violently. She would try to reach the Canongate bomber first. She had been so close when it happened, and in a sense the bomber had actually spilled her own blood (her fingers went to the tiny scar on her forehead), giving her a personal connection to him. She had obtained several bedraggled flowers from the memorial at the site and a fragment of broken glass from the chemistry classroom, plus the grubby sticking plaster Matron had put on her cut the day of the explosion.

The Canongate bomber's name was Andrew Wallace, his age nineteen, according to the newspapers, which also told Sophie his place of birth was Lanarkshire. Andrew had lost his father to the Great War and his two best friends to the government, the first dying overseas with the army, the second arrested for demonstrating in favor of the No Conscription Act and suffering a fatal asthma attack during his prison interrogation.

Sophie closed her eyes, touched the scrap of bandage to the cat's whisker, and let everything empty out of her thoughts. Andrew had loved football as a boy, hoped to be a car mechanic, and was fond of animals. A scene swam into focus in Sophie's mind: the black Labrador puppy called Fido, a present for Andrew's seventh birthday, now grizzled and slow and unable to understand the loss of his master. It was disgustingly sentimental, like something in a women's magazine, but Sophie couldn't help being moved. She saw the empty bedroom in his mother's little house, a football trophy on the chest of drawers. On the bedside table, a collection of childhood treasures, things prettier than a boy like this might be expected to have: a glass paperweight blooming inside with blue and yellow flowers, a diode of rose quartz, a piece of green glass polished by sand and sea until it was the perfect shape for holding in one's hand.

Somehow Sophie knew that the pebble had lived in Andrew's pocket and spent many hours in the warm hollow of his palm. Looking with her inner eye, she reached out for the pebble with her left hand and could almost feel it settle into place, her right hand steady all the while on the tuner.

Suddenly she felt herself there with Andrew in Canongate, right in front of a shop window full of tartan. Andrew was feeling reflexively in his pocket for the piece of green glass, heart leaping into his mouth when it wasn't there, then remembering he'd left it at home on purpose so that it wouldn't be blown to bits with the rest of him.

He raised a hand—naked without the pebble—to wipe away the sweat from his forehead.

Then he reached for the detonator.

"Speak to me, Andrew," Sophie said out loud, brows crunched in concentration, clutching the pebble so tightly that her fingers began to hurt. "Speak to me. Tell me what happened. Who's behind it? Andrew, did someone talk you into doing this?"

The scene before her froze: Andrew, trapped just an instant before the explosion.

She had to keep him there; she was afraid she might be blown up right along with him if she let time move forward.

"Talk to me!"

She slid the tuner slowly along the coil and paused when she heard something, a low murmur that resolved itself into words.

"It's worth it," the voice said over the headphones, sounding uncertain and unhappy. "Just remember why you're doing this. Remember Tim. Remember Tommy. This is for the two of them, and for all those others the government's killed. I'm doing it for them."

"Andrew," Sophie whispered intently. "Who helped you do it? Who gave you the explosives? Who set you up?"

The voice continued as if Sophie hadn't spoken.

"It's for them. Joining the Brothers of the Northern Liberties. Training for the mission. It's all for them. I won't live myself to see the Free Zone, but others will. The Free Zone. The Brothers."

Sophie feared she hadn't allowed for a proper mechanism to get her words to the dead boy. "Andrew, who were the others?" she said, trying to shoot the question at him like an arrow across the moat separating life from death. "Who's behind it all?"

"Cells. They've got us in cells so we won't know the others and bring them into danger. My team leader's Duncan, Duncan from Fife, Duncan the baker's boy. But Duncan's dead now. Dead, dead, all dead."

Sophie remembered that one of the bombers who killed

himself in April had been called Duncan MacDonald.

"May his soul rest in peace," she whispered to herself, her lips barely moving.

"Duncan's dead, Tommy's dead, Tim's dead," said the voice, gone softer now and sort of quavery.

She knew she hadn't much longer before the spirit of Andrew Wallace would retreat to the faraway place.

"Andrew," she said, speaking now in her full voice, her hand shaking with the strain of holding the slider in the right position. "Andrew, it's too many dead. Do you hear me? *Too many dead.* I need to find the person who's behind this and stop him. Not Duncan. The big one, the one who tells everybody what to do. We've got to stop this. Enough people have died already."

"Green glass," said the voice. "Green glass?"

Sophie knew she must be imagining it—the sound quality was poor, and spirit voices were not known for their emotional range—but she heard puzzlement in the Marconi waves.

"Duncan saw my lucky piece," the voice continued. "Green glass. The person's eyes were glassy green, he said. And me pestering him for a clue about our leader. Green as glass. Where's my lucky piece now? Where's . . ."

As the voice faded in and out, Sophie desperately sent thoughts of warmth and reassurance to the frantic disembodied spirit. Before long, though, whatever had been present was completely gone, lost in the atmospheric tangle of electromagnetic waves.

She fiddled with the tuner, but Andrew Wallace was no longer anywhere to be found.

It was past midnight, and Sophie felt bone-tired as she relaxed out of the position she'd held for the past hour, crouched over the apparatus and straining so as not to miss a single whisper of sound through the headphones.

Finding her left hand still clenched into a tight fist, she opened it and her heart seemed to skip a beat.

The green glass pebble lay in her palm, warmed to the exact temperature of her skin.

TWENTY-TWO

WAKING BLEARY-EYED on Saturday morning, Sophie drank a huge mug of tea and ate a piece of toast in the kitchen, then took her schoolbooks into the dining room, where she worked doggedly through a huge pile of homework. Peggy was away for the weekend at her second cousin's wedding in Kirkcaldy, both maids had been given the day off, and Sophie was in charge of meals.

After a supper of scrambled eggs and toast, Sophie climbed the stairs to her room, where she turned the key to lock the door and then retrieved the elements of the crystal set.

She thought she'd learned as much as she could from poor dead Andrew Wallace, and besides, she couldn't bear the idea of disturbing him again. The man who'd set off the bomb in Princes Street was a twenty-three-year-old engineering student called Malcolm Black, and Sophie had a few clippings and one of the dead flowers from the memorial (the one she'd picked up that day with Jean outside the electric showroom) to focus her tuning.

This time it wasn't nearly so easy, and she started to wonder if her success the night before had been beginner's luck. She focused like mad on Malcolm Black, repeating the name to herself until the syllables stopped making sense. She had a faint perception of presence, but it was as if the bomb had pulverized Malcolm Black's psyche along with his body.

More than half an hour passed before Sophie began to detect a pattern to her failures. Both times that she'd almost reached Malcolm, the same voice had cut in over his, a voice whose timbre and accent suggested a working-class man, perhaps middle-aged or even elderly.

There was something familiar about it, she thought. Could this be the voice of someone she had actually met? Someone who wanted to speak to her now?

She put aside all thoughts of Malcolm Black and concentrated on the new voice.

With a little adjustment, she found the place on the Marconi spectrum where it came through most clearly. Holding the tuner in place, she sent her own psychic energy to the unknown spirit.

Suddenly the words snapped into focus, no longer garbled. "Ma money," the voice said. "Where's ma money?"

And in a flash, Sophie knew who it was. It was the Veteran, who had been asking Sophie for money for years, every Friday afternoon, until he'd been taken away the week before, and who had called out something very similar as he attacked the minister at Waterloo Day.

But the Veteran wasn't dead! He was very much alive, held in a cell at the Castle. Could being imprisoned in a dark cell let a spirit fly free of its body?

She decided to venture a question.

"What money?" she said. "Was it your pension? Or did you get paid to kill the medium? Why were you at the Balmoral, and who paid you to murder Mrs. Tansy?"

"Ma money," the voice repeated. "Where's ma money?"

"Who paid you to kill the medium?" Sophie said.

"They took away my pension, and they said I'd not regret it," the voice said, falling into a four-beat line like something out of a poem.

"Who?" Sophie said impatiently. "Who was it who said you'd not regret it?"

"They said I'd not regret it," the voice said, sounding less certain than before. "They took away my pension. They gave me an assignment."

"What was it?" Sophie asked.

"They gave me an assignment, and they said I'd not regret it," said the voice, words falling into the same four-beat rhythm as before.

"What assignment?" she said.

"They told me the Balmoral," said the voice.

The promptness and precision of the response took Sophie so much by surprise that she lost hold of the tuner and had to fiddle about for a few agonizing seconds before finding the place again.

"—told 'em I was skint, and neither of 'em wanted to know," said the voice.

Sophie could have kicked herself. She'd missed the whole substance of his answer, with no guarantee she'd be able to get him to repeat it!

"And I said to him," the voice went on, in full flow, "'But where's ma money? Where's ma bloody money? You've no idea what it means these days, to live from week to week on a fixed income.' And so I took the other lady down, till they had to tear me off her and carry me awa'."

"Who wanted the medium dead?" Sophie asked, hoping to prompt the voice back to its earlier topic.

But it was no good.

"Ma money," whispered the voice, fading even as Sophie listened. "All I asked for was ma money. . . ."

And try as Sophie might, she couldn't find the voice anywhere on the spirit frequencies. It was all regular old everyday radio pirates blethering on about how to set up an illegal still or weatherproof a roof.

She listened for a few minutes to Dr. Freud rabbiting away about the Daedalus Complex: men inventing machines that caused the deaths of young people who ignored constraints on how the technology should be used. Before too long, though, she let go of the tuner and turned away from the apparatus in disgust.

She put away all the equipment and changed into her pajamas, got into bed, and turned out the light. But there was something she couldn't get out of her mind.

Sophie's crystal set picked up the voices of the dead at certain wavelengths, as well as living people broadcasting on the frequencies in between. Obviously she'd somehow tuned in to the Veteran's thoughts as well. But how would that work? The Veteran was alive and well.

It was just about possible that the force of the Veteran's obsession with the money had given his voice a special telepathic carrying power.

But wasn't it more likely that the Veteran, too, was now dead?

Sophie got up the next morning at half past six, hours before the usual time on a Sunday, and put on her slippers and dressing gown before creeping downstairs to retrieve the newspapers from the front doorstep.

Having lit the range and put a large kettle on the stove, she sat down at the kitchen table and spread the papers before her.

Half an hour later, the kettle had long since boiled and was now releasing clouds of steam, but Sophie didn't even notice, her whole attention fixed on a story in the left-hand column of the front page of the *Scotsman*:

The vagrant who was arrested last week for his attack on a member of the cabinet at the Waterloo Day observances of a well-known Edinburgh girls' school, and subsequently charged with the murder of Mrs. Euphemia Tansy, 56, at the Balmoral Hotel on the 15th of June, was found dead late Saturday evening in a cell in the Vaults at Edinburgh Castle. A spokesman for the authorities announced that to all appearances, the man—a veteran of the armed forces—died of natural causes. There were no signs of foul play, and the authorities have not scheduled an autopsy at this time.

The Veteran was dead.

He'd spoken to Sophie from beyond the grave.

And she had no doubt—despite the paper's bland assurances—that the death had been arranged, probably by the same person who hired the Veteran to kill the medium in the first place. Someone who feared that under interrogation the man might reveal what he knew and implicate his employer in that terrible crime.

What kind of person had access to a prisoner locked up in the country's securest stronghold?

Were Sophie and Mikael in danger?

TWENTY-THREE

ETWEEN WORRYING ABOUT murderers, IRYLNS, and the everyday threat of terrorism, Sophie felt like she was on the verge of a complete breakdown. And IRYLNS was almost the worst of it. It was shocking how different the city looked to Sophie after having been to IRYLNS.

The young women were everywhere. Sophie spotted more than a dozen of them before she'd even got halfway to school on Monday morning: the girl in the pink jacket on the tram, the girl wearing the plaid tam-o'-shanter and modest ankle-length skirt, the handsome young woman with black bobbed hair buying a cup of coffee from the stall at the corner of Waterloo Place. All their faces were as smooth and blank as wax.

In contrast, the girls in first-period English looked reassuringly ordinary. Even Harriet Jeffries couldn't be mistaken for anything other than a real (horrible) living breathing human, especially when she caught Sophie staring and shot her an evil grimace, then resumed her usual butter-wouldn't-melt expression before the teacher noticed.

But though the girls looked just as they should, Sophie still had a strange cloudy feeling of cobwebby things hanging at the edge of her vision. Half a dozen times that morning she felt a tap on her shoulder and jerked around to find nothing there, so that when Nan came to fetch her to lunch, Sophie ignored her until the others began laughing at her absent-mindedness.

Over lunch in the refectory—greasy little pellets of mince like rabbit droppings, dun-colored mashed potatoes, and turnips—Sophie caught up on the weekend's news. Having received special furlough from the headmistress on account of war preparedness needs, the others had gone home to Nan's family's house for a marathon session of driving lessons.

"Nan's brother's lovely," said Priscilla.

Nan beamed at her.

Jean put down her knife and fork.

"How's he doing with the prosthesis?" Sophie asked. It would be interesting to have a mechanical limb; it would make one into a kind of human-machine hybrid.

"Pretty well, I think," said Nan, though she didn't sound confident. "The worst of it is that he didn't lose the leg in combat. It was a Scottish mine that blew up the truck. When he first got home, he wouldn't do anything but sit in Father's armchair drinking whisky. But once they fitted him with the new leg, he began to feel much better. The best news is that there'll still be a position for him in his old regiment. Not just a desk job, either: he'll fight alongside everybody else. That's cheered him up no end."

Sophie privately found this perverse, but it would not do to say so.

"I daresay it cheered him up even more to have Priscilla hanging all over him," Jean said, sounding so bitter that Sophie looked at her with surprise. "I found it quite disgusting."

"They were just dancing," Nan said, rising at once to her brother's defense. "I thought it was lovely. If it cheered Tom up, what's wrong with that?"

"I certainly enjoyed myself," said Priscilla. She sounded almost angry. "Tom's a wonderful dancer. Nan, do you think he has a girlfriend?"

"No," Nan began, "he was engaged, but—"

The rest of the sentence was drowned out by Jean smashing her teacup down onto her tray so hard that the saucer cracked in two. She pushed back her chair and ran from the room.

Sophie looked around to see if any teachers had noticed, but there wasn't a single adult in sight.

What had happened? Usually at least two or three of them supervised at lunch.

Priscilla followed her train of thought without effort.

"Miss Henchman's called all the teaching staff to a special meeting," she told Sophie. "It's supposedly something to do with the government bill about the school learning age and war preparedness. It sounds as though certain programs will be able to pick which girls they want and—"

"It's wicked of you to tease Jean like that," Nan interrupted. "She can't bear it that people like you so much, and that you're so, well, *nice* to them all."

"By *people*, I suppose you mean boys?"

"Well, yes, but I didn't want you to think I was being rude," Nan said.

They didn't see Jean again until they arrived in Mr. Petersen's classroom after lunch and were greeted by three words on the chalkboard: POWER IN POWER, the motto of the Hanseatic League.

"Our topic for the day," said the teacher when all the girls had taken their seats, "is the relationship between science and politics. Everybody knows there's a pun in the Hanseatic slogan. Paraphrased and expanded, it might read 'Political power depends on the effective harnessing of new technologies and natural resources.'"

Oh, for goodness' sake, a man with this knack for making everything long-winded and tedious simply *couldn't* be in bed with the terrorists! Sophie began drawing an elaborately decorated letter P in her notebook.

"Speaking simply of the forms of power that actually make machines run," Mr. Petersen continued, "what are the traditional preferences of the Hanseatic states?"

Nobody answered.

"We generally prefer electricity to fossil fuels," Sophie said, feeling the rest of the class go stiff with boredom. "We've developed highly efficient technologies partly because of our relative lack of natural resources. Countries that've got a lot of coal tend to be almost *profligate* with steam power; it's precisely because we can't afford to use up all our supply running trains that we've developed ways of using electrical power to move vehicles far in advance of anything they have in Europe or the Americas."

"Part of what Sophie's saying," said Mr. Petersen approvingly, "is that human ingenuity can do a great deal to counteract so-called natural disadvantages. In Scotland, for instance, engineers have developed superb new technologies that quite make up for the fact that coal's in such short supply. And at the international level, the Nobel Consortium has been able to use its monopoly on top-quality armaments to secure political autonomy for the Hanseatic states. Weapons equal peace."

At the word *armaments* everyone groaned. Even Sophie wasn't sure she agreed with Mr. Petersen. Weren't explosives responsible for more evil than good in the world? Sophie remembered crying when she first learned about the seals trained to drag harnesses of explosives to blow up tankers. The poor creatures died in the service of a cause they didn't even understand, and that couldn't be right, could it?

"No, no, hear me out," the teacher said. "This weapons business is really important. What's the classic example of science directly affecting politics?"

"The establishment of the state of Israel," Fiona said. "Chaim Weizmann traded the secret of the acetone process—which lets you turn corn into acetone for manufacturing cordite—for the European Federation's support for the creation of a Jewish state in Palestine."

"Very good, Fiona," said Mr. Petersen. Sophie was *bursting* with jealousy. "Of course, politics can have very direct results on science and technology as well. The outcome of America's War of Secession depended very heavily on access to explosives. At the war's outset, almost all the gunpowder mills were located in the Northern states. The Northerners would have won and the United States of America would still exist as a single entity if Delaware hadn't seceded to join the

Southern cause. Why was Delaware so important?"

Everyone knew the answer to that.

"Delaware had the DuPont munitions factories," Jean said. Her eyes were still a bit red, Sophie noticed, but she didn't sound upset anymore. "Once the Southerners got hold of them, the Northerners had to let them secede."

"Mr. Petersen?" said Fiona, raising her hand.

"Yes, Fiona?"

"Weren't we supposed to do an experiment today? We've used up more than half our class time already."

Mr. Petersen looked at the clock and did a comical double take when he saw the time.

"We've not a moment to lose!" he said.

It turned out that Mr. Petersen had got hold of an old but functional pair of Caselli pantelegraphs, which allowed a person at one end to transmit an image to a receiver at the other. The sender wrote a message with nonconducting ink on a sheet of tin, which was then fixed to a curved metal plate and scanned by a needle. Telegraph wires carried the electrical message to the receiving machine, where it was transcribed in Prussian blue onto paper soaked in potassium ferrocyanide.

This was *fun*, Sophie thought, watching each set of lab partners take their turn to send a message, with much wrangling over who got to have the final product as a keepsake. Sophie and Leah were the last ones in line, and when their turn came, only minutes before the end of class, Leah took the sender's station and Sophie manned the receiver.

"I'm going to send you my famous drawing of a camel," Leah said, scraping earnestly at the tin with the writing instrument.

She came to join Sophie once she'd finished drawing and positioned the needle to do its work. As the clean blue marks began to appear on the paper, the two girls leaned over to watch, holding their breath.

"Look!" Leah said, jumping up and down and pointing. "There's the crescent moon in the background!"

Leah's camel posed in silhouette against a desert horizon, complete with palm tree and oasis and moon sliver. They watched with excitement as the triangular leaves of the palm tree and the camel's skinny head and neck began to emerge at the top of the page.

About a quarter of the way down, though, the line experienced a disruption. The stylus dug deep into the paper, racing back and forth.

"What's happening?" Leah asked Sophie.

The machine had gone haywire. After a minute the needle began to behave again, falling into its regular back-and-forth movement. But something was clearly awry. Beneath the horizontal strip of desert landscape with camel was a slice—growing even as they watched—of something quite different.

"What is it?" Leah asked Sophie, who shrugged again and shook her head.

"Some kind of a technical drawing?" one of the other girls said.

"Yes," said Sophie with impatience, "but what's it a drawing *of*?"

Leah peered at the line of text along the bottom. Parts of the diagram were labeled as well.

"Oh!" she said. "At first I thought the letters had come through all fuzzy because of the needle, but they're not even real letters!"

When Sophie looked, though, she saw something *quite* surprising: the letters were real, but they were in the Cyrillic rather than the Roman alphabet.

Beginning to puzzle out the words, she'd caught nothing more than the place and date lines—Sankt Peterburg, 21-02-23—and the words *serdtsevina* and *reaktor* when a hand snatched the page out of the calipers holding it in place. The stylus began whirring, and a wisp of smoke drifted from the guts of the machine.

Sophie looked up to see Mr. Petersen, his face pale and his hands shaking.

"What's wrong?" Leah said. "Mr. Petersen, why did you take our facsimile? We hadn't finished looking at it—do you know what went wrong?"

"Does the machine have a mechanical memory that it stores pictures in," Nan asked, "and could it have sent an old one by mistake?"

"No," said Mr. Petersen blankly, "there's no memory. I can't imagine what happened. Some kind of a misfire, I suppose."

"Oh," said Leah. "Will we get full credit for the experiment, even though it didn't work properly?"

"Certainly," said Mr. Petersen, a little color coming back into his face. He had rolled up the malformed image and tucked it into his breast pocket. "Full credit for the practical part, at any rate. I won't make any guarantees about your marks for the report. It depends on how well you write everything up; better than last time, Leah, I hope!"

The bell rang. Sophie lingered as the others left the classroom.

"I'm sure it was a technical drawing of some kind," she said to Mr. Petersen. "Had you any idea what it might be for?"

Mr. Petersen gave her a wary look. "Had you?" he countered.

Sophie shook her head. It was strange, but she could have sworn he seemed relieved.

"Do you think I could take it with me, and see if I can work out what it is?" she asked.

"No," said Mr. Petersen in a loud voice. "I need to hold

on to it," he added semiapologetically, "to help me learn what went wrong."

"All right," said Sophie, though she couldn't see how it would help him. In any case she remembered the drawing perfectly well.

Her first impression was that it was some kind of fortified chamber, something one might build to test a high-powered explosive reaction, but the real mystery was where it had come from. In spite of Mr. Petersen's dismissive answer to Nan's question, could the machine have retained the memory of something transmitted in the past?

It was an intriguing puzzle, one consuming enough that Sophie barged straight into Miss Chatterjee in the corridor outside the chemistry classroom.

"Sophie!" said Miss Chatterjee, using a handkerchief to wipe the hot coffee off her front.

"Really, Sophie," added Miss Hopkins, who had been walking alongside Miss Chatterjee, "you could hardly be more careless."

"I'm terribly sorry, Miss Chatterjee," said Sophie, feeling like the worst person in the world.

"*Sorry* doesn't put dinner on the table," Miss Hopkins commented. "Sophie, get the mop and bucket from the janitor's cubby and clean up that spill before someone slips and hurts herself."

"Yes, Miss Hopkins," Sophie said, not bothering to mention that mopping would make her late for her next class.

Of course it took ages to find the bucket, fill it with hot water and Nightingale fluid, and go back to clean up the mess. By then Sophie was mopping so frantically that it took her a minute to realize she was hearing a three-way conversation between Mr. Petersen, Miss Hopkins, and Miss Chatterjee in the classroom behind her.

"Are we protecting the girls," said Miss Chatterjee in her unmistakable cut-glass accent, "or are we simply protecting the country?"

"A ridiculous question," Miss Hopkins said. "There's no reason to see any conflict between the two. Myself, I think the latest development's more exciting than ominous."

"It all depends," said Mr. Petersen, "on what you think of the procedure itself. I remember—"

But Sophie was not to hear what Mr. Petersen remembered. A loud snort caused her to look around and see the unmistakable looming figure of Miss Henchman.

TWENTY-FOUR

"I ASSUME A TEACHER GAVE you permission to use the janitor's equipment?" the headmistress said frostily.

"I'm sorry to get in your way, Miss Henchman," said Sophie. She'd never seen the headmistress in the science wing; she hoped it wouldn't set a precedent. "I bumped into Miss Chatterjee and spilled her coffee, and Miss Hopkins told me to clean up."

"Quite right, too," said Miss Henchman.

Miss Henchman was surprisingly fair when it came to real accidents. She didn't have the irritable and unjust temper that led some teachers to punish one for mishaps resulting from carelessness rather than disobedience.

"Aren't you meant to be elsewhere by now?" the head-mistress added.

"Yes, Miss Henchman," said Sophie, thinking that she'd better not rush off until Miss Henchman actually dismissed her.

The headmistress nodded, and Sophie trundled the bucket as fast as she could back to where it belonged, then hurried to class.

There Miss Botham, rapt to the point of passion, was already in the midst of praising to the girls the nineteenth century's innovations in standard office practice, down to improvements in ordinary writing tools (the mass-produced lead pencil, the steel-nibbed pen, the patented reservoir pen with its ink stored in a kind of fountain inside the barrel).

"Typewriters, invented in the 1860s, shortly became indispensable," said Miss Botham, sounding like a braying donkey, "and the word *typewriter* soon came to be used interchangeably with *secretary* or *clerical assistant*. The machine became even more valuable with the introduction of the Dictaphone, which allows an employer to dictate a draft of a letter or a memorandum at any hour of the day or night in a medium the secretary may transcribe later on the typewriter."

The woman sounded like a paid advertisement, Sophie thought. Meanwhile Miss Botham drew a diagram of the Dictaphone on the blackboard.

"Girls who go to IRYLNS, girls who go modestly and without complaint to work in a local office, girls who stay at home to help their fathers with secretarial tasks," she rhapsodized, "all these girls do the country a service that may add up to precisely the difference between victory and defeat. Remember, your outlook is just as important as the skills you learn. To be a really first-rate secretary, one must know far more than shorthand and typewriting."

"And what's the correct outlook, Miss Botham?" asked Harriet, leaning forward in her seat with a disgustingly angelic smile.

"The perfect secretary experiences a sense of pleasure and excitement about each piece of work she undertakes," said Miss Botham, smiling at Harriet in a way that made Sophie want to be sick. "The perfect secretary is without morbid self-consciousness or sensitivity. She is a miracle of tact and discretion, and she is always in a good mood."

It was a relief when Miss Botham finally stopped and showed them how to put on the headphones and operate the foot pedal for slowing down or speeding up the rate at which the machine played back.

Sophie surprised herself by adjusting to the new technology with something like delight. She rapidly figured out how to turn herself into a highly efficient automaton—one had to leave one's brain entirely out of it, becoming a linked circuit of ears and hands and eyes without any conscious input. Thinking about any individual part of the procedure would only slow one down.

After a little practice, she was able to type the memorandum recorded on her particular cylinder (a terribly dull set of revisions to the school out-of-bounds rules—it was just like Miss Henchman to kill two birds with one stone by getting the girls to do her typing for free) without touching her foot to the slow-down pedal more than once every thirty seconds. Then she sped the recording up even faster than the ordinary speaking voice. Now her fingers flew over the keyboard, typing faster and faster until a pair of hands wrenched off her headphones.

Sophie looked up to see Nan staring at her, Sophie's headphones in her hands, a circle of girls surrounding them and Miss Botham fuming at the front of the classroom.

Sophie was bewildered. She'd really been in the flow of things. It was most annoying of Nan to interrupt!

"Sophie, you were typing so fast we thought you must be pretending," Nan said. "Fiona used her stopwatch and clocked you at a thousand keystrokes per minute—you were ripping those sheets out of the platen like nobody's business! I can't believe the machine didn't jam. Miss Botham thought you must be putting it on. She asked me to stop you and see whether you were really typing what was on the recording."

"Why should there be a problem?" Sophie said.

Her brain had been so far out of the loop of activity that she couldn't even remember what she'd just typed. It was always faster to type that way, even if one sometimes introduced awkward mistakes. Still, since Nan seemed worried, Sophie rolled the page out of the typewriter and hastily glanced at the first few lines.

"It looks fine to me," she said.

Nan took it from her hand, no longer so certain as before that something must be wrong. A few minutes later, though, she started laughing.

"All right, I admit it's a good joke," she said. "For a minute there, I really thought you'd acquired superhuman prowess as a typist, or crossed over into the fifth dimension or something. I still don't see how you got the machine to work so fast. What's the trick?"

"There's no trick," said Sophie, snatching the page back from Nan and reading it more slowly from the top.

Nan jabbed a finger at the middle.

"That's what you're looking for, I think," she said. "I must say, Sophie, I don't approve of that kind of language."

Many of the other girls had gone back to their work, but a few still stood nearby, Miss Botham hovering at the periphery.

Sophie followed the direction of Nan's finger and gasped. How had she made such an awful mistake? Would she ever survive the shame of Nan having seen it?

A quick look suggested that the previous pages were just as they should have been. This one, though, contained an appalling swerve from the straight and narrow.

In the numbered list of instructions she'd been typing, the break was painfully obvious:

48. No girl shall wear slippers outside the dormitories.
49. No girl

if the bloody bitch hadn't interfered i'd not be here at all i'd be living it up in one of the baltics damn them all to hell and the girl too for all she looked so young and that other harpy who paid me off in the first place and the gentleman too both of em up to no good i'd say but the young un worse than the old un and what's happened to my favorite little fellow i'd like to know

xajiodgoihovhoiahdoifhdaoifnoidasngoidnagoinadgoinagsoin doignadoignado;isgnoadsingoai;sdnaoisdhfiuoahughdoiaugna dskjnfgasdngdasiohgoiadshgoia

mind me girl it's not the one you think it's the other one make sure th

And the rest of the page was blank from where Nan had cut her off.

Sophie crumpled the paper into a ball and stuffed it into her pocket so that the teacher wouldn't be able to read it.

"Nan, I swear I didn't do it on purpose," she said urgently. "It must have been some kind of a fit. I think it might be related to what happened in Mr. Petersen's class just now. I'll explain—"

But Miss Botham had marched up to them, gathered up the stack of typed pages beside Sophie's machine, and laid her meaty hand on Sophie's shoulder.

"You'll not get away with creating a disruption in my classroom," she said, "not after being so disrespectful as to arrive late without an apology."

"But—," Sophie started to say.

Miss Botham jostled her so hard that Sophie almost fell, her leg crumpling under her.

"Put your things together," the teacher said in a cold voice, "and go straight to Miss Henchman's office. You've distracted the other girls and willfully created a nuisance."

Sophie waited wretchedly by the door as Miss Botham scribbled a note and sealed it in an envelope.

"That's for the headmistress," said the teacher, "and above and beyond whatever punishment she metes out, you'll type me ten clean copies of page three hundred and fifteen of

Walter Scott's *Redgauntlet*. A fine way for a big girl like you to behave! I expect to see a thoroughly reformed character the next time I lay eyes on you, Sophie Hunter."

Sophie trudged along the corridor toward the head's office with a strong feeling that the world was against her. It seemed incredibly unfair to get in trouble for something she had done in a trance, and worse to think of having fallen into an altered state without even knowing it.

She thought suddenly of Jekyll and Hyde and the way the transformation came on more and more easily until Dr. Jekyll actually lost his original form and became only Mr. Hyde. Had Sophie somehow opened herself up to this degradation by her own willful meddling in the spirit world?

She told the secretary that Miss Botham had sent her to see Miss Henchman, then took a seat on the bench. It was funny how horrible it felt to have to wait there outside the head's office, even knowing she had done nothing substantially wrong. It gave her a disconcerting glimpse into what it would be like to be one of those girls who got into trouble all the time.

Her thoughts intent on what had happened in class just now, it took Sophie a little while to notice that the voices in the office had become loud enough for her to hear them.

The person in the head's inner sanctum was none other than Sophie's Great-aunt Tabitha.

"I hadn't thought of it for her, possibly not at all and certainly not yet," Sophie heard her great-aunt say. "Let her complete the university degree first. There are far too few women in the sciences, and I have always argued that a handful of exceptional young women must be allowed to opt out of the scheme."

Sophie heard the murmur of the headmistress's voice, but couldn't distinguish the words.

"Nonsense!" said Great-aunt Tabitha.

Miss Henchman's more muted voice responded.

"Certainly not," said Great-aunt Tabitha.

Another inaudible statement by the headmistress.

"Well," said Sophie's great-aunt, sounding rather less certain, "I suppose I can't stop you."

They were arguing about what Sophie would do after taking her exams.

Great-aunt Tabitha thought Sophie should go to university.

Miss Henchman thought she should go to IRYLNS.

The headmistress was winning.

TWENTY-FIVE

SOPHIE DECIDED TO WALK home from school on Friday afternoon rather than taking the tram. Walking lubricated the thought processes, somehow. She decided that the incidents with the pantelegraph and the Dictaphone had to be related. Both came close on the heels of her using the radio to contact the dead. Had Sophie opened up some kind of doorway? Who wanted to contact her, and why?

The technical diagram from Mr. Petersen's class remained a mystery. Sophie had consulted a number of reference books without finding anything like it. When she asked Mr. Petersen the next day whether he'd worked out what had gone wrong, he brushed off her questions, avoiding Sophie's eyes.

Putting aside the drawing for the moment, Sophie could see a pattern.

The first dead bomber had revealed hardly anything. He had been too young, too confused, too remote from the heart of the conspiracy and, Sophie thought, too long dead.

The second voice had been the Veteran's. The Veteran had told her more than poor Andrew Wallace, but not with the kind of detail that would clear up any mysteries. He'd talked about the minister taking away his pension and someone hiring him for an assignment, probably the murder of the medium. He was clearly trying to say something else about the minister, but Sophie shrank from the idea of contacting him again. Let him rest in whatever peace he could salvage.

Then the next verbal communication, the words on the typewriter in Miss Botham's class. Sophie still had no recollection of hearing anyone on the recording other than Miss Henchman. She'd gone back afterward and begged Miss Botham to allow her to finish the typing job properly. That was just what Miss Botham wanted to hear, and so she let Sophie listen again to the whole thing, on the condition that she type out a clean copy. And there was nothing out of the ordinary, unless one found it extraordinary that Miss Henchman thought it possible to prevent girls from being seen in town during term time without the full, correct school uniform.

But there was no doubt in Sophie's mind that the voice

she'd heard belonged to the dead medium. The spirit of Mrs. Tansy had spoken of a bloody interfering bitch—Sophie mentally cringed, but mightn't she be talking about Great-aunt Tabitha? What if Sophie's great-aunt had interfered in some crucial way, perhaps by telephoning the ministry to ask for surveillance after that first séance?

Though the medium had alluded to an old one and a young one, Sophie didn't know who they might be. But she'd also mentioned a favorite young fellow, and it had come in a flash to Sophie at breakfast that Mrs. Tansy might have been talking about her cat.

She'd seemed to speak directly to Sophie, in any case, when she warned her "it's not the one you think it's the other one." But which was which?

Sophie tried to reason backward from the medium's words. Two people, a young one and an old one. Who might they be? And who was the man the Veteran had conversed with, the conversation that led him next to mention the attack on the minister?

The strap of Sophie's satchel pressed painfully into her shoulder, and a blister was forming in the place where her sock had worn through. Absently her hand found Andrew's green glass piece in her pocket. At the same time her eye fell on the pyramid of fruit in front of the greengrocer's: punnets of strawberries, raspberries, currants, and gooseberries beside a few lonely bunches of imported grapes.

The dead boy had said something about a man with eyes the glassy green of peeled grapes, hadn't he? All grapes were pale green once you peeled them, even red ones—the same green as the softly polished glass under her fingers. Green like gooseberries. Green like glass.

And in a blinding flash, Sophie saw it. What an *idiot* she was not to have thought of it sooner!

The dead boy hadn't spoken of green grapes, only of green glass. It was *Sophie* who'd met a woman whose eyes reminded her of peeled grapes, a woman whose assistant had eyes the exact same color.

The Veteran had attacked Joanna Murchison in public, asking where his money was. Not his pension, but his rightful payment for a commission?

Murchison's ministerial portfolio included Scotland's prisons as well as the army veterans' association. She would have had no difficulty having the Veteran killed in his cell.

Joanna Murchison—the minister of public safety— responsible for the Veteran's death, and for the medium's before that?

The thought struck Sophie like a thunderclap. What if the minister had ordered the medium killed because Mrs. Tansy had discovered she was the puppet master pulling the strings of the Brothers of the Northern Liberties, directing all the terrorists' actions from behind the respectable façade of the ministry, perhaps even supplying them with explosives?

What a *fool* Sophie was for not having seen it before! The great thing about the attacks, from the minister's point of view, was that they provided the perfect pretext for Scotland to go to war with Europe. The minister believed that only war would keep the country safe. That meant she would do just about *anything* to make sure people agreed, even if it meant killing hundreds of innocent citizens. Someone like the minister, Sophie felt certain, could easily persuade herself that giving explosives to terrorists was for the greater good.

Joanna Murchison had probably been tracking the Brothers of the Northern Liberties and planting evidence against the Europeans all along. When her plan came to fruition, she would make the evidence public, arrest all the remaining terrorists, and lead the country to war. Even peace supporters would want revenge for the deaths of so many civilians on Scottish soil.

The most shocking thing, if this was true, was the way the minister hadn't scrupled to sacrifice the lives of Edinburgh's citizens. Almost more than the murders of the medium and the Veteran, that showed what kind of person she was.

Wait, though. Was the *minister* the principal villain of the piece, or was it Nicko? *That* must have been what the medium was trying to tell her. It wasn't the old one, it was the young one! The green glassy eyes that Andrew's spirit had mentioned were just as likely to belong to Nicko Mood as to his master. The actual perpetrator, the person who dealt with the terrorists and hired the Veteran to kill Mrs. Tansy, surely wouldn't have been the minister. It was far more likely to have been Nicholas Mood, Nicko with his insatiable desire to please and his desperate impulse to advance himself. Why, it even seemed possible that the minister herself might not know about all of his stratagems.

Sophie didn't realize that she'd stopped with her key actually in the lock until the front door fell open, Great-aunt Tabitha on the other side.

"Sophie, what on earth . . . ?" she said. "I thought it might be some sort of salesman—didn't like the idea of someone lurking on the front doorstep without ringing the bell— thought I'd surprise the villain—never thought it might be *you*. Were you having trouble with the lock?"

Without waiting for an answer, she hustled Sophie into the sitting room and rang for tea.

"I'm off shortly," she told Sophie, "but I thought you'd like to see the results of last week's séance."

Sophie hung back. If only Great-aunt Tabitha would leave her alone!

"Come and see," coaxed Great-aunt Tabitha, her tone, Sophie couldn't help thinking, rather like the wolf's in "Little

259

Red Riding Hood." "At last week's Domestic Photo Circle, we captured a number of the dead on film. Look, this is my dear departed sister Alice, who died of diphtheria when we were children."

The picture looked like nothing so much as the blurry image of the cirronimbus cloud type in Sophie's geography textbook. It was hard to understand how even the most fond bereaved person could see a human being.

Great-aunt Tabitha didn't notice Sophie's lack of enthusiasm. She chattered away until Sophie's head ached, then left Sophie drinking a cup of strong, sweet milky tea while she got ready to go out. At least she didn't seem annoyed with Sophie any longer.

"I won't be late," she told Sophie before going upstairs. "If you're still awake when I get back, I'd like a word before you go to bed."

Afterward Sophie took the tea tray down to the kitchen, said hello to Peggy, who was grumbling because the price of eggs had gone up again for the third time since March, and went upstairs to her room.

Unpacking her satchel, she stopped dead in her tracks.

Photography! That was the way to prove her suspicions groundless or else get firm corroboration, especially given the need to find out who was more culpable, the minister or her assistant.

Spirit voices spoke in vague suggestive phrases. But if Sophie asked a spirit questions about the crimes and received an actual image of its perpetrator in response, the evidence would be irrefutable. Photos were by far the best way of identifying someone for certain.

In primary school Sophie had made something called a pinhole camera, which was a fancy name for an ordinary cardboard box with a hole poked through the side, used for watching an eclipse without hurting one's eyes by looking directly at the sun. If she worked out something like that, Sophie wouldn't need an expensive camera, just a box and some special paper covered with photographic emulsion, a low-budget substitute for the mechanically sophisticated image trappers used by the professionals.

And she knew the perfect place to get what she needed! Checking her watch, Sophie saw it was only half past five. Good. That funny little shop next door to the bookshop in Broughton Street Lane would still be open, the one that sold photographic supplies and spiritualist equipment.

She dug around in her bag to see how much money she had, then sifted through the dish of coins on top of the chest of drawers, superstitiously averting her eyes from the mirror.

That was where it all had started, with that pretty lady in the mirror on the day Mrs. Tansy had come for the séance. There was something painful in thinking about it. She very much wanted to see the lady again, and learn who she was—surely it must be a connection to Sophie's dead mother's family? The resemblance had been striking.

When she finished counting her money, Sophie pulled herself together to face facts. She didn't have much, she might well need more, and what *that* meant was that she'd have to break open the bank she'd had since age five, a hideous red clay pig with a rather sweet expression on its squashed face. The only way of getting the money out was to smash it open.

For ten years now Sophie had put money into the bank whenever she could spare it—against a rainy day, Peggy would say. It felt satisfyingly heavy when she shook it around, the jangling of coins muffled by a few ten-shilling notes from birthdays and Hogmanay.

Though it seemed to mark the destruction of her childhood, it was the work of only a moment to smash open the pig with the fireplace poker. Amazingly, she had over ten pounds.

She tucked away most of it beneath her underthings in the top drawer, then shoveled several pounds' worth of coins into the front pocket of her satchel. She'd have to find a dustpan and brush to clean up the wreckage, otherwise Peggy would want to know what she was up to, and Sophie had no intention of telling.

She did stop back in the kitchen to say she'd be out for half an hour. Peggy muttered something about people who didn't take their meals at regular times, but when Sophie promised to be back for supper at seven, Peggy kissed her on the cheek and told her not to hurry, they'd wait on her, fine lady that she was turning into.

TWENTY-SIX

WALKING THROUGH THE streets, Sophie's feet felt light, like in the kind of dream where one speeds effortlessly forward, four or five inches off the ground. For a moment she wondered whether she might be getting assistance from the spirit world, then felt silly when she realized it was just the effect of having emptied the schoolbooks from her satchel.

It was a great relief to find the shop still open. Sophie had never been inside before, having felt more aversion than attraction to the mysterious notices in the window ("Lady psychometrist seeks spiritualist gentleman, smokers need not apply"; "Train your powers of psychic communication in SIX EASY LESSONS").

It was a cramped room stuffed almost to bursting, the wall to the left dominated by a reproduction of Daguerre's famous photograph of the Champs Elysées. The picture made Paris look like a ghost town, the presence of the thousands of people who must have passed across the camera's field of view during the plate's exposure marked only by fleeting streaks of light.

Sophie heard someone clearing his throat. She turned to find a very young man with slicked-back hair, a spotty face, and a painfully prominent Adam's apple, who smiled and asked how he could help her in a pleasant but nasal voice.

Great-aunt Tabitha loathed and despised what she called jumped-up shop assistants, but Sophie thought this boy sounded nice. She decided to tell him the truth about what she needed.

"I want to buy a packet of photographic paper," she said, digging the coins out of her satchel and tipping them in a heap on the counter. "Whatever kind's best for capturing images from the spirit world."

"Hmm," the boy said, his fingers stroking a pitiful fringe of chin hair that only a dyed-in-the-wool optimist could have called a beard. "Tell me more. What kinds of spirit? Do you mean to use a camera, or do you prefer direct exposure? If I know exactly what you're wanting to do, I'll be better able to help you choose the right materials."

He had a good forceful way of speaking, and Sophie thought he'd be better off selling things over the telephone than in person, where extreme youth cut into his authority.

"I'm not exactly sure," she confessed, leaning her elbows on the counter and resting her chin in her hands. "I've been conducting an investigation, asking spirits quite practical questions and getting answers that are vague to the point of being actively unhelpful. What I want now is to get something more precise. I thought that photographs might make things clearer."

"So you'd like to use photography to persuade your spirits to narrow things down," said the shop assistant. "You'll not be wanting to take pictures of the spirits themselves, then?"

"Oh, no," said Sophie, a little shocked. "Why would I want to do that?"

"You'd be surprised what people want," said the boy. "You do see the difference between the two kinds of photography, don't you? I'm Keith, by the way."

"I'm Sophie," Sophie said.

They shook hands solemnly, Sophie revising her estimate of his age downward from nineteen or twenty to sixteen or at the very most seventeen.

"Yes, I know I look awfully young," said Keith, disconcerting Sophie by seeming to read her thoughts, "but I turned eighteen last week and I've been subbing for my older brother in the shop for years. He's off north to cover the Highland Games for the *Courant*—it might not sound like much, but the paper will put him on staff if he does a good job. He's not like me; he goes mad if he has to spend every day in the shop, so we're all crossing our fingers it'll work out."

Sophie promised to add her own positive finger-crossing powers in aid of Keith's brother's advancement, and Keith thanked her before turning over a flyer for an amateur photography competition and beginning to sketch a diagram on the back.

"Back to what I was saying," he said, "if you're simply trying to capture spirit presences, you don't need anything fancy. Think of Becquerel proving the existence of radioactivity by wrapping a photographic plate in black paper. All he did was lay a sample of uranium on top, and it emitted rays that fogged the plate. In the same way a spirit will often leave traces on film, so long as the room's really dark. Very often what people display as spirit photography, of course, really just shows they haven't sealed the room properly."

Sophie thought of Great-aunt Tabitha's latest effort and nodded.

"What you're wanting to do is something rather more interesting," Keith said, scribbling another diagram beside the first. "There used to be a superstition that the eyes of a murdered man could actually trap an image of the murderer. I don't know about that, but I do know that the police have been experimenting with a device that does something rather similar. They've mostly given up on it, though, because it won't work unless you've got a good psychic scientist on staff, and all they've got is a handful of crackpot spiritualist types. No offense," he added.

"None taken," said Sophie. Keith was *exactly* Sophie's kind of person.

"The basic idea," Keith said, so earnestly it was almost comical, "is that many serious crimes—murder's an obvious example—leave no witnesses aside from the perpetrator. So you want to get the dead to testify, but their words are often so vague as to be useless, not to mention that the 1921 decision in *Scotland v. Blavatsky* affirmed that recordings of the voices of the dead are inadmissible in court. They're simply too easy to fake."

"You really know your stuff, don't you?" Sophie said, impressed.

Keith nodded. "Yep, this is something I'm specially interested in," he said. "The legal aspects are fascinating—you should see the judge's opinion in—"

Sophie interrupted him by tapping the face of her watch with her index finger.

"Oh. Yes. Well, most of the same objections don't apply to images. Trickery's far from unknown in spirit photography, but it's relatively easy to prevent fraud if you know what you're doing. What you want is a setup capable of recording the last visual memories of the dead person. You get that by creating an arrangement that mimics the workings of the human eye—cornea, iris, lens, and so on—and using photographic paper as an artificial retina for recording patterns of light, which are organized by the psychic scientist and the dead person's spirit."

"Do you mean to say that ordinary spirit photography doesn't even require a camera, just a simple mechanism for recording images," Sophie asked, not sure she'd understood him, "but that what I want to do needs a very special kind of camera?"

"Yes, that's exactly right," Keith said.

"Would it be very expensive to get one?" she asked.

"I think there's a way around that," said Keith. "Sophie, it's funny you came in today. It's almost as if it was *meant*."

Sophie didn't like it when people suggested that perfectly ordinary minor coincidences signaled some deep pattern in the universe, but it was true she'd felt an instant connection with Keith.

"What are you saying?" she asked.

"I've been building cameras like that for years," he said. "It happens that I've got a new prototype I'm anxious to test. And though I'm far from being a medium myself, I've got a strong feeling—oh, call it a psychic premonition—that you're exactly the partner I've been looking for. What do you think? Are you willing to serve as medium?"

Then, when Sophie said nothing: "I haven't offended you, have I? You are a medium, I'm sure of it. Oh, I've got it all wrong as usual, haven't I? I'm sorry, Sophie, I didn't—"

"Be quiet," Sophie said. "I'm thinking."

What did it mean, that someone she'd only just met would guess that Sophie was a medium? She hated the very sound of the word. She wasn't any such thing. Or was she?

The struggle showed in her face, and Keith sighed.

"All right, let me guess," he said. "You're worried about whether you can trust me. I'm going to lay out all the advantages. First: you may not realize it, but you're talking about something technically quite difficult. Second: it's not a good idea to do this kind of work on your own. You need safeguards to make sure you're not simply capturing images from your own memory; you need someone to operate the camera, so that you can concentrate on the mental aspects; and you need someone to observe and certify the results."

"Maybe it isn't such a good idea," Sophie said, discouraged.

"Don't be an idiot!" Keith said, more cheerful than ever. "Third: I'm betting you don't have a license. But I've got my certification from the Glasgow Society for Psychical Research, Spirit Photography Division. Look!"

He whipped out his wallet, withdrew a card, and slapped it down on the counter between them.

Sophie picked it up and examined it. Printed on the back was the Dodgson Compact, a version of the Hippocratic Oath adapted for spirit photographers by one of the first scientists to enter the field. The text below identified Keith as a fully licensed psycho-photographic consultant, with authority to testify as an expert witness in courts throughout the Hanseatic states as well as to supervise spiritualist investigations by unlicensed practitioners.

"Aren't you going to tell me how young I am to have got this?" Keith asked.

"Certainly not!" Sophie answered. "Didn't anyone ever tell you it's bad manners to fish for compliments?"

Keith started laughing. "I think I'm still allowed to gloat," he said. "The card only came in yesterday's post!"

"Anyway, telling a person how young he is sounds more like an insult than a compliment, doesn't it?" said Sophie. "I think young people should be treated exactly like older ones."

"I couldn't agree more," said Keith, contemplating the document with great satisfaction before putting it away in his wallet. "But seriously, Sophie, I'm not fooling around when I say you'll get much better results this way. You don't think I'm trying to pull one over on you, do you? I won't charge you a penny; I'll even pay for the materials."

"No, I'm paying for the materials," Sophie protested, only realizing this meant she'd agreed to work with him when he whooped with delight.

He seemed so pleased, she dismissed the remaining scruples from her mind. She would make sure he didn't end up out of pocket, and she wouldn't tell him anything that would put him in a difficult or dangerous position.

"Ordinarily, my brother helps with the technical part," he said, "but since he's away, have you a friend you trust to stand in as our assistant?"

Sophie's thoughts went at once to Mikael.

"Yes, I've got someone," she said. "When shall we do it?"

"Tomorrow's good," said Keith. "I close up the shop around six, so we'd be able to get started soon after. Does that sound all right?"

"Oh, yes," said Sophie, amazed and grateful at how smoothly it was all working out. "Do you need me to bring anything?"

"No, nothing at all," said Keith.

"Thank you so much," Sophie said impulsively. "I can't tell you how little I was looking forward to this. I'm fine with machines—radios and such—but I've no affinity for pictures. And it's creepy dipping into the spirit world all by yourself!"

"Yes, that's something best done in the company of others," Keith said.

Then, as Sophie turned to leave: "Aren't you forgetting something?" he said.

"What?"

"Your money," he said, waving a hand at the pile of cash.

"Won't you take it toward the supplies for tomorrow?" Sophie asked, feeling magnanimous and rich.

Keith brushed away her offer, which he seemed ready to take as a reflection on his social standing, so Sophie scooped the money back into her satchel, where it jangled ridiculously loudly during her walk home.

For supper Peggy gave her a ham sandwich and a bowl of tomato soup heated up out of a tin. Afterward Sophie took a book and went to read on the window seat in the sitting room. It was so private there, it was almost like being in her own little house. The cushions and the curtains completely concealed her from the rest of the room.

Her eyelids kept drooping, and she jerked herself awake several times before deciding there was no reason not to give in and sleep.

She woke with a start.

"Minister of public safety, indeed!" said a familiar voice. It took Sophie a minute to realize it belonged to Miss Grant, Great-aunt Tabitha's ally from the Scottish Society for Psychical Research. She sounded absolutely furious. "It's a perversion of the language to suggest the wretched woman will bring Scotland to anything other than calamity and mass destruction."

"I couldn't agree with you more, Ruth, but we must put our minds to the problem and work out what to do next," said Sophie's great-aunt. "What do you think?"

"I've assigned several operatives to see if they can dig up anything to use against Murchison," said the younger woman. "I'm confident they'll find dirt, but it's a question of timing. If she goes public about Europe and the Brothers of the Northern Liberties before we come up with anything substantial, it's going to be difficult to stop things from moving inexorably toward war."

"I'm currently looking into the situation with the Brothers," said Great-aunt Tabitha. "I don't think she's told us the whole story, and it may prove a weak point in the defenses."

"What about Nicko Mood?" asked Miss Grant.

"I don't think he's capable of doing much on his own," said Great-aunt Tabitha, "but he may well have become an effective instrument. The real pity is that Joanna's come down so hard on the side of war. When we were younger, I worried about her politics, but I never thought it would come to *this*. On almost every other issue she's completely sound: she's the only member of the cabinet who agrees with me about the importance of higher education for women, for instance, and she's admirably tough-minded on the Highland fisheries."

"Why do you think she's come on so strong for war, then?"

"I'm not sure, though I suppose that if I were the only woman in the cabinet, I too might grow weary of having all the men roll their eyes whenever I spoke about peace. It is awfully tiresome when one's pacifist side is attributed solely to the fact of one's being a woman."

"A number of prominent men count themselves part of the peace party as well," Miss Grant objected.

"In the Hanseatic states as a whole, certainly," said Great-aunt Tabitha, "but in Scotland, at least over the last ten or fifteen years, willingness to speak boldly of war has become a kind of shibboleth of masculinity. No, if Joanna's used unacceptable means to put together the case for war, she must be exposed and brought to account, but I'm not saying I don't feel for her. We must see what we can do to stop her."

She fell silent, then spoke again. "One thing's certain, Ruth."

"What's that?"

"The program at IRYLNS must be expanded at once. I tell you, those girls provide the single most effective bulwark against the Europeans. There's not a moment to be lost."

They spoke for a few more minutes, then left the room.

Still in shock at her great-aunt's continued support of

IRYLNS, Sophie wondered if she should confess to Great-aunt Tabitha she'd overheard the whole thing. No, discretion sometimes really was the better part of valor. It was strange how often she'd benefited in the last few days from eavesdropping—though perhaps *benefited* wasn't the right word.

She opened the sitting-room door a crack and heard Great-aunt Tabitha let Miss Grant out, then lock the front door and descend to the kitchen for her evening cup of chamomile tea.

Sophie slipped upstairs to her bedroom, tore off her clothes, and threw herself into bed. Ten minutes later, when a knock came at the bedroom door, Sophie lay still as a dead mouse. The knock came again, but Sophie didn't answer. She could hear Great-aunt Tabitha's breathing outside on the landing. After a few minutes more, the sound of departing footsteps told Sophie that her great-aunt had decided not to disturb her.

It was a relief in a way to know that Great-aunt Tabitha hadn't just given in and accepted the ascendancy of the minister of public safety. If anyone could stop Joanna Murchison, surely it was Great-aunt Tabitha. But how could she speak with such approval of expanding IRYLNS? Why was she so willing to give the girls—except Sophie—up to the knife? And would anything intervene to halt the proceedings when Sophie's turn came?

TWENTY-SEVEN

"WE CAN'T DO IT, we simply can't," Mikael said, pacing back and forth on an isolate patch of grass in the Meadows the next afternoon.

"What's your objection, though?" Sophie asked. "I know you're not wild about spiritualism. But you were willing to pose as a client for Mrs. Tansy, and I don't see how this is different, except that the stakes are an awful lot higher now. You were the one who told me to see if the spirits could tell me anything about your brother!"

"I was *joking*!" Mikael shouted.

Sophie hoped nobody could overhear them.

"I wouldn't have actually sat in a séance, besides," he

added in a quieter voice. "Here you're asking me to take part in exactly the kind of shady transaction I most despise!"

"It won't be shady at all," Sophie said, struggling to keep her temper. "Keith says himself that most of what's presented as spirit photography is fraudulent. He wouldn't have anything to do with that sort of thing, he's mostly just excited about trying out his new invention. In fact, in a way it's us who'll be helping him, not the other way around. You'll see how good he is when you meet him."

"What is it with you, Sophie? You meet this chap and all of a sudden it's *Keith this, Keith that*. You're ridiculously impressionable! I don't think much of your loyalty to your old friends, I can tell you that much."

He picked up a large pebble and flicked it toward the ducks in the small ornamental pond nearby. The flock of birds flapped up off the surface of the water and flew away.

Mikael sounded almost jealous of Keith, though Sophie couldn't think why. She hadn't adopted Keith as her new best friend. People were so *silly* about things like this. Sophie had to push away a strong sense of irritation as she applied herself to the task of soothing Mikael's injured feelings.

Half an hour later, Mikael had agreed to help operate the camera that evening and to reserve judgment on the authenticity of the results.

"After all, we can't afford to waste time argy-bargying

when there's a murderer running loose," he concluded, look-ing smug.

It took all of Sophie's self-control not to roll her eyes.

To seal their reconciliation, they shared a dry hunk of cake pilfered by Sophie from the tin in the kitchen at Heriot Row.

"Aren't you going to eat yours?" he asked Sophie, who had picked off the icing and left the cake in several pieces on the greaseproof paper.

"I don't like cake very much," Sophie said. "The one really good thing about cake is that it's an excellent icing deliv-ery system."

"What an extraordinary thing to say! You don't mean to say you'd rather have icing than cake? Can I have yours if you don't want it?"

"It's all yours," Sophie said, and the cake vanished into Mikael's mouth.

"Wouldn't it make more sense, then," Mikael asked through a spray of crumbs, "not to bother with the cake at all, and to eat icing with a spoon straight from the bowl?"

Sophie passed him the bottle of fizzy lemonade.

"That wouldn't be the same at all," she said. "For one thing, the icing goes all lovely and hard when it's actually on the cake, with a sort of crust of crumbs on the side where it's attached. Picking it off and leaving the rest feels naughty and luxurious."

They finished the lemonade and put the rubbish into a bin nearby, already overflowing with refuse. In central Edinburgh all the bins had been removed because they provided such ready receptacles for bombs, but the city council had evidently spared this one, probably because the terrorists wouldn't waste their matériel outside the densely populated city center.

"How long have we got before our appointment with the Boy Photographic Wonder?" Mikael asked.

"Three hours," said Sophie, ignoring his sarcasm.

"Good. I'm dead set on seeing the exhibition."

"I don't see why we shouldn't walk through the displays," Sophie said. "They don't charge admission, except for a few of the pavilions."

"Right, then. What are we waiting for?"

Sophie led the way to the Bruntsfield Links, formerly a golf course, now home to the tents and permanent pavilions of the Hanseatic Expo. On the other side of the links were ancient burial pits supposed to contain more than ten thousand plague victims, and Sophie thought for one queasiness-inducing second that she could actually smell the half-decayed bodies. A moment later the smell resolved itself into an agricultural miasma rising from the first display area, a show of prize livestock proclaiming Scotland's superiority in the matter of pigs, sheep, chickens, and dairy cows.

They watched a Punch-and-Judy show, Sophie struck by a strong resemblance between the Judy puppet and Miss Henchman (could one of the puppeteers possibly have attended Sophie's school?), then sampled thirteen different kinds of jam, all made of fruit native to Scotland. Sophie was afraid that Mikael must have seen much better exhibitions in Denmark, but he seemed well entertained by what was on offer, particularly when it was edible.

The fair was thronged with buskers and beggars, most of them veterans of the armed services. Sophie gave away a few coins, although Great-aunt Tabitha always said not to because the money would just be spent on drink.

They coughed up the entrance fee for the Grand Pavilion, which housed a rotating set of scientific exhibits designed to demonstrate Scotland's achievements in technology. Outside it was impossible to tell exactly what they were paying for, but by the time the line snaked forward into the main tent Sophie was no less eager than Mikael to lay eyes on the Miracle of Life Extended.

Inside, two pretty girls in skimpy one-piece spangled out-fits posed on either side of a giant glass box. Mikael whistled his appreciation.

A person who wore something like that on the beach at North Berwick, Sophie thought sourly, would surely be arrested. That was to say, if she didn't freeze to death first! But she decided not to say anything in case Mikael thought she was jealous.

Closer up, the two girls looked older and less pretty, their long slim legs and acrobatic torsos belied by the wrinkles on their faces and the ropy skin of their necks.

As they got close enough to see inside the glass case, Sophie craned forward to read the label below.

Mikael suddenly clutched Sophie's arm.

"Tell me those aren't real babies," he said.

Sophie looked at him with surprise.

"Of course they're real!" she said, laughing at his expression. "If they were just dolls, what kind of a demonstration would it be?"

Six tiny babies lay almost motionless in the incubator. The legend below told the history of the artificial incubator, known to the ancient world in primitive versions but refined over the nineteenth century for hatching chicken eggs. At the turn of the century, the Irish obstetrician Oscar Wilde saw one of these chicken incubators in the Edinburgh Zoological Garden and realized it could be adapted for the care of babies delivered before the full term. The incubator box's double walls were filled with hot water for insulation, its lower half a reservoir containing roughly sixty liters of warm water. The preterm babies lay in the top of the box, where a thermometer kept track to make sure the temperature never fell beneath thirty degrees centigrade, a miracle of technology that Wilde and his colleagues had popularized by sending incubators to expositions throughout the Hanseatic states.

"Does it really seem a good idea to exhibit live babies like this?" Mikael said. "It's like an agricultural show! Whose babies are they, anyway?"

"I don't know," Sophie said curtly. If one had any choice, of course, one wouldn't let one's own baby be put on display like this. But Sophie didn't like it when Mikael criticized Scotland. "Probably babies born at the Lying-In Hospital for the Poor."

"Sophie, let's get out of here," said Mikael. "This place is too horrible for words."

They hurried out of the tent and back into the daylight. As they left the park and cut through the grounds of the Infirmary north toward Lauriston Place, Sophie couldn't get the sight of the infants out of her head. The rational part of her brain knew they wouldn't have been put there if the incubator hadn't represented their best, perhaps their only, chance of survival. But to be exposed in public like that would surely haunt one's dreams in later life, assuming one survived.

"Sophie?" Mikael said, sounding odd.

"What's the matter?" she said, stopping and turning to look at him. He grabbed her arm and hustled her onward.

"Hey, that hurts!" Sophie protested, trying to loosen his bruising grip.

"I don't want to frighten you, but I think we're being followed," Mikael said. Then, as Sophie reflexively began to turn her head to look in back of her: "No! Don't look. I don't want him tipped off that we've spotted him."

They sped up, Sophie soon gasping and frightened, despite herself, by Mikael's grim expression.

"This area's no good for losing him," Mikael said. "Anywhere that's public enough for us to be allowed in, he'll be able to follow us."

"Who is he, do you think?" Sophie ventured, hoping Mikael wouldn't be angry with her for asking. It was difficult enough just to talk at all, at this speed, and the leg on the side of her slight limp was already throbbing.

"Do you remember that beggar you gave a shilling to, back at the Meadows?"

Sophie remembered, though it was almost impossible not to look around and confirm it with her own eyes.

Something occurred to her and she let out a short sharp exclamation. "Mikael, I've just thought of something. What if the man following us is a kind of colleague of the Veteran? What if this man's working for the same person that hired the Veteran to murder Mrs. Tansy?"

What if he'd been hired to kill *them*?

"I think it's very likely he's working for the same person," Mikael said, speeding up again so that Sophie had to break into a jog. "It's possible that the true murderer has a whole pack of veterans working for him. If that's so, it might be another clue we can use to figure out who he really is."

Sophie hadn't breath enough to fill him in on her current state of thinking concerning the minister; it would have to wait till later.

"This wretch can't possibly mean to kill us in public, Sophie," Mikael added, though he didn't slow down. "If he did, he'd not have a dog's chance of getting away afterward. He'd have to be a really super marksman to hit either of us with a pistol at this distance, and it's easy to see he's not carrying a rifle. Still, I'll feel a lot better if we can lose him."

"Mikael?" Sophie panted.

"What?"

"I think he might have followed me from Heriot Row."

She had a sketchy memory of seeing a lame figure on the tram. It seemed very likely that it was the same man.

"We'll certainly assume that they know who you are and where you live," Mikael said. "But that doesn't mean we can't get some privacy for this evening. We'll go to the most crowded part of the Old Town and see if we can't give him the slip there. We're moving so fast he'll know that we've spotted him, but let's not slow down—I don't want him getting too close to us, just in case he's got a gun after all."

Sophie felt calmer because of Mikael having a plan. The most frightening thing was not knowing what was going on; putting even one's worst fear into words always made it less awful.

By now they'd reached Grassmarket, and they turned right and hurried toward St. Giles' Cathedral. They raced up Old Fishmarket Close to the High Street, where they slipped into a draper's shop. While Mikael peered out the window, Sophie watched a customer give a ten-shilling note to the assistant, who wrapped the money in the customer's invoice and packed it into an egg-shaped container that she pulled down from a wire hanging above her head. The container shot up and away through pneumatic tubes to the countinghouse, where a boy made the correct change. When the container shot back down, a bell rang and the assistant reached up and pulled out the change from its cocoon.

"He saw us come in," Mikael reported, pressing his face up against the window. "He's lurking now in the area down-stairs from the shop across the road. What we need to do is walk out of here, stroll up the High Street, and then make a break for it. We'll run up one of those little streets and hide before he can follow, and with luck he'll think we've only gone into another shop."

"And if he sees us?"

"Then we split up. You'll go ahead. I'll find a way to slow him down, then lead him astray and lose him. I can outrun him if I'm by myself. Then we'll meet up at the bookstall in Waverley Station."

"Good thinking," said Sophie, glad Mikael hadn't suggested splitting up as the first line of defense. He could run much faster than she could, but the thought of their being separated made her feel rather ill.

"Ready?"

Sophie nodded.

They pushed open the door and sauntered out into the street.

They crossed the road, the beggar stuck on the other side behind a line of schoolchildren.

"Now!" Mikael said.

They began running.

"Here!" Sophie grunted.

They turned into a narrow alley whose name she couldn't remember, running now through narrow streets of tenements like blond sandstone cliffs.

"I've got an idea," Sophie said, clutching the stitch in her side as they came out into Market Street. Her hip was pulsing like the devil, a dull pain that was quite tolerable so long as she didn't think about it. She couldn't hear the beggar's footsteps behind them, but that didn't mean he wasn't there. "Let's get a taxi!"

"Have you enough money?" Mikael asked.

"Yes," she said, grabbing his hand and practically dragging him to the nearest taxi rank. Fortunately there were three cabs waiting for customers—on a nice afternoon like this, a properly frugal citizen wouldn't waste money on a taxi—and they jumped into the backseat of the first one.

"What's all this, then?" said the driver when they asked him to drive in the direction of St. Mary's. "How am I to know this isn't just a silly game?"

Sophie scrabbled through her satchel and dug out a ten-shilling note and two half-crowns.

"I can't explain it," she said, "but it really does matter—we need to leave *right now!*"

As the words left her mouth, Mikael jabbed her in the side. The beggar had materialized at the opening into the street.

Sophie thrust the note into the drawer of the bulletproof plastic partition that separated the driver from his passengers, required by law after a terrible series of murders the year before.

"Just drive!" she said, almost shrieking in her anxiety to be gone.

Shaking his head, the driver pulled out into traffic and turned left onto North Bridge.

Sophie shuddered. They were going to pass the Balmoral Hotel once again.

"No need for hysterics," the driver said reproachfully as the car surged ahead of a bus and took them up Leith Street and into the New Town. "All you need to do is ask nicely, miss, and I'll take you wherever you like."

"Is he behind us still?" Sophie said to Mikael, speaking quietly to avoid attracting the driver's attention.

"No sign of him," Mikael reported. "This was a prime idea, Sophie. He wasn't dressed respectably enough to hail a taxi himself, even if he had the cash. Why, we're barely respectable enough ourselves!"

"It's quite true," said Sophie, looking herself and Mikael up and down and starting to laugh. They clutched at each other in a near frenzy when they saw how hot and dirty they were. Then a trickle of cold perspiration ran down into the small of Sophie's back; she broke off laughing, and caught her breath in something like a sob.

The driver let them off in Gayfield Walk, only five minutes from Broughton Street Lane. Sophie did not have the courage to ask for change back from her note; it was an awfully expensive cab ride, but then again it had possibly saved their lives.

TWENTY-EIGHT

OUTSIDE THE PHOTOGRAPHY shop, Mikael paused.

"Must we really do this, Sophie?" he asked.

"We have to," she said. "It's our best chance. We must learn what happened to the medium; we can't go around like this forever, with our lives perhaps in danger and not even knowing whom to suspect."

"All right, then," said Mikael, breathing hard and running a hand through his hair. "What are we waiting for?"

They pushed open the door and walked into the shop, the electronic chime sounding its welcome.

At first Mikael and Keith acted like two dogs circling around and deciding whether they're going to fight. But once Keith had locked the front door and drawn the blinds and rather stiffly offered the visitors a hot drink, Mikael unbent enough to accept a cup of coffee, and after that the obligations of the guest-host relationship forestalled any direct hostilities.

Sophie cupped her hands around a mug sporting a patchy image of a black standard poodle. The warmth of it in her hand was a comfort. Taking a sip, she thought what a good thing it was that Sir Humphry Davy had put aside his chemical experiments long enough to invent the dehydrated coffee sachet. Instant coffee was far nicer than the real coffee in Italian sandwich shops, especially with lots of condensed milk, which made it taste almost like cocoa.

"So what exactly have you two got planned?" Mikael asked.

Keith didn't seem to notice the edge to his words.

"We're going to test a new camera I've developed," he said. "Well, to be strictly accurate, it's not really a new camera, just a modification of an existing one. Its purpose, as I've designed it, is to capture the images seen by a dead person."

Seeing Mikael about to snort, Sophie kicked him in the ankle.

"So, Keith," Mikael said, glancing sideways at Sophie and rolling his eyes, "what parts do we play?"

"I'm going to look on," Keith said, ignoring Mikael's rudeness. "That may sound lazy, but in spirit photography the photographer's own memories and desires tend to interfere with things. We can't do anything with the results of this evening's experiment unless we know I haven't affected the images we receive, either by accident or by fraud."

"Fair enough," Mikael said. "What do you need me to do?"

"Mikael, you'll operate the camera," Keith said. "It'll be mounted on a tripod, so you won't need to point it in any particular direction, but the machinery needs a human hand to advance the film to the next exposure. Don't worry if you don't have much experience with a camera, any old idiot can do it."

"What about me?" Sophie asked, putting her hand on Mikael's arm to stop him from reacting badly to Keith's tactlessness.

"You've got the toughest job," Keith said. "All I have to do is document everything I see in writing, and your friend here will simply advance to the next frame each time one or the other of us gives him the go-ahead. You're the one who has to find the spirit we want and shape the series of questions. It's best to be as specific as possible: requests like 'show me your loved one' are liable to backfire."

"Oh, I've already thought of what I want to ask," Sophie said. The questions had been circulating at the back of her head all day, except for during the chase, when she had been too frightened to think about spirit photography. "But how do

I get in touch with the spirit in the first place?"

"You'll call it to you, of course," Keith said. "Don't worry, it won't be difficult. It's often tricky to get spirits to come and let you take pictures of them, but that's not what you're asking. You just want to know what they *saw*. Dead people aren't so different from living ones, really: even folks who run and hide when there's any risk of their being photographed are usually quite happy to take a photograph as a favor. I've got a good feeling about this, Sophie."

"So who exactly are you going to contact, Sophie?" Mikael asked, smirking a little.

Before Sophie could say, Keith held up one hand, palm toward them.

"It's best we watch with an open mind," he said. "Sophie, don't tell us a thing until afterward. Are you ready to get started?"

Sophie and Mikael looked at each other, then nodded.

They followed Keith from the small lounge to a tiny darkroom at the back of the shop. As Keith switched on the infrared lamp, they looked warily at each other in the spooky orange glow.

Keith showed Mikael how to operate the camera, then told him to load a clean roll of film; the factory seal was unbroken. He asked Sophie whether she'd rather sit or stand.

"Stand," she said.

She stayed quite still while Keith fastened a blindfold over her eyes.

"All set," he said after that. "Mikael, I'll tell you when it's time to release the shutter. Sophie, it's all yours."

Sophie took a minute to slow her breathing back down to the normal rate. There was no point being nervous. She was among friends, wasn't she?

The room felt small and cramped and airless. Sophie could smell sweat through the photographic chemicals. It was strange having no visual input at all. She put up her hand and tweaked the blindfold into a more natural position. She hoped it would stay properly fastened; Keith hadn't really tied it tightly enough.

She had actually worked out her plan the night before in bed. It had to be Mrs. Tansy she would contact, though Sophie was frightened of the medium's strongly malevolent personality and her almost palpable desire to come back and make somebody pay.

Sophie focused on breathing in a slow, regular pattern as she waited for the spirit to find its way to the darkroom.

"You're not far away," she said. "You found me the other day in Miss Botham's class. You worked out how to speak to me through the Dictaphone. Now I've got something different for you, something even easier because you won't have to put any of it into words. I'm going to ask you some questions.

When you answer, I don't want names, just faces. My friend Keith's built a special camera and after each question, you'll picture the face of the person I've asked about. Mikael and I will help you print the pictures; together we'll organize the light so that the image can be laid down on the film in the camera."

She stopped to take several deep breaths, then readied herself to begin.

"I want you to put yourself in a very particular time and place," she said slowly. "It's the fifteenth of June—a Wednesday—and you've checked into a grand suite at the Balmoral Hotel."

Mikael coughed, and Sophie lost her concentration for a second.

"It's midday and you're waiting for your next appointment," she went on after a minute. "It's the young man booked by the night receptionist. There's a knock at the door. You open it and show the boy in. Now, the first thing I want you to give me is a shot of that boy."

Sophie squeezed her eyes tightly shut behind the blindfold, wrapping her fingers around her thumbs, and concentrated as hard as she could to help the spirit lay down the memory of Mikael's face onto the film in the camera. This would be a kind of control for the rest of the experiment. It was a good way of getting a feel for it, and the medium's experience with this kind of work would surely make everything easier.

She kept her eyes closed until she felt a kind of sliding-into-place, like the *snick* when a jigsaw piece slots into the right spot.

"I think that's it," she whispered.

"Mikael, advance the film, please," Keith said, sounding quite calm. "From now on, I'll tap you on the shoulder to let you know when it's time. Sophie, you're doing very well."

"All right," Sophie said, speaking not to Keith but to the spirit, who felt very close by. She hoped the medium hadn't actually materialized: an ectoplasmic embodiment of her too, too solid flesh would be beyond awful.

"You had another visitor after that. That's the person I want you to picture for us now. Before you answered the door, you bundled Mikael into the wardrobe and locked him in. Then you answered the door. Who did you see there?"

She waited without feeling anything, then realized she had to give the medium a little more help.

"What was it?" she said, breathing deeply and feeling suddenly as if her rib cage had come into alignment with someone else's, two hearts pumping, two pairs of lungs expanding and contracting. "Oh. You answered the door and at first you thought that nobody was there."

She paused to get a clearer sense of the scene.

"You're looking straight ahead and you don't see anybody. You're thinking someone's knocked and then run away, like those awful children in the street where you used to live."

The words were coming fast to Sophie's tongue.

"You look left, then right. And then you hear someone chuckling and you look down. . . ."

The *click* from before echoed again in Sophie's head. Keith seemed to hear it too, for he muttered encouragement to Sophie.

"The man comes into the room. He's at ground level. Now he's coming toward you and throwing his arms around your knees in something like a rugby tackle. He's bringing you to the floor. He's got a straight razor and almost before you know it, he's clambered up onto your body and slashed your throat and you roll back away from him as the blood starts gushing out. Look—look right at his face. Look at the face of the man who's just killed you. There—give it to us now."

Snick. Louder and more definite than before.

"And your spirit's leaving your body now, hovering over it. But I need you to answer a few more questions. Mrs. Tansy, did you ever talk to someone from the Nobel Consortium? The police seem to think you were in contact with someone— is there a person I can talk to and find out more?"

Sophie felt the spirit *waver*. It was rather like leaning over a boiling saucepan and letting the tiny waves of warmth hit one's face like hot invisible jelly.

She concentrated hard. "Nobel," she said again. "Did you speak to someone of Nobel's?"

Click. Faint but firm.

"Forward to the next frame, Mikael," Keith whispered. "I'm sure we got an image there."

"Just two more things," Sophie said now, trying not to betray the importance of these last questions.

"We think you had strong suspicions about who was behind the bombings. Did you identify anyone in connection with them? And if so, who was it? We might need this picture to track the person down," she added, "so it will be especially helpful if you can give us a really good shot."

Click. The unmistakable sound of a picture being taken. Sophie heard Mikael advance the film to the next exposure.

"One more," said Sophie softly. She felt drained and exhausted from concentrating so hard. "Just one more thing. Can you tell us who you think hired the man who killed you? Who sent the Veteran to kill you, Mrs. Tansy?"

SNICK. This time the click was quite loud. Sophie heard one of the boys swear—she couldn't tell which—as he failed to catch a jar of chemicals that slid off a shelf and smashed on the floor.

"Time to stop this," Mikael said in a loud voice, angry and afraid.

"Don't worry," Keith said, his voice more excited than fearful. "Telekinetic disturbances often accompany this kind of manifestation. Sophie, can you hear me? Are you ready to stop?"

Sophie reached up to take off the blindfold, but paused to thank the medium first. She did it silently, not wanting to sound silly to the others, but the words in her head were heartfelt. Thank you. Thank you so much. That was really helpful. And I promise you I'm going to bring your true murderer to justice. The Veteran's dead. I expect you know that. But I swear to you I'll do everything I possibly can to find the person who sent him to kill you. I'll stop that person, if it's the last thing I do.

She hoped the medium would go away now. She still had a slight unpleasant sense of the woman's presence in the room.

Taking off the blindfold, she found the other two staring at her.

"What's wrong?" she asked.

"Are you all right, Sophie?" Keith asked.

Sophie considered the question.

"I've got a bit of a headache," she said. "Not too bad, though. How soon will we know whether we've got any results?"

Keith looked at his watch.

"It's half past seven," he said. "Even working with high-speed chemicals, it's going to take me at least ninety minutes to process the film, make a contact sheet from the negatives, and blow up the prints. Why don't you two leave me to it for now and come back just before nine to take a look at what we've got?"

"How do we know you're not going to pull a switcheroo on us and substitute another film for the one in the camera, or give us a completely different set of proofs for that matter?" Mikael asked, advancing on Keith, his right hand clenched.

Sophie shrank away from Mikael's fist, but Keith just sighed and held his ground.

"Look," he said, "I suggested that Sophie mix in questions she knew the answers to with ones she didn't, if you see what I mean. I don't even know Sophie's last name or where she lives, let alone what she's just been talking about."

"Don't you read the papers? You must have recognized the details—the murder of the woman at the Balmoral—"

"*Now* I do, but I couldn't have had pictures prepared in advance. You're going to have to trust me on this. You can certainly stay and watch if you like, but it's awfully cramped in here and the smell of the chemicals gets to you after a while, especially if you're not used to it. Sophie needs to eat something—she's just expended a huge amount of mental energy, and I bet her blood sugar's low. Do me a favor and go to the chip shop around the corner, get her something to eat, and let me do my part of the job in peace and quiet, all right?"

He let Sophie and Mikael out the back door into an alley full of garbage, a pack of feral cats nosing through it for their dinner.

TWENTY-NINE

"WAIT FOR ME!" Sophie called out as Mikael navigated through the rubbish.

Mikael turned around to look at her, arms folded across his chest, face expressionless. Sophie couldn't tell what he was thinking.

"What is it?" she said, her voice faltering as she caught up with him. She felt quite sick to her stomach.

"Don't tell me you really don't know," Mikael said, not meeting her eyes as he kicked an empty tin across the way.

"I really don't know!"

"Sophie, this whole spirit business—well, for a long time I didn't believe in it at all. Recently I haven't been so sure. Some things you *have* to take seriously, and I can see that tonight's one of them. So you can cross me off the official skeptics list."

Sophie just looked at him. What did he mean her to say in response? Something flat in his delivery made his words more hurtful than reassuring.

"Good," she said uncertainly.

"Just don't think this whole 'medium' business makes you special," he added. It was frankly almost a relief to hear the anger overtly now in his voice, easier than having him angry with her and insisting he wasn't. But she didn't understand *why* he was so angry. "Mediums are creepy, and that part of my opinion's never going to change. You'd better be very careful you don't start picking up bad habits, Sophie."

Letting him browbeat her like this was hardly any different from encouraging him to punch her repeatedly in the stomach, but Sophie felt immobilized by submissiveness. They were standing outside the chip shop by now, its grease-smeared windows all steamed up on the inside, and the sight of a random beggar out of the corner of her eye forced her to speak.

"We've got to go into the shop," she said urgently. "It's too dangerous hanging around outside like this. For all we know, there's a whole *gang* of homeless veterans out looking for us."

Mikael let himself be dragged into the storefront, where

the smell of hot fat enveloped them like a cloak of invisibility.

"I'm starving," he said, sounding surprised. He turned to Sophie and laid a hand on her elbow, an apology fluttering in the softness of his touch. "Let's get some food. Have you any money left?"

They ordered two fish suppers and an extra portion of chips and mushy peas. Though the chips were soggy, the fish was shockingly good, its flesh falling into fragrant white flakes under the crisp batter shell.

"So what do you think?" Sophie asked when the ruins of the meal lay on the table between them.

Mikael swigged the last of his Iron Brew, a rust-colored fizzy drink ("Made in Scotland from Girders"). He burped and wiped his hands on a paper napkin.

"On the basis of that beggar following us this afternoon," he said, "I think we're justified in drawing a few conclusions. Are we in agreement that (a) the same person may be responsible for the terrorist attacks as well as for the murder of Mrs. Tansy, and (b) he's also potentially running a whole network of those army veterans you see begging on the streets?"

Sophie nodded. She supposed there was no point saying that it might be a woman; they would have to see what the pictures showed.

"It's possible, of course," Mikael continued, "that the beggar following us today isn't working for the same person who hired your Veteran to kill the medium—"

"Possible, but not likely," Sophie interrupted.

"That's right," said Mikael. "Which means that (c) this person's found something out about our investigation and alerted his gang to follow us wherever we go. How would you say we attracted his attention, Sophie?"

"When you were taken to the Castle and questioned," Sophie said, "that would have sent up a red flag. And I was there too. Because of the Veteran being killed in his cell, we know the villain must be someone with pretty good access, maybe even someone who's part of the government. . . ."

"Well, whoever he is," said Mikael, "it wouldn't have been hard for him to have had one or both of us tailed."

"Both, most likely," said Sophie.

They looked at each other, their faces pale and frightened.

"I don't see what we can do about it," Sophie said finally.

"We'd better both be very careful," Mikael said.

Shortly before nine o'clock, they bought a paper poke of chips for Keith and returned to the door in the alley.

"You're not going to believe what good shots we've got," Keith said in greeting. "Oh, thanks," he added as Mikael handed him the chips. "Just let me lock up back here, and I'll show you everything."

He ushered them again into the darkroom, where sheets of photographic paper were clipped to washing lines with ordinary clothes-pegs, amid a strong smell of chemicals and the sound of dripping water.

"They're exceptionally clear," Keith said, stuffing chips into his mouth and gesturing to the suspended prints. "I've printed two sets, Sophie, one for you and one for me. You must promise you'll work with me again. I've never seen anything so good."

Sophie was just relieved he didn't use the word *medium*. She tried not to look at Mikael.

"Each time Sophie asked a question," Keith continued, tactfully directing the explanation toward Mikael, "it was framed in such a way that all the spirit had to do was focus on a single face. With the first question, she asked the spirit to provide an image of the young visitor that day. And look!"

He held up a head-and-shoulders portrait that was so unmistakably of Mikael himself that even Sophie wondered for a split second whether Keith could have rigged a secret camera. Then she dismissed her suspicions. She had *felt* the medium's presence, after all.

She cast a quick look at Mikael, but it was impossible to tell what he was thinking.

"After that, Sophie asked the spirit to focus on a second visitor. Here's where Sophie made really imaginative use of her knowledge of what must have happened. Look, this print shows several superimposed images; it's rather like what happens when an ordinary camera jams and gives you multiple exposures in a single frame. It's a little dizzying, isn't it? You two aren't so used to it as I am. But look at the picture's different layers. See, here's where the dead woman—not that she was dead yet, of course—opened the door of the hotel room and looked straight ahead. If you look closely, you can see she's actually captured the pattern of the wallpaper on the other side of the corridor."

Mikael leaned forward to look more closely.

"I recognize that fleur-de-lis pattern," he said, his voice hoarse with surprise. "That's exactly the wallpaper they've got on the hotel walls, a sort of bumpy velvety stuff."

"These blurry marks show her moving her head from side to side," Keith continued, politely ignoring Mikael's shock. "And then she finds the target: she looks down and sees the person Sophie asked about. We're facing down toward a figure—an elderly man, pretty scruffy-looking—who's sitting for some reason on the floor in front of the doorway. Look, it's so clear that you can actually see the weave of the carpet behind him."

"He's not really sitting on the floor," Sophie said. "He's a double amputee, a war veteran, and if you look closely you can see he's on a sort of cart."

Keith looked, raised an eyebrow, and wrote a few lines in the fat exercise book lying open on the counter.

"The next one's a bit gruesome," he warned, pausing for a moment before he held it up for them to see.

Sophie and Mikael stared in silence at a picture all the more horrifying for not showing any actual gore.

All that could be seen was the Veteran's contorted face, much too close up.

Sophie could almost feel the flash of the razor across her throat and the pressure of the man's powerful arms holding down her shoulders as she tried to roll away from him, his breath hot and horrible in her face.

She suddenly wished she hadn't eaten all those chips. She hoped she wasn't going to be sick.

"Sophie asked next about the Nobel Consortium," Keith went on. "I suppose she's trying to get a sense of the woman's political entanglements. Well, there's a pretty clear answer on this one. I've got no clue who the man is, but it's an extremely clear photograph, and perhaps one of you has some ideas about where to look for him. . . ."

And the photograph he held up? It was *Mr. Petersen*!

She was conscious of a fierce bubbling excitement—*now* they were getting somewhere, this made sense of so many other things, of course Mr. Petersen was working for Nobel!—and was about to open her mouth to identify him when she felt Mikael painfully grip her upper arm. "Don't say anything," he said in a voice just above a whisper. "We'll talk about it later—there's no reason to let Keith in on it."

Keith politely ignored the conflict—he really was an unusually patient and well-mannered boy, not like Mikael, whose fingers were bruising Sophie painfully. How did Mikael know what she was about to say? She supposed her face must be more transparent than she thought, or else Mikael just knew her very well.

"All right," she whispered angrily to Mikael, "but stop making such an ass of yourself, it's not polite."

"Polite?" Mikael yelped, but he let go of Sophie's arm and said a gruff "Sorry, mate" to Keith.

Sophie was consumed now with impatience to see the last two photographs, of the person Mrs. Tansy suspected of being behind the bombings and the person who'd sent the Veteran to kill her at the Balmoral.

It was conceivable that the picture would show the face of some entirely unknown and quite ordinary-looking person, one impossible for them to track down. If the man had never been arrested and wasn't a public figure, a picture wouldn't necessarily yield a name. Sophie felt sure, though, it wouldn't simply be some anonymous face. Joanna Murchison, Nicko Mood—she had thought about it for many hours and she was certain that one or both of them must have been involved. Mrs. Tansy had almost certainly understood that to be the case.

"Let's take a look," said Keith.

Sophie envied him the luxury of having only a technical interest in the results.

"These last two pictures are quite astonishing," said Keith. "Sophie, this is really one for the history books! I've never seen anything like it. And the level of detail in the faces, given the nonrepresentational quality of the design—all I can say is that it's quite extraordinary."

"Show us!" Sophie said.

"Oh," said Keith, looking surprised. "I forgot you hadn't seen them yet."

Sophie almost tore the pictures out of his hands. Their beauty knocked the breath out of her. With Mikael close by her shoulder, she laid the two photographs on the table. At first glance they were virtually identical; both pictures, though they were the same size as the previous ones, looked less like ordinary snapshots than like blown-up images of the court designs from a deck of playing cards. They even had the suit and designation in the corners—how on earth had *that* happened, and what did it mean?

The image produced in response to Sophie's question about who sent the Veteran to kill the medium? The knave of clubs—and the face of the right-side-up knave was *unmistakably* Nicholas Mood's, his features clear in every particular although he was dressed as if for a costume ball, with hair hanging about his shoulders and the strange flat cap and embroidered waistcoat the knave always wore in decks of cards. But the most surreal thing was that when the card was rotated a hundred and eighty degrees, it should have been the knave again (of course) but it wasn't. The hair and clothes were the knave's, but the face belonged to Joanna Murchison, as if Mood and Murchison were conjoined twins.

The next card—the medium's best guess about the person behind the bombings—was the queen of clubs. This time, the minister's face could easily be discerned peeping out from the wimple and brocade—but the upside-down face at the other end of the card was Nicko Mood's.

"She's telling us something about a man and a woman," said Keith.

"Do you suppose they're real people?" Mikael asked.

Sophie had almost forgotten the others were there, let alone that they wouldn't recognize the faces. "They're real people, all right," she said grimly.

"How do you know?" It was Mikael, of course, sounding distinctly skeptical.

"Because I know who they both are," said Sophie. "I've met them. They came to my great-aunt's house for supper, and I'm not in the least surprised to see their faces again here."

"But who *are* they, Sophie?" said Keith. "You must tell us!"

"The man's name is Nicholas Mood, and he works for the

woman, who's called Joanna Murchison."

"Joanna Murchison," said Mikael. "Sounds familiar—seems to me I've seen that name in the newspapers recently. Oh, no, Sophie—you're not serious. . . ."

"I'm dead serious," she said. "She's the minister for public safety, the person responsible for bringing terrorists to justice and keeping Scotland safe."

"But—"

This time it was Sophie who silenced Mikael by turning and catching his eye and making a tiny gesture with her head toward Keith.

"Don't worry, you two, the politics of it really aren't my business," Keith said comfortably into the awkward silence that ensued. "You can explain the whole thing to him later, Sophie. I can see you've got a pretty clear idea of the way things must have happened, you and that spirit were on the exact same wavelength."

Sophie shuddered.

"What I'm really impressed with," Keith added, "is the way the medium's left you with a nice puzzle."

"A puzzle?" Sophie asked, feeling by now as if her brain was barely functioning. "What puzzle?"

"It's obvious what he means, isn't it?" said Mikael, picking up both prints and looking back and forth between the two. "Which one of them really did it? Did Mrs. Tansy simply *not know*, and implicate them both as suspects? Was Nicholas Mood working primarily as the minister's agent, and is she the one to hold culpable? Or is it the other way around, with Mood having gone beyond his mandate as the minister's tool?"

Sophie gave Mikael a warning look. She had said too much already, no need for him to compound the problem. They thanked Keith and promised to tell him what happened, though it made Sophie feel distinctly cheap to leave him so much out of things.

THIRTY

MIKAEL INSISTED ON walking Sophie home.

"Boys and girls are perfectly equal," Sophie said when he wouldn't let her go by herself.

"Yes, of course they are, but Sophie, there's something we must talk about."

To Sophie, it all seemed quite clear. Convinced that Scotland had a moral obligation to go to war with the European Federation, Joanna Murchison must have channeled funds (under the pretense that the money came from the Europeans) to the impressionable and easily directed young Brothers of the Northern Liberties. If the minister could only implicate Europe in the deaths of Scottish citizens, Scotland would be able to go to war—and the rest of the Hanseatic

League would have to join them.

The medium must have learned something about the minister's role in the bombings and tried to extort money from her. But the minister was not the sort of woman to be blackmailed. She hired the Veteran, probably using her loyal assistant Nicko as a go-between, and the woman's death was assured.

When the Veteran spoke about money—"Where's ma money?" he'd cried out as he attacked the minister—he was talking about the money he'd been promised for the hit, promised but never paid. It would have been safer and easier for the minister or Nicko to send another assassin to the Veteran's jail cell than to leave the man alive.

Meanwhile the pair of them prepared to expose the terrorists' "European backing" and mobilize the country for war.

"Haven't we already talked it all to death?" Sophie said, barely stifling a huge yawn. It was as though a chemical fog had descended on her brain to prevent thinking.

"Sophie, this is really important. Look, isn't there somewhere near your house where we can find a safe place to talk? I can see you're quite done in, but we must have a word."

In the end they took shelter behind a shed in Queen Street Gardens.

"Give me those pictures," said Mikael.

Sophie handed him the manila envelope, her hand brushing against his in a way that made her skin tingle.

He fanned them out and then picked the picture of Mr. Petersen from the rest. Oh, god, Sophie had almost forgotten about that. She would have to ask the teacher about Nobel, that was for certain, but first she must get some sleep . . . *sleep* . . . her head nodded forward, eyelids drooping.

"Sophie?" said Mikael, speaking very loudly into her ear.

"What?" she asked. Oh, if only she could lie down and close her eyes, just for a minute! She would give a hundred pounds to be allowed to go to sleep right here and now.

Wait. The picture. Mikael.

Still swaying a little with tiredness, she looked from the photograph of Mr. Petersen back to her friend's face with mounting incredulity. How on earth had she never seen it before? Why did it take her being practically *dead* with exhaustion to put two and two together?

"Mikael," she said slowly, her tongue sticky and thick in her mouth, "your surname isn't Lundberg, is it?"

"No, that's my aunt's name," he said, sounding surprised. "Sophie, don't you know my full name? We've been friends for *years*!"

It was strange to realize she didn't know Mikael's last name. How different the real world was from the world of school! There, one could hardly think of anybody without their entire name coming to mind. Harriet Jeffries would stay "Harriet Jeffries" long after she married and took her husband's name—

not that anybody sensible would want to marry Harriet Jeffries; she would be one of those awful wives who laid down vinyl over the carpet to stop it from getting soiled.

Sophie tried to get a grip on her meandering thoughts. Mikael's next words seemed inevitable.

"My name's Petersen, of course, Mikael Petersen. And this picture—Sophie, it's my *brother*."

Sophie groaned and dropped her head into her hands. Oh, she might as well be the village idiot for all the intelligence she'd shown up to this point!

She lifted her head back up and took the picture from him.

"Your brother," she said, "and my chemistry teacher. Mr. Petersen."

"You're not serious," said Mikael, looking horrified.

"I'm completely serious," she said. "He came in March—our old teacher left to be married, under slightly strange circumstances."

"Sophie, tell me, is he safe?"

"Yes, of course," Sophie said. "At least, I haven't seen him since yesterday, but he was perfectly all right then."

Mikael let out a huge breath.

"Mikael," Sophie asked, "what can your brother possibly be doing in Edinburgh? Do you think he came here for the teaching job, or is it something more nefarious? Could the Nobel people have sent him here for some reason?"

"He was always as likely to be here as anywhere else," Mikael said. "The Nobel Consortium posts its operatives throughout the Hanseatic states, and he'd certainly be quite comfortable in Edinburgh—his English is much better than mine because our parents lived here for a few years when he was little. Nobody would be able to tell he wasn't Scottish born and bred, not if he put his mind to it. But the main thing is that I must see him and talk to him as soon as possible! I'll be able to ask him about the knife, and find out how he's doing—oh, my aunt will be awfully relieved when I tell her. And of course we must ask him what we shall do about the minister and all that."

"Will you come to school, then, and see him there?" Sophie asked. She could see Mr. Petersen would be the best person to consult; there was certainly no point going to Great-aunt Tabitha—and yet it didn't sit altogether well with her to hand the problem off to someone else like that. Just because she and Mikael weren't adults didn't mean they weren't fully capable of taking responsibility. "I don't know where he lives, though I expect I could find out."

"No, school's fine," Mikael said. "Shall I come on Monday?"

Sophie thought about it.

"Tuesday's better," she said doubtfully. "You see, I work for him and I've got a regular appointment with him on Tuesday afternoons, so we'll be sure to find him alone. Can—

can you wait that long, do you think?"

"I suppose I must," said Mikael. "It's only a few days. The thing is, I'm leaving for København next Saturday."

"What?" His remark took Sophie's breath away. "Are you going for a visit? Why didn't you tell me sooner?"

"Sophie, I live there," he said, sounding so annoyed that Sophie shrank back from him, she couldn't help herself. "I'm not going back for a visit, I'm going *home*. Don't you remember? I never stay in Edinburgh for more than a few weeks."

"But I thought you'd stay longer this time!"

The prospect of his departure made Sophie realize how much—how very unwisely—she'd come to depend on Mikael. She slumped down and hoped he couldn't tell she was upset.

"Well, I've got no say in the matter," said Mikael. "My passage is booked on the *Gustavus Adolphus*, leaving from Leith a week from today."

Sophie was too tired to feel as shattered as she might have otherwise.

They made an arrangement to meet at the side of the school in the middle of the day on Tuesday, Sophie beginning to fret now about the lateness of the hour.

"One other thing," Mikael added, laying a hand on Sophie's arm. "Will you promise me something?"

"What?" Sophie said, suddenly breathless for a reason she didn't understand.

"I'm worried about what's going to happen after I go back to Denmark," Mikael said.

Sophie made a noncommittal sound.

"Yes, I know you're capable of superhuman displays of fortitude and willpower. But all this has proved pretty overwhelming. I can't help thinking the danger's going to get even worse if I leave you to face this alone. I suppose I might be able to delay my departure somehow," he added, "but it would create difficulties at home."

"No, you can't possibly do that," Sophie said fervently. "Your aunt would never forgive me, for one thing."

"She'll never forgive you if you get yourself killed, either," Mikael said, sounding really angry now. "Edinburgh's the most dangerous place for both of us right now. It would be much better for you to go to København as well. You really could come with me, you know. It would be a lot safer than staying here. My mother won't mind putting you in the spare bedroom; she's good that way."

"I'm not leaving the country," Sophie said, at once annoyed and elated that he should have suggested it. "Aside from everything else, it's illegal for children under eighteen to leave Scotland without a special visa, and it's supposed to be almost impossible to get."

"I know, I know," said Mikael. "I'm not going to force you to do anything against your will. But I want you to promise me you'll think about it."

"I can't!" Sophie said. "Why, even if I could get a visa, I've got my exams at the beginning of August—I'm sure there's no way to take them abroad, and besides, I'd miss the last weeks of prep—no, Mikael, it's kind of you to offer, but I really couldn't think of it."

"It's all very well to talk of exams," Mikael said furiously, "but what if someone's planning to cut your throat?"

When Sophie began to explain again why the exams were so important, Mikael cut her off.

"Don't say it," he said, speaking in a crisp, irritated way. "I know you'd have to be dragged on board ship kicking and screaming. You'd rather risk death than miss sitting your stupid exams. I *know* all that. I'm not asking you to promise to come with me, I'm just asking you not to dismiss the idea out of hand. Depending on how things go, it might look a lot more appealing this time next week."

Finally Sophie said she'd think about it. Then she hurried the rest of the short way home, where she had to endure Peggy's scolding as well as an endless stream of questions about the supper served in the private rooms at the Balmoral Hotel (Sophie had invented a cover story involving Priscilla's birthday and a meal at the hotel), before begging exhaustion and hauling herself upstairs to bed.

THIRTY-ONE

ON MONDAY EVENING Sophie resolutely put everything else out of her head and concentrated on working her way through a huge set of sums, pausing now and then to rub out a mistake.

Nan was struggling on the other side of the room with an essay on "The Rime of the Ancient Mariner."

"Oh, it's hopeless," she said for about the fifth time, laying down her reservoir pen and rubbing her eyes. "If I went to a wedding and one of the other guests plucked my sleeve and tried to tell me such a ridiculous story, I'd smack the stupid man!"

Priscilla and Jean were in the middle of a quiet but intense conversation at Jean's desk.

"It's not like you to make so much fuss about homework," Sophie said. "That essay won't take much longer, will it? Anyway, I like the part where they reach the equator and the ship won't go. The doldrums, that's what they call it."

"Doldrums is right," said Nan, tipping her chair onto its back legs and running both hands through her hair. "All this is a complete waste of time. Whether or not that bill goes through Parliament, I'm joining the Women's Auxiliary Corps the moment I turn sixteen."

"When's your birthday?" asked Sophie, who could never remember people's birthdays.

"August fourteenth," Nan said. "The first day of those wretched examinations, in case you'd forgotten. I've given up on the idea of having any kind of a party; it's not worth the trouble. I suppose I've got to take the exams, though. It will only mean a week's delay, and it's an awful waste doing all this work if I don't sit them after all."

Nan always came solidly in the top third in maths and science, and she did better than that in history, the only subject she really liked.

"It's not really a waste, is it?" Sophie asked. "Isn't it worth learning all this for its own sake, apart from the exams?"

Nan stared at her.

"Sophie, you're mad," she said. "I'd be far better off starting my training right away. We might well be at war within the

323

next few weeks, and it's frustrating to think I won't see combat before January at the earliest."

"You sound as though you *want* to see combat!"

"Well, of course," Nan said. "What's the point otherwise?"

As Sophie tried to explain to Nan why she found this so extraordinary, the other two girls' voices rose in a full-scale row.

"What's up, you two?" Nan asked, switching her attention away from Sophie.

"Jean's being even more impossible than usual," said Priscilla.

"I'm not!" Jean shouted.

Sophie hoped the hall monitor wouldn't hear them.

"Sophie," Jean said in a more moderate voice, "what do you think? Isn't sixteen too young to get married?"

"I don't know," said Sophie. "I suppose it depends on the person. It sounds awfully young to me."

"Scottish law has always allowed minors to marry without the permission of their parents and guardians," Nan objected. She put her essay aside and rested her elbows on the desk. "That's why English couples in the old days used to elope to Gretna Green, because it was the first place you came to over the border. If you were a young man who'd run away with an underage heiress, you could marry her there legally, and her family wouldn't be able to stop it."

"But don't you think that must have happened more often in novels than in real life?" Sophie asked Nan.

"Oh, can it, you two!" Jean shouted, scowling at them. "We're not talking about history or novels. We're talking about the modern world, and in the modern world sixteen's much too young!"

"In the modern world," said Priscilla, "lots of girls marry at sixteen."

The color had risen in her cheeks, and she looked both very pretty and seriously annoyed.

Only now did Sophie register what was going on.

"Priscilla, you're not thinking of getting married, are you?" she said.

"Why not?" said Priscilla, preening a little under Sophie's horrified look. "If the government bill concerning school-leaving age goes through, being married is likely to become one of the only ways of getting an exemption—at least that's what my father thinks. I've had two proposals already, and I'm certainly not going into the ghastly Women's Auxiliaries. That uniform is terribly unflattering!"

"You're hopeless," Nan said, shaking her head. "But really, Priscilla, surely Jean's right and you're much too young? If you wait a little longer, you'll have a much better chance of getting a really good husband."

"I don't see why that should be the case," said Priscilla. "My mother met my father when she was fourteen and he was nineteen, and they married as soon as she'd left school."

"Just because it was right for them," Sophie said, "doesn't mean it would be good for you. Besides, doesn't your father want you to take a degree?"

"Oh, he doesn't really mind one way or the other," Priscilla said, "and in any case, the situation may change at any moment."

"Well, I can't stand it," Jean said, sounding quite grim. "What about our flat? I won't be able to afford it without you, Priscilla. You mustn't let me down like this."

Priscilla shrugged. "You'll work something out," she said. "Besides, you know I haven't said yes to anybody yet!"

As Jean groaned, the door to the study opened, and the earnest freckled face of Miss Hopkins appeared in the crack.

"Nan, are you there?" she said.

"Yes, of course, Miss Hopkins," Nan said.

"Miss Henchman would like to see you at once in her study," the teacher said.

The girls looked at one another.

"Don't worry," Miss Hopkins added, though her voice faltered. "Nan's done nothing wrong."

After Nan had left, Miss Hopkins came all the way into the room and shut the door behind her.

"Girls, I'm afraid something very dreadful has happened," she said.

Sophie thought she looked almost as bad as the day she'd told them about the bombing in Princes Street.

"It's one of Nan's brothers, isn't it?" she said, though she could not explain how she knew.

"Yes," said Miss Hopkins simply. "Her oldest brother, Sam, has been killed in a skirmish in the Urals. Nan's father's downstairs with Miss Henchman; they've decided it'll be best for her to stay at school until the day of the funeral. Her mother's not taking it too well."

"How awful," Priscilla said. All the color had left her face and her hand had gone straight to Jean's. They sat next to each other, looking much younger than before. "What can we do to help?"

"Treat her gently," said the teacher. "Encourage her to see Matron if she's not eating or sleeping properly. Beyond that, I don't know that there's anything we can do."

"Will we have permission to go to the funeral?" Priscilla asked. Sophie suddenly and desperately hated her for always knowing the right thing to say.

"Well," said Miss Hopkins, her voice trailing off, "I don't know. . . ."

"Surely we'll be allowed!" Jean cried.

"It's not that, Jean," the teacher said, clearing her throat.

"It's just that until the army returns the—er—the *remains*, they won't be able to have a funeral. It may be some time."

Having silenced them entirely, she asked if they needed anything. They said no, and she sighed, shook her head, and left.

Lights-out had come and gone before Nan crept back into the room. As she undressed and changed into her nightgown, Sophie decided to speak.

"Nan?"

The other girl didn't answer, but her muffled sobs kept them all awake for a long time.

In the morning Nan's eyes were red and swollen, though she insisted she felt fine and said a soldier's highest honor was to give his life for his country.

Breakfast was sad and quiet. Everyone knew what had happened, and several girls came up to Nan to tell her how sorry they were about her brother.

"Priscilla?" Jean said just before history class was due to start.

"What?"

"Don't let's argue anymore."

"All right."

They shook hands on it as Miss Chatterjee came into the room to begin the lesson. But the day went on feeling strange and sad, and even Sophie had to fiddle with her handkerchief and pretend she'd got a bit of dust in her eye when the teacher spoke a few words of condolence to Nan.

As the bell rang and Sophie began to put away her notes, she looked up to see Nan at her side.

"Sophie, I need you to do something for me," she said. "Something really important."

"Anything," said Sophie.

"Promise?"

"Promise."

"We all know what really happened last week in class," Nan said. "That weird drawing in Mr. Petersen's class, and the stuff you typed off the cylinder for Miss Botham. You're a medium, Sophie, aren't you? You've been hearing the voices of the dead."

It didn't take psychic powers to predict what Nan was going to say next.

"The thing I can't stand," Nan said, now crying outright despite the fact that they were absolutely *surrounded* by other girls putting away their things and pretending not to listen, "is knowing I never said good-bye to him. On Sam's last leave, he was only home for forty-eight hours, and my parents didn't want to break up my school week. Oh, if only I'd seen him then! But Sophie, you'll be able to fix things. You'll help me speak with him, won't you?"

Then, when Sophie said nothing: "Sophie, you promised!

Of course I won't blame you if we try it and it doesn't work. I know you can't always control these things. But I must speak with him one more time, if it's humanly possible, and say a proper good-bye to him."

Was this Sophie's punishment for dabbling in the spirit world? All her old ambivalence about the supernatural flooded into her mind. It *couldn't* be right to want to talk to a loved one after he or she died, it simply couldn't.

But Sophie had made Nan a solemn promise. With an awful sense of foreboding, she said they'd talk about it later.

"You'll do it, though, won't you?"

"Oh, all right," said Sophie, though she couldn't see any good coming of it, and the thought of opening herself up again to spirits made her quite sick.

Nan just pressed her hand and sobbed.

THIRTY-TWO

JUST BEFORE LUNCH Sophie slipped away from the other girls to meet Mikael at the school's side entrance. He was at the door already, wearing a cap and a navy blue shirt and trousers and carrying a brown paper parcel; he could easily have been mistaken for a delivery boy, which was exactly the idea.

Sophie led him through the halls to Mr. Petersen's classroom. The teacher wasn't there yet, though they could hear him talking on the telephone in the office at the back. Sophie had arranged to be there earlier than usual because it suited Mikael better.

They heard him put down the receiver. Sophie and Mikael looked at each other.

"I still can't believe it's really him," Mikael whispered. "Do you think—?"

Then Mr. Petersen appeared in the doorway. He saw Mikael at once. His face went white and then red, and the two of them rushed into each other's arms.

Seeing them together like that made Sophie inexplicably angry. She could hardly remember why she liked either of them in the first place.

"Mr. Petersen!" she said.

"What is it, Sophie?" he asked.

He and Mikael were smiling like idiots; Sophie sourly reflected that they hadn't even thanked her for helping them to be reunited.

"There are things I need to ask you about," she said.

Mikael looked at her curiously. Could he tell how angry she was?

"Arne, you must tell me the truth about this first," he said urgently to Mr. Petersen, reaching into his trousers and pulling out the pocketknife. "I found—"

"My pocketknife!" said Mr. Petersen. "But how—?"

"It had fallen into the back of the couch in the suite at the Balmoral," Mikael said. "The suite where the medium was killed."

"What?" said Mr. Petersen.

They had all taken seats around the lab table at the back

of the classroom, and Sophie's teacher looked genuinely horrified.

"I misplaced that knife a month ago," he said, "but however can you know it turned up at the scene of the crime? I certainly never heard a word from the police, though I wondered whether they would contact me; I had several appointments with Mrs. Tansy in the weeks preceding her disappearance, though I was as surprised as anyone else to hear of her death."

Sophie wanted to ask about the appointments, but Mikael spoke first.

"I was *there*," he said stubbornly. "That's how I know about the knife."

"There at the hotel? You mean, when the medium was killed?" said Mr. Petersen. "That can't be!"

Sophie could see they were going to go on at cross-purposes if someone didn't set them straight, so she gave a clear short explanation of how Mikael had come to be at the hotel.

Mr. Petersen looked terribly worried.

"The knife must have got there by way of the Veteran," he said. "You know the man I mean, Sophie, don't you? I don't think I've ever been so horrified in my life as when I saw him attack the minister. After that, it was less surprising to learn he'd also been implicated in the death of the medium. But it still sends shivers down my spine to think of my own involvement with him. I can't quite forgive myself—I felt awful when I heard about how he died, and I fear I may bear some of the responsibility for the crimes he committed along the way."

"How so?" Sophie asked.

Before Mr. Petersen could answer her, Mikael asked another question. "Why did the Veteran want to implicate you? He could have framed anyone he wanted. Was there something about your dealings with him that might have given him a dislike for you?"

"He knew I worked for the Nobel Consortium," Mr. Petersen said thoughtfully. "Hmm . . . I must mull that one over."

"But why are you *here*?" Sophie burst in. "Are you still working for Nobel? Why did you meet with the medium and the Veteran?"

"That I can't tell you," said Mr. Petersen, sounding quite annoyingly apologetic. "Confidentiality. Sorry."

There were all sorts of other things Sophie wanted to learn too. It would drive her mad if he wouldn't answer any of her questions!

"Did you pay off our old chemistry teacher so that you could take her place?" she asked.

"Why do you say that?" said Mr. Petersen warily.

"Jean and I spotted her in the electric showroom in

Princes Street, still using her maiden name and spending money like water. It was clear she hadn't got married at all, but on the other hand she had much more money than before. It was most odd. Then I accidentally saw the travel visas in your passport—I do apologize, I couldn't help it, I was looking for something to write you a note with and it was right there in your desk drawer. I couldn't understand why you'd been traveling back and forth so often to Stockholm without saying anything. It made me wonder whether your job here was just a cover for something else."

"Damned fool!" said Mr. Petersen. "Sorry, Sophie; not you. Miss Rawlins is really the most impossible woman. I'm not surprised to hear of her behaving so foolishly. Well, that's another little job for me. . . ."

"You're not going to kill her?" Sophie asked, aghast. She didn't like Miss Rawlins, but that didn't mean it was all right to talk about disposing of her as one might an unattractive garden shrub.

"Kill her?" Mr. Petersen looked quite horrified. "Certainly not, Sophie. Whatever must you think of me? Oh dear, I see you've got hold of the wrong end of the stick completely. God, what a mess!"

He jumped out of his seat and began pacing back and forth. "You've got no reason to trust me, Sophie," he said. "But by the most solemn oaths possible, I swear I mean you no harm. On the contrary, your safety's vitally important to me."

"What about the bombings?" Sophie asked. It was her deepest darkest worry, especially now that the Nobel connection had been proven. "If you had anything to do with those deaths, we can't keep it secret."

Mikael might be satisfied simply to know his brother hadn't been at the murder scene, but Sophie couldn't let things go so easily, even if it *was* her beloved Mr. Petersen.

"Sophie, I swear to you on my mother's head that I'm not involved in any way with the Brothers of the Northern Liberties," said Mr. Petersen. "I'd never intentionally harm another human being. I'm deeply committed to pacifism. Look, I can see why you're suspicious. Those entry stamps in the passport must have been a bit of a facer! Indeed, I must confess that I *was* involved with one of the bombings, the one at St. Giles' Cathedral."

"The one where nobody was killed?" Sophie said, confused. "But—"

"I was asked to find the device and, if possible, to defuse it without detonating it. Unfortunately the bomb went off as soon as I sent in the first mechanical probe. It wasn't supposed to work that way, but at least it prevented the bomb's going off in the middle of morning services, as it was meant to."

"A mechanical probe?" Sophie asked, curious despite herself.

Mr. Petersen looked for a moment as if he would like to indulge her curiosity. Then he shook his head.

"Another time, Sophie, I'll tell you all about the latest antiterror gadgets," he said. "All you need to know now is that I was there with the full knowledge of the police—indeed, at their request. They contacted the Nobel Consortium, and someone there told them I was nearest by."

"Oh," said Sophie. "Mr. Petersen—"

She was going to ask why he had taken the teaching job in the first place, but she stopped when Mikael started chuckling quietly. She supposed he thought it was funny, the way she kept calling his brother by his formal name.

"Stop it!" she said, so annoyed she actually reached across—she couldn't believe she did it—and whacked him in the stomach, a hard backhanded blow that took him completely by surprise. He reached over and grabbed her arm and forced it back until she begged him to stop.

Now it was Mr. Petersen laughing.

"I can see you two are old friends," he said. "Oh, it's so good to see you again, Mikael!"

He clapped Mikael on the shoulder, and the two of them looked at each other affectionately.

At that moment Sophie had a revelation—a *horrible*

revelation. She let her arm go limp so suddenly that Mikael was put off balance and couldn't stop her from snatching it back from him. She didn't want to touch him; she couldn't let him touch her for even a moment longer.

For months Sophie had believed herself to be in love with Mr. Petersen. Everyone knew about it and joked about it, and even Sophie had grown comfortable with the idea. *Of course* Mr. Petersen would never fall in love with Sophie—that was a given.

But Sophie wasn't jealous of the love she could see in Mr. Petersen's face as he looked at his younger brother. It was *Mikael* whose affections she begrudged; she could hardly bear seeing even an *iota* of love in his eyes for someone else, even for his brother.

It was really Mikael Sophie had been in love with all along! Oh, how awful, how shameful; it was the most humiliating—the most *unforgivable*—thing she had ever done. Falling in love with her best friend!

The other two were looking at her curiously. She couldn't say a word to explain why she'd gone silent. She was briefly consumed with a powerful and irrational dislike for both of them. Why couldn't they have stayed in Denmark where they belonged?

"Forgive me for saying so, Sophie," said Mr. Petersen, after a quick look at his watch, "but I have a strong feeling you're going to be in very hot water if you don't make haste to lunch."

"Oh, golly," said Sophie. At least it was an excuse to leave right away.

"Give me a week to sort things out," the teacher said. "That's all I ask. Then I'll tell you everything I can."

"But Mikael will have gone by then!"

"I'm traveling to Denmark next week in any case," said Mr. Petersen. "I'll explain everything to him then; it will be easier that way."

But when would Sophie get to see Mikael?

"Away with you now," said Mr. Petersen. "Don't worry, Sophie, it will all come right in the end, with a bit of luck."

"Come to tea on Thursday," Mikael called after her as she left. "I'll tell Arne now about everything else that's happened, and then you and I can talk on Thursday about what to do next."

She waved a hand to show she'd heard, but didn't look back. Probably they would enjoy having some time alone together. It wasn't hard to tell when she was superfluous. Realizing she was in love with Mikael only drove home how peripheral Sophie was to his life. She would have to be *scrupulous* in making sure he caught no glimpse of her feelings; she would rather die than be exposed.

THIRTY-THREE

THAT EVENING SOPHIE plowed steadily through an enormous pile of homework without letting anything distract her. Schoolwork was *nothing* compared to everything else that had happened recently.

Jean and Priscilla had yet to resolve their argument, but agreed to put their differences aside. Nan herself spent the evening in bed with her history textbook. She could hardly have turned more than a page or two, but if she was crying, she did so very quietly.

They all talked softly in bed until eleven o'clock, much too keyed up to feel in the least sleepy. Once the last inspection had come and gone and the corridor lights been put out, they joined Nan on her bed, Priscilla wearing a very fancy pair of blue silk pajamas, the other three in the distinctly less glamorous regulation ones.

"Did you find the things I asked for?" Sophie asked Nan, speaking softly, though not actually whispering. Nan's bereavement would keep them from being punished for breaking the lights-out rule only so long as their offenses were not too glaring. Quiet voices and a single candle would be safest.

In silence Nan laid a series of objects on the bed: a snapshot of Sam with his arm around Nan's shoulders; a little double-action revolver, formerly Sam's, usually kept in the rifle-club cabinet and illegally borrowed for the evening; an Azerbaijani woven bracelet Sam had sent his sister for Christmas; half a dozen postcards.

"Don't you need anything else?" Jean asked Sophie. "Some incense, or a crystal ball?"

"I've got a powder compact with a mirror in it," Priscilla suggested, "and there's also my transistor radio."

Her willingness to contribute her most treasured possession (Priscilla's father had obtained the radio from one of the men who had actually invented the transistor) set Nan off into tears again.

"We won't need anything like that," Sophie said, trying to project confidence. "We'll just use these things as a way of connecting with Sam."

Sophie didn't want Nan to hear her brother's voice directly. There was something upsetting in the sound of a disembodied voice even when it didn't belong to someone you loved, and hearing Sam's spirit talk in its present thinned-out, incoherent state could do Nan no possible good.

"How does it work?" Nan asked. She seemed to be trying hard to behave as though everything was all right.

"It's a technique called psychometry," Sophie explained. "Every object retains impressions of the people who've handled it. They sometimes do it at séances—people put things like a pen or a watch into a tray, and the medium gives readings from them. It doesn't have to be something of your own—people often get readings on an object belonging to someone they're worried about."

She felt incredibly silly stating the obvious like this, but the things taught in the mandatory Spiritualist Instruction class were all airy-fairy nonsense and none of the others came from the kind of family that had Friday-night séances. It wasn't a question of social class, more of different cultures: Great-aunt Tabitha's civil-service-oriented and rather mandarin circles practiced spiritualism very regularly, while most other people felt that it was all very well but not the sort of thing one did in one's own home.

Priscilla and Jean stayed cross-legged at the foot of the bed, Nan at the head, while Sophie crouched on the floor beside them.

"Put the candle on top of your locker," she told Nan, "and then touch each of these things, saying your brother's name every time."

The others watched Nan touch each relic in turn, her lips moving as she faintly sounded the name.

Once Nan had finished her pass along the row of objects, Sophie let her own fingers brush over them, forcing her mind to become as receptive as possible. Sophie had met Sam a few times over the years, but her mental image of him as distinct from the other Harris brothers remained blurry. Best of all would have been something that had been on Sam's body right at the moment he died, for his spirit would cling to it afterward. Most of the things here gave off a much clearer sense of Nan than her brother, and it was with some discouragement that Sophie made a second pass over them, this time letting her hand rest a little longer on each item.

As she came to the pistol, the candle guttered and a breeze swept through the room.

Jean yelped, Priscilla shushed her, and even Sophie (by now more or less hardened to the presence of the uncanny) almost lost her balance, stopped from toppling over only by Nan grabbing her shoulder and holding her upright.

"It's not *really* glowing," Priscilla whispered as Sophie's fingers closed over the pistol's grip. "That's just a reflection of the ambient light."

Nobody bothered to correct her.

Sophie couldn't imagine Nan hadn't unloaded the pistol as a safety precaution, but she double-checked the cylinder to make sure the chambers were empty. Then she took hold of the gun and let her mind go blank.

Next thing she knew, she found herself standing in the middle of the room, trapped between Jean and Priscilla, who were each holding one of her arms. All her muscles hurt, and her throat felt raspy and sore.

"Be quiet!" Jean hissed. "You've been shouting loud enough to wake the dead!"

"Surely that's the point of the exercise?" Priscilla murmured, dragging Sophie back over to Nan's side.

"Nan, was it any good?" Sophie asked. She couldn't remember a thing—a strange and frightening feeling.

The others looked at one another.

"I'm not sure if *good*'s the word," said Nan, sliding over to make room for Sophie as the others resumed their places at the foot of the bed. Her face was very white, and she swallowed several times as if trying not to be sick. "It was too much of a jumble for us to make much sense of. Sophie, I'm sure it was Sam speaking through you. He speaks—used to speak—very quickly when he's excited, not a stutter exactly but a sort of jerky pattern. The way you were talking just now was exactly like it."

"And what did I say?" Sophie asked.

She hadn't meant to give voice to Sam's thoughts, just to receive a message she'd be able to pass on later to Nan, but clearly her control wasn't as good as she imagined.

The others exchanged glances.

It was Priscilla who spoke.

"It was pretty much what you'd expect," she said, "from someone fighting hand to hand and knowing he's about to die."

"Oh, Nan, I'm sorry," Sophie said, tears springing to her eyes. She clasped Nan's hand, and Nan flinched at the contact.

"It's not your fault, Sophie," she said, detaching her hand from Sophie's. "That's war. We all know it can end like that. But Sophie, he really wasn't *himself*. I think the pistol took things in the wrong direction. Too violent. Do you think you could try one more time? What I need is to say good-bye, and feel at least for myself that he hears it. I can see it's horrible for you, Sophie, but it would mean the world to me if we could do it."

Sophie gave Nan a doubtful look, then sighed. What did she think she was saving herself for, anyway?

"All right," she said. "I'm going to try something different this time. I think there's something I can do with the post-cards. I only thought of it just now, but it should be better than the gun. That was a mistake."

She sat and thought for a minute, the others afraid to interrupt. Then she picked up the little sheaf of postcards and looked at them closely. She laid them out writing side up on the coverlet like a game of solitaire.

"I need to get a few things from the other room," she said. "Back in a minute."

She tiptoed across the room and into the study, where she found an exercise book and a plumbago pencil.

"All right," she said, back beside the others and amazed at the steadiness of her own voice. (It was a good thing she'd gone to so many of those wretched séances over the years.) "I need you all to work with me this time. We're going to form a small sitter's circle, the kind they use at real séances. You'll all join hands, but I need to keep mine free, because I want to try letting Sam communicate with Nan in writing. That's been the pattern of their contact over the last few years while he's been abroad."

Priscilla took Jean's hand and Jean took Nan's. Sophie asked Priscilla to rest her right hand lightly on Sophie's left forearm, Nan doing the same on Sophie's other side. Then Sophie took up the pencil and let it rest on the exercise book, her left hand pressing the page flat to the surface of the bed.

This time she spoke aloud. She didn't think her concentration had been good enough the last time, perhaps because she'd had little conviction that Nan would benefit from hearing what her dead brother had to say. But she couldn't protect the others, not really. They were living through bad times, and whatever happened, there would be many deaths.

She raised her head and closed her eyes.

"Sam," she said. "This is Nan's friend Sophie at school. Nan's here with me right now, and so are two other girls we share a room with, Jean and Priscilla."

She stopped speaking and felt for some kind of a response—anything, really. She felt a little tug or a tweak, like a dog whistle pitched high above human hearing.

"Sam, your sister's right here and she wants to say good-bye," Sophie said, tipping her head in Nan's direction and hoping she'd have the sense to speak.

"Sam?" Nan said. "I just wanted to tell you how sorry I was to miss you on that last leave. I'm so proud of you, and I love you. That's all. I hope you're at peace now."

The words would mean nothing in a storybook, but the sound of them being spoken by a real person she actually knew made Sophie want to cry. She heard some sniffling, and one of the others pulled up a clasped pair of hands to wipe eyes on a sleeve.

Sophie forced herself to stop thinking so much and tried to make her mind blank. Then, suddenly and startlingly, something began to happen.

Her left hand felt for the edges of the exercise book, gripping the upper right-hand corner of the page, her forearm pressing it down flat along the top. Meanwhile her writing hand adjusted itself into a different grip on the pencil and began to move in fits and starts over the paper.

The feeling was altogether so strange that Sophie couldn't help opening her eyes to look. She stared as the words took shape.

Two, three, four lines of writing. Sophie hoped it would be enough.

Just then she had a flash of him, the agonizing presence of whatever remained of Sam Harris, the shreds left over from the pain of his last moments (he'd died in *fire*, Sophie realized, gagging), his own self weakened by months of deprivation and the unrelenting hostility of the people he was meant to be protecting.

Within the agony, though, she sensed the solid core of his self intact. Even without having seen what he'd written, Sophie knew that none of Sam's agony or his ambivalence about the army's so-called peacekeeping mission or his doubt as to whether the sacrifice of his own life had any meaning would feature in the message to his baby sister.

Sophie found her lips moving, silently mouthing, "Please let him be at peace; oh, please be at peace, Sam," repeating it over and over until the pencil fell still in her hands and she slumped forward onto the bed.

She came to herself a moment later in a scene of quiet chaos: Priscilla in tears, Jean's arm around Nan's shoulders, Nan herself shaking with hysterical sobs as she read the words on the page.

"Are you all right?" Priscilla asked Sophie.

"Quite all right," Sophie said. She couldn't shake the memory of how Sam *felt*—the fear and the sorrow and the self-disgust and the awful sensation and smell of burning, and yet through it all something human and real that had to do with his love for his family and his old life in the world. "Does the message make any sense?"

Nan thrust the exercise book in Sophie's direction, then got up and staggered across the room to the basin, where she ran water to splash on her face.

Sophie held the book under the small pool of candlelight and read the dim scrawl wandering up and down across the ruled lines.

"My dearest little Nanny goat don't spare me another thought. So proud of you. Confident you'll find your heart's desire in Women's Auxiliaries but do be careful Nan it'll be harder than it seems at home. Look out for Mum and Dad they'll need you now and take care of your good self with all love for evermore from your loving brother Sam."

The gap between Sam's message and the torrent of pain

and anger she'd felt from him struck Sophie hard. What must it have cost him to send these loving words? They had none of the vagueness Sophie associated with the run-of-the-mill spirit message—the postcard template had helped him write something very much like what he would have inscribed in life.

Sam telling Nan she'd thrive in the army, after his own experience and in full knowledge that she too might lose her life, showed a generosity and willingness to sacrifice that Sophie couldn't begin to emulate.

The loud tread of the teacher patrolling the corridor brought them all back to the real world. Sophie blew out the candle and practically leaped back into her own bed, while Jean and Priscilla scurried across the room. Only Nan remained out of bed and over by the sink, the tap still running.

The steps paused outside for a moment. It was easy to imagine the teacher leaning down and checking the crack under the door to see if they had a light on, and then deciding not to bother the poor things.

"Nan?" Sophie whispered, after five minutes had passed and it seemed reasonable to assume the corridor was clear.

"I'll come to bed soon," Nan said.

"I'm so sorry," Sophie said. "I didn't mean to hurt you."

"No! You can't imagine what you've done; it's all I hoped for. Thank you, Sophie. I don't know how I can ever repay you."

Sophie felt wretched. This couldn't be right. Wasn't one supposed to judge an action by its fruits, and hadn't the night's work only brought Nan more pain?

What if Nan asked Sophie to contact her brother again, wanting more messages? What if she became addicted to crossing the boundary between life and death?

Sophie buried her face in the pillows. First thing in the morning, she'd swear the others to silence. She certainly had no intention of becoming the on-call psychic for the whole of the fifth form. She fell asleep to the background of Nan's quiet sobs and a faint whispered conversation between the other two girls.

THIRTY-FOUR

WAKING MUCH EARLIER than usual, Sophie arrived at breakfast in time to bag one of the two much-coveted private tables, tables that seated only four instead of fourteen and were usually snapped up by groups of sixth-form girls who had no scruples about rousting out anyone who dared encroach on their territory. Several older girls loitered nearby with their trays, but Sophie glared at them until they went away.

Nan got there next. She and Sophie ate their cereal in silence until they saw the other two girls at the head of the food line. Then Nan turned to Sophie.

"I know you hate being thanked," she said, "but it *mattered* to me to have that last word from my brother."

Sophie felt awkward and irritable.

"I can't ever do it again," she warned, "and you mustn't tell anybody else what I did, either."

"Why ever not?"

"Because it's too horrible, that's why," Sophie grumbled, mashing the Weetabix with her spoon.

"How can you say that?"

"It's playing around with people's emotions, and I really hate it."

Jean and Priscilla slid into the seats across from them.

"You must swear never to tell a soul about what happened last night," said Sophie, so loudly that one sixth-form girl looked over from the next table to see what was going on.

"We swear," said Priscilla, her face drawn and tired.

"You two," said Jean, "we've got important news."

Sophie looked more closely and saw that Jean looked as tired as Priscilla, but more at peace with herself than she had seemed for months.

"We talked it all through last night," Jean continued, "and Priscilla's changed her mind. Assuming they'll take us, we're both going to join IRYLNS as soon as we've got our exam results."

"IRYLNS?" Sophie said stupidly.

"That's wonderful," said Nan, mustering more enthusiasm than Sophie would have thought possible. "You two aren't cut out for the army, and IRYLNS is the best other way of serving."

"Yes, and we have to thank you and Sophie for showing us the way," Jean said, smiling at them. "The idea of service—it really makes sense of everything, doesn't it? It did for your brother, Nan, and it does for you. And now it will for us as well."

Sophie was so horrified she couldn't speak.

"We're going to see Miss Henchman straight after breakfast," said Priscilla, "and tell her what we've decided."

"You can't!" said Sophie, finding her voice at last. "You simply can't!"

She couldn't believe that she'd contributed to this decision by her participation in the séance. She'd never forgive herself.

"Why not?"

"Because—because—"

She couldn't tell them about what she'd seen, could she? The strict prohibition of the Official Secrets Act closed up Sophie's throat so that she could hardly breathe.

But she had to tell. She simply had to. She fought to get control of her lungs and larynx and tongue so that she could speak the warning.

"Because IRYLNS will destroy you," she found herself saying. She hoped she didn't look as wild-eyed as she felt.

"They make girls into *monsters*—you mustn't do it."

Meanwhile Priscilla regarded her suspiciously, then broke into a delighted chuckle. Even Nan was smiling a little.

"Oh, Sophie, you can't fool us," Priscilla said. "It's a good idea, to try and get back at me for teasing you about Mr. Petersen. But a tale about the gothic secrets of IRYLNS— we're living in the twentieth century, after all!"

Sophie stared at the others. This was worse even than she'd imagined. She'd thought of the possible consequences of telling, the chance that she might have to endure prison and even perhaps torture or death. But it had simply never occurred to her that she might not be believed. Whatever would she have to do to convince them?

"Give it up, Sophie," Nan said. "You know yourself it's the best thing for these two."

"I'm sorry about all that teasing," Priscilla added, sounding really remorseful. "I don't know what gets into me. My father always says there's a kind of devil inside me that thrives on tormenting others. But I'm determined to become a better person, Sophie, and you have to believe me when I say that IRYLNS will be the best way for me to do that."

Your teasing and Jean's jealousy, they're *parts* of you, Sophie desperately wanted to say. You can't just wipe them out like mistakes in your calculus homework. You mustn't—

But there was no point saying it. It would only be her fate,

Cassandra-like, not to be believed. What powerful additional security for the secret keepers at IRYLNS!

"Aren't you going to congratulate us?" Priscilla said.

"I must go," said Sophie, piling her breakfast things onto the tray. She had to work out a way to convince them, but nothing she said now would change a thing, and it would make Nan think she was a bad person if she kept on saying bad things about IRYLNS—and Nan's good opinion *mattered*. She needed hard evidence. But how would she get it? "I've got a few things to do before class."

Then she stopped, inspired.

"If I had to make an excuse to go and see a very eminent doctor," she said, "what do you think I should say?"

The other girls looked at one another as if Sophie had gone mad.

"You don't need an excuse," Jean finally said. "You've always got your limp."

Sophie felt as if she'd been punched in the stomach.

She almost always forgot that she had a limp.

Did everyone think of Sophie as a person with a limp?

Did Mikael?

THIRTY-FIVE

I N THE SCHOOL LIBRARY, Sophie headed straight for the city directories, the outlines of a plan taking shape in her mind.

The others would never believe what she said about IRYLNS. Telling them that she'd actually been there with Great-aunt Tabitha wouldn't make any difference—it would just make her sound like a silly, self-important girl boasting about her influential relations.

But what if Sophie went back to IRYLNS, sneaked in illicitly, and took *pictures* of the abuse? Then she could show the photographs to Jean and Priscilla and persuade them to change their minds. Sophie might still risk prison or worse, but she felt she couldn't *not* do it. She put out of her head the thought that in another few months, it might be not just Jean and Priscilla but Sophie herself who would need to be saved.

She'd no hope of getting into IRYLNS through the front door. They took security seriously there. But IRYLNS stood alongside research institutes where doctors actually saw patients. She could steal into one of those and find a way to slip out the back, reach the garden behind IRYLNS, and get into the building that way instead.

The city council compiled a really useful directory that listed every Edinburgh street and its occupants, so that one could easily find, say, the names of every householder in Heriot Row, or the professor's neighbors in back of the school tennis courts.

Sophie flipped to the entry for Buccleugh Place and made a list of names and telephone numbers on the flyleaf of her history textbook.

It was never easy to find a telephone at school. Girls were not supposed to telephone home without permission, so they had no regular access to one. Where could she find a telephone, and when would she be able to use it?

Just then the librarian appeared and Sophie slammed the directory shut and blushed. At least there was nothing racy about what she had been reading, not like that mortifying time she'd been caught returning an overdue copy of *Mesmeric Love*.

"Don't worry, I wasn't going to look," said the librarian,

smiling at her. "I wonder if I could prevail on you to man the helm, though, while I run down to the refectory for a cup of coffee?"

"Of course," said Sophie, who'd had a holiday job in the library the summer before. "Is there anything you'd like me to do while I'm here?"

"Well, you could go through the file and check for overdue books," said the librarian. "I'll be back in fifteen minutes."

Sophie took her place behind the desk, sorted out the cards for the overdue books, and wrote out the notices. All the while, the telephone squatted like an alluring toad at the back of the office.

She wished she'd asked the librarian for permission to make a few calls. Surely she wouldn't have said no, and then Sophie wouldn't feel such a heel for taking advantage. It might be days before she got another shot at a telephone, though, and by the weekend all the doctors' offices would be closed, so the phone at Great-aunt Tabitha's wouldn't do her any good. Anyway, she was contemplating breaking into a top-secret government facility. It was ridiculous having scruples about making a telephone call without permission.

A minute later Sophie had the receiver in her hand and was asking the operator to put through a call. She let the phone ring for ages at the Osteopathic Consultancy and then at the Clinic for Research into Disorders of the Thyroid, but nobody answered. Well, it was only just after eight o'clock. Most offices didn't open until nine or even half past.

She put through a third call, fearing that she'd need to find another telephone later on in the day—the librarian would be back at any moment—when she was startled by a young woman's voice.

"Braid Institute for Neurohypnosis," said the telephone receptionist. "How can I help you?"

"You come very highly recommended by a friend," Sophie said, trying to sound adult, "and I wonder whether you might squeeze me in for an appointment."

She was proud of having used the word *squeeze*; it seemed like the kind of thing a woman in her thirties might say.

"We're terribly busy just now," said the receptionist, sounding genuinely sorry. "That is," she added in a brighter voice, "unless you'd be able to come in at very short notice."

Very short notice was exactly what Sophie wanted. She said as much, then listened to the girl on the other end of the line flip through the clinic appointment book.

"We've got a cancellation tomorrow afternoon—that's Thursday the seventh—at four thirty. Would you be able to take it?"

Sophie felt like doing a celebratory dance right there in the office. Why, it couldn't have been better if she'd picked the time herself!

The receptionist sounded delighted when Sophie accepted the slot.

"You'll not regret it," she told Sophie confidentially. "Our Mr. Braid's a remarkable man, quite remarkable. And don't forget your national insurance card, all right, hen?"

Sophie replaced the receiver in its cradle with relief. She'd have no trouble getting to that appointment—she'd go along with the others to tennis practice, pop in to say good-bye to Mikael (she ignored the feeling of her stomach turning inside out), and then take the tram down to the university. Since her appointment fell near the end of the day, it shouldn't be hard to arrange to be somehow left behind when the building closed. The Braid Institute stood right next door to IRYLNS, and she could easily climb over the wall in the garden and go on from there.

Shortly after three o'clock the following afternoon, Sophie wriggled through the gap in the wall into the professor's back garden. Mikael knelt by one of the flower beds, a heap of weeds at his side.

Beside him, the professor's handsome Great Dane lay sprawled on the warm flagstones of the garden path, too lazy to do anything more than raise his head and greet Sophie with mournful eyes. It was ridiculous how sad that dog could look, she thought, leaning to scratch the ridges of his harlequin brow.

"Sophie!" said Mikael, scrambling to his feet and wiping his hands on his trousers. "I was afraid I might not see you before I left."

His brisk, careless manner rubbed Sophie the wrong way.

"I can't stay long," she said, hating how stiff she sounded. She had Nan's camera in her pocket with fresh film in it—Nan could refuse Sophie nothing now (a haunted generosity of which Sophie had promised herself not to take advantage). "I've got a doctor's appointment near the university at half past four, and I mustn't be late."

Mikael gave her a sharp look.

"Anything I should know about?" he said.

She avoided meeting his eyes—oh, why did she have to be in such *turmoil*? "No, nothing," she said, "just an ordinary appointment."

Mikael frowned.

"Then why are you skiving off from tennis practice? Wouldn't your school usually send you to the doctor with a teacher, or something like that?"

Sophie had forgotten Mikael's quickness.

"All right," she said, "it's not just an ordinary appointment, but I've promised not to say anything about it."

"Why can't you trust me, Sophie?" Mikael said. He sounded angry, and it turned Sophie's heart stony.

"I do trust you," she said, patting the dog's mastodon

skull. "But sometimes the fewer people who know something, the better."

Why did she have such a strong impulse to punish Mikael just now, and how did it come about that not telling him things seemed the best way to do it?

Mikael looked hurt, then pensive.

"It's almost as if you *want* me to be angry with you," he said.

They went through into the house. The professor was out, but Mrs. Lundberg stepped out of the kitchen to give Sophie a kiss, throwing up her hands in despair when she realized that Mikael actually intended to wear his filthy gardening trousers outside in the street.

"Back shortly, Aunt Solvej," he said. "Sophie's not stopping for tea; she's got a doctor's appointment. I ban you from lifting even a finger in the garden while I'm gone—I'll have plenty of time to finish the weeding before tea."

At the tram stop in Canongate, they checked the timetable. Sophie had just missed a tram, and it would be ten minutes before the next one.

She and Mikael looked at each other, neither quite knowing what to say.

"Don't worry, Sophie," Mikael said. "You'll work it all out. Look, can I buy you an ice cream?"

The unexpected niceness of the suggestion caught Sophie off guard. Mikael smiled back at her, and some of the tension between them fell away.

"So what about that ice cream?" Mikael said, pointing to the small shop on the other side of the road.

"I'm not really hungry," Sophie said, realizing with dismay that she could hardly *bear* the thought of Mikael leaving.

"But it's Luca's! You can always eat an ice cream from Luca's, can't you?" Mikael said.

It was true that Luca's ice cream, manufactured in Musselburgh and sold in shops and kiosks all over Edinburgh, was smoother and whiter and colder and creamier than anything you could imagine, like something the twelve dancing princesses might have eaten out of crystal goblets at their nightly balls.

So Mikael bought two ice cream cornets and they sat and licked them on the bench at the tram stop, Sophie trying hard not to jump up every minute to look out for the tram.

"Sophie?" Mikael said.

"What?"

"I really want you to come with me to Denmark."

Sophie had prepared herself to greet such an observation with indifference, but she felt a deep stab of regret that she couldn't shuck off her responsibilities and go with Mikael to København. Adults would laugh at the idea of a schoolgirl having responsibilities, but they'd forgotten what life at this age was really like.

Tears welled up in her eyes and she shook her head with great vehemence instead of answering Mikael in words. Oh, if only she hadn't realized she was in love with him! She couldn't shake the feeling of Mikael making this offer out of something like pity. She would be *damned* if she'd accept an invitation chiefly motivated by pity. Better to stay and risk the consequences.

"I know what you'll say," Mikael went on, ignoring Sophie's psychic plea for him to shut up. "Your exams. Your great-aunt. Your school friends. The minister of public safety. The Brothers of the Northern Liberties."

As he ticked each item off on his fingers, Sophie painfully regretted not having told him anything about IRYLNS, in some ways the most clear and present danger of all. If he knew about that, he'd insist on her coming with him. If only she could tell him!

She clamped her lips tightly shut.

"You can change your mind, you know, Sophie," Mikael said. "Changing your mind isn't a bad thing. You're free to decide you're not responsible for the whole world. My mother will take you in, no question, and there's a good English-language high school that's even on the right tram route. I can't imagine your great-aunt would kick up much of a fuss, not if she thought you really wanted it. I don't know—I can't explain, exactly—but something in you just isn't *thriving* in Edinburgh."

With great relief, Sophie saw the tram come around the corner. She surprised herself by flinging her arms around Mikael. Then she pushed him away and got in line to board.

But Mikael's hand rested again on her arm, the stickiness of the ice cream attaching his fingers lightly to her skin.

"Won't you go now?" she cried out.

"Sophie, my ship's the *Gustavus Adolphus*, sailing on Saturday at nineteen hundred hours—that's seven o'clock in the evening—from pier sixteen at Leith. Will you remember that? Just in case something blows up between now and then—"

Sophie winced.

"No, not literally, you idiot. Figuratively. If something goes terribly wrong and you decide things have changed—that it's too dangerous to stay here and you'll come with me after all—you can still change your mind, as long as you reach the ship in time. Don't worry about the visa. There are ways of getting around it. My brother will help you if you need it. Oh, Sophie, just be careful, won't you?"

"You, too, Mikael," she said. "Do take care!"

The driver had stopped. If she didn't hurry, she'd never make the appointment on time.

She tore herself away from Mikael and up the steps into the tram.

THIRTY-SIX

I T TOOK HARDLY ANY time at all to get to Hume Close. Sophie crossed the road and walked into Buccleugh Place with a good fifteen minutes to spare, feeling terribly exposed as she walked past Adam Smith College.

The receptionist inside the Braid Institute took her national insurance card and showed her where to wait. The hall outside the waiting room had an exit at the back into the garden, a heavy door with panels of frosted glass. If Sophie could just nerve herself up, it wouldn't be hard to open and shut the front door as a decoy, so that it sounded as though she'd gone, and then race down the hall and let herself out the back door into the garden. And hope she didn't find herself trapped there, she added to herself, though there was almost always some way out of a garden.

Just thinking about sneaking around was making her pulse race so fast she was practically hyperventilating. To calm herself down, Sophie picked up a sample of the waiting-room literature, an odd-looking pamphlet called *How to Magnetize*.

It was not long before Mr. Braid appeared in the waiting room, his face humorous and weather-beaten, an attractive contrast to the impeccably polished attire of his navy pin-striped suit and gleaming dress shoes. He shook Sophie's hand; if he felt the sticky remnants of the ice cream, he was too polite to show it.

Inside the consulting room, they established that Sophie had come to see if he could do anything about her limp.

"In ordinary life," said the specialist, "mind and body work together in tandem, with no clear ascendancy of the one over the other. In the trance state, the mind's power over the body emerges in its full force. Under these conditions, the mind is sometimes able to cure the body of ailments as diverse as gallstones, ulcers, varicose veins, even broken limbs."

Broken limbs! How absurd. Sophie stifled the desire to laugh.

"The magnetic trance makes sense of a host of otherwise inexplicable phenomena," Mr. Braid continued, gesturing enthusiastically in the air. "Surely it's only an illusion that humans have a finite and self-contained center of consciousness or will—I would venture to say that there is no such thing as a coherent self."

Sophie was pretty sure that *she* had a coherent self, and she thought Mr. Braid was probably sure *he* had a coherent self as well, but she schooled her expression so that he wouldn't be able to tell she disagreed with him.

"I am quite sure that we *all* possess a second self," the doctor continued, "a self that lives an independent mental life and has ways of acquiring knowledge off limits to our everyday self."

Sophie's second self wanted to laugh, but she didn't give in to the impulse. Some of the most powerful theories of the twentieth century had elicited laughter, after all, and often from people who should have known better. Think of how many jokes one heard about Wittgenstein's Uncertainty Principle, silly jokes whose punch lines stupidly made fun of the Austrian physicist's incendiary hypothesis that one could know either the position or the velocity of a subatomic particle but never both at once.

"Well, then, Miss Hunter," said the doctor, "the order of the day will be to obtain from your second self an account of the accident that led to your limping."

"But I was a very small child," Sophie protested. "I don't remember anything about it."

"Your mind contains reservoirs of knowledge to which

your conscious self lacks access," said Mr. Braid, settling into his chair and rubbing his hands together in a gesture that might have been sinister if he hadn't seemed so transparently well intentioned. "We won't be able to do anything about the limp until we have learned as much as possible of its etiology, both physical and psychological."

Then, when Sophie continued to look skeptical: "Trust me, Miss Hunter. I've been doing this for twenty years, and I still see new things every day, things that fill me with awe and gratitude that I am able to pursue this work. We'll try a spot of automatic writing first. I'll hypnotize you and then ask you to lay out whatever you can remember about the accident and your body's own awareness of the physical damage that remains. Afterward you won't remember anything that's happened—"

Sophie hoped this wouldn't be the case. . . .

"—and I will keep the statement back from you until the end of your course of treatment, in case the knowledge should prove traumatic for your conscious self in these early stages of our working together."

What wouldn't Sophie's conscious self be able to face? She prided herself on her pragmatism and willingness to face facts.

"How long is the usual course of treatment?" she asked the doctor.

"It varies from case to case," Braid said, "but twelve weeks wouldn't be at all out of the ordinary. On your way out, ask Miss Tiptree to schedule your next appointment."

"Shall we begin?" said Sophie, unable to stop herself from looking at her watch. Twenty to five. Not bad. If she left it too much later, there'd be nothing to see next door but girls spooning mush into their mouths at supper.

"Let me explain exactly what I'm about to do," said the doctor. "In the early days, the mesmerist put his client into the trance state by means of an extraordinarily showy set of passes in the air. Do you know the sort of thing I mean?"

"Yes, of course," said Sophie.

"It's not nearly as flashy as the comic-book version, of course, but I will use my hands to help you pass into the mesmeric trance—"

Sophie was suddenly much more nervous than she'd imagined about the prospect of being hypnotized. What if, when the doctor hypnotized her, she revealed to him her plan to infiltrate IRYLNS by way of Mr. Braid's back garden?

"—and then I'll ask you a series of questions, to which you will write your answers with the pencil and paper I provide. I have found," the doctor added as an afterthought, "that patients are less disturbed by the idea that their second self can communicate by means of writing than by the idea of another speaker borrowing the vocal machinery."

Well, that was sensible enough. Just like a séance. . . . Now the doctor began to motion with his hands. Sophie waited for his questions and prepared herself to make some illegible scrawls on the paper in front of her. Really it couldn't be too hard to fake. . . .

"Very good," said Braid, rubbing his hands together. "*Remarkably* good, for your first time. How very glad I am, Miss Hunter, that you telephoned my office!"

Sophie looked at him with amazement, slowly realizing that her right hand ached where she'd been clutching the pencil. A heap of pages of semilegible writing lay on the table between herself and Braid, pages he now swept up and out of her view before she could decode a single line.

But he'd only just begun! Surely she couldn't have fallen into a mesmeric trance without even realizing it?

She looked at her watch and saw that almost thirty minutes had passed since she'd last checked. But that had only been a few minutes ago!

Braid refrained from laughing at Sophie's incredulity.

"Everyone's taken aback the first few times," he said in a kindly manner. "Disconcerting, isn't it?"

"What did I say, though?" Sophie said, leaning forward and gripping the edge of the table, her knuckles white. "Did I say anything . . . *bad* ?"

"Miss Hunter, I assure you that you need never worry

about the confidentiality of what passes in this room," said the doctor. "All communications between us are privileged—and when I say 'us,' I include your other self, the self that emerges under hypnosis."

"So I do have another self? A self that wrote things down in answer to your questions?" Sophie asked, hardly able to believe it.

"Yes, and the nature of that self's responses has already suggested to me some further avenues of inquiry," Braid said.

"Can't you tell me what I wrote?" Sophie begged.

"No, I'm afraid I can't," said Braid, "for that might jeopardize the force of the therapeutic intervention later on. But we have some interesting weeks ahead of us, Miss Hunter, and I look forward very much to our collaboration."

He stood and shook hands with Sophie. It was strange to think that just half an hour earlier, she'd been eager to rush in and out of Braid's office at top speed so as to get on with her real mission.

Well, she would learn no more of her history today. She made an appointment for the following Thursday and asked the receptionist if she could use the washroom in the hall.

"Of course," said the young woman. "It's the first door on the left, toward the back."

"Thank you."

"Will you be all right letting yourself out?" the secretary asked.

Sophie looked and saw she was poised to go, scarf tied over her hair, handbag packed up, keys in hand ready to lock up.

"You see, usually I leave just at five," the girl continued apologetically, "and I've still got the shopping to do before I go home."

"I'll be fine," Sophie said, inwardly thanking the god of illicit investigations for this lucky break.

They left the office together, the receptionist locking the hall door after them ("Mr. Braid will be there hours longer," she explained) and rushing out the front door while Sophie let herself into the lavatory. She was so nervous by now that she thought she might be sick, but the sight of the toilet fixture calmed her stomach, and in the end she simply washed her hands and splashed cold water over her face.

She peered out into the hallway. Seeing nobody, she raced down the hall and out the garden door. Thankfully it hadn't an alarm system, just a dead bolt that opened quite easily from the inside. She entered the garden and pulled the door closed behind her. As it closed, she realized she might have stuck a bit of cardboard in the jamb to prevent it from shutting all the way.

Oh well, perhaps it wasn't locked.

She tried it.

Locked.

So that bridge was burned. She'd have to find another way out when she was finished.

She located a series of footholds on the sturdy wooden fence that separated the Braid Institute's garden from that of IRYLNS next door. Very cautiously, she lifted herself just high enough up to see over into the garden.

It was completely empty. Taking a deep breath, she pulled herself up and over the fence, then gracelessly dropped down to the ground on the other side, twisting her ankle, and stumbled forward. It felt like enemy territory, and the movement of a tabby cat on the other side of the garden almost made her scream.

THIRTY-SEVEN

S OPHIE'S OBJECTIVE ALL along had been to get into the locked ward. Even just a few pictures of girls like the ones she'd seen that day in the garden would surely make Priscilla and Jean take Sophie seriously. The windows at the back of the building were tiny and high off the ground and opened barely wide enough to allow a very small person to pass through, but there was no hope of getting by the guards at the front.

Some gardening equipment lay abandoned near the fence, and Sophie, feeling like a criminal (she supposed she *was* a criminal), dragged a wheelbarrow over to beneath the window, climbed up onto it, and peered inside.

The scene might have come straight from one of the famous photographs of the alienist Flaubert's patients at the

Salpêtrière in Paris. A host of young women in white hospital gowns wandered up and down a narrow central ward; others were visible through the doorways leading to the secondary wards.

About a third of the patients were in bed, a handful more in wheelchairs. Those lucky enough to remain ambulatory looked dazed and unhappy and somehow *damaged* in a way Sophie couldn't explain. She took Nan's camera out of her pocket and snapped a picture, but she would have to get nearer for the photographs to really be any good.

There were no nurses or other authority figures in sight, so far as Sophie could tell. She'd take the chance and go in.

Crossing her fingers for luck, Sophie hissed a few words through the window: "Hey! You, there!" Then, when a girl slowly turned her head toward Sophie: "Yes, you! Look, I need to get inside. Can you help me through the window?"

The girl's face showed an utter lack of understanding. Another girl, though, had stopped pacing up and down and come near.

"What is it?" she said, her speech slurred.

"I need to get in. And the window's got one of those security things; the screw's keeping me from pushing it up from the outside."

Some expression flitted across the girl's face, but Sophie couldn't read it.

At that point the wheelbarrow tilted beneath her, tipping her to the ground. After remounting, bruised and rather dirtier than before—thank goodness the camera wasn't broken—she found the other girl's face only inches from her own, her fingers fumbling with the screw over the sill.

Sophie tried another friendly overture. "What's your name?"

The girl looked up and opened her mouth, then closed it again, her face puzzled and pained.

"Don't remember," she mumbled finally, finding words with difficulty. "Been here for ages. No name. Don't remember coming here."

Despite the uncertainty of her fingers, she managed to loosen both screws and raise the window. She placed her hands on Sophie's wrists as Sophie fought to lift herself up onto the sill. It was a struggle, but she made it in an awful scrambly way that left her shaky and out of breath. It wasn't hard after that to swing her legs over the sill and slide in through the window.

Inside, Sophie found herself in the midst of a small mob. The girls thronged around her, congregating from all over the ward, and for a moment Sophie almost panicked.

Then one of the girls—it was hard to tell them apart with their identical gowns and cropped hair, here and there a bandage covering the downy tufts—stepped forward and leaned over her, as if to confide something important.

Sophie froze.

"They. *Watch*. Us," said the girl, using the pauses to tell Sophie something important. "Watch. Us. From. Off. Ward."

She looked inquiringly at Sophie, who caught on and said, "You have to block me from view?"

The girl gave a slow nod.

She must be heavily dosed with tranquilizers, Sophie thought. Or else—much worse—could it be massive neurological damage from the surgical procedure?

Sophie wanted to ask them all what had happened, to listen to each and every story so as to go out and bear witness. But she had, she thought, at most half an hour before the odds of being discovered would become disastrously high, and all she could sensibly do in that time was to gather enough evidence to persuade Jean and Priscilla to change their minds.

"I need to see the very worst," she said now to the girls pressed around her, speaking softly in case the authorities were monitoring the ward for sound. "I can't stay long—I mustn't be found here—but I've got two friends at school, and I need to tell them exactly why they shouldn't come to IRYLNS. I'll take pictures of whatever you show me, if you don't mind."

The girls consulted briefly with one another in garbled sentences she couldn't understand. Then three of them took

Sophie between them and moved her down the ward in a formation like fighter planes escorting a bomber, weaving in and out to mislead the watchers.

They stopped short next to a bed whose occupant seemed little more than a narrow, bolster-shaped lump under the covers. Maneuvering Sophie into position, the girl who'd first helped her climb through the window drew a set of curtains around the bed and made a series of gestures (easier for her than speech, Sophie guessed) to tell Sophie she now stood out of the watchers' sight.

Movements tentative, Sophie knelt by the bed and put a hand out to the place where she thought the girl's shoulder must be.

The girl in the bed groaned and rolled toward Sophie. One of the other occupants of the ward pulled down the covers so that Sophie could see the girl's face.

The girl in the bed was unmistakably Sophie's former idol Sheena Henshawe.

Her body was thin to the point of emaciation, and her arms and neck were covered with sores and rough discolored patches. Most of her hair was shaved down to uneven stubble, the remaining strands thin and colorless. A shunt taped to Sheena's head drained through a tube into a basin full of pus by the side of the bed (the smell was almost intolerable). An IV delivered fluids into her arm, and the bed was surrounded with a frightening amount of medical equipment.

This emptied-out shell of Sheena grunted and tried to pull herself up into a sitting position. Lacking the strength, she had to let the other girls prop her up.

Though it might have been more a function of her own desire than of anything really there, Sophie believed she saw a glimmer of recognition in Sheena's face.

"Sheena!" she cried out. "Whatever happened to you?"

Sheena shook her head. "Can't . . . tell," she said, her blistered lips hardly moving as she spoke. "Why . . . here?"

"I'm not here to undergo the training," Sophie said quickly. "I'm trying to stop my friends Jean and Priscilla from joining IRYLNS, and I thought if I could tell them about what really happens here, I'd be able to persuade them not to. Oh, Sheena, it must be stopped! Look at you. . . ."

The girl shook her head, too weak to answer.

"What *happened* to you, Sheena?" Sophie cried out.

She didn't know which transformation disturbed her more: the real Sheena into the gleaming, perfect secretary that day on the bridge, or that beautiful, well-groomed mannequin into the degraded wreck lying before her.

"Emotion . . . overload," Sheena mumbled. "Seizure. Surgery."

Her eyes appealed to Sophie for something Sophie couldn't identify. She tried and failed to come up with a tactful way of asking about Sheena's prognosis. Would Sheena ever get back to anything like normal health?

As a compromise, she said, "What will you do when you're well again?"

She was horrified to see the tears spill out of Sheena's eyes and down her rough, chapped cheeks.

"Only thing in the world I ever wanted," Sheena said, her words suddenly much clearer. "Best thing in the world. Serving my country. Can't do it now. Don't want to live."

Sophie stroked her arm and felt a furious surge of hatred for the people who had done this to Sheena.

"Sophie," Sheena said, clutching her hand so hard that Sophie jumped. "This place . . . all for good. Good of others. Greater good. Good of country. Highest good, IRYLNS. Friends . . ."

"But don't you think it should be stopped?" Sophie asked. "Sheena, look what they've done to you!"

Sheena shook her head, pulling herself up a little and digging her nails into Sophie's arm.

"More important, Sophie. You and the others . . . must come to IRYLNS. The country needs . . . Serve. You must."

Then she fell back onto the bed, shattered by the short conversation.

Sophie's horror exceeded anything she had ever felt before. She'd been so *sure* about this venture, so sure that the girls who'd been destroyed—destroyed not once but twice over—would welcome any chance to get the word out and save a few others. And here was the worst thing imaginable, Sheena Henshawe—Sophie's hero Sheena—reduced to this wreck of skin and bone, and yet still rehearsing the most coherent version she could manage of the message about duty and service and self-sacrifice.

It was the last thing in the world Sophie had expected, that she would find IRYLNS's most pitiful victim and be told that nothing was more important than giving oneself up for the cause.

She stared at Sheena and didn't know what to say.

"I won't tell the others," she said finally. It was the least she could do. She didn't have the right to go against Sheena's wishes, not really. "I won't say anything at all, if that's what you want."

As a faint smile came to Sheena's lips, the other girls who'd clustered around them suddenly froze.

Sophie looked up. "What is it?" she said.

Before she got an answer, though, she heard two familiar voices approaching the bed.

There was no way to escape discovery.

"Let's have a look at Sheena Henshawe," said one of the new arrivals.

"There's no chance she'll be of any further use," said the

other. "Will you send her to the asylum at Rothersay?"

"I think so," said the first speaker, "assuming she recovers from the infection. The worst-case scenario is that we'll have to place her in a nursing home. They're not really equipped at Rothersay for the level of care that girls like Sheena are liable to require."

A hand swept back the curtain around the bed, and Sophie found herself under the eyes of Great-aunt Tabitha and her friend Dr. Ferrier, the Institute's director and its most fanatical supporter.

THIRTY-EIGHT

FTER A HUMILIATING and painful interlude in which two burly male nurses hauled Sophie out of the ward and down the corridors to the director's office, Sophie found herself at the receiving end of a tirade from Great-aunt Tabitha.

The guards had confiscated Sophie's film and returned the camera to her with contempt.

As phrases like "I'll never trust you again" and "criminal trespass" rolled off Great-aunt Tabitha's tongue, Sophie had a sudden horrifying revelation, something to do with Mr. Braid's words about multiple selves.

"The J and H procedure—*J* and *H* don't just stand for *joy* and *happiness*, do they?" she said, breaking in on Great-aunt

Tabitha's speech. "The letters mean *Jekyll* and *Hyde* as well. . . . You split the girls off, into a good self and a bad one."

Silence followed Sophie's naming of the two selves in Robert Louis Stevenson's tale.

"I suppose Sophie might as well hear the real explanation," said Great-aunt Tabitha, exchanging a glance with Dr. Ferrier.

"Oh, yes, she might as well," said Dr. Ferrier. "I don't see how it can hurt *now*."

They had dismissed the guards. Sophie wasn't sure what her punishment would be, but she no longer thought she'd be thrown into prison.

"It began when I invented the machinery," Great-aunt Tabitha said. "The machine is the Emotional Battery, its logical complement is the J and H procedure, and as you've guessed, the abbreviation stands for something more—something *other* than 'joy and happiness.' Jekyll and Hyde . . . it has often been said that men are more rational creatures than women. I believe that men and women alike suffer from having emotions, but IRYLNS trains women to become repositories for all of the destructive emotions experienced by the men they work for, many of whom are politicians and diplomats who quite simply cannot *afford* to have a bad day. Wives have always known that part of their job is to bear the things their husbands cannot. We have simply taken the process one step further, fully modernized it, and put it on a technologically sound basis."

Sophie was speechless. Aside from everything else, it seemed so terribly unfair that the women should pay such a high price for what was after all the men's problem! Almost without knowing it, she put her hand up to her open mouth.

Now Dr. Ferrier took over. "Girls who undergo the surgical procedure must be regularly hooked up thereafter to the Emotional Battery," she told Sophie, "or else they will be less than supremely fit to do their jobs. We install a conduit in the brain that works like the electrical equivalent of the tap one inserts into a maple tree to drain off the sap to make sugar. Purged regularly in this manner, all their emotions stored in the battery, the girls soon become quite incapable of experiencing negative feelings. They make perfect empty vessels, then, for the rage of the men they work for. To sustain their peace of mind, we hook them up to the battery twice a week at a local service center, where the treatment can be administered in a modern and fully hygienic setting."

Sophie had a very vivid picture of Sheena's devastated body; thinking about what had happened to Sheena's mind was even worse.

"Sophie," said Great-aunt Tabitha, her voice softer than before, "it's pretty certainly going to come into law within the next few months that IRYLNS shall have every girl it asks for, the minute she turns sixteen. At that point, there won't be anything I can do to keep you out of it."

"So I'm going to have to come to IRYLNS?" Sophie asked, feeling like the stupidest person in the world.

"I wish you'd never seen any of this," said Great-aunt Tabitha, sighing and adjusting her body in her chair. "You've seen only the worst. There are wonderful aspects to the work we've done here too. Really wonderful! I'd have given anything to spare you this terrible foreknowledge."

"Anything?" said Sophie. "Then why can't you—"

Great-aunt Tabitha cut her off. "Anything but break the law," she said. "At this point, just when we're about to expand IRYLNS on a far grander scale than before, it would be a public relations disaster if anyone found out that one of the scheme's originators had pulled strings to get an exemption for a relative. And there's every reason to believe your conversion will go quite smoothly, without any negative impact on your health. It's only a very few girls who don't do well under our regime. Some of them even get married in the end— there's no real reason they shouldn't. You understand what I'm saying, don't you, Sophie?"

Sophie understood.

"Susan, do you think we can handle this without the police?" asked Great-aunt Tabitha.

"Certainly," said Dr. Ferrier. "No need for them now—I

388

can see Sophie quite understands what's required of her. We won't see any repetition of this little incident, will we, Sophie?"

Sophie shook her head.

"I'm going to take you back to school in a taxi," Great-aunt Tabitha said. "Peggy will collect you after school tomorrow, and from now on, there won't be a moment when you'll be allowed out of sight of one or the other of us, except when you're at school. I'll notify your teachers that you need to be kept under close supervision because of a security threat. We'll keep this up through the time when you actually get admitted to the program at IRYLNS. And within a week of coming here, you'll no longer have the faintest desire to leave."

No longer have the faintest desire—Sophie thought her heart might actually stop beating, she was so frightened by her great-aunt's calm certainty.

They sat together in silence until Great-aunt Tabitha moved to collect her things.

"Thank you, Susan," she said, shaking the director's hand.

"I'll look forward to meeting you again under happier circumstances, Sophie," said the director to Sophie.

Sophie muttered a few words in return, but nobody—not even herself—knew exactly what they were. The older women let the lapse in manners pass.

"I won't be sixteen until December," Sophie said in the car. The words sounded pitiful, even to her, but it was too late to take them back.

Great-aunt Tabitha just looked at her. Sophie hung her head. There was nothing more to say.

Sophie's great-aunt dropped her back at school, coming in herself to make sure Sophie wouldn't be able to skive off. What she said to the housemistress, Sophie would never know, but back in the girls' bedroom, getting ready to lie down, Sophie thought she'd never survive the others' idle chatter.

"Any more tales about the horrors of IRYLNS?" Priscilla even asked, laughing when Sophie shook her head and got into bed without saying good night.

As she lay in bed, trying and failing to fall asleep, dreading the prospect of Peggy arriving tomorrow to pick her up as if she were still a little girl, hardly knowing how to console herself at the prospect of months of virtual imprisonment followed by a transformation in which she would permanently lose herself, Sophie thought that perhaps she should overcome her scruples and run away with Mikael after all. Would she even be able to get away to meet him, though? And without a visa, how would she get onto the ship? Knowing what she did now about IRYLNS, she wondered whether that wasn't the reason Scotland regulated travel visas so strictly, much more strictly than any of the other Hanseatic states.

Sophie drifted through the day on Friday and met Peggy in the front of the school without saying a word. In her bedroom at home, she found the planchette she'd used as a toy when she was younger, and idly set it up on its little table. Resting her fingertips on the little rolling platform, she asked the spirits whether she should try to leave with Mikael.

But rather than moving to *yes* or *no*, or spelling out words by pointing to letters of the alphabet, the planchette simply meandered over the table.

In a dull stupor, Sophie went downstairs and put a telephone call through to Mikael.

The professor answered, and Sophie exchanged a few words with him before asking to speak to Mikael.

She thought Mikael might be able to tell something was wrong, to read her mind and somehow break her out of the cloud preventing her from exercising proper self-determination. If he would only say he *wanted* her, if he himself only felt about Sophie the way she felt about him, all her difficulties would vanish and she would go *joyfully* with him.

But when Mikael came on the line, he sounded distracted. After thanking her for calling, he fell silent. And then, even as Sophie cast about for a way to broach the topic of København—there *had* to be some fashion in which she could take him up on his offer without being a burden, there just *had* to be, and he had said himself that Mr. Petersen might find a way around the visa difficulty—Mikael cut her off.

"Look, I'm sorry, Sophie, but I've got something I must go and do now, something really important."

It was as if he'd dug a skewer straight into her eye socket. *Something really important!* It wasn't as though *Sophie* was important, of course, not even when her sanity—her life—was at stake. Some small part of her could smell the self-pity—the silliness—in the way she was handling all this, but she didn't have the energy to change course.

"Best of luck, Sophie. I'm sure it will be all right. You'll write me a letter as soon as anything happens about you-know-what, won't you? And you know you can ask my brother for help at any time."

Then Mikael put down the telephone before Sophie could even say good-bye.

Sophie had imagined *she'd* be the one to cut their conversation short, in an understated but noble gesture of self-sacrifice.

It must be more fun to be the person leaving than the person left behind. Who knew how much longer she would remain the person she was now, anyway?

Sophie had never felt so alone in her entire life.

Great-aunt Tabitha popped her head around the study door and gave Sophie a sharp look, making Sophie fear she would never be allowed a moment of privacy again, but she kept her face still and submissive. There was no point seeming outwardly rebellious.

"You'll be ready to go first thing in the morning, won't you, Sophie?" said Great-aunt Tabitha.

"Go where?" Sophie said. Surely not to IRYLNS, not yet?

"It's the annual outing of the New Town Women's Spiritualist Association," her great-aunt said. "I expect you to come with us so I can keep an eye on you."

"No!" said Sophie, feeling for the first time as if she might break down and cry. She hadn't been dragged on one of these trips since she was quite a small child; she always stayed at home with Peggy instead. Her great-aunt *knew* how self-conscious it made Sophie to trail around after the idealistic middle-aged ladies who made up the cohort. "Please, Great-aunt Tabitha, please don't make me go. . . ."

But Great-aunt Tabitha was adamant.

"You've forfeited the right to be treated like an adult," she said. "How can I trust you, Sophie, after you broke your word not to pry? No, I want you under my own supervision when you're not at school."

Seeing there was no chance of her great-aunt relenting, Sophie went upstairs and packed her overnight bag. At first she put in just the bare essentials—toilet bag with toothbrush and flannel, pajamas, clean underclothes. But the valise seemed to sit there and reproach her.

Something grew in her as she stood there in the middle of the room, a feeling so unfamiliar she wasn't even sure at first what it was.

Sophie was furious.

She was absolutely enraged!

She felt like one of the avengers in a Greek tragedy. How dare Great-aunt Tabitha paper over the violence being done to hundreds of girls in the name of patriotism? Did she not care about them at all? How could she be willing to sacrifice *Sophie*?

It came to Sophie in a flash that she had to leave, she couldn't *not* leave. She supposed she would honor Sheena's wishes by not telling the others about IRYLNS. But she, Sophie, was not bound to immolate herself for the greater good.

She had the right to make her own choice. And she chose not to destroy herself.

It was amazing how much calmer Sophie felt now. She lay down on the bed and began to think about what to do.

She could slip out in the middle of the night, lie low somewhere until the late afternoon, and then meet Mikael at Leith. But she didn't have a visa. Without one, they wouldn't let her aboard. And Mikael was angry with her, or else why would he have cut short their conversation like that? The last thing she wanted was to force her company on an unwilling partner.

She had to find a way of getting an exit visa, and then make her own plans to escape. Mr. Petersen would help her. She would go and speak to him first thing Monday morning. With his Nobel connections, he would almost certainly be able to get her a visa and a safe place to go to, perhaps even in Stockholm rather than København so that it wouldn't look as though she were chasing after Mikael, and then everything would be all right.

Now that she'd come to a decision, the idea of waiting even until Monday seemed almost unbearable, but it wouldn't do any good to fuss. Still, she added to her bag a few other things she felt funny about leaving behind, just in case she got a chance to escape this weekend after all: her passport, the beaten-up leather slippers that had once belonged to her father, a photograph of her parents on their wedding day, the small soapstone elephant named Horatio that usually lived on Sophie's bedside table. She crammed all her money into her purse and tucked it out of sight at the bottom of the case. It would be silly not to have it with her if some opportunity for flight presented itself. As an afterthought, she tucked in her chemistry textbook.

She got a surprisingly good night's sleep, the best one she'd had for ages. Decision-making as a remedy for insomnia—now, there was a thought. If only she could speak to Mr. Petersen right away!

THIRTY-NINE

THE VEHICLE HIRED FOR the expedition was a bright maroon charabanc, its seats covered in a lurid bottle-green leather substitute. A green-and-yellow-striped fringed canopy had been raised to protect the ladies' complexions from the Saturday morning sun. As president of the New Town Women's Spiritualist Association, Great-aunt Tabitha had designated Heriot Row for the morning rendezvous, and as the driver leaned on the hood of the charabanc smoking a cigarette, she scanned the horizon for stragglers.

The ladies of the NTWSA were scheduled to arrive at the Nobel dynamite factory by midmorning—Sophie was particularly dreading this part of the trip, as it brought to mind her parents' untimely deaths at the factory's Russian counterpart—then take a tour of the facilities, to be followed by a late lunch. In the afternoon they would pick wildflowers in the countryside, spending the night at the Ayrshire Temperance Hotel and visiting Culzean Castle and the Electric Brae the next day before returning home in time for Sunday afternoon tea.

As the last few ladies arrived, Peggy ran out the front door and pressed a packet of barley sugar into Sophie's hand.

Tears came to Sophie's eyes. Only Peggy ever remembered that Sophie got carsick.

"Thank you, Peggy," she said, and wished the housekeeper a nice weekend, though the words seemed quite inadequate to her feelings.

Peggy snorted at the idea of herself having a nice weekend, but she stayed outside and waved at Sophie from the front doorstep until the bus turned the corner.

As they drove out of Edinburgh to the main road that ran west to the coast, Sophie found the movement of the charabanc distinctly sickness inducing. She popped a piece of barley sugar into her mouth and sank down low in her seat. She would have been quite interested to talk to Miss Grant again—she might know more by now about the minister and Nicko Mood, mightn't she?—but Miss Grant sat in the front seat, sequestered in conversation with Great-aunt Tabitha.

Once they reached the main road, Sophie stopped feeling

so queasy, and when Miss Gillespie passed around the inevitable Kelvinsulated flasks of warm milky tea, Sophie accepted a cup and a shortbread biscuit. There was plenty to look at on the way, and she was surprised by how quickly they reached the tiny coastal station where they would board the train for the very last part of the journey to Ardeer.

The Nobel factory lay on an industrial estate served by a private road, but a narrow-gauge railway ran all the way in to the gates of the factory, where the private train station admitted workers and a few select visitors.

Sitting in the railway carriage as they traveled toward the compound, Sophie looked out over the isolated coastal landscape and remembered Alfred Nobel's notorious loathing for this place. He had written of Ardeer to his brother, in a letter reprinted in the leaflets the train conductor gave them with their tickets:

> *Picture to yourself everlasting bleak sand dunes with no buildings. Only rabbits find a little nourishment here; they eat a substance which quite unjustifiably goes by the name of grass. It is a sand desert where the wind always blows often howls filling the ears with sand. Between us and America, there is nothing but water a sea whose mighty waves are always raging and foaming. Now you will have some idea of the*

place where I am living. Without work the place would be intolerable.

But Sophie found it rather beautiful.

It was no accident, of course, that the factory had been built in such a desolate place. The English Explosives Acts of the 1860s made it impossible to build dynamite factories south of Hadrian's Wall, but Scotland welcomed them, so long as they were built far from populated areas and in accordance with the provisions of the Carriage and Deposit of Dangerous Goods Act. The Ardeer factory was now owned and operated by the Nobel Consortium, the sophisticated transnational holding company that managed what had once been Nobel's personal empire.

They got off the train at a platform lacking even the most basic railway-station amenities—no newspaper stall, no flower seller, not even a coin-operated chocolate machine—to find stringent security measures in place. Guards with Alsatians patrolled the barbed-wire perimeter, and the security officer at the gatehouse checked each woman's national identity card against the names on the prearranged list of visitors. Fortunately Great-aunt Tabitha had telephoned ahead to add Sophie's name to the list, or she would have been left under the supervision of the guards while the others took their tour.

They were all asked to deposit their bags in the gatehouse,

along with any personal items made of metal, which led to great indignation on the part of two ladies who had to retire and take off their steel-boned corsets and another one who didn't want to put aside her cigarettes and lighter. Though smoking was not at all the thing in Great-aunt Tabitha's circle, this lady was an old-fashioned Decadent who wore vegetable-dyed handwoven scarves and smoked a special mentholated tobacco to clear her airways. She left behind her smoking paraphernalia only after a serious dressing-down from Great-aunt Tabitha. They would be searched again, of course, before being allowed to enter the buildings where nitroglycerin was actually produced.

"We've got a very special lecturer for the occasion," said Great-aunt Tabitha as she herded the ladies away from the gate to the building where the tour would begin. "He'll be here any moment now. Sophie, I think you'll enjoy this bit of the tour, I don't know why you're looking so sullen."

In the minutes that followed, Sophie's great-aunt checked her watch a few times, irritation growing.

When their guide finally appeared, Sophie almost fell over in shock. It was Mr. Petersen!

He greeted Great-aunt Tabitha with a firm handshake, apologizing profusely for keeping them all waiting. Great-aunt Tabitha introduced him to all the ladies and he shook everyone's hand, including Sophie's.

"Nice to see you, Sophie," he said quietly.

Sophie couldn't help the surge of pleasure that rose in her heart at finding him here. Now if only she could snag him for a few minutes of conversation, she could tell him she'd decided she must leave and ask for his help. It was progress, distinct progress!

"Mr. Petersen," Great-aunt Tabitha told the others complacently, "is a research chemist in the employ of Mr. Alfred Nobel. He has kindly agreed to show us about today, and will take questions afterward."

"The Nobel Consortium produces more than half the world's dynamite," said Mr. Petersen as they walked toward the first building. Oh, he was in his element here, all right! If ever a person loved talking about explosives, it was Mr. Petersen. "Dynamite is used most frequently for the purpose of demolition, as in mining and tunneling. It's also used in bombs, warheads, and mines, but not in guns, as the rapidity and intensity of the blast would shatter a metal barrel. By the end of the last century, it had become illegal to manufacture nitroglycerin and dynamite in Europe and the Americas, and the production of dynamite has since then been almost exclusively the charge of the Hanseatic states."

"Isn't it awfully dangerous, though?"

The words came from Miss Grant, whose calm confidence made the question sound almost mocking.

"Well, it's true that nitroglycerin's immensely volatile," said Mr. Petersen, "but we take every possible precaution. And the compound we call dynamite's actually quite safe: it burns rather than exploding when it's set on fire, and aside from deliberately detonating it with caps and fuses, the only way to ignite it involves compression and a high degree of heat. All the explosives manufactured here are tested for stability in two subsidiary departments known as India and Siberia; in India, as you might guess, the explosive material is subjected to extreme and protracted heat, whereas in Siberia, the temperature is kept very cold."

"But there must be some risk?" said Great-aunt Tabitha. "It's an immensely powerful explosive, after all, isn't it?"

"Pound for pound, the explosive force of Dynamite Number One is four times that of gunpowder," said Mr. Petersen, looking solemn, "and it's also much denser, so that the same volume of explosive ends up being over seven times as powerful."

Most of the ladies shivered. Sophie thought they were enjoying this measured flirtation with destruction.

Half an hour into the tour, Sophie was so stunned and impressed by what she was seeing that she'd temporarily forgotten the troubles pressing down upon her. The factory was self-contained, with steam provided by a central boiler house, and electricity and compressed air produced at the on-site power station. Though the four-hundred-acre industrial compound was mostly open to the air, the clustering of tunnels and tramways and pipelines gave parts of it the semienclosed feel of a railway yard. It was quite extraordinary to think that only seventy years earlier, this had been a barren waste of sand dunes stretching down to the sea.

There were more than three hundred buildings, many of them with their own chimney stacks, and Mr. Petersen enumerated some of their functions: the acid works and acid-recovery plant, the mills for processing ammonia and potash and kieselguhr, the steam- and powerhouses, the departments for washing and carding and bleaching the fleecy fiber that would be nitrated into guncotton, the pulping mill and box factories, all connected to one another by the rather sweet little narrow-gauge railway.

The workers wore color-coded coveralls so that the factory superintendents could see at a glance whether a worker was out of place—dark blue for the runners and carriers, light blue for workers assigned to the smokeless powder factory, scarlet for the nitroglycerin house—and the pattern of the colors made the scene look like a modern painting when Sophie squinted a little. There were lots of other things to look at too, including a pond that was blown up once a week by a safety officer to destroy the dregs of nitroglycerin that drained into it and an armory attached to a shooting range where they tested explosives for rifles and shotguns. Sophie stopped being sorry at having been made to come and started—amazingly—actually to enjoy herself.

At the acid works where the constituent parts of nitroglycerin were made, they learned that whereas glycerin—a natural byproduct of soap making, in which fats were boiled with wood ash or some other alkali—was quite safe to produce, nitric acid was extremely dangerous. It was manufactured in enormous steel retorts, six feet across and bricked up like ovens, from oil of vitriol shipped by canal from Laurieston and then combined with nitrate of soda. The acid was subsequently forced in the form of a suffocating reddish gas through an elaborate system of pipes to condense in jars on shelves. The liquid would then be pumped by compressed air into tanks at the top of the nitroglycerin hills, artificial grass-covered embankments (mostly conical, often sixty or seventy feet high) built to contain accidents.

The factory compound contained four of these hills, each with two separate nitrating houses, frail-looking white shingled cabins. The liquid nitroglycerin would flow back down the hill to the processing rooms, propelled only by the force of its own weight so as to minimize the risk of accidental detonation.

Security at the nitroglycerin hut was much tighter than anywhere they'd been so far. A guard at the entrance checked their visitor's passes for a second time, and a female searcher examined each of them.

Mr. Petersen told them that even workers who came in and out of the building three or four times a day would be searched every time they passed through the door. Sophie thought him naïve for believing this—it was human nature to become lax—but she hoped everyone had been checked properly today, at any rate. Thinking about it made her feel slightly sick, her parents' fate at the forefront of her mind.

Several of the other women seemed to share Sophie's worries.

"Are you really sure none of these workers break the rules?" one of them asked.

The female searcher laughed. "It's hardly in their own interest to break the rules, now, is it?" she said. "They're the ones who'll be blown up if they do. There's a long list of prohibitions. The young women aren't allowed to wear pins in their hair, metal corsets, or metal buttons; you can see they've all got their hair plaited and the ends fastened with elastic. A few years ago, a band came to play at a factory dance, and one of the musicians lit up a cigarette without thinking. There was practically a riot! I thought the girls would tear him to pieces—they had him on the ground in a flash, with his arms pinned so he couldn't endanger anyone."

Once everyone had been checked, they stepped into

rubber overshoes provided by the company. NO SHOE THAT TOUCHES THE GROUND OUTSIDE MAY TOUCH THE FLOOR OF A DANGER DEPARTMENT, a sign warned, and Mr. Petersen explained that it was because the grit might produce friction and spark an explosion.

At the center of the nitroglycerin hut stood two lead cylinders, each five feet in diameter and six feet deep, sunk into the floor and protected with dome-shaped tops, the lead pipes curling in and out of them. By each tank, a scarlet-clad man watched the thermometer while sitting perched on one of the strangest contraptions Sophie had ever seen, a one-legged stool that would topple to the ground if the watcher relaxed his attention even for a second. Mr. Petersen explained that the special stools had been designed as a safety measure to stop the watchers from falling asleep and missing the kind of temperature fluctuation that would merit an evacuation.

What really caught Sophie's imagination and made her skin crawl was the sheer volume of the liquid nitroglycerin. Thousands and thousands of gallons of it ran throughout the building in pipes that spewed out *waterfalls* of nitroglycerin, cream-colored streams shooting out of lead gutters into enormous tanks where the explosive rose to the surface to be skimmed off by young women wielding gigantic aluminum ladles like washbasins with handles. From there it was poured into tanks to be rinsed, first with cold water and then with warm water mixed with carbonate of soda.

One of the guards who'd checked them in appeared and took Mr. Petersen aside for a quick word. When he came back, he looked worried, though not excessively so.

"Will you excuse me, ladies?" he said. "I must take a telephone call. Many apologies."

Fortunately the women of the NTWSA were so thoroughly immersed in learning about working conditions and the inequalities of pay between men and women that they hardly minded his going, particularly when one of the managers offered to take the next part of the tour.

"Sophie, would you mind coming with me?" Mr. Petersen said to Sophie while nobody was listening.

"If you like," said Sophie, suddenly very nervous.

What was all this about?

FORTY

THE GUARD LED THEM around an obstacle course of hills and outbuildings to a place called the communications room. It struck Sophie as an awfully fancy name for a hut with a telephone switchboard, until they got inside and saw the row of telephone operators, girls as slick and professional-looking as one could imagine.

"Our telephonists are trained by the General Post Office in Glasgow," said the guard, sounding very proud.

But Sophie thought they had that look, the look that said IRYLNS, and she shrank away from their glossy sameness.

"Your call should come through in about ten minutes," said one of the operators, giving Sophie and Mr. Petersen an impersonal smile. "Perhaps you'd like to wait in the lounge next door. Can I fetch anyone a coffee?"

She showed Sophie and Mr. Petersen to the small lounge opening off one side of the shed, then brought them each a cup of coffee.

"I must admit this was a ploy on my part," said Mr. Petersen once they found themselves alone together.

"What do you mean?" Sophie asked.

"I didn't lie when I said we needed to come here to receive a phone call," said Mr. Petersen. "But I'm afraid I was a bit cavalier with the truth, Sophie. The telephone call's not for me. It's for you."

Sophie felt the blood pound in her ears.

"It's not—," she began, then couldn't think how to say it. "That is—"

"What?" said Mr. Petersen, setting down his coffee cup and looking at her with concern. "What's wrong, Sophie?"

"It's not a telephone call from a *dead* person, is it?" she asked.

Mr. Petersen looked startled.

"Why would you think I'd put you on the line with a dead person?" he said, sounding rather wary.

"It's just that I seem to have had an awful lot of spirit communications recently," Sophie confessed. "I thought this might be another one."

Mr. Petersen did a double take.

"You mean the drawing that came over the pantelegraph wasn't the only one?"

"Far from it," said Sophie. It struck her that she could speak to him now almost as one adult to another. No trace of that painful crush remained. "At least the others made a bit more sense. The drawing—well, let's just say I don't have a clue as to who sent it or why."

A little old lady in a flowered coverall came in and cleared away their cups, giving the table an aggressive wipe.

"We'll have to look into this," said Mr. Petersen. "I want to hear more about it, but now simply isn't the time. Sophie, assuming the operator is able to put the call through, you're about to receive a person-to-person call from Mr. Alfred Nobel."

"Alfred Nobel?" said Sophie, now more perplexed than frightened. "You're pulling my leg, Mr. Petersen, aren't you? When people say *Nobel*, they mean the company, not the man. If Alfred Nobel were alive today, he'd be over a hundred years old. And in any case, alive or dead, what could he possibly want with me?"

The charwoman had come back in during Sophie's speech—she must have been cleared by security, or Mr. Petersen would have prevented Sophie from saying anything in front of her—and she now surprised both Sophie and Mr. Petersen by looking up from polishing the side table and saying, "Oh, he's not alive, dearie, not really. They say it's his brain, sitting in a very superior jam jar somewhere in the countryside in Sweden!"

Mr. Petersen gave her a repressive look and she subsided, but not before a picture flashed into Sophie's head of a brain in a jar, rigged up to a speaking trumpet from which the pronouncements of Alfred Nobel were broadcast to his underlings.

"I suppose the truth's not so far off," Mr. Petersen admitted.

Would he have said anything if the old woman hadn't brought it up?

"Alfred Nobel exists in a kind of limbo," the teacher continued. "He is highly selective these days about what business he attends to, but there are a few things he won't let go of, including his dream that one day weapons will have become so advanced that two armies may mutually annihilate each other in a second. At that time, of course, the civilized nations will recoil with horror and disband their armies, which will in turn lead to world peace. Here's the thing, Sophie: The scientists who work for him are probably only months away from creating precisely the explosive he's dreamed of, a bomb so powerful that the world's great powers may abjure war for once and for all."

Sophie had never quite accepted Theodor Herzl's famous

proposition that the man who discovered a terrible explosive would do more for peace than a thousand of its milder apostles, but Mr. Petersen certainly seemed to believe what he was saying. Could it be true? Why was Mr. Petersen telling her about it *now*?

"What does all this have to do with me?" she asked. "Me in particular, I mean, not me as a person who in general might like there to be world peace?"

"I've been privileged to serve as one of Mr. Nobel's personal assistants," said Mr. Petersen. "He has sworn an oath that he won't die until certain conditions have been fulfilled, and my job is to help bring about those conditions, for Mr. Nobel is tired of life, Sophie, or rather of the half-life he now has. Without your help, nothing can go forward."

"That's ridiculous!" Sophie said.

"Sophie, what do I have to say to persuade you that your potential to affect the course of events in the Hanse is simply enormous?"

The girls and boys who experienced untoward events in storybooks always pinched themselves to make sure they were awake. Sophie gave herself a hard pinch now—somehow it was almost impossible to give oneself a really painful pinch—and found it altered nothing.

"Why me rather than anybody else?" she persisted. "There's nothing special about me."

"I was sent by Mr. Nobel to teach you and to protect you," Mr. Petersen repeated. "Also to persuade you that you must leave Scotland for the next stage of your education."

"You were *sent*?" Sophie said, seizing on the part of the pronouncement that made the least sense of all. Leaving Scotland, now, well, *that* sounded like an extremely sensible idea. . . . Was he really going to help?

Mr. Petersen sighed.

"Sophie, I really must apologize to you. Because of Miss Rawlins's poor judgment, you've already gathered that I obtained my position at school under false pretenses. I'd been asked to do whatever was necessary to get the position, at the behest of my employer, Mr. Nobel."

"Wouldn't you have been more useful to him doing your real job than messing about teaching us chemistry?" said Sophie. Something about the way he spoke of Mr. Nobel annoyed her; it was almost *worshipful*. "Why did he want you in Edinburgh?"

"Why do you think?"

"To help the police prevent any more bombings?" Sophie guessed.

"At least you've given up the idea that I was the éminence grise running the Brothers of the Northern Liberties! You know, I was on the verge of telling you all this that day weeks ago before we were caught in the blast from the Canongate

413

explosion, but I thought the better of it."

It all would have been much easier if he'd told her everything then, but there was no point regretting it. Sophie didn't believe in looking back and wishing things had gone differently. If only she had known Mikael's real last name, she would have realized much sooner that Mr. Petersen could be trusted. All this put her in mind of the most urgent question. "Mr. Petersen, do you think you can get me an exit visa?"

"It may not be necessary," said Mr. Petersen, looking mysteriously pleased with himself. "The main reason Mr. Nobel sent me to Edinburgh was to persuade you to come with me when I leave the country."

"Me?" Sophie asked, by now completely stymied. She hadn't even explained yet about IRYLNS, and here he was anticipating her request! "Why would he care about me? How did he even know I existed?"

"I still can't tell you that, Sophie. But the telephone call we're waiting for will reveal more. You're about to talk to Mr. Nobel himself. It's a very great honor—he hardly communicates with anyone outside the organization these days."

At that moment one of the operators appeared and beckoned to Sophie to follow.

She looked back at Mr. Petersen as the young woman led her toward the main room, but he simply settled down more comfortably in his chair, crossed his arms across his chest, and smiled.

"Go on, Sophie," he said. "It's just a telephone call. It can't hurt to talk."

FORTY-ONE

W HEN THE FOLDING DOOR closed and she found
herself alone in the mahogany-lined telephone
booth, Sophie felt a wave of claustrophobia so
intense she thought she might actually pass out. She leaned
her forehead against one side of the booth—an electric light
had come on overhead when the doors closed—and tried to
collect her thoughts.

It was just a telephone call. What was she afraid of?

She picked up the receiver and held it to her ear.

"This is Sophie Hunter," she said into the mouthpiece, hearing nothing but a mild hissing on the line. "Is anybody there?"

"Sophie," a voice whispered. "I am so very glad that we
are finally in touch with each other."

Nobel's voice sounded familiar, but she couldn't think from where. Had she heard a speech of his on the radio? As she cast about for the memory, he continued to talk.

"I do not have much strength, and so we will not speak long. There is much, in any case, that I cannot say to you until we meet in person. My enemies have a long reach, and even a secure telephone line presents risks. When you come to me in Sweden, we will be able to talk freely."

The country's name gave her the clue she needed. She was so surprised, she blurted the words right out.

"You spoke to me already! Yours was the spirit voice that came through Mrs. Tansy that night in Heriot Row. You told me to be careful and to keep my own counsel, and you promised me a journey over water! How—? Why—?"

"I had my own reasons for contacting you in that way," said the voice, sounding wearier and less hopeful than anything Sophie had ever heard in her life. "Reasons I mustn't reveal until we meet in person. I spoke to you that night under quite peculiar circumstances. Obviously I am not dead, though I find myself in an equivocal state of embodiment these days. One of my agents—indeed, it was your Mr. Petersen—paid Mrs. Tansy a substantial sum to ingratiate herself with your guardian, serve as the medium for that night's séance, and make sure you were involved from start to finish."

"That was why she asked for me to come and see her

checked beforehand!" Sophie said, the pieces of the puzzle falling into place.

"You were known to be skeptical about the manifestations of the spirit world," said the voice. "I thought that would be the best way of inclining you toward belief. The medium had no idea, though, that I actually meant to use her body as a vessel through which to communicate with you."

"But I still don't see what you wanted with me!" Sophie said, almost more confused than before.

"My life's work has been to give the world peace," said the voice. "Fifteen years ago, we were on the verge of making what I'd dreamed of, a weapon so powerful that the very threat of its use would cause grown men to quake in their boots: the holy grail of deterrence and the necessary precursor, or so it seemed to me, of world peace."

The voice fell silent. It was still hard to think of it as belonging to Alfred Nobel; Sophie was trying not to concentrate on the whole "brain in a jar" end of things.

"What happened then?" Sophie asked.

"A tragedy," said the voice. "The work had been conducted in the utmost secrecy in an enclave within a Russian munitions factory. For security reasons, there were no records outside the facility of the key mechanism; even I myself had only a vague idea as to how the thing worked. And then the factory blew up, destroying all records and killing its creator, along with many others."

"Fifteen years ago," Sophie said slowly. "Was that—"

The voice cut her off. "Yes, Sophie. That was the factory explosion that killed your parents, and your father was the inventor of the miraculous weapon. All these long years, I have believed there to be no way of recovering what was lost. But recently I learned that a second set of plans survived the blast. We must lay hands on it before it can be used by the wrong people, people who wish to dominate the world rather than give it peace."

Sophie's head whirled with a million questions. She didn't know where to start.

"I will tell you more," said the voice, "when you arrive at my estate. Petersen will instruct you about the journey. Meanwhile, I ask you to give him your complete confidence. Au revoir, Sophie."

"Wait!" Sophie shouted.

But the voice had gone.

When the operator came on the line to ask if she needed to place another call, Sophie put the receiver back in its cradle and slumped onto the shelf at the side of the booth, head in her hands.

A knock came at the door.

Sophie opened it partway and saw Mr. Petersen peering through the gap.

"Well?" he said.

Sophie shook her head and glared at him. "I can't believe you've been keeping all this from me," she said.

"I was afraid you'd feel like that," said Mr. Petersen. "All I can do is apologize and say—"

But at this juncture they were interrupted by the same guard who'd appeared to summon Sophie and Mr. Petersen for the telephone call.

They could see at once that something was wrong.

"Sir?" he said, his face pale and sweaty.

"What is it?" said Mr. Petersen, sounding annoyed.

Sophie crossed her fingers and prayed there hadn't been an accident. Surely they would have heard the explosion?

"We've got a, well, a *situation*," the man said.

"A situation?"

"Well, what I'd call a situation, sir."

"Can't you be more specific? What kind of a situation?"

"There's an intruder in the dynamite house."

"What sort of intruder?"

"We don't know yet," said the guard, "but it doesn't look good. The ladies had just got to that spot on the tour, so we've got a high civilian presence even beyond the workers."

Mr. Petersen turned to look at Sophie. "Every bone in my body's telling me to get you away safely out of here, but I'm going to do you the courtesy of treating you as an adult.

Do you want to come with me?"

Sophie nodded.

They raced outside and hopped into one of the carts for transporting people and goods. En route, Mr. Petersen told Sophie what to expect in the dynamite house, a long wooden cabin where liquid nitroglycerin soaked into the porous siliceous earth called kieselguhr to become dynamite. The mixture was transported in a wooden box on a handcart known as a bogie to the mixing area at the other end of the building. There the young women would give the boxes another stir and then tip the blend into smaller boxes with brass sieves in them, rubbing the dynamite through small holes in the sieve. The loose, crumbling, coffee-colored dynamite went next to the cartridge houses, where the workers pulled pump handles to force rods through hoppers, jamming the dynamite down brass tubes at the bottom. A parchment square was wrapped around the bottom of each tube, folded off at the lower end, and tamped down. Each three-inch cartridge had its top folded over and was then dropped through a slide in the wall, where it rolled into a box of finished cartridges. The five-pound boxes would be grouped into fifty-pound wooden cases and taken by bogie down to the beach, where the narrow-gauge lines ran straight to the sea. From the jetty at the southeast end of the peninsula, the cases would be loaded into boats and then into the company's own steamers for shipment all over the world.

Still a few minutes short of their destination, Mr. Petersen showed no sign of stopping his bizarre account of how dynamite was manufactured.

"Why are you telling me all this?" Sophie said finally.

"Oh, gods," said Mr. Petersen. "I'm sorry, Sophie. I suppose rambling on like this is the way I calm myself down in times of trouble. What I wouldn't do right now for a cigarette! But obviously that's out of the question. . . ."

"What are we going to do when we get there?" Sophie asked.

"Whatever we can," said Mr. Petersen, suddenly sober.

Inside the dynamite house, they could see at once that the situation had escalated. This wasn't a simple question of an unidentified intruder. The unexpected arrival—of all people in the world!—was Nicko Mood. He had a gun in his hand, his clothes were disheveled, and in short he looked remarkably like a man about to blow up hundreds of people (including himself) without a second thought.

"Sophie Hunter!" he said when he saw her.

On the other side of the room, all the workers and lady visitors stood with their hands on their heads.

Mr. Petersen pushed Sophie behind him, but Mood wrenched her arm almost out of her socket and dragged her to his side.

Great-aunt Tabitha looked on dispassionately as he held his gun to Sophie's head.

"It's still possible for you to escape with your life," Sophie's great-aunt told Mood. "If you commandeered one of the ships at the jetty, you could be away in no time. Even if you don't give a fig for the rest of us, surely you'd rather live than die?"

"It may be hard for you to believe, Tabitha, but I have nothing left to live for. The deal you cut with Joanna leaves no place for me. She has forced me to write a letter of resignation, and made me promise to retire from the public eye. Life as I know it is over, and with my career ruined, I don't know that I care much for the little bit of living that's left to me. I might as well take a few of you with me when I go."

Mr. Petersen was making faces at Sophie while Nicko looked in Great-aunt Tabitha's direction. His gestures and her own common sense told Sophie they should try to keep the man talking to spin things out as long as they could. It would take Mr. Petersen quite a while to come back with help.

As the teacher crept away, Mood fell silent.

"What I want to know," Sophie said hastily as Nicko Mood began fiddling with his gun (it had just occurred to her that a bullet puncturing a tank would be enough to set off an explosion), "is why you thought you'd be able to get away with the murders on top of everything else. When you hired the Veteran to kill Mrs. Tansy, you left a trail of evidence that any halfway decent investigator could have uncovered. How did you think you'd ever get away with it?"

Nicko looked angry, but at least he stopped waving the gun around.

"The plan was flawless but not foolproof," he said. "The Veteran was supposed to frame Nobel's man for the medium's murder, but he flubbed the business, as he fouled up everything he put his dirty little hands to."

So that was how Mr. Petersen's knife had ended up at the hotel!

"We had set up all the evidence to implicate Europe in the terror attacks," Nicko said. "All I had to do was wait for a discreet interval to pass, and the minister would have had the whole government in the palm of her hand. But your wretched great-aunt has foiled me! Joanna will stay in office, and I will serve as scapegoat."

"One of you was always going to have to pay the price," said Great-aunt Tabitha, coming forward and giving him a scornful look. Her courage was heartening. "How did you think you would get away with it?"

"Once the Veteran was found dead in his cell," said Nicko, "all traces of our part in the affair were gone."

"Nonsense!" said Great-aunt Tabitha.

Nicko bristled, and Sophie wished her great-aunt would

approach the conversation with a bit more tact. If the man got really annoyed, he was capable of blowing them all up at any moment—or of shooting Sophie in the head!

"Miss Grant and I had already assembled a dossier," Great-aunt Tabitha continued, "and you can be assured that we would have been able to demonstrate your involvement in the murders as well as the bombings. I don't know why you thought the minister wouldn't cut you loose at the least sign of trouble; it was bound to happen. Of course I believe her when she says that she had no idea at the time what you were doing out of that misguided impulse to protect her."

Miss Grant took over the narrative. "It was only after Tabitha witnessed the attack on Waterloo Day that we really became suspicious again and started to dig around," she said. Her words seemed to cut into Nicko, who visibly slumped as he listened. "The less said about the minister, the better—but you'd left your fingerprints all over the business, metaphorically speaking."

"All I needed was a little more time!" Nicko cried. "I almost pulled it off!"

He tucked the revolver under his arm—Sophie wished she thought she could get the gun away from him, but it wasn't worth the risk, not with the chance of a stray bullet blowing them all to kingdom come—and felt in his pocket for his cigarette lighter. He flicked it on and held the flame up high.

The women of the NTWSA and the dozen scarlet-clad young women who worked in the hut gazed at him with horror.

Out of the corner of her eye, Sophie saw Mr. Petersen moving toward them from about twenty feet away, silently but frantically gesturing for her to keep Mood talking. Fanned out behind him were a half dozen guards.

"How did you manage to get past the searchers," Sophie asked, desperate to fend off the explosion, if only for a few more seconds, "without them finding the gun and the lighter and taking them away from you?"

"It was child's play," Nicko boasted, preening. His responsiveness to flattery was the only thing that helped Sophie hope they might after all escape with their lives. "I showed them my identification from the ministry—it hasn't yet been taken away from me; Joanna gave me a week to straighten out my affairs. And that's precisely what I'm here to do. I'm not sorry, either, Sophie, to take you with me as well as your wretched great-aunt; you and your little friend gave me considerable anxiety, and it was only a matter of time before you'd have had to be put out of the way."

Mr. Petersen and his men slunk a little closer.

Sophie crossed her fingers and prayed. All things being equal, she really would prefer not to die in an explosion.

"Those searchers are extraordinarily careless," Nicko

added with satisfaction. "I can't think why they don't get properly qualified people to do the job."

"Don't you have any qualms," Sophie asked, trying very hard not to look in the direction of the guards, "about taking all these innocent people with you? What about sending away some of the women who work here before you blow us all up? None of them ever did anything to hurt you."

"Why should I want to save any of them?" said Nicko, looking genuinely surprised. "A few factory girls are no great loss!"

And at that moment one of the young women simply *threw* herself forward at him, four or five others instantly following, yelling as they went. In the blink of an eye, they had knocked him to the ground, and he vanished (so did the lighter!) beneath the heap of flailing limbs.

Everything happened next in a blur. Mr. Petersen and his men could do nothing without risking Mood letting off a bullet that would send them all to their deaths. They rushed up and simply stood in front of the heap—with all the girls, it was like the picture of Orpheus and the Maenads in Sophie's book of Greek myths.

A minute later, Mood lay supine on the floor, a woman holding down each of his arms and legs, while the girl who'd first thrown herself on him had jumped up and was waving the extinguished lighter and gun in the air.

"Give those to me," said one of the guards, struggling to keep his voice calm.

He took them and left the building, his deliberate pace more than anything else reminding everybody what a close shave they'd just had.

Two other guards handcuffed Mood in special plastic manacles and dragged him away with them. Sophie had to look aside as he wept and pleaded with the officers to let him go. He must have gone a bit mad in the end, she realized. Only a madman would have thought he could successfully orchestrate such a complex plot. Mr. Petersen went with them to escort Mood to the vehicle that would take him to jail.

Great-aunt Tabitha strode over to the girl who'd saved them—she had an amazingly pretty pink and white complexion, the result of breathing nitroglycerin every day—and pumped her hand.

"A quite remarkable effort," she said. "It's not necessary for me to say how very much we are in your debt."

Then Great-aunt Tabitha turned to Sophie. "I suspect you know rather more about all this than I imagined, but I won't inquire as to how that came about," she said.

"Is everything going to be all right?" Sophie asked, still terribly worried about the consequences of the minister's politicking. "Surely the minister must be brought to justice as well; it can't have been only Nicko Mood who plotted those deaths!"

Great-aunt Tabitha looked quite triumphant. "The minister wants war, I want peace, but we've agreed to set aside our differences and work together in the short term for Scotland's good. There won't be any more money flowing in the direction of the Brothers, and as a token of her goodwill, the minister has accepted my candidate to replace Nicko Mood. Ruth Grant will make a superb chief of staff. . . ."

Miss Grant to work for the minister?

Looking at Miss Grant, Sophie underwent a startling realization: Miss Grant had been looking forward to this moment for months. She'd planned to get Nicko's job all along!

It rubbed Sophie the wrong way to think of the minister surviving unscathed. But at least surely now they'd be able to abolish IRYLNS. After pulling off this triumph of investigation and politicking, Miss Grant and Great-aunt Tabitha could do anything they wanted.

"You'll be able to do away with IRYLNS!" Sophie said.

But instead of giving Sophie the ready affirmative she expected, the two women exchanged significant looks and smiled.

"Do away with it?" Miss Grant said. "Why ever would we do that?"

"IRYLNS is one of the country's most precious resources," Great-aunt Tabitha added. "We need every weapon we can get."

"But at least you'll stop the bill that says IRYLNS has the right to claim any girl once she turns sixteen from being passed into law?"

Their silence made it clear that neither woman meant to do anything of the sort, although Great-aunt Tabitha had the grace to look slightly ashamed.

Sophie found herself speechless.

Mr. Petersen appeared now to tell them that Nicholas Mood was safely in custody.

"Sophie, the most important thing is to get you out of here," he said then. "None of this is necessarily going to prevent Scotland from continuing on a collision course with Europe, and meanwhile the risk that you might be sent to IRYLNS is too great to chance your staying here."

"You know about IRYLNS!" Sophie said. "But how?"

"We have our ways," said Mr. Petersen, making a wry face. He had taken Sophie slightly aside, though Great-aunt Tabitha and Miss Grant were close enough to listen in. "Sophie, you must leave the country, and now's the ideal chance," he said. "You've got more than enough time to meet Mikael and sail with him to København. There's a driver waiting for you outside the gates as we speak."

"How will I get out without a visa?" Sophie asked. It was all happening much too quickly—she'd only just decided to leave, and already they were conspiring to send her away without further delay. She had a sudden powerful urge to drag her heels. Wouldn't she get to say good-bye to Peggy first? And what about her friends? Who would protect *them* from IRYLNS if Sophie just left?

"We've got a plan," said Mr. Petersen.

"Couldn't I stay until after my exams?" Sophie said, not liking the plaintive note she heard in her own words but unable to suppress it. "Then I could say good-bye to everybody first. Do I really have to decide right now?"

After looking around to make sure nobody but Miss Grant could hear their conversation, Great-aunt Tabitha unexpectedly joined her voice to Mr. Petersen's.

"Sophie, you must leave at once," she said firmly.

Sophie looked at her with enormous surprise.

"If Mr. Petersen whisks you off now and makes you disappear, I'll be able to deny knowing anything about it," Sophie's great-aunt said. "The longer we wait, the riskier it becomes. Seize the day. If you stay, I can't promise I won't hand you over to IRYLNS."

She leaned over and kissed Sophie's cheek.

All Sophie's energy was focused now on not crying.

Her eyesight was blurry as Mr. Petersen led her out of the building and across the narrow-gauge tracks, back toward the gatehouse at the main entrance.

Just before they reached it, Mr. Petersen turned to Sophie.

"We'll speak again before long," he said.

Sophie stared at him. "Aren't you coming with me now?" she asked.

She didn't understand it. They'd been walking for ages without him saying anything. If they weren't to go on together, his silence became not surprising so much as completely infuriating.

"I can't," said Mr. Petersen. "I've got loose ends to tie up, and we can't afford to have you waiting around while I take care of them. The commander you met that night in the Castle will be here within the hour, and once he gets his hands on you, it'll be impossible to spring you."

"Oh," said Sophie, feeling somewhat bereft.

"Don't worry," he said. "I'm handing you over now to somebody who will take extremely good care of you."

They reclaimed Sophie's bag from the guard and passed out of the compound into the sandy flat area in front of the gatehouse. There she looked at Mr. Petersen, and he looked back at her, and both of their faces expressed a shared sense of unfinished business.

Sophie waited to see whether he'd say anything else, but he didn't. And she wasn't about to say anything herself.

After a few minutes, a Crossley roadster pulled up in front of them. Mr. Petersen shook hands with the driver, then turned to give Sophie an awkward hug.

"Have a safe journey," he said. "I'll be in touch."

In a daze, Sophie fumbled with the door and let herself into the passenger seat.

"Thank goodness you're all right," said the driver. "Hostage situations are always touch and go. I was extremely relieved when Mr. Petersen radioed to let me know you'd survived unscathed."

The driver was Miss Chatterjee.

FORTY-TWO

T HE HISTORY TEACHER'S unexpected appearance as get-
away driver made Sophie feel confused as well as
relieved. It was a better thing, of course, to be handed
over to someone familiar than to a complete stranger. But
what was Miss Chatterjee doing here?

The teacher took a left turn onto the feeder road that
would take them to the highway leading east back to
Edinburgh and the port of Leith. "Surprised to see me?" she
said.

Sophie just nodded.

"I must make my confession," Miss Chatterjee went on,
politely ignoring Sophie's distress. "Mr. Petersen was not the
only teacher at the Edinburgh Institution for Young Ladies

who served two masters. Like him, I have been on the payroll of the Nobel Consortium for some time. Indeed, the Consortium paid for my education and set me up in Edinburgh more than ten years ago. It is very much the Consortium's way to prepare for all possible eventualities, taking the longest view."

Sophie turned and stared at her. This was utter betrayal, worse—*much* worse—than learning the truth about Mr. Petersen. Was that what Miss Chatterjee had meant the night she warned Sophie not to think of her as a hero?

"I can imagine how you feel," said Miss Chatterjee when Sophie didn't say anything. "I wish I could have told you before, but the Consortium is quite strict about us keeping our identities concealed. If I had let you in on the secret, I would have been recalled to the central office in Stockholm, where I could have done you no good."

Sophie was tallying up all the clues she'd missed: Miss Chatterjee's lovely clothes, well beyond what one might purchase on a teacher's salary; the elevated circles she moved in; most of all, the air she had of life being interesting and important. She remembered Priscilla's canny observations about Miss Rawlins and wished she'd thought of asking her about Miss Chatterjee. But the thought of Nan and Priscilla and Jean, and not being able to say good-bye to them, made Sophie start crying in earnest.

Miss Chatterjee offered a silk handkerchief, and Sophie wiped her eyes and blew her nose and generally tried to pull herself together.

"The day the headmistress called a special meeting for all the teachers," Miss Chatterjee said when Sophie had collected herself, "it became clear that things were in a parlous state. Her news—that Parliament was certain to take virtually all of you girls for IRYLNS—made us see that you were in even graver danger than we had anticipated. Neither Mr. Petersen nor I was quite sure what happens at the Institute, but enough stories have trickled out that we thought we'd better come up with a plan to get you out of danger. In that sense, all this business with the minister and her assistant just precipitated things a little sooner than we expected."

Sophie remembered overhearing Miss Chatterjee ask on the day of the coffee spill whether the decision to send the girls to IRYLNS was really a matter of protecting the girls or just of promoting the interests of the country. That must have been the day they decided Sophie had to be rescued.

"You didn't send me a little metal toy iron by way of the medium, did you?" Sophie asked. "As a kind of warning?"

Miss Chatterjee gave her a blank look, and Sophie wondered whether the medium had given Sophie the warning of her own accord. Many secrets must have gone to the grave with Mrs. Tansy; as much as she had disliked the woman in life, though, and resented her for getting Sophie mixed up in the whole business to begin with, Sophie still felt she owed her something.

"Miss Chatterjee?" Sophie asked.

"What is it, Sophie?"

"What can be done about the other girls? Can't you stop Jean and Priscilla from going to IRYLNS?"

Just then a radio receiver in Miss Chatterjee's handbag, on the floor by Sophie's feet, now began emitting short sharp bursts of speech.

"Would you mind passing me the radio?" Miss Chatterjee asked.

Sophie dug around in the bag and found it. It was one of the new transistor ones, like Priscilla's.

Both Miss Chatterjee and the person at the other end spoke in code, so Sophie couldn't follow most of what they said, but there was an ominous change in Miss Chatterjee's body language. She didn't drive any faster—she probably didn't want to alert whoever might be watching—but she looked suddenly much tougher than before.

"Sophie, it's bad news, but nothing we can't deal with," she said after signing off. "Apparently our old friend Commander Brown has cottoned on to the fact that a crucial witness has left the scene. He's put out an all-points bulletin and instructed the police to mount a series of roadblocks.

We're still miles away from Leith, but we've got to hide you right away so that if the car's stopped, they won't see you."

Sophie didn't know how to respond.

"Don't worry," Miss Chatterjee added. "We planned for this contingency, and the risk is minimal."

The word *risk* made Sophie's stomach hurt, but she thought she'd rather know the details than not.

"What's the plan, then?" she asked.

She knew Commander Brown wouldn't kill her, but his finding her would surely initiate exactly the series of events she most wanted to avoid, beginning with a serious interrogation in the Vaults and almost certainly ending with matriculation at IRYLNS.

"Well, let me put it this way," said Miss Chatterjee. "How do you feel about small enclosed spaces?"

Five minutes later Miss Chatterjee pulled over at a spot where the road got wider and opened the boot of the car to show a steamer trunk—quite a large one, though it didn't look big enough to hold a person, which was part of the point. It had a false bottom and breathing holes, and Miss Chatterjee assured Sophie that there was really plenty of room for her inside.

When she saw Sophie's doubtful look, she sighed. "Yes, I know it's awful, and I wouldn't like it much either," she said. "But I borrowed it from my friend Harry, who's a stage magician and twice your size, and he gets inside it every night."

She showed Sophie the safety latch that she could use to let herself out if she accidentally got stuck in the hold of the ship, rather than in Mikael's cabin as planned. She would have ended up in the trunk sooner or later, even without the road-blocks, Sophie suddenly realized, for this was how they intended to get her on board ship without the proper visa.

"What about Jean and Priscilla?" she asked urgently. "You must tell them they can't go to IRYLNS!"

"Don't worry about them," said Miss Chatterjee, handing Sophie a flask of water. "Your job now is to protect yourself. We can't afford to lose any more time—get into the trunk!"

Despite her conviction that a police car might come into view at any moment, despite her horror at the idea of being taken into custody, despite her fear of IRYLNS, something in Sophie rebelled at the thought of shutting herself up in this awful cramped box.

"Do I really have to?" she said.

"You must," said Miss Chatterjee.

The sky had become cloudy and overcast.

"Hurry up, Sophie!"

The unfamiliar note of anxiety in the teacher's voice provided the necessary spur. Sophie reminded herself that she didn't dislike small dark spaces, but climbing into the trunk still made her feel as if she were going voluntarily into her own coffin.

"If things go as they should, I won't see you again for a long while, so I'll say good-bye now," said Miss Chatterjee. "Sophie, it's been a pleasure teaching you. And I swear to you I will deliver this trunk into the keeping of your friend Mikael on the *Gustavus Adolphus* if it kills me. Mr. Petersen was most precise in his instructions!"

The top of the trunk closed over Sophie and she found herself in pitch blackness, clasps shutting loudly over her head.

Would Sophie escape? What would happen to Jean and Priscilla?

Within five minutes these concerns looked trivial beside the need to prevent herself from being sick.

Sophie had already felt nauseated sitting in the front seat of the car. It turned out that the motion of the car as it affected her now was about a hundred times more sick-making than on an ordinary car ride. She wished she'd thought to retrieve Peggy's barley sugar from her bag before Miss Chatterjee had tucked it in beside her in the trunk's secret compartment, but there was hardly any space to move about in. Besides, even the slightest movement made being sick that much more likely.

The car twisted and turned, it sped up and slowed down, it even stopped a few times for long enough that Sophie would have been absolutely terrified had all her attention not been engaged in the desperate struggle not to throw up.

It seemed an eternity before the car came to a halt. The engine stopped and Sophie heard the passenger door open and close again. She thought she wouldn't even mind if Commander Brown was outside and about to order the car searched, so long as she never again had to endure such a ride.

Someone opened the boot and the whole car shook. Sophie hoped the last little bit of movement wouldn't trigger actual vomiting. She was only barely holding on. Aside from the sheer unpleasantness of it, the sudden sound and smell of a person throwing up inside the trunk would let the authorities know that something was very wrong.

The trunk somewhat muffled the sound of their voices, but Sophie was relieved to hear Miss Chatterjee negotiating the fee with a porter rather than, say, explaining her actions to a police officer. Then the trunk was heaved out of the boot of the car and slotted onto some kind of handcart. Someone outside thumped the trunk a couple times; it might have been Miss Chatterjee bidding Sophie farewell.

She could hear the shrieks of gulls and smell salt air even through the dark masculine scents of the trunk, but it continued to be a great effort not to be sick as they rolled up the steep gradient of the gangplank and she began to feel the quiet movement of the ship.

Had there ever been such a test of the power of mind over matter?

It seemed an interminable wait, with lots of jerking around and sudden sharp yaws and pitches in unexpected directions, before Sophie's trunk finally came to rest on a flat floor. She heard a boy's voice saying "That's for your help" and an older man thanking him and then the sound of a door opening and closing.

The top of the trunk opened now, and though Sophie was still trapped beneath the false bottom, she couldn't help letting out a groan of relief.

The next thing she knew, Mikael had lifted up the decoy shelf above her and leaned down to help her out.

Her arms and legs were incredibly stiff, but Sophie struggled out as fast as she could.

"Thank goodness," said Mikael. "I'd begun to be afraid—"

Sophie cut him off.

"Where's the basin?" she gasped.

"Right there. Sophie, you must tell me everything! What happened—"

But though superhuman fortitude had helped so far, Sophie couldn't hold it in for another second. She doubled up and to her great shame and mortification began to be sick into the porcelain basin on the washstand.

FORTY-THREE

FOLLOWING A DISCREET interval involving towels and large quantities of warm water (storybooks never said anything about the crying and vomiting part of having adventures), Sophie and Mikael crept up to the top deck of the merchant steamer for a breath of fresh air. The ship was still at anchor, shortly to depart.

Sophie still felt extremely queasy, but as her stomach was now completely empty, she thought there wasn't much chance of being sick again. She sipped small mouthfuls of fizzy lemonade from a bottle, having rejected with a shudder Mikael's offer to procure some brandy (supposed to be good for seasickness) from one of the stewards.

"Are you sure it's safe for us to be on deck like this?" she asked.

They were quite alone, for the weather had taken a definite turn for the worse and everything more than about fifteen feet away was wreathed about with the cold mist called the haar.

"We're quite safe," Mikael said. "For one thing, the police haven't a clue where you are. For another, as soon as you came on board ship, you passed out of Scottish sovereignty. Miss Chatterjee visited me yesterday afternoon to give me all the paperwork I'll need if anyone questions your right to be here; the Danish embassy has accepted her application on your behalf for asylum, and I've got that and a proper ticket for you as well. We won't have any difficulties."

The word *asylum* had a harsh sound, but there was nothing to be done about it. They sat in the deck chairs, wrapped up in blankets to protect them from the cold damp fog.

"I'm awfully glad you're here, Sophie," Mikael said. "Everything will be fine from now on."

"I don't have much luggage. . . ."

"That's all right. There's a small commissary on board. And my mother will fit you out properly once we're in Denmark."

"Your mother doesn't even know me!"

"Sophie, you're looking awfully green again. Are you all right?"

As it started to rain, they raced back down to the cabin

just in time for Sophie to be sick for a second time.

"I'm afraid I'd better lie down," she said. "I'll tell you the whole story later on."

"That's fine," said Mikael. "I won't bother you; I'm sure resting will make you feel better."

She lay down on the nearest bunk, and he sat on the opposite one to watch over her. It was strange to think of sharing a cabin with him, and even stranger to contemplate living together with his mother once they got to Denmark.

"I almost didn't come," Sophie said after a minute.

It was a more confessional statement than she would usually have made, but she was feeling so sick and sleepy that the usual mechanisms of self-censorship seemed to have stopped working.

Mikael didn't say anything.

"When I telephoned you yesterday evening," she continued, "I was sort of on the verge of changing my mind, if only you'd tried to persuade me, but you sounded as though you didn't even want to talk to me. I swore not to make a fool of myself by going where I wasn't wanted."

She was distracted by a funny sound coming from the heap of luggage in the corner of the cabin. She turned her head and saw a wicker basket fall to the ground.

"The ship must have embarked," she said, though she hadn't detected any obvious change in its motion.

Mikael followed her eyes to the basket and started laughing.

"You know, I had a very good reason for not being able to talk yesterday," he said. "There was something really important I had to do, I told you that. Look at the scratches!"

He leaned over to show his hands to Sophie. They were covered with puffy, sore-looking red scrapes.

"I'll let him out now," Mikael added. And to Sophie's amazement, when he unfastened the clasp on the basket, a huge black cat leaped out.

"What's that cat doing here?"

"It's Mrs. Tansy's cat. Don't you remember? That was what I had to go and do last night when I couldn't talk on the telephone."

And Sophie had been so sure that Mikael cut their conversation off like that because he was angry with her. . . . It was a good reminder not to jump to conclusions.

"I took that landlady at her word when she said she'd put the cat on the street. And even though Blackie here's a tough customer, I didn't fancy his chances with those terrible kids."

Sophie didn't have the energy to make a joke about the originality of the name. The cat didn't seem to mind one way or the other. It stopped racing around the tiny cabin long enough to press its muzzle against Sophie's outstretched fingers. After a minute or two of sniffing around the bunk, it curled up next to her and began to lick its hindquarters.

"Well, will you look at that?" said Mikael, sounding more than a little piqued.

Lying on top of the bed, the cat's warm body pressed against her side, part of Sophie still couldn't believe she was about to leave behind her entire life in Scotland.

Though she had learned things in the past few weeks that completely changed her view of the world, there were still an awful lot of mysteries to be solved.

Nobel's motives remained an enigma. What did the Swedish industrialist want with her?

Why had Mr. Petersen been so cagey about the curious technical drawing that appeared over the pantelegraph, and had it anything to do with Nobel's missing plans?

What had really happened to Sophie's parents? Would Nobel be able to fill in the story for her, or would she have to live with the gaps?

She was surprised how little it took to reconcile herself to missing the exams. The thing that really gave her a pang, strange to say, was the thought of missing the appointment with Mr. Braid the following week. What a pity! She was curious, most curious, to know what her second self had written under hypnosis. Would the doctor keep the pages quite safe until she could come back and find him again?

Though it was galling not to know the answers to any of these questions, there was still something comforting about having questions one cared enough to ask. Surely everything would come right in the end. If only she could know in advance that Jean and Priscilla and Nan would be safe. . . .

"Sophie!" Mikael said, breaking into her thoughts. "Do you want to come out on deck with me now? Surely the fresh air will do you good."

Sophie's legs felt like cotton wool, and Mikael had to drag her up several steep staircases, but she was glad she'd come. The haar had cleared a little, and they could just about make out the shore.

As they watched, the foghorn blew and the crew lifted anchor. The ship began to make its way down the Firth of Forth to the open sea.

Though the ship was really moving away from shore, it looked as though the land was receding from the ship. The country vanished in a mist that made it hard to believe Scotland even existed, as if all life up till now had been a dream, and this the awakening to a new day.

AUTHOR'S NOTE

I HAVE ALWAYS BEEN in love with the idea of north. In the summer of 2000, I took a long-awaited trip to St. Petersburg and found myself absolutely in thrall to the sheer beauty of that northern landscape, the magic of Russia's imperial past, and the heartbreakingly shabby grandeur of the present-day city's buildings and parks. I was surprised, though, by how much St. Petersburg reminded me of Edinburgh, a city I visited regularly as a child, since my Scottish grandparents lived just a few miles outside of it in a town called North Berwick. The similarities between the styles of building and ways of living, the visual quality of those long evenings of summer light, the closeness to the water, and the lingering Enlightenment presence: all these things made me feel as though I had entered a strange secret northern world with the feel of a Hans Christian Andersen fairy tale.

Over the next few years, I went to Tallinn (in Estonia) and Stockholm, then to Copenhagen (or København, as it is spelled by the Danish), and I began to dream about what it would be like to live in an alternate universe in which these northern cities, so strongly united by culture and geography, were also politically connected. What if the medieval northern European trade alliance, called the Hanseatic League, had found a second life in the modern era, due to calamitous developments in European politics? This world would have split off from our own when Napoleon beat Wellington at the Battle of Waterloo on June 18, 1815.

What would it be like, I asked myself, to be a fifteen-year-old girl growing up in a Hanseatic-identified Scotland that was still being run along the principles of the eighteenth-century period known as the Enlightenment, with its passion for rationality and science? At a time when the world—as it did in our own version of 1938—seemed to stand on the brink of total war?

As in our own world, the 1910s in Sophie's world saw a Great War; here, though, it lingered on into the 1920s and ended with England falling to Europe. Now the countries in the Hanseatic League, including Scotland, are able to hold out against the Europeans only because they also happen to be the world's premier suppliers of top-quality munitions, which Europe needs. This is the legacy of Alfred Nobel, the Swedish chemist and industrialist whose invention of dynamite in 1867 changed the landscape of *The Explosionist*'s Europe even more decisively than it changed our own. (The real Alfred Nobel lived from 1833 to 1896—assuming he was born in the same year in this world, he would be almost ninety-five years old, though the old lady at the factory hints to Sophie that Nobel only survives as what she calls "a brain in a jar.")

Nobel's name is best known today for the awards he funded, including prizes in Physics, Physiology or Medicine, Literature, and Peace, for one of the paradoxes of the dynamiteur's life was that he was also a devoted pacifist. The Nobel factory at Ardeer where the novel's final showdown takes place really existed, and the abandoned buildings of the dynamite factory can be visited to this day.

The world I imagined comes out of real places and real history but also out of fairy tales and counterfactual paths not taken. The people in this world are preoccupied with technology (everything from electric cookers to high explosives) but also with spiritualism, a movement our own world largely abandoned in the early twentieth century. Sigmund Freud is a radio talk-show crank, cars run on hydrogen, and the most prominent scientists experiment with new ways of contacting the dead.

Some of the same figures are prominent in this world's history as in our own, in many cases for roughly the same reasons (the scientists Kelvin and Faraday and James Clerk Maxwell are mentioned, for instance, as are the psychologists Pavlov and William James). But in this world, Wittgenstein is a physicist rather than a philosopher, and Harry Houdini (born in 1874) is still alive—in fact, he's the real owner of the trunk used in Sophie's escape.

In general, I have relied very extensively on actual historical sources. In our world, we can't talk to spirits—but some of the most respected scientists of the late nineteenth century devoted a great deal of energy to trying to show that we could. Most valuable of all to me were memoirs of Scottish life in the 1920s and 1930s, including Muriel Spark's autobiography *Curriculum Vitae* and her brilliant novel of education *The Prime of Miss Jean Brodie*.

Technology developed quite differently in this world than in our own. The fuel cells that Sophie learns about during her driving lesson would have been unobtainable in the real-world 1930s. On a more peripheral note, the transistor technology that's alluded to several times was only invented in our own world in 1947–48 but seems to have been discovered here in the early 1930s, perhaps because the continual threat of war proved such an effective spur to scientific inventiveness. Transistor technology is also required for the aerial assault drone to which Great-aunt Tabitha is likened—a point first noted by my father, whose background as a native Scot with an engineering degree has made his advice particularly indispensable to me while writing *The Explosionist*.

My enormous outright breach of the unofficial rules governing alternate history concerns Arthur Conan Doyle's Sherlock Holmes stories and Robert Louis Stevenson's tale of Dr. Jekyll and Mr. Hyde. Both writers were born in Edinburgh—Stevenson in 1850 and Conan Doyle in 1859. It has often been observed that Stevenson's tale of double selves, though it is set in London, casts more light on Edinburgh. Meanwhile, though Sherlock Holmes also resides in London, Conan Doyle based his most famous character on Dr. Joseph Bell, one of his medical school professors at the University of Edinburgh. The story of *The Explosionist* is so deeply indebted to these tales that it seemed to me they had to have shaped the imagination of my fictional characters as well as my own.